PEGASUS

By Danielle Steel

DANIELLE STEEL

PEGASUS

A Novel

**Doubleday Large Print
Home Library Edition**

Delacorte Press | New York

DELACORTE PRESS and the HOUSE colophon
are registered trademarks of
Random House LLC.

ISBN 978-1-62953-218-9

Printed in the United States of America

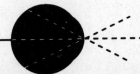

**This Large Print Book carries the
Seal of Approval of N.A.V.H.**

To my beloved children,
Beatie, Trevor, Todd, Nick, Sam,
    Victoria, Vanessa, Maxx, and Zara,
To history, magic, survival, and new lives,
To the Pegasus in each of our lives, to carry
    us forward,
And the courage to pursue him bravely
    and embrace him.

I love you so very much,
Mommy/d.s.

PEGASUS

Chapter 1

It was already nightfall when the stable boys heard the horses approaching. Their hooves sounded thunderous like a distant drumbeat, long before the uninitiated would have known what it was. The riders were returning from the hunt, and minutes later the boys could hear the voices calling out, the laughter, the horses snorting as they brought in their riders. When they entered the courtyard of Schloss Altenberg and approached the stables, it was obvious they were in high spirits and it had been a good hunt. One of the earliest arrivals said the hounds had gotten the fox, which they'd expected, as

the horses pranced around, still excited
from the exhilarating day. Riders and
mounts alike had enjoyed the cold October
weather, and the men in "pinks," their scar-
let riding jackets, with white jodhpurs and
tall black boots, looked like a portrait as they
dismounted and handed the reins of their
horses to the stable boys, who helped several women dismount too. A number of
them were riding sidesaddle, which looked
very elegant, but was no mean feat on a
hunt. The group that had gone out that day
had been riding together for all the years
they had known one another and were old
enough to hunt. For all of them, horses were
their passion, and riding their favorite sport.

Alex von Hemmerle was known to be
one of the finest riders in the county, and
had been breeding extraordinary horses
since he was barely more than a boy.
Everything in his life was born of tradition,
which was true for all of them. There were
no newcomers or surprises here. The
same families had inhabited the area for
centuries, visiting each other, following
long-established rituals and traditions, in-
termarrying, running their estates, and
cherishing their land. Alex had grown up in

Schloss Altenberg, as generations of his ancestors had, since the fourteenth century. He held a ball there at Christmas, as all his forebears had done. It was the most glamorous event in the county, and everyone looked forward to it every year. His daughter Marianne had been his hostess for the first time the year before, when she turned sixteen.

Now seventeen, Marianne had the same striking ethereal beauty her mother had had, with finely chiseled features. She was tall like Alex, with almost translucent porcelain skin, her mother's nearly white blond hair, and her father's electric blue eyes. She was one of the most beautiful young women in the region and as famous a rider as he was. He had put her on horseback before she could walk, and she went on every hunt, so she had been furious not to go with him that day, but she had a bad cold and a fever, and he had insisted she stay home. She was sturdier than she looked, despite her delicate beauty, unlike her mother, who had been far more fragile, and had died from blood loss and a severe infection the day after Marianne was born. It was not unusual for women to die in childbirth, but

losing her had marked Alex severely.
There had never been an important woman
for him since. And although he had discreet dalliances in the county occasionally, his daughter was the only woman he
truly loved now, and he had had no desire
to remarry since his wife Annaliese's
death, and knew he never would. They
had been distant cousins and childhood
sweethearts, although he was several
years older. He had never expected to find
himself widowed at thirty, but in the seventeen years since he'd lost her, his life with
his daughter and his friends was all he
wanted, and he always warned the women
he saw quietly not to expect anything permanent from him.

Running his vast estate kept him busy,
and breeding the Lipizzaner horses he was
so proud of filled his life nearly as much as
his daughter, and she shared his passion
for them. She loved admiring the new foals
and watching her father train them. His
snow-white Lipizzaners were said to be the
finest, and the easiest to train, and his
bloodlines the purest. He was rigorous
about which stallions he used for breeding,
and which mares he chose to reproduce,

and he had taught Marianne all about them since she was a little girl.

She had been to the Spanish Riding School in Vienna with her father often, and thought their rigorous precision exercises looked like ballet, as she watched the splendid white horses dance and go through their incredibly intricate paces. She held her breath as she watched them prance on their hind legs in the "capriole" or "courbette" or leap into the air in the "croupade," with all four legs tucked under their bodies. It thrilled her every time she saw it, just as it did Alex. And he had trained some of his horses in these exercises as well. Marianne wished that she could become a rider at the school, and she was capable enough to do it, but the Spanish Riding School did not accept women, and her father said they never would. So she was content to see her father's horses perform at home or in Vienna and help him train them before they left. Once in a great while, he allowed her to ride them, but very seldom. But he did allow her to ride any of the Arabian horses he kept in his stables and bred as well. Her riding skill was instinctive, and she had grown up with some of the finest horses in Germany, and learned everything her father taught her. Horses were in her blood just as they were in his.

"Good hunt today," Alex commented, looking happy and relaxed as he and his good friend Nicolas von Bingen threaded their way through the other riders, who were chatting animatedly in the courtyard. They were in no hurry, even after the long ride. It had grown bitter cold as night fell, and the ground had been hard, but nothing stopped them, since all of them had good mounts, though perhaps not quite as fine as their host's. Nicolas had been riding a new Arabian stallion that Alex had lent him and had found him an excellent ride.

"I might like to buy him from you," Nicolas said, and Alex laughed.

"He's not for sale. Besides, I promised him to Marianne, after I train him for a while. He's still a bit rough."

"He suits me that way," Nicolas said, smiling at his boyhood friend. "Besides, he's too much horse for her." He liked his horses lively and a challenge to control.

"Don't tell her that!" Alex said, smiling. Marianne would never have tolerated an insult like that, and her father wasn't sure that was true. She was a better rider than Nick, although Alex would never have dared say that to him. Nick was a little overly zealous with his horses at times, and Marianne had gentler, better hands. He had taught her himself, with exceedingly good results.

"Where was she today, by the way? I don't think I've ever seen her miss a hunt," Nick commented, surprised that she hadn't come along. She was a familiar sight at their hunts, and always welcome with her father's friends.

"She's sick. I nearly had to tie her to her bed to keep her home. You're quite right, she never misses a hunt," Alex said with a worried look.

"Nothing serious, I hope." Nick's eyes were instantly concerned.

"She has a bad cold and a fever. The doctor came around last night. I was afraid it was going to her lungs. He ordered her to stay at home. I knew my word wouldn't suffice, and I didn't think his would impress her either, but I think she was feeling worse than she wanted to admit. She was asleep when I left this morning, which is very unlike her."

"Should you have the doctor back tonight?" Nick had had his own bad experi-
ences with influenza, and had lost his wife
and four-year-old daughter to it five years
before, after an epidemic in the county and
a particularly hard winter. He had been devastated to lose them both, and like Alex, he
was widowed now, in his case with two
sons, Tobias and Lucas. Tobias had been
ten when his mother and sister died and still
remembered them both, and Lucas was
only six now, and had been barely more
than a baby when they died. Tobias was a
quiet, gentle boy, who worshipped Marianne, who was two years older. And Lucas
was a lively, mischievous child, full of fun,
and happy wherever he was, particularly if
it was on a horse. Tobias was far more like
his much gentler mother, and Lucas had all
the energy and fire of his father. Nick had
gotten up to all kinds of misadventures
when he was younger, and was still the talk
of the county at times, when he started an
affair with some woman, occasionally even
married ones, or took a bet racing a horse
at breakneck speeds. He was an extremely
competent rider, though not of Alex's super-
lative skill. He had never had the patience

to train a horse the way Alex did, although he was fascinated with Alex's Lipizzaners, and what he was able to do with them. Even before they left for the Spanish Riding School, Alex had already begun to train them in the intricate figures for which the beautiful white horses were famous.

"Do you have a minute?" Alex asked him as they walked past the stables. The others slowly began to disperse and called out their goodnights when they got into their cars.

"I'm in no rush to get home," Nicolas said, smiling casually, as the two men strolled toward the barn. They had been friends since their childhood, although Alex was four years older, and they had gone to boarding school in England together when they were young. Alex had been the better student, and Nick had had far more fun, which was still the case. Nicolas von Bingen enjoyed everything about his life. He was a good friend and a good father, and a kind person, although Alex knew he was a little too fun-loving and irresponsible at times. Widowhood had only dampened him a little, and for now he was not yet burdened with running his estate. His father was still alive and very much in control, which left Nick a considerable amount of time to play, unlike Alex, who had run his own estate and fortune since his early twenties, when his father died. In many ways, Nick still acted like a boy, while Alex had been very much a man for more than two decades. But they complemented each other and were more like brothers than friends.

Nick followed Alex into the barn, and Alex led him to an immaculately kept stall where one of his finest Lipizzaner mares was nursing a foal she had given birth to only days before. The coal-black foal was standing unsteadily on its legs as the mare looked at them both with her big dark eyes. Nick knew that Lipizzaner foals were born dark brown or black, so he wasn't surprised by its color, as it stood in sharp contrast to its snow-white mother. He knew it would take five or six years for its coat to turn white, just as he knew it would be ten years old before it was fully trained. The foal would spend four years with Alex, and six at the school in Vienna. The training of the remarkable Lipizzaners happened over long, careful, diligent, and meticulous years.

"He's a beauty, isn't he?" Alex said

proudly. "One of the best I've seen. He was sired by Pluto Petra"—who Nick knew was Alex's finest stallion, whom he used to breed—"and this little mare did very well. I'm going to have fun training him." He looked as proud of the newborn horse as any father, and Nick smiled at him.

"You're a wonder," Nick said affectionately, as the two men walked out of the barn together. Alex would have asked Nick to join him for dinner, but he wanted to have dinner with Marianne in her room.

"Do you want to ride with me tomorrow to the north border?" Alex asked him. "I'm thinking of clearing some of my forests. I thought I'd take a look. I want to get an early start, and be back at noon. We can have lunch after our ride."

"I'd love to," Nick said regretfully, as he stopped at the Duesenberg he had left parked under a tree. He much preferred his Bugatti, but had decided to be more respectable when he came to join Alex for the hunt. "I can't, though. I have to meet my father. There's something he wants to talk to me about. I can't for the life of me think what it is. I haven't done anything to annoy him in weeks." They both laughed at what he said. Nick enjoyed a close relationship with his father, although his father frequently scolded him over rumors he had heard, of Nick's womanizing, or his galloping around, or driving at insane speeds. Above all, Paul von Bingen was always trying to get Nick involved in the running of the estate. He assumed that that was what his father wanted to discuss with him the next day. It was a recurring theme. "I think he wants me to take over managing the farms, which sounds like dreadful work to me."

"You'll have to do it one day. You might as well start now," Alex said sensibly.

They still had farmers on their land who had been indentured servants, and now rented their farms from him for pennies. But they were a necessary part of the system, and the traditions that had ruled them all for years. They weren't really part of the modern world, but living here in the countryside allowed them a tranquil life away from the cities. Germany had been troubled for years, since the chaos and poor economy after the Great War, and the Depression. The economy had improved under Hitler, but the country's problems weren't over yet. Hitler had tried to give Germans a sense of pride again, but his fervent speeches and rallies at fever pitch didn't appeal to Alex or Nick. Alex thought he was a troublemaker, and had a strong dislike for most of his ideas, and his annexing Austria in March was a disturbing sign of his ambitions. But whatever Hitler was doing seemed very remote to them here in their peaceful Bavarian countryside. Nothing could touch them here, and nothing ever changed. Their families had been in the area for centuries, and would be, doing the same things, in another two hundred years. They were insulated from the world. And both men were comfortable knowing that their children and great-grandchildren would still be here one day.

Alex and Nick had been brought up to be noblemen, and very little else. They had been blessed with enormous fortunes, which they never discussed and rarely if ever thought about. They had tenant farmers and servants, and vast estates, which in turn would pass on to their children, in a totally protected life and world.

"I don't see why I should take on the farms now," Nick said, as he slipped his long legs into the Duesenberg and looked at his friend. "My father is going to live for another thirty years, and he does it far better than I ever will," he commented with a wry smile. "Why should I screw it up now? I'd much rather do something else. Like ride with you tomorrow morning, but my father will be upset if I don't at least pretend to listen to him." Nick knew all of his speeches by heart, chapter and verse.

"You're shameless," Alex chided him, but he was also aware that Nick was more responsible than he let on. He was wonderful with his boys, and had vastly improved the lot of his tenant farmers, using his own funds to improve their homes. He cared about them as people, but he just didn't want to be responsible for their land and farms, which he found incredibly tedious and thought his father seemed to enjoy. Nick was more interested in the welfare of those less fortunate than he, and bringing up his boys, with whom he spent a great deal of time, just as Alex did with Marianne. They had in common that they were both devoted fathers and family men, steeped in the traditions of their familiar world.

"Sorry I can't ride with you tomorrow," Nick said regretfully as he started the car.

"I'll come by after lunch and watch you train that stallion of yours." Nick had been watching Alex work with the young Lipizzaner for months, and was as always in awe of his skill.

"I still have so much work to do with him. I promised him to the riding school in January. He's the right age, but I don't think he's ready yet." The four-year-old stallion showed a lot of spirit, and Nick never got bored watching Alex take him through his paces. The Lipizzaner stallion would have impressed anyone just as he was, except Alex, who was a perfectionist and rarely satisfied with his results. "Come over whenever you want," Alex invited him, and a few minutes later, Nick drove off with a jaunty wave and headed toward his own estate a few miles away, as Alex walked back into the schloss, to visit his daughter and see how she was.

Marianne was lying in bed, looking bored with a book, and she still appeared feverish but better than she had the night before. He touched her forehead with a gentle hand, and was relieved to find her cooler, although her eyes were still dull and her nose was red.

"How do you feel?" he asked, as he sat down next to her on the bed.

"Stupid for lying here. Did you have fun at the hunt? Did they get the fox?" Her eyes lit up as she asked him. She had thought about everyone hunting all day.

"Of course. It wasn't nearly as much fun without you, but I'm happy you stayed home. It was freezing today. We're going to have a hard winter, if it's cold as early as this."

"Good. I like it when it snows." She was happy to see him. "Toby came to see me today." She brightened a little, speaking of Nick's son. He came to visit all the time and worshipped her. He'd had a crush on her for years, and she treated him like a little brother. Toby could hardly wait for the day when he could pursue her, and she'd take him seriously. Marianne knew that day would never come. "Don't tell his father he was here. You know how Nick is when anyone is sick." He had been nervous about illness ever since his wife and daughter had died of influenza, and he was particularly cautious about his sons. "We played chess. I beat him," she said happily as her father smiled at her.

"You should be nicer to him. He thinks the sun rises and sets on you."

"That's just because he doesn't know any other girls." She was completely unaware of her beauty, and her effect on men. Several young men, and even their fathers, had been looking longingly at her for the past few years, and Alex was relieved that it never turned her head. She was much more interested in her father's horses, and spending time with him, than she was in men. There was a childlike innocence about her still, which touched his heart. He couldn't bear the thought of parting with her one day if she got married and moved away. But even if she did, he knew she wouldn't go far.

Marianne attended the local school, with the children of other noble families, and she had no interest in going to university in another city, particularly now that there was so much unrest and disruption in the cities and towns. His own father had insisted that he attend university in Heidelberg, and he had been happy to come home again, to what he thought was the most beautiful place on earth. And Alex was relieved that

Marianne agreed with him about it. Sometimes he felt guilty for depriving her of a bigger life, but with turmoil around the country, she was better off here. He liked keeping her close to him, where he knew she was safe.

"Can I have dinner with you downstairs, Papa?" she asked, ready to get out of bed, although she was still pale, and Alex shook his head with a stern expression.

"No, you're not well enough yet. And it's drafty downstairs. I asked them to bring us trays here. Marta will be upstairs with them in a minute. I want you to get well so you can come and see the new foal in the barn. He's a beauty, even better looking than his father. I took Nick to see him after the hunt. You can come and watch me work with Pluto tomorrow if you like. He's doing well." Her father gave her the latest report, and Marianne sank back into her pillows with a sigh, and he could see she didn't feel as well as she claimed. He was greatly relieved that she hadn't gone out that day. It would have been madness if she had, but she was stubborn enough to try.

Marta and one of the housemen came in a few minutes later, with their dinner on trays, and her father let her get up and sit next to the fire, wrapped in a blanket, while he told her all about the hunt. She looked tired afterward when she went back to bed, but she was cool when he felt her cheek and kissed her.

"Goodnight, my angel," he said, smiling at her, as she looked at him with gentle eyes.

"I'm the luckiest girl in the world, to have a father like you," she said softly, and he melted at her words. He felt the same way about her. And then she thought of something she had forgotten to tell him at dinner. "I listened to the radio today, and there was some kind of rally in Berlin. You could hear the soldiers marching in precision, and they sang a lot of songs that sounded like there was a war on. The Fuehrer made a speech asking everyone to pledge loyalty to him. It scared me. . . . Do you think there will ever be a war, Papa?" She looked young and innocent as she asked. Hitler had convinced everyone that occupying Austria would avoid a war, and that "lebensraum," annexing Austria, would be enough.

"No, I don't," he said reassuringly, although Hitler had mobilized the military two

months before. "I don't think it's as dangerous as it sounds. And nothing will touch us
here. Sleep tight, my darling . . . sweet
dreams. I hope you feel better in the morning. But I still want you to stay home from
school for a few days. You can keep me
company in the barn."

She smiled as he left the room and she
felt better after what he'd said. As she listened to the Fuehrer's speech that afternoon, she had felt a chill of fear, as though
the whole world were about to change. Hitler had said it would, on the radio. But she
was sure her father was right. Their leader
was just speaking to the masses to excite
and inspire them. It had nothing to do with
them here at home. She fell asleep thinking about their Christmas ball, and how
much fun it was going to be. She had to
start planning for it, it was only two months
away. And Nick had said that Toby could
come this year for the first time. He had told
her that day that he was going to get his
first tailcoat and top hat, and she had
laughed at him. He was a handsome boy,
but he still seemed like a child to her. She
felt like one herself, as she drifted off to
sleep. She could hardly wait to see the inky

black Lipizzaner foal in the barn. She remembered the first time she had seen one and had been so shocked it wasn't white. And then it had grown up to be a beautiful snowy creature like the others that seemed to dance in midair. She was dreaming about her father's Lipizzaners as she fell asleep. They were magical beings in a perfect world. A world where she knew that nothing bad could ever touch her, and just as her father said, she would always be safe.

Chapter 2

In the morning, Nick drove his bright blue Bugatti to the large manor house where his father lived on their estate. He had moved there when Nick married, and he had given Nick and his wife the use of the schloss, as he thought was fitting for his son and his bride. He'd been urging Nick to run the estate then, and he was still trying to get him to do so, without success. Nick was perfectly content to visit their tenants, spend time with his friends, and tend to his sons, which he claimed was full-time work, since they had no mother to take care of them now. Paul von Bingen was pleased that his son was so attentive to his children, but he would have liked to see him more interested in their land, and learning how to manage it himself one day. At forty-three, Nick was convinced that that time was so far off that he had years to learn what he needed to know. Nick still felt like a young man. His father was sixty-five and always seemed younger than he was as well. Paul von Bingen was still a handsome, vital man, but Nick noticed that his father didn't look well today. He appeared tired and pale and was frowning when Nick strode into the library, greeted his father and sat down in a chair near his desk.

"Are you well, Father?" Nick asked with concern.

"I am," Paul said, sitting at his desk, and gazing at his son with a somber expression, and then he got up and closed the door. Nick could tell it was going to be a serious discussion, possibly even a lecture, from the look on his father's face. He was sorry he hadn't gone riding with Alex instead. This wasn't going to be fun, but periodically he had to subject himself to his father's speeches about responsibility and obligation and what duty and their heritage required of them. Nick knew the main themes of the sermon by heart, and braced himself for what was about to come. His father sat down at his desk again and seemed to be weighing his words, which was unusual for him. Ordinarily, he launched right into a well-rehearsed list of what Nick should be doing and wasn't. Nick had been hearing it for twenty years, and waited patiently for him to start.

"I want to tell you about some things I've never discussed with you before," Paul began in a measured tone, and Nick glanced at him in surprise. This was new, and he couldn't imagine what it was. "I was very much like you when I was young. Actually I was a great deal wilder than you are, or ever were. You seem to have a fondness for pretty women and fast cars, but there's no harm in that, I suppose. And you're a wonderful father, and a devoted son."

"So are you a wonderful father, Papa," Nick interrupted him with a loving look in his eyes. "And you're very patient about my not wanting to run the estate. I just think you do it better than I ever will, and it would be a shame to have me make a botch of it, if I took it over from you now." His father smiled with a wintry expression that Nick had never seen before. Something was different today and he had no idea what it was. There was a sense of sadness around his father that frightened him. He hoped he wasn't sick. He was growing increasingly worried as he watched his father grope for words. "Is something wrong?" He cut to the chase, and his father didn't answer, which was unlike him as well.

"When I was twenty-one," Paul went on, avoiding Nick's eyes, "I met your mother. I was twenty-two when you were born. She was a very beautiful girl, and very young. She had dark hair and dark eyes like you, although other than that, you don't resemble her at all." Nick knew he was the portrait of his paternal grandfather, except for the dark hair. "She had very exotic looks, and I thought we were the same age. We had a brief and passionate affair one summer when I had nothing else to do, and she got pregnant, almost immediately. Later, I discovered that she was just fifteen, and she was sixteen when she had you. Needless to say, my parents weren't pleased. And even less so, when they discovered who her parents were. Her father was one of our tenants, or actually, his cousin was. Her father had come from the city with his wife and children to work the farm with his cousin, which was why I'd never seen your mother before. I was besotted with her immediately. Their cousins, our tenants, had originally been our serfs, which my father found particularly unamusing. I insisted I was in love with her, and perhaps I was. I'm not sure that anyone knows what love is at that age, or what can happen as a result, all the ramifications and consequences and things that can go wrong. When she told me she was pregnant, I did what I thought was the right thing and married her in a small ceremony in the chapel on the estate, in utter disgrace with my parents. My father struck an agreement with hers. No one was ever to know that I had married her, and we agreed that when she gave birth to you, we would be divorced immediately afterward. My father was able to arrange it with an attorney in Munich. And she agreed to give up the child when it was born, which was part of the contract my father made with them.

"I went abroad for a year, to Spain and Italy. I had an extremely good time, although

I felt bad about her. We were divorced as soon as you were born, as she had agreed, and they left the farm. She and her parents and brothers and sisters went back to the city, and my father bought the farm from their cousins for a very handsome price. After two hundred years on our land, they felt disgraced by what had happened and wanted to leave. I eventually returned from my travels, having allegedly married a young countess in Italy, who supposedly gave birth to you and died in childbed of a fever, which was common at the time. No one ever questioned the story when you appeared with me on my return, and everyone felt sorry for me. To be widowed so young and have a child on my hands. Your grandmother helped me take care of you, and no one ever knew the truth, except my parents, your mother and her family who were gone, the priest who married us, and the nurse who took care of you. And no one ever talked. I never saw your mother again, which was a dastardly thing to do. But I barely knew her, and you were the result of youthful lust, a brief summer fling.

"And the only real love I felt was for you. I fell in love with you the moment I saw you, and I never regretted having you for an instant. In fact, I think it turned me responsible early on, which was probably a good thing, since my own parents died when I was still relatively young, and I had to learn everything you've resisted learning all your life. I had no choice. I had a child, and a large estate to run, and I have done so for you, so that I can turn it all over to you in good order one day."

He looked bleak as he said it, and Nick could see that his father's confession was weighing heavy on his heart. What he didn't know was why he had chosen to tell him about his history now. Nick was trying to sort through what his father had said and what it meant to him. What shocked him most was hearing that the mother who Nick had always believed had died in childbirth, actually hadn't. And she wasn't an Italian noblewoman, she was a young girl on one of their farms, the daughter of a farmer or their city cousin, but the impact of that hadn't hit him yet. Nick was more shocked to realize that his mother was probably still alive, particularly since she'd been so young when he was born.

"Are you telling me that my mother is still

alive, and always was? Why are you announcing that to me now, Father?"

"Because you have to know. I had no
other choice now but to tell you. And I don't
know if she's still alive. I assume she is. She
was told never to contact us again, and she
hasn't. She was a decent girl, and she kept
her word. I have no idea where they moved
to, but I'm sure we could find out. I imagine she's still alive, she'd only be fifty-nine
now, which isn't very old. And I'm very sorry
to tell you all this. I never intended to tell you
any of it."

He had even covered his tracks by saying that her family had blamed him for her
death when she died and never wanted to
see him or the child again. That had explained the absence of maternal grandparents in his life, which Nick had never
questioned, and he had such a happy childhood that, although he missed having a
mother, he had lacked for nothing and
basked in his paternal grandparents' attention when they were alive, and most of all
his father's, who could never do enough for
his only son. Paul had never remarried, and
Nick couldn't help but wonder why now,
since he hadn't been mourning a child bride

he had loved. Perhaps the circumstances had been so traumatic and distasteful, Nick imagined, that they had cured him forever of wanting to form a permanent attachment, although he knew his father had had several long relationships that never led to marriage. He always said that the only family he needed or wanted was his son.

"Now that I think about it," Paul went on, "I vaguely recall hearing that she married a short time later. I think my father's attorney knew that, after he handled the divorce. I was relieved for her. I remember my father saying something about it, but I didn't pay attention. I had you, which was all I cared about by then. And if she did remarry, I'm sure she had other children. She was a lovely, healthy girl. But all I ever had or wanted is you." He and Nick exchanged a serious look, and neither man spoke for some time.

Nick was stunned by what his father had told him, and to realize that the father he had always believed would never lie, had told him nothing but lies about the circumstances surrounding his birth. It was a shock to learn that he had a mother somewhere who had probably sold him for a healthy sum. His father hadn't mentioned money, but it was obvious that that would have been part of the arrangement, to induce her and her father to agree to their terms to divorce and give up the child.

"What was her name?" Nick asked in a low voice, suddenly wondering what she looked like. There had never been any photographs or portraits of her anywhere, which his father had always said would have been too painful for him, and Nick had never questioned it for a moment, and respected his father's feelings about his "tragic loss."

"Hedwig Schmidt." Nick nodded as he felt the name carve itself into his brain. And then his father took a long breath and went on. "I am telling you this now because I had a visit two days ago from a man I haven't seen in years. We were friends as young men. He went to live in Indonesia, and I haven't seen him since. He's a general of the Wehrmacht now, and he came to see me as a favor. I don't know where or how he got it, but he had the record of my marriage, and the divorce, and he knew about you. People tell things nowadays that they never did before. There is information flying

through the air all over Germany, in this
very ill wind that is blowing from Berlin."

Paul looked hard at his son. "My friend
Heinrich von Messing tells me that your
mother was half Jewish. I didn't know it at
the time, and it wouldn't have mattered to
me. The circumstance of who she was was
enough to make our marriage unsuitable,
by reason of her birth. Her parents were
cousins of our tenants, and apparently, according to my friend, her mother's family
were Jews, which makes her half Jewish,
and you a quarter Jewish, and your sons
one-eighth. And according to Heinrich, being even part Jewish is very dangerous
these days.

"We've all been well aware of that for
several years, since the Nuremberg Laws."
Jews had been defined as a separate race,
and stripped of their citizenship. Since then,
one hundred and twenty more laws had
deprived them of further rights, and having
any "non-Aryan" blood in one's ancestry
had become a very bad thing. Paul had
never imagined that the plight of Jews in
Germany had anything to do with them,
and now it had everything to do with them,

and especially his son. The news had come as a shock to Paul.

Tears filled Paul's eyes as he went on, but he didn't move from his seat. He could see that Nick was already stunned by everything he had said. "He came to warn me, so that I could alert you. He said that someone has started a file on you, and your ancestry through your mother is known. This could be disastrous for you and your boys. It takes very little to tip the balance now. You and your children could be seized and sent away, and not allowed to remain here, or own property. Heinrich feels that to be safe, you and the boys must leave Germany at once. If not, with the dossier on you and your heritage, it's only a matter of time, and a very short time he believes, before the three of you will be sent to some kind of camp for 'undesirables.' It is almost a crime now to be a Jew in Germany, and even being a quarter Jewish puts you and the boys at great risk. They have been using Dachau, near Munich, for 'undesirables' of all kinds, which now applies to you and your children." Tears rolled down Paul's cheeks as he said it.

"Heinrich said it's going to get worse. I asked if I could speak on your behalf, or if we could get some kind of special dispensation when they go after one-quarter Jews, but he told me without question that anyone with any Jewish blood or ancestry is in danger in Germany." As he said it, Paul coughed to cover a sob that lodged in this throat like a fish bone. He looked as if his heart were about to break. "My darling son, you and your children must leave. Now. Soon. Before anything happens to you. According to Heinrich, there is no time to waste." There was an endless silence in the room as Paul's tears ran off his cheeks onto his desk. Neither of the two men moved as Nick stared at him, and it sank in.

"Are you serious? I have to leave? That's ridiculous. I'm not Jewish. My mother may have been, but you're not. I'm not. I didn't even know. And the boys are even less." Their mother had been Catholic and was related to a bishop.

"Not to them. Not to Hitler's government. If you have any Jewish blood at all, whatever religion you practice, you're a Jew," Paul said bitterly. "It's not about religion, it's about race, and you're not a pure-blood Aryan German in this country now."

"That's absurd." Nick stood up and walked around the room, unable to believe what he'd just heard. "I have nothing against the Jews, but I'm not one of them." Nick was dumbstruck.

"You are as far as they're concerned," Paul repeated. "I won't have you taken from your home and sent to a labor camp. My friend in the Wehrmacht said they could come here to take you away, and almost surely will, to make an example of you. They don't care who you are or how you're living—people of Jewish ancestry must go, or risk what will happen if they stay. And who knows what they'll do next. They're sending Jews to labor camps now and calling them a 'criminal element,' in order to make it more acceptable to lock them up, along with homosexuals, Gypsies, and anyone else they don't want in Hitler's Germany. Jewish teachers cannot work, Jews are being eliminated from their businesses and fired from their jobs, they can't go to parks or swimming pools. Where do you think this will go next? You can still get a passport to leave Germany, with special permission. You have to take the boys and go while you still can, before it gets worse." And now Paul was beginning to believe it would. He spoke to Nick with a tone of urgency.

"How much worse can it get?" Nick said, skeptical. "We are respectable people, Papa. You own one of the biggest estates in Germany. We come from one of the oldest families," Nick argued with him with a look of desperation. He was fighting for his right to stay in the only place he knew that was home.

Paul said miserably, "As far as they're concerned, a half-Jewish mother cancels out the rest. They don't care how old or honorable our family is, by ancestry, you are Jewish, even if you don't agree. And Jews are no longer welcome here, that is precisely what the general said. He took a great risk himself in coming here to warn us. He said that your file has already crossed someone's desk in Berlin. They are checking all the old families, all the town records, marriages, births, they are systematically looking for Jews. He said we have to move quickly. They could come here in a matter of weeks."

"What am I supposed to do?" Nick nearly shouted at him, but there was no one to shout at, no one to rail at but the fates. Because of a mother he had never known, or even knew existed, Nick and his sons would have to leave their home and flee. "What do I have to do? Run away?"

Paul looked at him with heartbreak in his eyes and nodded. "Yes. Heinrich said that people are leaving for America, if they can get sponsors and jobs, which isn't easy. I made a list of people I know there, but I don't know if they'd be willing to help. I want to write to the headmaster of your school in England—perhaps he can assist us. We have to reach out to everyone we know, to get you out of here. But to do that, you have to have a job."

"And what will I do, Papa? Be a chauffeur? I don't know how to work." He felt like a fool saying it, but they both knew it was true. The world he lived in and their circumstances didn't require him to work, or to know how to do anything productive. He hadn't even learned the little he should, to manage his own land.

"Perhaps you could work in a bank," Paul said hopefully. "You can't take more than a certain amount of money with you. They don't want any large fortunes leaving Germany. I'll give you whatever I can." Paul looked distressed. He had thought of the same things himself. "You have to be able to take care of the boys."

"Nothing in my life has ever prepared me for this," Nick said, with a tone of desperation. "We're brought up to do nothing except ride horses and drive cars, be civil at dinner parties and dance at balls. What part of that would make me eligible for a job?"

"We'll have to think of one quickly. There's no time to waste. You could teach German once you got there. You speak English well—it's why I want to write to your headmaster. Perhaps he could get you a job in a school, in England or the States. It's a respectable profession and it would feed you and the boys."

"And what am I supposed to tell my children?" He couldn't imagine what to say, it was all so convoluted, so ridiculous, and so sick. Toby wouldn't understand it at fifteen, and Lucas even less at six. He didn't understand it himself. "That we have to leave Germany because we're considered criminals? My sons don't even know what a Jew

is. And I'm supposed to tell them that because a lunatic is running Germany, we're
now being forced to leave home, to go to a
place where we have nothing and know no
one. Papa, this is insane."

"Yes, it is," Paul agreed, "and when things
calm down, which I'm sure they will eventually, you can come back, but for now you
have to leave. Heinrich made that very clear
to me, and I believe him. You have no other
option. I'll write the letters, and you need to
think if there is anyone you know who can
help, either sponsor you or give you a job."
Nick sat down in silence again for a moment, dumbstruck by all he'd heard. And
Paul was surprised by what he said.

"The men I went to school with in England
do the same thing we do. Hunt, ride horses,
and manage their estates. They don't have
jobs. And I'd like to try to meet my mother,
at least once. Even if she wants nothing to
do with me, I'd like to see who she is." It
suddenly mattered to him, although he
wasn't sure why. He was curious about the
mother who had given him up at birth. And
since she was probably still alive, he wanted
to see her face.

"I understand. I'll help you do that." Paul

looked as though he meant it, although he wasn't happy about it. She had been gone for forty-three years, and he had no desire himself to exhume her from the past. But they had more important things to tend to first, than satisfy Nick's curiosity about his mother. "We have no time to waste now. We have to get you and the boys out of Germany as soon as we can." Neither of them could think of a way to do that yet, but they knew they had to find a plan. Nick and the boys' lives depended on it, or their well-being certainly. Nick was horrified at the idea of going to a labor camp with his sons, and Paul couldn't think of anything worse, although his friend the general had hinted that that might only be the first step, and there could be worse to come, and he didn't want that happening to them. The general paying Paul a visit to warn him had been an immeasurable gift. Paul shuddered now, thinking of what might have happened if he hadn't come. They would have been taken by surprise, and Nick and the boys would be gone.

"Let's talk about this later," Nick said with a look of distress. "I need some air."

"Where are you going?" his father asked, panicked, fearing what Nick would do next.

"To Altenberg, to see Alex." As always, in times of unhappiness or joy, he wanted to see his friend.

"Are you going to tell him?" Paul was worried.

"I don't know. I just want to be there for a while. Of course I'll tell him when I leave. And I need to think about who to write to and where to start. I don't know anyone in the States." It might as well have been on another planet, and he couldn't see himself teaching at a school in England. He couldn't imagine leaving Germany at all. To where? To do what?

"I know some people in the States," Paul said quietly. "I will write them all letters asking them to sponsor you and the boys, and give you a job."

"I can work as a stable boy, or a dance instructor," Nick said ruefully, and he was only half-joking. They were among the few things he knew how to do. He hadn't tended to his own horses since he was a boy himself, but he knew he could.

"I'll try to get you something better than

that," his father said sadly, horrified by the situation they were in. He was willing to do anything to save his son and grandchildren.

A few minutes later, Nick drove away in his Bugatti, and both men were lost in thought. As he drove the beautiful sports car, Nick realized that life as he knew it was about to end, for years if not forever. And Paul was trying to adjust to the idea that he was about to lose his entire family and be separated from everyone he held dear. He thought of going with them, but he couldn't abandon the estate. He had a duty to be there for the land and their tenants, and to uphold his heritage and everything he had been brought up to respect. And he felt too old to go. The last thing Nick needed now was an old man on his hands to worry about. He would have enough to do with his boys. Paul knew he had to stay here. But Nick and the boys **had** to leave. Soon.

When Nick got to Altenberg, he parked his car and walked to the stables, and found Alex already working with Pluto. He was driving him hard through his paces, making him switch directions with split-second timing, and training him to stand motionless on his hind legs, which was called a "levade" and was something Lipizzaners were born to do. Nick noticed that Pluto had improved remarkably in recent weeks, since he had last seen Alex practicing with him. The result of hours of training was extremely good. Pluto was a natural performer, and he would do well when he left for Vienna in a few months, although Alex still wasn't satisfied. Alex waved when he saw Nick perch himself on the fence to watch his friend and the Lipizzaner at work.

"How bad was it with your father?" he called over his shoulder, and Nick shrugged. He didn't want to lie to him, and he didn't want to tell him the truth yet either. He was still digesting what he'd heard. It was just too hideous to believe. He and the boys had to leave Germany in a matter of weeks, with nowhere to go, and no way to support his sons when he got there. What his father had told him that morning was a nightmare, and all Nick wanted to do was wake up and hear it was a joke. But it was no joke. He thought about his mother, too, as he watched Alex work with Pluto, this time adding a hopping motion to the horse's erect stance, which Nick knew was called a courbette. He had seen Alex train horses to do that

for years, as well as the ultimate, the capriole and the croupade, in which the exquisite white horses seemed to fly through the
air in a perfectly choreographed ballet. Alex
referred to the maneuvers they did as "airs
above the ground." Alex was brilliant at training their Arabians, too, in **haute école** and
line training, and it soothed Nick a little to
watch Alex work with Pluto all afternoon. It
was dark outside when he stopped, and a
groom came to lead the horse away. Alex
talked to Pluto and calmed him for a few
minutes before he left, as though thanking
him for his hard work and a fabulous performance. Pluto had done better for him that
afternoon than ever before, and Alex looked
pleased when Nick jumped off the fence
and walked over to join him.

"I have no idea how you get them to do
that," Nick said admiringly. "I've watched
you do it a thousand times, and it still looks
like magic to me, as though you will the
horse to rise in the air. I swear you're a
magician."

"It's in their blood. They **want** to do it,"
Alex assured him modestly. "I just give them
the courage to try. Once they know they
can, it's easy, and fun for both of us." Nick

looked unconvinced and distracted as Alex met his eyes. "Was everything all right with your father?" Alex asked him, worried. It had suddenly dawned on him that Nick's father might be sick. He hoped not, but Nick looked deeply unhappy and upset.

"Yeah, he's fine," Nick said vaguely as they left the stables. Alex watched him closely. Nick's whole body looked tense, and his eyes were two deep pools of pain. They had been friends for too long for Alex not to notice.

"You don't have to tell me," Alex said cautiously. "You don't owe me anything. But I know you're lying. If I can do anything to help, tell me."

Nick shook his head, and against his will, in the face of Alex's kindness, tears sprang to his eyes, and he turned to look at the friend who was like a brother to him. It was Alex who had consoled him when his wife and daughter died, and who had been there for him for every major event in his life, good or bad. They had celebrated and cried together, and shared every grief and joy like the brothers they felt they were.

"My mother is still alive. . . . My father lied to me for all these years about who she

was. And he just found out she was half
Jewish. He didn't know. He has a friend in
the Wehrmacht who came to tell him, and
that the boys and I will be sent away somewhere, possibly to a labor camp, if we don't
leave. I have to leave Germany in the next
few weeks, because I'm now considered a
'Jew.' I need a job and a sponsor in America or England, or anywhere I can get to.
Alex, I have no idea what I'm doing, or how
I'm going to support the boys when I get
there. About the only job I'd know how to
do is be a stable boy or a groom or a chauffeur." There were tears in his eyes as he
said it. He looked panicked. Alex stopped
walking and stared at him as he listened.

"You're serious? This isn't some kind of
joke?" Alex couldn't believe it. Nothing he
had just told him was credible, least of all
that his mother was alive, and Nick was part
Jewish. But far worse was the news that he
and the boys could get taken to a labor
camp and had to leave immediately. It was
beyond comprehension.

"Do I look like I'm joking? What the hell
am I going to do?"

"Find a sponsor and a job, and damn
quickly," Alex said solemnly. They both

knew what had been happening in Germany since the Nuremberg Laws, instigated by Hitler. They just hadn't known that it applied to Nick and his boys. That was very, very bad news, and justified how Nick looked.

"A job doing what?" Nick said grimly. "At least you can train horses. I can't even do that. I just ride them after someone else does."

"Are you sure there's no way to buy your way out of this or talk to someone to change their minds?" Alex still couldn't believe it, nor could Nick, but it seemed to be terrifyingly true.

"Not according to my father. His friend, the general in the Wehrmacht, said we have to leave immediately, within a few weeks if not sooner. I have no idea what we're going to do. And why would anyone want to sponsor me and the boys, or hire me for a job I can't do?"

"We'll think of something," Alex said, trying to be helpful. But beyond finding Nick a sponsor and a job, he was grappling with the idea that his boyhood friend who had been his soul mate, brother, and partner in crime for forty years was about to leave

Germany, possibly forever, or surely for a long time, until Germany returned to normal, and who knew how long that would take? "Do the boys know yet?" Alex asked, panicked for him.

"I just found out this morning, and I'm not going to say anything to them until I know what we're doing. What if I can't find anything, and they send us away?"

"You'll survive it if that happens. But we have to make sure that it doesn't." He couldn't bear the thought of the three of them being taken away. It would be just too cruel, and what if one or all of them didn't survive it? Alex wanted to do anything and everything he could to help. He tried to imagine what it would be like if he and Marianne had to leave Germany, just as Nick and his children did. It was beyond anything he could understand, and he would have been just as terrified for the well-being and safety of his daughter as Nick must be now about the boys. Nick had a look of desperation as Alex walked him to his car and they stood there talking. Alex had never been so frightened for anyone in his life as he was for them now. It reminded him of when Nick's wife and daughter got sick. He was just as agonized for Nick and his sons now, and he felt sick himself thinking about it. "We'll think of something," he tried to reassure Nick as he got into the Bugatti. Nick stared up at him with sorrow in his eyes, and a look of despair. Neither of them could ever have dreamed that something like this could happen in their beloved country. Their lives had seemed safe and secure forever, into all the future generations, and now Nick was being forced to leave. It was impossible to absorb and fathom, let alone find a miracle to solve something so enormous.

"I don't know what I'm going to do," Nick said honestly. "What if there is no solution?"

"There will be," Alex said quietly. "There has to be, although this never should have happened. Never. Not in a civilized country like Germany. Who cares if your mother was half Jewish?"

"I want to see her," Nick admitted sheepishly. "I'd be angry at my father for not telling me the truth for all these years, if the rest of this weren't happening. But I can't be mad at him now. The poor man is terrified for us, and heartbroken that we have to leave. But I'd like to see who she is. Even if we have nothing in common, she's still my mother, and I've always wondered about her." Alex nodded. He could understand that, although it seemed so much less important than his other problems now.

"Does it really matter?" Alex asked.

"It does to me," Nick said solemnly. "Although I have to find a sponsor and a job in the States or Britain first. I need someone who can employ me so I can support the boys."

"I'll think about it tonight," Alex promised.

Nick reached out to touch his arm through the open car window. "Thank you," he said, "for everything . . . for being my friend for all these years." Alex nodded, unable to speak for a moment, and moved to tears himself. There was nothing he could say to express what he was feeling or how much Nick and his children meant to him. He hated the Nazis more than ever now, for what they were doing. The country had gone mad if they were following this little monster who wanted to chase respectable people from their homes and send them away with their children. Nick von Bingen and his family were the backbone of Germany, its heritage, and the essence of what mattered. And treating people like him and his family as if they were criminals was going to leave a gaping wound in the soul of the country Alex had been proud to call his homeland. And all he could think of was how much he was going to miss Nick and the boys. He couldn't bear to think about it yet. He was still reverberating from what Nick had told him, and as he walked into the schloss, he wiped his eyes. He was crying for his friend, his sons, his father who would be heartbroken to be separated from them, for himself, and for the country he had loved and could grow to hate now, for banishing his friend. What was about to happen was an immeasurable loss to all of them, and a frightening sign of the times. Their safe, peaceful life had been shattered, and Alex was certain that nothing in his life would ever be the same again.

Chapter 3

The days after Paul told Nick that he had to leave ran into each other with endless stress and a constant undercurrent of shock and fear. Nick still couldn't believe what was happening, Paul spent his days writing letters to people he barely knew in America, hoping to find a sponsor and a job for his son, and explaining their plight to anyone who would listen.

Lucas was oblivious to the tension surrounding them, but Tobias picked up on it quickly and asked his father what was wrong. It was one of the most painful moments in Nick's life to explain to his son what was happening, and why they had to leave their home. It made no sense to any of them.

After bursting into tears and saying he wouldn't go, Tobias took off on his bike to tell Marianne. She was just leaving the stables when he found her. She had been watching her father train Pluto, and was over her flu by then, although she still had a bad cough, and she had a red scarf wrapped around her neck. And the moment she saw Toby, she knew he'd been crying, and she was afraid that something terrible had happened. Her father had said nothing to her about what the von Bingens were facing. He didn't want to tell her until the boys knew and they knew where they were going, which would be something concrete, rather than the raw terror that was seizing Nick and his father at the moment. Their worst fear was that no one would help them, and that Nick and the boys would wind up in a labor camp after all. Their days of freedom were numbered, and time was racing. If they were going to get out of Germany, they had to find something soon.

"We're leaving!" Tobias shouted, as he threw down his bicycle, untangled his long adolescent legs, and ran toward her.

"Leaving for where?" She looked startled and uneasy, and the devastation on his face frightened her immediately. His eyes were filled with tears.

"We don't know yet. But it's going to be soon. America maybe, or England. Papa and Opa are working on it. Papa's mother was half Jewish, and she isn't dead after all. She went away somewhere, and they got **divorced**," he said in a conspiratorial tone. "And now we have to leave because they think we're Jewish too."

"That's ridiculous." Marianne tried to dismiss what he was saying as she stared at him. He was as tall as she was, and she could see that he was shaking, from fear and shock at what he'd been told, as much as from the cold wind that swept her white blond hair across her face. "You're not Jewish. Who said you have to go, and go where?"

"The **Reich** says we're Jewish, even if only a little bit. Because of Papa's mother, and he's never even seen her. She left when he was born and gave him to Opa. Papa just told me. I won't go," Tobias said, frightened. "I want to stay here. This is our home." He burst into tears, and she reached out and put her arms around him and held him close as she began to cry too. "Papa said if we don't go, they'll take us away somewhere. Maybe a labor camp. I don't want that to happen either."

"Does Lucas know?" she asked, instantly worried. They were like her brothers. She knew that Tobias had a crush on her, but she paid no attention to it. He was just a child to her, even though he was only two years younger. But at seventeen and fifteen, it made a difference. A big one.

"He's too little. We can't tell him." He echoed what his father had said. "Papa has to find a sponsor and a job."

"What kind of job?" She was shocked at the idea, as well as everything else Tobias had just told her.

"I don't know." He was confused.

"What can he do?" She looked surprised, as she led Toby to the house to get them both out of the chill wind.

"I don't know," Toby said, as they walked into the drafty main hall, with ancestral portraits lining the walls. He followed her to the kitchen, where she asked for hot chocolate for both of them, and then took him upstairs to her father's study since he was out. It was

a cozy book-lined room, with a fire burning
in the grate for when her father would come
back from the stables. It was her favorite
room in the vast, drafty house. The larger
rooms were hard to keep heated in the
winter, but this one was always warm and
inviting, especially when her father was in
it. She loved sitting and talking with him
here. And Tobias liked it too.

"This all sounds crazy," Marianne said
sensibly, unable to believe his story, or the
dire implications of it for them. "Are you sure
you have to leave? Why would they send
you away? Your father's not a common
thief."

"Of course not, but they think he's a Jew."
Tobias appeared desperate as he said it.

"Are they sending Jews to labor camps?"
Marianne looked horrified, as though she
didn't believe him.

"A general who is a friend of Opa's came
to warn him. He's the one who said we had
to leave, or they'll take us away." Marianne
was pale, and her hands were shaking
when Marta brought the tray in, with a cup
of hot chocolate for each of them. Marta
could see that they were upset about something and left quietly, sure that it was an ar-

gument of some kind between them and they'd work it out. They always did. They had been squabbling as children for years. Marianne usually won because she was older, and Tobias was still a child in many ways. Marianne was growing up, particularly in the last year, and Marta thought she was as beautiful as her mother had been, perhaps even more so, and she had her father's spirit.

"This all sounds like a crazy story to me," Marianne said with determination, as they sipped their hot chocolate. She didn't want to believe what he'd told her, but the terror in Toby's eyes told her it might just be true, unless he had misread the seriousness of the situation and thought it was worse than it really was. She hoped so. "Does my father know?" she asked him.

"I don't know. Papa didn't tell me," Toby answered, and as though they had conjured him up, her father walked into the room. Marta had told Alex they were in his study, and she appeared shortly afterward with a tea tray for him. He helped himself to a cup of tea, and looked at both children with a serious expression.

"What's going on here, you two?" He

wasn't sure if they'd had an argument, or if Toby had told her the news, if Toby even knew it himself yet. Nick had said he wouldn't tell his boys until he was sure where they were going, and he wasn't yet. Nick had told Alex that himself.

"We're leaving," Toby said sadly, and told him the same story he had told Marianne minutes before. Alex nodded, and they could both see he already knew.

"Your father told me a few days ago," he said quietly. "That is very, very bad news, for all of us," he said. And the way he said it told Marianne that it was true, and tears filled her eyes immediately.

"How is that possible, Papa?" she asked him in a choked voice. "Why are they sending Jews to labor camps? And the von Bingens aren't Jewish."

"Nick and the boys are part Jewish, it turns out. And apparently that's all the Reich needs to hear. They have been slowly banishing them from our society for the past five years. They seem to want all Jews isolated from the rest of us, or out of Germany, or confined in camps if possible. Toby's right, they have to leave. And very soon too. His father and grandfather are working very hard on it." He had sent off several letters himself, but had no responses yet. "I'm very sorry, Toby. I'm sure your father will find a solution. It's just hard not knowing where it will be."

"Can we go to visit them?" Marianne asked quietly. It was the worst news she'd had since her father told her that Toby's mother and sister died five years before. She remembered it perfectly. She had been very fond of Toby's mother, and very sad when she died, and equally so about his little sister.

"It depends where they are," Alex said honestly, "but we'll certainly try." Marianne and Toby exchanged a look then, which said everything they felt about being separated. Toby couldn't bear the thought of yet another important loss in his life, not only his dearest friends but his home too. And he didn't want to leave his grandfather behind, but he and Toby's father had said that his grandfather had to stay. They didn't want to leave their ancestral seat unattended with all the upheaval going on, even if the schloss was far from any city. It was hard to say what would happen now.

They talked for a long time, and Marta

brought them more hot chocolate and tea, and some freshly baked biscuits. It made Marianne suddenly realize that her friends might not be living this way anymore, and she was grateful that she and her father didn't have to leave too. And after a while, Alex offered to drive Toby home, but he said he'd be fine on his bicycle and left a few minutes later, after kissing Marianne on the cheek. She thought of him more than ever like a little brother when he did it, and not the man he wanted to be.

"That's an awful story, Papa," she said sadly, still unable to believe that it was true. She was shocked by everything she'd heard that afternoon. It was truly inconceivable.

"Yes, it is. I don't know what they're going to do. It's not so easy to pull a job out of a hat, and a whole new life, in a matter of weeks. It takes time to organize, and that's the one thing they don't have."

"And if they get sent to a camp?" she asked, holding her breath.

"They'll have to be very brave and survive it," he said matter-of-factly, trying to convince her that they'd be okay, but he didn't believe that himself, not by a long shot. He thought Nick and the boys should leave Germany as soon as they could, but for now they still had nowhere to go.

He and Marianne talked about it all through dinner, and Marianne thought she could detect a small smirk of disapproval on Marta's face when she heard that Nick and the boys were part Jewish, and then she left the room to tend to her duties in the kitchen.

Marianne thought about them all night, and finally slept fitfully, and in his room, Alex was still awake when he heard the birds begin singing the next morning, while it was still dark. But he sat bolt upright in bed then. He had an idea. He got up, dressed quickly, and hurried downstairs to grab a coat and his car keys, then rushed to the garage, to drive his Hispano-Suiza over to the von Bingens. He used the big brass knocker to pound on the door, and their head housekeeper appeared a moment later. Alex asked to see Nick immediately and was told he wasn't up yet, and then she reluctantly agreed to check. Nick appeared a few minutes later, wearing a silk dressing gown open over his pajamas and slippers. He was surprised to see Alex pacing in his front hall, as though he had come to make some kind of announcement, which was the case.

"I have an idea, and I think it will work," Alex said excitedly. He didn't want Nick to leave, but under the circumstances, it was their only hope. And with the risk of being sent to a labor camp, he didn't want them to stay either.

"Why are you here so early?" Nick asked with a pained look, as he tied the belt of the dressing gown. He had been up until two, but no great ideas had come to him.

"I'll give you two of my Lipizzaners, and some Arabians. All we have to do is contact a circus, and ask them to give you a job and sponsor you. And with eight horses, two of them Lipizzaners, I'm sure they would." Nick looked at him in disbelief and burst out laughing. He laughed so hard he nearly cried, and then he had to sit down. He rang for coffee for both of them, and looked at his friend.

"You're crazy, but I love you, Alex. I can't join a circus, for God's sake, no matter how fabulous your horses are. I can't do a circus act. You're the horse trainer, not I. And I can't take your horses. And not the Lipizzaners surely. No circus would hire me. I'd have no idea what I was doing."

"I can teach you. And the Lipizzaners know their job. All you have to do is guide them through it, by voice command. Leave the hard part to them. You can ride one of the Arabians and gallop around the ring. Nick, you're one of the best horsemen I know. And you can do it, if it will save you and the boys." Alex saw it as their only way out.

"I can't join a circus," Nick said. "What would I do there?" He looked horrified, but Alex was determined.

"You'd be saving your sons, and yourself, from disaster here. The situation for Jews is getting worse not better, and your father's friend said they have a file on you. What choice do you have?" Nick didn't answer for a long moment as he thought about it, and then he nodded, and looked at Alex. Everything his friend had said was true.

"I can't take your horses. Eight of them, and two of them Lipizzaners. If I do it, I'll pay you before I go."

"I won't take your money. You're like a brother. If the circus will take you, they're a gift from me."

"I can't do that," Nick said firmly, and then he grew pensive again. "How would I find a circus from here?"

"There is one called Ringling Brothers. I've read about it. I think they merged with another circus, and they're based in Florida. We can call the embassy in Berlin and ask."

"They'll think we're crazy," Nick said, smiling. He was beginning to feel hopeful, even though he still thought it was a crazy idea, and probably wouldn't work. Circuses didn't just hire men with horses to perform a circus act they didn't know how to do. It sounded far-fetched to him. But they called the embassy later that morning, and they were given the address of Ringling Brothers Barnum & Bailey Circus in Sarasota, Florida. It was based there for the winter before it went on tour. The woman at the embassy knew all about them, and Nick didn't tell her why he wanted to contact them. He was afraid she'd think he was crazy too.

Nick and Alex drafted a letter then, asking them to hire and sponsor him, with a description of the horses he could bring with him, and explaining the documentation he needed from them. They drove to the post office to mail it, and then they went to the manor house to tell Paul what they'd done. He thought it was an intriguing idea, although he insisted on paying Alex, too, if it worked. Nick would be taking some of his best horses. And Alex said he had an old railroad car they could use for the ship to transport them. He was even beginning to convince Nick as they discussed the plan. Nick wanted to go riding after that, but Alex wouldn't let him. He said they had work to do.

"What kind of work? Do you want to look at your forest land again?" Nick liked that idea too. It would distract him and get his mind off his problems.

"You have a circus act to learn, my friend," Alex said in a stern tone, "and after we teach you what you need to know, we'll work with the boys." Nick could see he was dead serious, and this time he didn't laugh. They drove back to Schloss Altenberg, and Alex pushed him hard all afternoon, showing him how to work the Lipizzaners, and how to direct them by voice commands. And then he had him ride Pluto around the ring, again and again, taking the big white stallion through his paces and everything he knew how to do. And then he had him work with Nina, the Lipizzaner mare, and an Arabian stallion.

"Your horses are a lot smarter than I am," Nick said finally. "I keep forgetting what to do. They don't." They were impeccably trained.

"They'll remind you. They're smarter than I am sometimes too." Alex had done nothing but instruct him, with infinite patience, all afternoon in his style and their liberty commands. And he made Nick repeat what he learned again and again. He was a hard taskmaster, and incredibly patient, and Nick was impressed.

It was an arduous week in Alex's hands. He was relentless in his training of Nick, teaching him how to work as one with the horses, and then he included the boys. Responses to Paul's letters began to drift in, all of them negative. No one had a job for Nick or felt they could sponsor him and the boys. Their only hope now was the circus, and as they waited for an answer, Alex continued to work with Nick and the boys. Paul came to see them in the stables several times, and was impressed by what he saw, and Marianne came every day after school to watch them. They looked very professional to her by then. Toby was still a little shy, but Lucas was irresistible and a natural. He rode one of the Lipizzaners bareback, and Alex taught him how to leap from one to the other, and both the mare and the stallion were willing to let him do that. If the circus hired them, Alex was going to give them Pluto, and the mare called Nina. She was ten years old, but beautifully trained and a steady ride. And he had already handpicked six Arabians for them, all from his best stock. He insisted that he could spare them, and that he had so many horses that he would hardly notice. But Nick knew that Pluto had been promised to the Spanish Riding School, and Alex would have a hard time replacing him. And Alex persisted in refusing to be paid.

A full two weeks after Nick had sent the circus the letter, he finally got a response. Nick's hands were trembling as he tore open the envelope in front of Alex and his father and read what they said. There was dead silence. Alex was afraid that they had turned him down. It had been almost three weeks since the general's visit, and the threat of labor camp, or worse, was becoming more real by the day. Ringling Brothers was their last hope. Nick met Alex's eyes when he put down the letter, and there were tears in his eyes as Alex gently touched his arm to console him.

"My God, they want us," he whispered, "it's all here. Everything we need. They're even going to post bond for us. We can leave." The tears rolled down his cheeks then, and Alex gave him a hug, let out a war whoop, and they could see that Paul was crying too. It was both happy and bitter news. With luck, they could avoid being sent to hard labor, but it meant they were leaving Germany forever, and it had to be very soon. Time was running out.

Paul regained his composure quickly, congratulated his son, and said he would book passage on a ship to America as soon as he could. He hurried off to make some calls and was back half an hour later. He had booked Nick and the boys in first class in two cabins, on the luxurious **Bremen,** which was leaving in four days for New York. It was willing to take the boxcar and the horses with its cargo, and Nick and the boys would have to tend to them. It was going to be their last voyage in luxury, possibly ever, or for a very, very long time. Who knew when or if they would ever come back to Germany? The atmosphere was one of jubilation and sorrow, excitement and despair. And when Nick told the boys they would be leaving, everyone cried.

The six of them spent the next four days together, and Alex was relentless rehearsing their act with them. Nick and the boys actually looked like an experienced circus team by the day before they left. And Marianne and Alex and Nick's father were planning to accompany them to the boat. They were going by train to Bremerhaven, via Nuremberg and Hanover, and boarding the ship there. And on the last night, Alex and Marianne had them to dinner at Schloss Altenberg. The meal was superb, there were many toasts, many silent moments filled with emotion, and a constant flow of tears. It was hard for all of them. Lucas was the most excited, but he had no real concept that they might never come home.

Their documents were in order, Paul had paid their emigration tax, and thanks to the general, the Reich had given its seal of approval to the plan. It was satisfied to see them leave. As far as they were concerned, there would be three fewer Jews in Germany, which appeared to be what they had in mind, to either force them to leave or strip them of all the rights they had ever had, or find some excuse to treat them as criminals. Hitler was "reclaiming Germany from the Jews," and now suddenly Nick had become one of them, and so were his boys.

By the time they boarded the train from Bavaria to Bremerhaven, and saw the boxcar with the horses loaded onto the train as well, all six of them were silent when they took their seats for the long ride. There was nothing left to say. They had said it all the night before: their hopes, their dreams, their regrets, their fears for one another, their sorrow to be parting. They watched the countryside slip by, as Toby and Marianne held hands, and they all fought back tears. Nick had a lump in his throat the size of a fist when the train pulled into the station in Bremerhaven, and Alex got up to help him oversee the move of the boxcar by crane onto the ship. The two men looked at each other for a long moment, as they watched it with their hearts in their mouths, terrified the boxcar would slip, and at that moment,

Nick knew exactly what Alex had done for him with his plan and his incredible gift. He had given them a new life, safety, and freedom. Nick hoped he could do as much for him one day, but it didn't seem possible. Alex had saved them from an unknown fate and given him and his sons the chance for a future. And as they watched the boxcar gently set down on the deck of the ship, Nick whispered silent thanks, and Alex put an arm around his shoulders, as both men wondered when they would meet again.

Chapter 4

Once the horses were safely on the ship in their boxcar, the six of them stood on the dock, looking at each other. Passengers and their guests were boarding the ship, to stroll the deck and visit the cabins, but Nick didn't want to leave the pier. This would be the last time he would stand on German soil, and once he boarded the ship, he would lose everything he loved and knew. He couldn't bear the thought of his father being alone, and he turned and spoke to him quietly, out of earshot of the others.

"Will you come, Papa? Please? I don't

want you to stay here. You can come to the circus with us. I'm sure they would sponsor you too." He could come on the next ship—he wasn't in the danger that Nick and the boys were and could take more time to leave. But Paul slowly shook his head. All the pain he was feeling over their departure was plain in his eyes.

"I can't. I can't abandon everything we have here. I need to take care of it for you and the boys. I don't trust these people in the Reich. They're going to destroy the country if they can. I want to at least protect and preserve our small part of it for you." A sense of responsibility and duty was keeping Paul in Germany, but his heart was leaving with Nick, Tobias, and Lucas. After they left, there would be nothing for him in Germany, except their land. Paul was the guardian of their property now, and nothing else. And he ached with an almost physical pain to see them all leave. He was grateful, too, that he and Nick had done some fancy footwork the previous year to keep Toby out of the Hitler Jugend. Their doctor had given him a letter saying he had asthma and couldn't attend meetings. Paul wanted to contribute nothing to Hitler's Reich, least of all his grandsons. Paul hated the Nazis even more now. He would never forgive them for making Nick and the boys leave.

"I'm going to miss you, Papa," Nick said softly, and Paul nodded and lowered his eyes, unable to speak. He would miss them, too, beyond measure.

They stood there for a few minutes then, in silence, and Alex came over to them to talk to Nick.

"I want to check on the horses." He looked concerned. There were eight horses in the boxcar—Pluto, Nina, and six Arabians, of which two were stallions and four were mares—and he wanted to be sure they were all right after the train ride and having the boxcar moved onto the ship. He wanted to see for himself that none of them had been injured and that they were relatively calm, although they would sense something different happening. Alex had given Nick and the boys all the instructions they needed, and even some fancy bridles to use in the circus. And to the very end, he had refused to let Nick pay him. It was an enormous gift, which Nick knew he could never repay with an equally important gesture, other than his love and loyalty forever, but Alex had had that from him for years and always would. The two men looked bleak and despondent at the prospect of saying goodbye.

Only Lucas was in good spirits as they boarded the ship. He was itching to go exploring, but Nick told him to wait until later after they set sail. Nick and Alex went to look at the horses, and they were skittish but fine. Alex said they would settle down, and he hoped it would be a smooth trip.

And while Nick and Alex were busy with the horses, Lucas stood talking to his grandfather, and Toby stood quietly chatting with Marianne. She had been dabbing at her eyes with a lace handkerchief since they left home, and she looked at Toby sadly now.

"I'm going to miss you so much," she said miserably. He was like her little brother, and had been since he was born. "Write to me every day, and tell me what the circus is like. I want to know everything." She tried to distract both of them. He nodded and promised to write, although he usually didn't like writing letters and seldom had, but he said he would for her.

"Will you visit Opa?" Toby asked her wistfully, and she nodded as they glanced at his grandfather. Lucas was chatting animatedly with him, and even managed to make his grandfather laugh, which wasn't easy today.

They visited Nick's stateroom, and the boys' cabin next door. Both rooms were very elegant, and Nick knew this was the last grandeur they would see for a long, long time, until they returned to Germany. He had been allowed to take ten reichsmark with him. And Paul had slipped a wad of cash into Nick's hand unseen, which he concealed under his clothing once he was in his cabin. It was all they had now, other than the bond posted by the circus and the salary he'd earn once he was hired. He couldn't imagine living on his salary, but they would have to. He had left his Bugatti with Alex and told him to use it. And they had brought several trunks with them, including two filled with evening clothes to wear when they performed with the horses. He had several tailcoats and two top hats with him, and another set for Toby.

As they stood chatting in Nick's stateroom, the boat horn gave the signal for all visitors to disembark. The mere sound of it filled them with panic, and Toby clutched Marianne as though he were drowning, and they both burst into tears, and Nick hugged his father and then Alex. The two men closed their eyes as they stood in a last embrace, like brothers who were about to be separated for life. And then Nick hugged Marianne, and she bent to kiss Lucas on the cheek.

"You be a good boy, and don't marry the fat lady in the circus before you come back to me," Marianne said, and Lucas guffawed and promised he wouldn't. And then Paul hugged his grandsons again, and looked longingly at his son, as though to engrave every detail of him into his memory. Nick and the boys walked them to the **passerelle,** and they all hugged one last time before Paul, Alex, and Marianne disembarked. Nick had no idea why the other passengers were leaving Germany, for pleasure or as emigrants, but their own departure was so emotionally charged and so painful that their three visitors could barely tear themselves away, but finally did. All of them were in tears except Lucas, who was too excited by the ship to be as sad as everyone else.

And joining the circus still seemed like fun to him. The agony of their leaving Germany was somewhat lost on him, since he was only six.

Nick moved away from the **passerelle** and stood at the rail farther down the deck to watch them, and Toby stood beside him, as Lucas came and went, talking to sailors, or other passengers, and returning to his father like a puppy. Nick and Alex exchanged a long look between the pier and the ship, and Marianne could no longer stop crying as she waved to Toby, and he was fighting back tears. Paul's chest was heaving with the sobs he was holding back, and at last the **passerelle** was put away, and tugboats slowly moved the giant ship from the dock, as the boat horn sounded continuously, and Nick waved at the three people he loved standing on the dock. He heard Toby choke on a sob next to him, and he put an arm around his shoulders and held him close to him, and then Lucas came to stand next to them and waved at the others on the dock.

Nick, Toby, and Lucas waved for as long as they could see them, and the three on the pier never moved from the spot, until the ship was too far away to see anyone on it anymore, and they slowly turned to go home. The SS **Bremen** had set sail with everyone they loved on it. The three of them were pensive on the trip home, and never said a word. The only sound was Marianne blowing her nose discreetly from time to time, and then she put her head on her father's shoulder, and exhausted from the emotions of the day, she fell asleep, with her handkerchief still in her hand. They had all cried rivers that day.

Nick wanted to check on the horses again after they set sail, and he tried to convince Lucas to come with him, but he wanted to explore the ship, so his father let him. Toby was sitting in their cabin, looking destroyed, and too upset to do anything. His eyes were rimmed with red from crying.

"We'll be back," Nick said gently, and Toby nodded, to be polite, but he didn't believe him. They were outlaws and outcasts in Germany now, displaced persons who had no right to occupy their own home. They had been banished like common murderers and thieves. And the stamp on their passports said "Deported," although they

hadn't been and had left of their own ac-
cord. And there was a red J stamped on
their passports now as well, for "Jew,"
"Jude." They were political refugees, and
their German citizenship had been canceled as Jews.

When Nick got back from the horses,
Toby was gone, and Lucas was visiting the
elegant swimming pool and the kennels.
There was a smoking room, a lounge, and
a famous ballroom as well. He had said he
wanted to see the dogs, and Nick strolled
quietly along the deck, and stood at the rail
looking out to sea. He had noticed several
pretty women when they boarded, but he
had no interest in pursuing them. All he
could think of was the world they had just
lost. The elegant ship was the last vestige
of it. Lucas didn't understand that, and Toby
grasped it to some extent, but Nick fully realized what was happening to them and just
how painful it would be. The fact that they
were joining a circus in a foreign country
was even stranger, and hard to fathom or
imagine what it would be like. He didn't even
want to think about it now, as he stood looking out to sea with his heart full of Alex, and
his father. Nick hadn't felt so bereft and dev-

astated since his wife and daughter died. He stood at the rail until he got too cold, and then went back to his cabin, and lay on the bed for a while, hoping to sleep. When he couldn't, he went below to visit the horses again. He picked up one of the brushes Alex had given them, and began currying Pluto, as the stallion turned toward him with a pleased look.

"Good boy," Nick said, patting his snowy neck, and continuing to brush him. All of the horses were tethered on short lead lines to secure them so they wouldn't get hurt, and they'd have to do without exercise for several days. Nick just hoped that the sea wouldn't get rough, so they wouldn't be injured. He didn't want to lose any of them before they even arrived. He had brought a loaded pistol with him, in case he had to put one of them down. It had been Alex's suggestion, and he hoped he wouldn't have to use it. Particularly for the Lipizzaners— they were precious cargo on the ship, and Nick's ticket to a new life.

He stayed with the horses for a long time, and then went back on deck, where he ran into his boys playing shuffleboard and talking to two young girls. Nick smiled when he saw them. Toby looked happier than when they'd set sail, and Lucas ecstatic, wielding the shuffleboard paddle that was taller than he was, and trying to impress the girls, who giggled at what he said. They were closer to his age than to Toby's, and eventually they scampered off, and Lucas lost interest in the game, and came to where his father was sitting in a deck chair with a blanket, to tell him what he'd been doing. And from the sound of it, he'd been everywhere on the ship, in first class, since the lower decks weren't accessible to him.

"Can we go swimming later, Papa?" he asked excitedly, and Nick agreed. It distracted him from his miseries to be with his children, and he wanted the trip to be a happy time for them, before they faced the unknown, and joined the circus.

The two boys went to a movie at the cinema later that afternoon, and Nick continued to stroll the deck, and visit the horses periodically. One of the other passengers questioned him about it, when he went indoors for teatime. There was an elaborate buffet set out for the first-class passengers, and the German equivalent of high tea. The food was supposed to be notoriously good on the ship, but Nick couldn't eat. All he wanted was a cup of tea, which he followed up with a stiff malt whiskey.

"I understand that you're traveling with a boxcar full of Arabians," the man who'd asked about the horses commented with interest. He was American, said he was from Kentucky, and that he owned horses himself, and had been in Germany buying hunters and two racehorses, but they were being sent to the States on another ship, with handlers he had brought over. He said his name was Beauregard Thompson. "Where are you taking them?" he asked, in a heavy Southern accent Nick could barely understand. He was used to British inflections and not an American accent from the South.

"To Florida," Nick said simply, and the man nodded, impressed by what he'd heard about Nick's horses. Transporting eight Arabians was a sign of great wealth.

"You're smart to have them on the ship with you," he complimented him. "You can keep an eye on them yourself. I'd love to have a look at them sometime," he suggested politely, and Nick nodded as he took a long sip of the whiskey. He needed it, it had been a hard, deeply emotional day.

"Of course," Nick said pleasantly. "Only six are Arabians actually. The other two are Lipizzaners," he said casually, not sure the man would know what they were.

"Oh my God," the man said, awestruck. "Now, **that** I'd like to see. Are you taking them to show them?" Nick nodded with a wry smile. He was taking them to be "shown" in a circus. He was sure that if Thompson knew that, he'd be shocked. There was nothing gentlemanly about the circus.

"I'll be happy for you to see them," Nick volunteered, and Thompson left after that, to find his wife, who he said was shopping at the ship's boutiques.

Toby and Lucas came to find Nick in his stateroom after the movie. They went swimming, and then Nick and Toby went to clean out the horses' stalls before they went to change for dinner. Nick hadn't done stable boys' work in years, but he found it easier than he remembered, and not totally unpleasant. It was a good chance for him to get to know the horses, as he moved between them, patting them now and then. Pluto was the most responsive to him, and nuzzled him each time he walked by, as though to say hello. Nina, the Lipizzaner

mare, was the most upset. And the Arabians still seemed nervous, but all right. And
all eight horses were eating and drinking.
Nick was careful to notice that.

And once he and Toby had cleaned out
their stalls, and disposed of the manure as
they'd been told to, they went back to their
cabins to bathe and dress. Dinner that night
was white tie, for him and Toby, and Lucas
was going to eat in their cabin with a steward. He was too young for the formal sitting
in the dining room, and it sounded boring
to him anyway. And the young steward had
promised to take him to the kennels again.
According to Lucas, the ship was full of
dogs. Theirs were the only horses.

Nick and Toby introduced themselves
once they were seated at the captain's table. There was a very glamorous-looking
couple from Berlin—he was from a well-
known banking family, and they were planning to visit relatives in New York. There
was a relatively famous German actress,
who eyed Nick with interest, a sentiment he
didn't return. She was twenty years older
than he was, and drank way too much at
dinner. There was an Italian couple, and a
British writer Nick had heard of but not read,

and a very pretty French woman named Monique, who mentioned that she was widowed. Her husband had been German, and they had a schloss in the Tyrol. And there were two other German couples of no particular interest whose only attribute seemed to be that they had a great deal of money, but they were neither fun nor attractive.

After dinner, they all moved upstairs to one of the bars on the upper deck for coffee, cigars, and liqueurs. A band started playing, and there was dancing. And just as they began playing, Toby asked his father's permission to slip away, which Nick granted. And after Toby left, Nick danced with Monique, and was still dancing with her when the captain and some of the others left. The bar was full of passengers, and everyone seemed in good spirits and very lively, and although it had been a hard day for him, Nick's spirits improved as he chatted with the attractive French widow, who was an exceptionally good dancer and very pretty. There was a surreal feeling to all of it for him, as he hung suspended between two worlds. And for a moment or two, in the glamorous context of the boat, he could pretend that nothing bad had happened, but he knew it had, and it weighed on him heavily between drinks. He was working hard to flee the truth. The young French woman sensed that something was wrong in his life, but was polite enough not to ask.

"Are you visiting friends in America?" she asked discreetly, and he nodded. He had no intention of telling her that he and his sons were joining a circus, and had fled Germany to save their lives. "So am I," she said, with a small sigh. "Germany is so dreary these days, with all those rallies and marches and speeches. My husband died six months ago, and I need a change. I'm going to Boston to visit my sister. She lives there with her husband. She seems to like it. They married last year, and they're expecting their first baby, so I thought I'd go over to see her." She said she lived near Munich, and had no children. And judging by the jewelry she was wearing, Nick sensed that her husband had left her a vast fortune. She mentioned once while they were dancing that her husband had been forty years older than she was, and she looked to Nick to be about thirty.

She was a lovely woman, and they danced several waltzes and foxtrots, and she was particularly impressive doing the tango. She and Nick looked very striking on the floor, and several people stopped to watch them, and afterward she and Nick laughed. It had been fun. It was obvious that Monique found him attractive. He found her equally so, but he was in no mood or position to start a shipboard romance with anyone. His life was a shambles, and he was enough of a gentleman not to inflict that on anyone, although she looked like she was willing. They sat and talked for a while afterward, and at two in the morning, he walked her to her cabin, while she told him how much she had enjoyed the evening.

"So did I," he said, smiling at her. He hadn't expected to enjoy the first night so much, but she had boosted his spirits. And he always liked to dance, and was good at it.

"I met your little boy today," she said, when they stopped outside her door. "He's adorable."

"Yes, he is, thank you," Nick agreed warmly. "I think he met everyone on the ship today, including all the sailors. He's having fun."

"So am I," she said, looking wistfully at Nick. "I loved dancing with you tonight. I haven't been dancing in months."

"You're a wonderful dancer," he said sincerely. She wished he wanted more from her than that, but she could see he didn't. There was something profoundly sad in his eyes, and she could sense this was not a happy trip for him. He was putting a good face on it, and he was every inch a gentleman, but there was something sad and remote about him, as though he had lost someone he dearly loved. In fact he had lost a country that day, and said goodbye to his father and best friend. She assumed he had lost a woman, but he had given up a great deal more. He had abandoned an entire life.

"Thank you for the compliment," she said, flirting with him. "Perhaps we can do it again tomorrow. I think tomorrow is the casino night, and the day after that the masked ball." There were special entertainments planned every night, and she had brought a different gown for each occasion. From what Nick had seen that night, her wardrobe and her figure were exquisite. For the right man, she would be a glorious catch, but not for him. Not anymore. He had the good manners and good sense, in his current circumstances, not to get involved. He felt as though that part of his life were over now too. He had nothing to offer anyone, surely not stability, or even a pleasant way of life. All of that was gone. He resisted the urge to be melancholy, but he was still reverberating from everything that had happened. And to some degree, he was still in shock, and she could see it.

"I'd be very happy to escort you to the casino," Nick said pleasantly, although he had no intention of gambling with the little he had. His father had paid their first-class passage, and he needed the money they had brought with them, to take care of his sons. Overnight, he had become responsible, despite his carefree, self-indulgent ways of the past. Those days were over. He had grown up instantly. And a random night of shipboard gambling, give or take even a few hundred reichs-mark, was no longer possible for him. For her, he could tell it would be small change. The difference in their circumstances now made even a casual flirtation with her seem dishonest. He was no longer of her world. He had become an outcast in his country, and what had previously been his life. Nothing of all that was visible to her. But he knew the difference, between what he had once been, only days ago, and what he was now. And in another week, he would be nothing more than a performer in the circus. It was horrifying to think about and still impossible to absorb.

"Goodnight. I'll see you tomorrow," she said with a seductive glance as she disappeared into her cabin, and Nick walked slowly back to his own, feeling pensive. He didn't really want her, but if he had, she would have been untouchable for him now. Their lives were miles apart.

Before he went back to his stateroom, he checked on the boys. Both were sound asleep, and he gently covered Lucas with his blanket, as he clutched the teddy bear he had brought with him, that he had slept with all his life. And he was wearing pale blue pajamas. Toby was sleeping, too, with the peaceful face of the boy he still was. And then Nick went back to his own room, sat down quietly in a comfortable chair, and lit a cigar. He had much to think about these days. He poured himself a cognac from the decanter in his room, and sat in the dark, in the moonlight, watching the smoke from his cigar, and the brightly lit end, wondering what the future had in store.

Chapter 5

The casino night with Monique was as pleasant as the night before. They danced after the gambling, and it was a lively evening Nick enjoyed. He had always liked gambling, within reason, but he only played roulette twice that night, for modest amounts, and lost. Monique won five hundred reichsmark, and he didn't play again. He was being cautious.

Both boys were enjoying the ship, the weather was fine, and the horses were doing well. And on the night of the masked ball, halfway through the trip and far from land, they hit a November storm. And the ship began pitching and rolling. With apologies to Monique—who didn't suffer from seasickness it turned out—Nick went to see the horses, after he checked on his sons, who were fine in their cabin. The horses were frantic and wild eyed in the storm, and Nick stayed with them for several hours trying to calm them. There wasn't much he could do, except be there and try to reassure them as best he could, patting and stroking them and speaking to them in a soothing tone. It didn't make much difference, but he didn't want to leave them alone, in case one of them got hurt. They were crucial now for him and the boys, and late into the night as the storm seemed to get rougher, if that was possible, the worst happened. Pluto looked at him and quietly lay down, a dreaded sign in horses. Nick was well aware of the consequences as soon as the beautiful stallion lay down, and there was nothing Nick could do to stop him. He was equally aware that if Pluto didn't get up again on his own within hours or a day at most, he would be dead when they arrived in New York. And he couldn't appear in Florida with only one Lipizzaner, and particularly without the stallion he had promised. Pluto was by far the more impressive of the two Lipizzaners, although Nina was lovely too. But she was outclassed by the stallion in breeding, looks, and size.

Nick stayed with him all night, and by morning things had not improved. The storm continued to get worse, and with a feeling of panic, he returned to his cabin to change and went to the dining room for breakfast. Neither of his boys was feeling well, and they decided to stay in their cabin. He didn't tell them about Pluto. There would be time enough for that piece of bad news later, if the horse refused to get up. Nick was still hoping he would, perhaps when the storm was over.

He ran into Beauregard Thompson at breakfast in the dining room, and they were among the few passengers at the buffet that morning. Most people had stayed in their rooms, seasick from the storm, including the Kentuckian's wife, who he said was very ill. But Thompson was a hardy soul, and Nick had always been a good sailor. Nick mentioned that he was having a problem with one of his horses and asked for Thompson's advice.

"There's nothing much you can do, except hope he gets back up on his legs again," he said, sharing Nick's concern. "That's a death sentence for your stallion if he's lying down. How many hours has it been now?" Nick told him, and he nodded. "I had a mare do that to me last year. I thought she'd get back on her feet again and survive it, but she didn't. It killed her after two days. We put her down, but she was nearly gone when we did. She would have died on her own within two more hours. If this damn storm would calm down, you'd have a chance, but with all this going on, I doubt you'll get him up. He's probably seasick," which was contributing to the problem. "I'll take a look at him after breakfast, if you like," he promised.

Nick led him downstairs to the boxcar when they both left the dining room. The Arabians were still frightened, but holding up, and Nina looked desperately unhappy, but she was still standing. Pluto was in the same spot where Nick had left him, on the ground. He hadn't budged an inch, and looked up at Nick with an expression of de-

feat and despair, and then laid his splendid head down on the floor of his stall, as
Beauregard marveled at him.

"My God, what a spectacular creature,"
the man said in amazement. "How big is he
standing up?"

"Just over sixteen hands," which was on
the tall side for a Lipizzaner.

"I've never seen anything so beautiful,"
he said in open admiration. "He's incredible." Pluto looked woebegone as he lay in
his stall, but he was still strikingly handsome. "You've got to save him."

"Yes, but how?" Nick said, frightened. He
could feel Pluto slipping right between his
fingers. And Nick would hate to tell Alex that
the beautiful young stallion had died before
they arrived.

"There isn't a damn thing you can do except hope and pray he decides to survive
this. He's young enough to make it through
it if he wants to." All Nick could do was hope
he wouldn't die.

Beauregard Thompson stayed with him
for a while, and then went back to his own
cabin to check on his wife, and Nick stayed
alone in the boxcar with the horses for
the rest of the day. The room stewards

had promised to watch over the boys. And he knew that Toby could entertain Lucas. The storm finally calmed a little, but Pluto didn't move and barely made a sound even when Nick stroked him and talked to him. He seemed to be getting weaker.

By the end of the day, Nick was in despair. It was obvious that the stallion wasn't going to make it, and it was only a matter of time before he died, maybe hours. And there was no way to feed him or even give him water while he lay there. Nick knew enough about horses to realize that he was watching the beautiful young stallion's final hours. At one point, he even thought of being merciful, and using his pistol to put him down, but he didn't have the heart to do it. He sat down next to him instead, and continued stroking his neck and crooning to him, and his eyes filled with tears. It was heartbreaking to watch the Lipizzaner slowly die.

And finally, he laid his own head down against Pluto's massive shoulder, and knowing no one was there to hear him, Nick begged him to stay alive.

"I know this must sound stupid to you," he said in a low voice to the horse, "and you deserve better than life in a circus, but I need you for my boys. Without you, they probably won't want us in Florida, and if they don't, I have no way to feed Toby and Lucas. If you don't come to the circus with us, we're really in a bad spot here. Pluto, if you'd just stay alive for me, I swear I'll take care of you forever, and I'll owe you my life. My boys are depending on you and so am I. Please don't die ... please ... we need you so desperately. . . . I need you. . . . I'll do everything for you I can. I promise. . . ." Tears slid down Nick's cheeks as he spoke to him.

He suddenly noticed that the storm had calmed completely. The pitching and rolling had stopped. And as though he had noticed it, too, Pluto turned his head to look at Nick, lying alongside him, and he shook his head as though to nod. And then he gave a gigantic shudder, which Nick was terrified would be his last, and with enormous effort, and a loud whinnying, Pluto fought his way to a standing position on shaking legs. Nick watched, unable to believe his eyes. Pluto was up! He had made it, and with any luck at all, and some sustenance, he wouldn't die! It was as though the stallion had made his own decision, and a supreme effort for his new owner.

Nick put his arms around the horse's neck and sobbed. He had never been so grateful for anything in his life. The horse dying on their way to Florida would have been one blow too many in a series of brutal shocks that had turned their life upside down. And now it felt right-side up again. He offered the horse some water, which Pluto took gingerly with a grateful glance at Nick, and then he turned to look at the other horses, and Nina whinnied to him from her stall, as though to say welcome back. Nick stayed with him for another hour to make sure he didn't lie down again, but the stallion was eating and already looked better when he left.

Nick went to find Beauregard Thompson immediately, and knocked on the door of his cabin when he didn't see him on deck. He came to the door, was surprised to see Nick, and said he had been ministering to his wife.

"How is he?" he asked in a somber tone, referring to the stallion. And he was sure Nick had come to tell him he was dead. He hadn't expected him to survive, he had already been lying down for too long.

"He's up," Nick said with a broad smile, and Thompson stared at him.

"I can't believe it. When I saw him, he was nearly gone." Nick nodded in agreement. "What did you do?"

"I talked to him. I pleaded with him to get up, and he did." Nick looked ecstatic, and was enormously relieved.

"You're a better man than I am. I couldn't get my mare to get up last year, no matter what I did. I had the vet in to see her three times, and we still lost her. But I have to admit," he said, laughing, "I never asked her to get up. Well, good for you." He pounded Nick on the shoulder. "We'll have a drink to celebrate after dinner."

"Thank you. I just wanted you to know." Nick was hoping to see Monique that night after dinner. He had been too busy with Pluto and worried about him, to see her at all ever since the horse had lain down. She had continued to show interest in him, and had sent a note to his cabin with a bottle of champagne saying that she missed him. She was trying hard. And at another time in his life, she would easily have succeeded in seducing him. But right now, there was just too much going on to pay serious attention to her.

When Nick went back to his stateroom, he was smiling broadly. Pluto had survived, and as much as it could be right now, their future was safe. Just as Nick had asked him to, Pluto had saved his life.

Chapter 6

For the last day of the trip, Nick kept a close eye on Pluto and the other horses, but they all seemed to be doing fine, and the stallion seemed stronger than ever once he was on his feet and eating and drinking again. He seemed to have formed a deeper bond with Nick after his illness, and whinnied with pleasure whenever Nick came to the boxcar. It was as though he knew how much he meant to him now, and what was expected of him. Nick felt as though they had made friends.

Nick spent his daytime hours with his sons, playing shuffleboard, swimming, shooting skeet with Toby, and walking around the deck together. And with Pluto back on his feet again, he spent the evenings with Monique. They danced until the wee hours, admired by everyone who watched them. They made a splendid couple, and were obviously having a good time. Their tangos were legendary on the ship, and they looked dashing whenever they were together. Monique had a sense of showmanship and was enjoying the attention they got, and being with a man as handsome as Nick. And finally, when he took her back to her cabin, since it was the last night, Nick kissed her. He'd had a little too much champagne, celebrating Pluto's recovery, and he couldn't resist Monique's charms as they stood in the light of the November moon, bright and heavy in the sky. They would be reaching New York the next day.

"When are you going back to Germany?" she asked in a whisper, after he kissed her for the second time. She was anxious to see him again, and continue the pleasures of the trip.

"I'm not," he said quietly, and she looked at him in surprise.

"I thought you were only visiting, to show your horses somewhere."

"I'm staying," he said, not wanting to say why or tell her that he'd be showing his horses as a circus act. He was embarrassed about the life he was about to lead, among circus people, whom he could only imagine as freaks. And now he was one of them. He hadn't adjusted to it yet, and wondered if he ever would.

"Is there some reason why you're not going back?" she asked, looking startled and suspicious. She knew other people who had left the country in the past few years, afraid of what was happening in Germany, and fearing for their lives. But she could think of no reason why Nick would be one of them.

"Yes," he said as he leaned against the rail in the moonlight. He didn't want to lie to her, and would have preferred not to explain it, but he could see that she wanted an answer of some kind.

"Are you Jewish?" she asked him with a curious expression. She didn't think it likely. He was obviously a nobleman of high rank, as his name, looks, and title suggested.

"Yes, and no," he said honestly. "In the

real world, as we knew it until recently, no, I wasn't. In Hitler's Germany, apparently I am. I never knew my mother. My parents divorced when I was born, and my father and I discovered recently that she was half Jewish, which makes my sons and me Jewish according to the Nazis. We had to leave, we might have been sent to a labor camp if we stayed, so we're going to America." She looked shocked at what he said, and for a moment he wasn't sure which part of the story had alarmed her, the fact that he had barely escaped being sent to a labor camp, or that his mother was Jewish.

"How horrible of them," she said, suddenly sympathetic. "And how absurd. What will you do?" She looked worried and sad for him and the boys, which confirmed to him that she was a good person. And he laughed at her question.

"I didn't have a lot of choices. I have no profession, nothing I know how to do. I suppose I could have been a dance instructor"—he smiled at her—"or a chauffeur or a stable boy. I can't say that any of those options appealed to me, and I only had a few weeks to figure it out. A friend gave me the horses I have with me. Two of them are Lipizzaners, trained for exhibition. I'm joining the circus as an equestrian act," he said with a wry expression. "My six-year-old son is enchanted. I can't say I feel the same way about it, but I'm grateful that I could get them out of Germany and found something I can do. So, my dear, you have been dancing your nights away with a circus performer. I daresay your friends would be shocked, and so would mine." Saying it out loud to her made it both worse and better. Worse because it made a reality of it, and better because it was so ridiculous even to him that it made it laughable instead of something that made him want to cry. Not knowing what else to do, Monique laughed.

"Are you serious?" She thought he might be teasing her. But from the look in his eyes, she could see he wasn't. It was the oddest story she'd ever heard. She had heard of doctors and lawyers who had left Germany, all of them Jewish, but never aristocrats like Nick.

"I'm entirely serious. When we land in New York, I am taking my sons and the horses to Florida, where we were hired by the Greatest Show on Earth. They sponsored me to get us out of Germany, and offered me the job, and I'm very grateful that they did. So I'm afraid you've shown up a bit late in the day. A month ago I could have courted you properly, and visited you when you go back. Now I'm going to be wintering in Florida with freaks and clowns and circus acts, and touring with them nine or ten months a year. I can send you post-cards from all over the States."

As he said it, she looked truly shocked this time, particularly at the look in his eyes. He was clearly still grappling with the im-pact of what had happened to them.

"I can't even imagine it," she said hon-estly.

"Neither can I, but it's better than a la-bor camp on the Czech border. Or having my children die of malnourishment or some disease. We really had no choice."

"You're a brave man, Nick," she said qui-etly, impressed by what he had said.

"No, I'm a man who was driven out of his homeland, by a lunatic who wants to purify the master race and take over the world. And Jews are not welcome in it, or part of his plan. And suddenly, by a quirk of fate, I have become one. It's more than a little humbling, to say the least. I slipped from the top to the bottom of the ladder, literally overnight."

"Do you think Hitler is really that bad?" she asked thoughtfully. From Nick's perspective, he certainly was, but it was still hard for her to believe that he was as dangerous as Nick said. Thus far, nothing Hitler had done had affected her, except that her favorite seamstress had moved away, and her doctor in Munich had been obliged to close his practice. But other than that, she had suffered no ill effects. And her doctor had been about to retire anyway.

"I actually think he's considerably worse than we all realize," Nick said with a bitter tone about Hitler. "Now that I know what he's up to firsthand, I think he will make changes that will frighten and affect us all. The boys and I are certainly a good example of that. And if my father were still married to my mother, he'd be a criminal for being married to a Jew. That's against the law now, for a Christian to be married to a Jew. Luckily, he divorced her. He would never survive this, being uprooted and having to leave everything he's ever known, disappearing like a thief in the night."

"Will he come to the States too?" she

asked, curious about them now. He had become a real person to her with his confessions, not just a handsome man in a superficial way. Nick shook his head in answer to her question about his father.

"He's staying to protect our land. Which, other than me and my children, is the only thing he's ever loved. He's a man of duty, honor, and tradition. He stayed to run our estate until I return. And God only knows when that will be. Probably not until Hitler steps down, or someone runs him out of town, or shoots him, which sounds like an excellent idea to me." He could say that openly now, having escaped. "And even if I can return to Germany safely later, I can no longer inherit my estate till the laws about Jews are changed. My children and I can't own property anymore."

"Do you think there will be a war?" she asked Nick, looking slightly nervous.

"I don't know. They say not, but all signs seem to point to it, to me. His rallies sound like calls to arms. I don't think he'll stop until he takes over all of Europe. Germany will never be enough. Taking over Austria was only the beginning." He was convinced of that now.

"He is ambitious," Monique agreed, "and there seem to be soldiers everywhere these days. There were an incredible number the last time I went to Munich. And most of them seem to be SS, the elite corps."

"I've noticed it too," Nick agreed with her. "I managed to keep Tobias out of the Hitler Jugend, because he had asthma as a child and we have a sympathetic doctor. I didn't want him parading around in a uniform, parroting the party line. And now instead, he's going to be in the circus, playing with the clowns. It's a hell of a choice."

"I'm sure they'll let you come back eventually, probably very soon," she said to encourage him. But Nick wasn't sure of that at all.

"I'm not convinced. And, my dear, until then, I'm afraid that the person I will become when we get to Florida isn't even suitable for you to know."

"Don't be ridiculous," she scolded him, and then lowered her voice conspiratorially. "I was a manicurist when I met my husband. He married me and changed my life. It wasn't the circus, but I wasn't born into the lofty world you were. I only got there because of Klaus. And he got very upset whenever anyone said anything about it. He hired a teacher to show me how to speak and act like a lady." It was an amazing confession that Nick found fascinating and endearing in its honesty. And when he thought about it, only the way she danced gave her away. It was a little too intimate, a little too flirtatious and outrageous for a lady of rank, and she did the tango in a way no respectable woman would dare. But he didn't care. She was a nice woman, and he liked talking to her. And what did it matter now?

"If they ever throw you out of Germany," he said wryly—trying to make light of the fact he had been, which still smarted to his very core. He was far more aristocratic than any of the idiots he knew in the Third Reich—"we could form a dance team, or you could join me in the circus. But I don't think they'll be sending you away, as long as you're not Jewish."

"I'm not," she confirmed, "but neither are you, in any real way."

"That's not what they believe, or exactly correct. I'm part of the race they want to stamp out. According to them, it's a race of criminals and half-breeds."

"Will I ever see you again?" she asked

sadly, and he looked at her for a long moment before he answered.

"Probably not," he said quietly. "I don't see how. You'll have a nice visit with your sister and her baby, when it's born. And you'll go back to Germany, to the life you know, that your husband gave you. And I'll be here, in the circus. Not 'at' the circus, **in** it, just like the clowns."

"Don't say that," she scolded him with a catch in her voice. She felt so sorry for him.

"Why not? It's true. And I'd better get used to it quickly. That's not a life you want, Monique." She didn't deny it because what he said was correct. "We can write to each other. But for now, that's the best I can do." She realized now that the reason he had held back till then, even from kissing her to any great extent, was because of everything he had just explained, not because of her. He had been so distant with her at first, except on the dance floor, and now she knew why. He had been nothing but a gentleman with her, out of respect and kindness. He didn't want to pull her into his mess, or the life he was about to lead. He didn't even want her to see it, and he knew she never would. She would go back to

Germany in a month and lead the life she had, since marrying her husband. A life that Nick would never live again. He had been born into it, and she hadn't. But she had been allowed to stay and he was a refugee now. The irony and unfairness of that did not elude either of them.

Nick liked Monique, and the fact that she was straightforward with him. And she liked him for being truthful as well. He hadn't tried to cover up what was happening to him, and he was bitter about it, but not with her. He was as lovely as she had thought at first. Even better now. He wasn't just a handsome, dashing aristocrat, he was a real human being. And she was sorry to hear everything that was happening to him. She felt now as though she'd made a friend. He kissed her again then, but there was no passion to it. She was a pretty woman, but suddenly their lives were too different. As a circus performer, he didn't feel very dashing. He felt anything but, as he kissed her on the cheek, chastely this time, and then walked back to his own cabin. It was hard to imagine what his life would be like now, but surely like nothing he had ever known. And he wasn't anxious to find out.

He lay awake in his bed for a long time that night, and finally he put a coat on over his pajamas, and went outside to stand at the rail. It was nearly daybreak by then, and the sun came up slowly as they steamed into New York Harbor. The rest of the passengers were asleep, and he watched as they slid by the Statue of Liberty. The tugboats had come to lead them in, and at seven o'clock in a bright morning sun, they pulled into the dock. They had arrived. And whether he felt ready for it or not, their new life had begun.

Chapter 7

Nick made sure that the horses were all safely tethered, and Toby helped him clean out their stalls before they disembarked. Lucas gave them all water, as his father had shown him how to do, and oats in their feed bags. Nick commented that the three of them had become able stable boys during the long trip. And he watched closely, once he was dressed, as the crane lowered the boxcar carefully onto the dock.

From the pier on the Hudson River, the boxcar would be taken to the station, and their trip to Sarasota would begin. Nick barely had time to find Monique to say

goodbye, before he left to join the boys in
the car he had hired to take them to the station. He found her as her endless stack of
steamer and cabin trunks was being re-
moved by cabin boys and porters. She was
wearing a heavy fur coat, and a spectacular hat with a veil, and white kid gloves.

"You look very beautiful," he said, smiling
at her. "Thank you for our lovely evenings.
I haven't danced that much in years." And
he realized that, mostly thanks to her, the
respite from reality on the boat had done
him good. It was his final farewell to a life
he had been forced to give up, and he had
enjoyed spending time with her.

"Take care of yourself," she said, looking
longingly at him, wishing things were different, but they weren't. "Write to me sometime."

"I will," he promised, but neither of them
was sure they would, and he thought it unlikely. What could he possibly have to say
that would interest her now, in her safe world
in her husband's schloss in the Tyrol, once
she returned from Boston? In a strange way,
she had inherited the life he had been born
to, and he had lost it. They were ships passing in the night. He kissed her gently on the

cheek through her veil, smiled, and then was gone, as she stood watching from the rail as he got into the car with his boys. Lucas was hanging out the window, looking up at the ship they had just left, and a flat-bed truck was carrying the boxcar with the horses. Nick had stolen a minute to thank Beauregard Thompson for his kindness and support during Pluto's experience of nearly dying. They shook hands, and the horseman from Kentucky wished him luck.

As they drove to Penn Station, Lucas was gazing out the window, fascinated by everything he saw and chattering excitedly, while Toby drifted into pensive silence. Nick kept a lookout to make sure that the boxcar was stable and the luggage car was following with their trunks. He had never had to handle so many details and arrangements on his own. Until then, servants and underlings had handled everything he had to cope with now himself, and he had a new respect for how talented and dedicated they had been, and how complicated it was to manage all the details, particularly with the horses. And as they hurried to their train, he stopped at a Western Union office in the station to send telegrams to his father and Alex, saying that they had arrived safely in New York. Lucas was insisting that he wanted to see the city, the Chrysler Building, and the Empire State Building, which was the tallest building in New York, and Nick said they didn't have time.

It seemed like a herculean feat to get the boxcar onto the Seaboard Air Line Railway train, and half an hour later they were settled into their compartment with their trunks all around them. It was a relief when they finally left the station, even though they had seen nothing of New York. Nick couldn't help thinking of Monique, on her way to Boston, and how simple her life was. She could return to Germany whenever she wanted, and he and his sons had fled. The cruelty of fate didn't escape him, but it was the way of the world now. He thought, too, about his mother, as they rode south on the train. He would have liked to try to find her before he left Germany, but he hadn't had time. And in an odd way, for the first time he felt angry at her for abandoning him, but she'd been a young girl, probably with no choice in the matter. He was determined to find her one day, and meet her, but he knew that now it was a long way off, if he could ever return to Germany at all. If Hitler remained in power, Nick would be a man without a country for the rest of his life.

"We're not going back, are we?" Toby said softly, once Lucas fell asleep from the rhythmic motion of the train, several hours out from New York.

"I don't know," Nick said honestly. He didn't want to lie to him and give him false hope. "It depends on what happens in Germany. For now, we have to make our home here." They had no other choice.

"With the circus? Forever?" Toby was appalled.

"For a while."

"I miss Opa," Toby said sadly, and Nick nodded. He missed his father too. Terribly. And Alex. And their comfortable home and life.

"So do I. I'm sure he misses us too," Nick said sadly, as the train to Florida rolled on.

It was long after dinnertime when Nick's telegram arrived at the manor house at the schloss that night. Paul had decided to remain where he was—the main house would be too lonely now without Nick and the boys, so he didn't move back. And staying in the manor house was a way of convincing himself they would return. The main schloss was their home.

He was relieved to read in the telegram that they had arrived safely in New York, and were on their way to Florida with the horses in good condition. Nick had signed it from him and the boys, and Paul had tears in his eyes when he read it. His life had been bleak for the past five days without them. He couldn't even imagine a whole lifetime without them now, and he had aged visibly ten years overnight.

When Alex got Nick's telegram at Schloss Altenberg, he showed it to Marianne, who had been sitting in the library with him. And they had been nearly as lonely as Nick's father. Nick and the boys' absence was sorely felt in everyone's life. Alex was relieved to read that the horses had traveled without mishap. Nick hadn't told him that Pluto nearly died. It would only have worried Alex for no reason, since all was well now, and Pluto seemed healthier than ever. At least for now, their future was safe.

When the train made several stops as it wended its way south, Nick got out and checked the horses, and gave them fresh water. The boys were excited to have dinner in the dining car, and afterward the porter set up their sleepers. They weren't due to arrive in Sarasota until the next morning, and would be traveling through the night. And Lucas loved the little blue light over his bed in the compartment. He thought everything about the trip was exciting. And Toby cheered up a little after dinner, as they watched the countryside slide by. Nick was exhausted by the stress of their travel, and constantly worried about either his sons or the horses. There seemed to be so much to take care of now. He had had no idea how complicated running one's own life was, and he was not enjoying the process. No matter how bad it was, it would be good to get to Florida, and finally stop moving around. He felt as though they were coming from the far end of the earth to get there. And they hadn't arrived yet. He was grateful that they wouldn't have to travel again for the next three months, since the circus was settled in its winter quarters, and wasn't leaving on tour until March. After that they would be on the move, going from city to city, for nine months. But they would have time to adapt to their new life now, with only a light schedule of occasional performances in Sarasota. It would give him and the boys a chance to adjust and settle in, and perfect their act. He wished Alex were there to help him improve further, and tried to remember everything Alex had taught him about putting the Lipizzaners through their paces.

And after not sleeping at all the night before on the ship, Nick fell into a deep sleep on the train, with the hypnotic rhythm and the sounds of the wheels on the track. It was morning, in a bright sun, when they finally got there. Nick had woken the boys an hour before, so they could dress and have breakfast, in the dining car again. Lucas ordered nearly everything on the menu, and tried to order in German. Nick forced him to use his halting English instead of translating for him. Toby had learned enough English to speak a little, although not well. He had to struggle for his words, but the people he spoke to were patient about it. Nick let Lucas order for all of them, and he did a decent job of it, and got everything right, except for the pancakes, which he called "crepes" and confused the waiter.

Both boys spoke a smattering of French, which they'd learned from a nanny they'd had when they were younger and still remembered, and enough English to get by.

When the train finally stopped in the Sarasota station, they felt as though they'd been traveling for weeks or months, not a mere six days on the ship and twenty hours on the train. There were roustabouts from the circus removing the boxcar, when Nick got off the train with the boys, and two porters carrying their trunks. He had no idea what to do next, when a man in a shiny blue suit, a lavender shirt, and a red tie came up to them, wearing a fedora pushed back on his head, and brandishing a foul-smelling cigar like a magic wand.

"Mr. von Bingen?" he asked, and the two boys stared at the man, silently echoing their father's unspoken thoughts. They had never seen anyone like him. The man smiled broadly the moment Nick acknowledged who he was. It was obvious that the man in the shiny blue suit was from the circus, and had come to meet them. And he confirmed that the moment he spoke.

"Welcome to Florida and the Greatest Show on Earth," he said grandly, waving the cigar in Lucas's face. The boy scrunched up his nose at the evil smell and turned away, while his father shook the man's hand.

"Thank you for coming to meet us," Nick said sincerely, grateful for the help.

"Of course. Joe Herlihy," he said, pumping Nick's hand until Nick thought his arm would fall off. Joe instructed the handlers to load the boxcar onto the flatbed truck he had brought with him. The logo of the circus was emblazoned on the door of the panel truck he was driving, and it was strange to see it now. It made everything suddenly seem more real. "How did the horses do on the trip?"

"Surprisingly well," Nick said in the clipped British accent he had when he spoke English, because that was where he had learned it, in boarding school. The man with the cigar spoke in a Southern drawl that was hard for Nick to understand.

"Do the boys speak English?" Joe asked with interest and a friendly glance over his shoulder at the boys in the backseat of the truck. The boxcar was following on the flatbed.

"A little. They're learning. We came over

on a German boat, so they really haven't had to speak it yet," Nick explained.

"They can go for years without ever learning it here," Joe said with a grin. "We have thirty-two nationalities at the circus, and over thirteen hundred performers and workers. It's a small village, or actually not so small, maybe more like a small city." When he spoke, he did so with obvious pride. "I've been with them for twelve years. I'm usually a scout, in the States anyway. Mr. North does the scouting and hiring himself in Europe. And they use me to meet and greet sometimes, for people like you. We have a lot of Germans, as well as Czechs, Poles, and Hungarians—they all speak German too. You should feel right at home there." Nick knew it was going to take more than a common language for him to adjust to his new colleagues and surroundings, but if many of them spoke German, it would be nice for the boys, and he knew Lucas would be relieved. He wanted to make friends quickly, he always did. Toby wanted to practice his English, and so did Nick. There were a lot of American expressions he didn't understand. "There are many French, Italian, and Spanish too. We have a group of Japanese acrobats, and a family of Chinese gymnasts and jugglers. They speak English, although I can hardly understand them. And almost all of the big cat acts are German. It must be very popular in your country." Nick smiled as he said it. If it was, Nick had never heard about it. He had never known any lion tamers at home, nor acrobats or jugglers. He couldn't even remotely imagine what they would be like. But he was about to find out.

Both boys were wide-eyed as they drove through Sarasota. It was a pretty little town, and Joe pointed out minor landmarks to them. As it turned out, it was a short drive to the winter headquarters at the fairground, and when they got there, Nick saw a huge spread of land of many acres that was teeming with activity. There was a gigantic tent, a big top, where their performances would be while they were there. There were menageries, tents, practice rings, workshops, railroad yards, and what looked like a sea of trailers in several vast parking lots. There were hundreds of them. And they rolled past the gates of an enormous structure that looked like a house, only bigger, which Joe said was Ca' d'Zan, and appeared to be a Venetian palace sitting on the bay.

"The Ringlings live there," he explained. Nick already knew that they owned the circus, and that John Ringling North had become president the year before, after his uncle John Ringling died. It was entirely a family-run business, with six of the actual Ringling brothers presiding. They had bought the Barnum & Bailey Circus many years before, in 1907, and the Ringlings were now in full control. They had merged two powerful, successful circuses and turned them into an astounding whole, with more than thirteen hundred employees, more than eight hundred animals, a hundred and fifty-two wagons, and a fifty-nine-car train. And everywhere Nick looked were people in odd costumes, women and young girls in tutus and ballet clothes, and men and women in gymnastic clothes. There had been a rehearsal for the clowns that day, and Lucas stared at them as they walked by. They were talking animatedly with each other, followed by dogs in varying shapes and sizes, in funny outfits, that were part of their act.

"We have more horses than any other animal. But yours are the only Lipizzaners in the country," Joe explained to him. Nick looked around when they got out of the car—it seemed more like ten or twelve circuses banded together in one location. It was more circus and everything that went with it than any of them could have dreamed.

"Wow! It's so big!" Toby whistled softly, and his father was thinking the same thing. It looked as though one could easily get lost there. Lucas was jumping up and down, wanting to meet the clowns.

"You'll meet everyone eventually," Joe reassured both boys. "And there are lots of kids for you to play with. You'll all be tutored together once we're on the road. When we're in Sarasota, all the performers' children go to the local schools. There are too many of them for just one school. And you two boys will be going to school too." It suddenly appeared to be a real community, with families, not just all the odd characters in the circus.

"We're actually here for the winter early this year. We had an actors' strike that shut us down till almost July. So we came down to our winter quarters earlier than usual, although we did a few extra shows in the Midwest." It had turned out to be a blessing for Nick, since they were already there and not still on tour when they arrived. "And I think we're going to leave later this spring, which will give you plenty of time to rehearse and settle in before we tour. We usually start in February or March. We're planning on early April now. We open in New York."

Joe checked a note he had in his pocket, and looked up the number of their trailer, and consulted a map in order to find it. It was in the third enormous parking lot, and when the truck pulled up next to it, Nick noticed that it was particularly long, although not very wide. And when they stepped into it, it looked like an inexpensive hotel room, but it had everything they would need.

His breath caught as they walked into the trailer. This was their new home, and he had never seen anything like it, with two tiny bedrooms and a miniature kitchen. His parking space for the Duesenberg had been bigger than this, and he tried not to let what he was feeling show on his face. The boys peeked into the bedrooms, exploring. Lucas seemed satisfied, and was anxious to go outside and meet the children he'd just seen wandering around. They had just come home from school on several school buses. Toby collapsed on the trailer's only couch with an exhausted, dazed expression. Everything was simple and clean, but none of them had ever realized that people actually lived like this. Nick reminded himself that if they had been sent to a labor camp, it would have been far worse. Or if they had been forced to leave their estate, as Jews. Where would they have gone?

"We have a tent set up on the fairgrounds for your horses. We got it as close to your trailer as we could. It's warm, so they'll be fine in a tent. We'll use a trailer for them when they're on the road. We can store your boxcar here, or put it on one of the trains," he informed Nick, who nodded. He was feeling overwhelmed by all the information and the tiny trailer they'd be living in, which was generous by circus standards. The two bedrooms were the size of the beds. It was all so vastly different from anything they'd ever known, and Toby looked like he was about to burst into tears, which Nick hoped he wouldn't. It would upset Lucas if he saw his older brother distraught. And Nick had to worry about both of them now. He tried to put a good face on it for their sake. He then asked Joe to show him to the tent where their horses were, so he could tend to them. He suggested that Toby and Lucas come with him, to keep them busy.

"Mr. North wants to see you at four this afternoon," Joe told Nick. "I'll pick you up and take you to meet him. And you have rehearsal at ten tomorrow morning. He'll be attending that as well. You're an important act for us," he said generously. "He likes to see all the acts when they come in. He particularly likes horses, so I'm sure he'll enjoy yours. He's a very accomplished horseman himself. And he wants to see your Lipizzaners."

"I hope he likes our performance," Nick said vaguely. He couldn't imagine being able to find his way around the maze of trailers, tents, workers, performers, and roving bands of people who swarmed the area like ants. He had never seen so many people in one place in his life. The boys were fascinated by it. Nick saw Toby watching a group of girls in ballet costumes with sparkles on them. They were pretty girls with good figures, and he hoped that would cheer them up a little. And Nick suddenly found himself missing Monique, who was at least familiar with his world. He felt as though he had been dropped on another planet, nothing looked like anything he'd ever seen before. Even the tropical landscape was strange and different, and it was warm.

Joe pointed out the cookhouse in another huge tent, where they could get their meals, or they could cook their own in the trailer if they preferred, but none of them knew how. Nick had never cooked in his life, and he'd have to learn that, too, if he was going to feed the boys. Going to the mess tent with hundreds of people for every meal sounded exhausting to him. And he realized quickly that the one thing they would lack here was privacy. There were so many people, living so close, seemingly on top of each other. He could touch with his hand the next trailer from his own. It would be hard to get away for a quiet moment alone, or have a family life that hundreds of people weren't encroaching on.

After Joe left, they walked a short distance to the tent where their horses had been put in stalls and safely tethered. They turned their heads when Nick and the boys entered, and Pluto shook his fiercely the moment he saw Nick, as though to say hello to him, and Nick smiled. Here was something familiar at last. He went quickly to the big stallion and stroked him, deriving more comfort from touching him than he was giving. He needed to see Pluto at that moment, and Nina, and the others. They were the final gift from his lost life, a last piece of Alex, a tiny remnant of the world they had known that had disappeared so quickly and so totally, on the other side of an ocean, in a country where they weren't welcome anymore. This was all that was left. Eight horses, and his two children.

They decided to stay and curry the horses before they went back to the trailer. He put a bridle on Pluto that someone had taken out of the boxcar and hung on a hook near his stall. There was a makeshift tack room in the tent, and their feed had been put in it.

A moment later Nick slipped onto the stallion's back, and suddenly as he sat there, life felt real to him again. Whatever else happened, or wherever they went, they had this. Each other and the horses Alex had given him. He had Pluto who had come back to life for him, and as he leaned down close to the horse's head, he whispered "thank you," and knew that for now, the Lipizzaner was his only friend in this frighteningly unfamiliar world. The Lipizzaner stallion would carry them through. He already had, when he decided to get back up on his feet again. And for that, and for this opportunity, Nick was infinitely grateful, no matter how strange it all seemed.

Chapter 8

Although he made every effort not to let it show, Nick was nervous before his meeting with John Ringling North, "Mr. John," as Joe called him. He had no idea what to expect, any more than he knew what life in the circus would be like. He felt like he'd been dropped onto a different planet, as he watched hundreds of circus performers and employees milling around, talking to each other in groups, or heading for rehearsals in costumes or workout clothes. He had heard the tigers roaring that afternoon, and a string of elephants had walked by when he and the boys went back to the trailer.

Everything they saw was unusual, new, and different.

Joe Herlihy came to meet Nick at the horses' tent later that afternoon to pick him up for the meeting. And he looked admiringly at the beautiful white stallion.

"The two Lipizzaners are incredible," he said, as he watched Toby brush Pluto. The stallion tossed his head back with a loud whinny, as though saying thank you. "They do a liberty act, don't they?" he inquired, which meant they responded to voice commands and signals.

"Yes, but I also ride them," Nick answered. Nina was easier to ride, she was older and calmer and had had more training. But Pluto was more exciting.

"That must be a sight to see. Your older boy too?" Nick nodded. Alex had worked with Toby before they left. He was no circus performer, but he rode very well, and had all his life. And he had taught Lucas a few simple tricks so he could join the act if the circus wanted him to.

"The Arabians are all liberty trained too." Nick smiled at Joe, who, if possible, was wearing an even louder suit than the one he had worn that morning. It was gray with a silver sheen to it. He was portly, and there was a lot of it, and he was wearing a bright blue tie and a pink shirt. But it looked almost normal against the backdrop of the circus and the oddly clad people all around them, many of them in bright colors and costumes. Nick was wearing an impeccable suit from his tailor in Berlin for his meeting with John Ringling North. He had no idea what to expect or why the president, who was the owner of the circus, wanted to meet him.

Before they left, Nick told Toby he'd meet him at their trailer afterward, and to keep an eye on Lucas. He had been exuberant all day and said he wanted to meet all the clowns. To Nick it felt surreal that he now lived among them, and they were about to become part of his everyday life. Lucas, of course, was thrilled, and Toby didn't know what to think. He had barely spoken since they'd arrived. He seemed to still be on some kind of emotional overload from the trip, and the strange place where they'd landed.

Nick rode in Joe's panel truck with the circus logo on it, and a few minutes later they got out and walked into a building on

the fairgrounds. Joe led him to North's office, where two secretaries looked as so-
ber and respectable as they would have in
any lawyer's office or bank. And a moment
later, when John Ringling North came out,
he was wearing a dark pinstriped suit,
similar to Nick's although not as well tai-
lored, a white shirt, a dark blue tie, and impeccably shined shoes. He had a good
haircut and wavy black hair and a wide
smile as he greeted Nick pleasantly and
shook his hand and invited him in. At least
here Nick felt as though he were in a familiar world. John Ringling North was serious and well spoken, and looked like an
intelligent man. He invited Nick to sit down
across the desk from him. Joe had vanished when they walked in.

"Welcome to Florida, and to Ringling
Brothers," the president of the circus said
kindly. "I hope you had a good trip, and your
horses traveled well."

"They did," Nick assured him, trying not
to think of Pluto's nearly dying during the
storm. But he was fine now, and in good
health. "I wanted to thank you," Nick said
quickly. "I am very grateful to you for spon-
soring me and my sons. You saved our

lives, literally. Germany is not a safe place to be these days. For us, anyway. It all happened very quickly for me and my family, and we were warned to leave as soon as we could. You helped us do that. "

"I understood that from your letter," John North said carefully. "I have to admit, I was a little confused though. People with a last name like yours, with a 'von,' are not usually subject to religious persecution. What's going on now in Germany? Were there some political issues I don't know about? Were you vocally opposed to the current government?" He knew that some were, with potentially disastrous results.

"I only discovered a few weeks ago that my mother, who I've never met, was half Jewish. It changed everything for us overnight. We were at great risk. We received a private warning from the Wehrmacht, the army, from a friend of my father's, to leave. He's a general and he did us a great favor by alerting us to the impending danger. He said things are going to get much worse. And if you are a Jew they're already pretty bad." He had begun to learn that firsthand. "And with my ancestry, that I never knew about, my boys and I were suddenly at great risk. You can't predict how far that kind of hatred and prejudice will go. They might have wanted to make an example of me and my boys, and show that even aristocrats who turn out to be Jews won't be tolerated and aren't welcome in Hitler's Germany." John Ringling North looked distressed by what he said, but not surprised. He had heard similar stories recently, and they had hired other Jewish performers who had left Germany in the past few years. Despite all they had left behind, after 1935, they thought it was safer and wiser to get out.

"You and your horses will be a great addition to the show. We've never had Lipizzaners before, there are none in this country, although I'm familiar with them. They'll be a treat for our audiences to see. Beautiful beasts. I'm anxious to see yours. You'll go on before the intermission with the animal acts. The high-wire acts and performers go on afterward. We generally open with the big cats in the center ring. I'd like to bring you out right after that, also in the center ring." It was a great honor, which Nick didn't yet know. "Which also brings up the matter of your name. We travel all over the country, to big cities and small towns. Americans aren't good with foreign names, and we'd like to give you a name they can remember. I was wondering if you'd mind shortening your name to Nick Bing—just as a stage name, of course. And I was also wondering if you have a title." The "von" suggested that he did, or might. Nick looked embarrassed when North asked, and startled by the change of name. But Nick Bing certainly did sound American, and would be easier to remember than von Bingen.

"Actually, my father has a title, but he doesn't use it. He's much more modern in his thinking, and he finds it unnecessary. He's a count."

"We could use that," North said pensively. "Count Nick Bing. The count," he tried it on as he said it. "Would you prefer duke?"

"Actually, no," Nick said modestly about claiming to be a duke, which sounded embarrassingly pretentious to him. "Do I really need a title?" He was horrified at the dishonesty and arrogance of it. He was a viscount, thanks to his father, but seldom if ever used the title.

"It's theatrical, and Americans love royalty. Let's settle for count. The Count, Nick Bing. I think that'll work. And what about your horses' names, the two Lipizzaners?" North was responsible for the successful financial operation of the circus, but he was also acutely aware of all the more important performers, who they were, and what they did. He knew everything about the circus, and attended performances often. And he traveled with them when they were on the road, in his ornate private Pullman car with a silver dome. He had become president a year before, and was doing an excellent job running the complex operation. And he intended to watch Nick's rehearsal the next morning in the main tent. It was a command performance.

"The stallion is Pluto Petra, and the mare is Nina. They follow tradition in that the stallion is named for his sire and dam, mares only have one name, but their names always represent their bloodlines. They're easier to follow that way. And in the purist tradition, there are six names of the original stallions that date back to the eighteenth century. Breeders of Lipizzaners are very proud of their ancestry, and very solemn about their names."

"I'm sure that's true," North said respect-
fully, "but we don't want your stallion sounding like a cartoon character. And I'm afraid
that Pluto will remind them of the dog in
the Disney cartoons. We want something
a little grander. Maybe you can think of a
better name for each of them. We want to
start advertising and putting out stories
about your stallion as soon as possible.
Maybe some press interviews and photographs with you, before we go on tour. It
won't be for another five months, but I like
to plan ahead. See what you can come up
with for both of them. What about the Arabians?"

"They all have Arab names, which relate
to their bloodlines too."

"That'll work," he approved. They discussed salary then, and what he offered
Nick was respectable, although not stag-
gering. But Nick hadn't expected it to be. It
would be enough for him and the boys to
live on, and the circus provided them many
benefits, the trailer to live in, free food at the
cook tent, and health care when needed.
There would be no luxuries, but they would
be protected and secure, and he was employed, which seemed miraculous to him.

"Thank you very much," Nick said with considerable emotion. He was grateful for all of it, and particularly that he and the boys were safe, no matter how unusual their situation was. He had never expected to join a circus, but his life had been full of surprises recently. And Ringling Brothers was the least of them. He had given up a country and a way of life, left his family and his home, become a criminal due to circumstances beyond his control, and discovered that the mother he had mourned all his life wasn't dead after all and had relinquished him at birth. It was a lot to digest and absorb.

"I'm looking forward to your rehearsal tomorrow morning," John Ringling North said warmly as he escorted Nick out of his office. "I'll have the contract ready for you. We'll give it to you after the rehearsal." Nick was well aware that he was still on trial, and there would be no contract if the president didn't like their performance. He was going to have Toby ride with him, and have Pluto go through everything Alex had taught him so carefully. He just hoped that the stallion would be willing to give it his utmost in the unfamiliar surroundings. Nick was going to have a talk with him that afternoon. He was nervous about the circus president watching the show. What if he didn't hire him after all? Then what would they do? It didn't bear thinking. He couldn't go back to Germany now. His performance with Pluto was going to have to be outstanding if there were to be a contract.

After the meeting, Nick found Joe in the parking lot, leaning against his truck and smoking a cigar. He was wearing a light gray fedora to match his suit, which, as always, was pushed back on his head. It was a perfect look for him, and he smiled at Nick as he approached.

"How did it go?"

"Well, I think. He's coming to our rehearsal. And he changed my name." Nick grinned wryly—he had expected none of this. He hadn't known what to expect at all. "I'm Nick Bing now."

"It suits you. Sounds a bit British, like your accent when you speak English." They both laughed.

"I hope he likes our act," Nick said nervously as he got into the truck with him. Joe was about his age, and seemed to understand how Nick felt, and he was trying to make Nick and the boys feel welcome and at home.

"Don't worry. He'll like it, I'm sure." Joe tried to reassure him.

"He wants me to change the Lipizzaners' names too. The man who bred them would kill me for that, but I don't have much choice, do I?" Nick glanced at Joe questioningly, and Joe looked sympathetic. This was a whole new world for Nick, and it showed. Most of the performers they hired, except a few very young ones, had been in circuses before.

"The circus is all about drama and excitement, 'hype' we call it. Everything is bigger and better and more dramatic, or smaller and more exotic. I figured he'd want you to change Pluto's name," Joe commented as he started the truck.

"I'll try to think of something." But he had no intention of telling Alex once he did. It would seem like a sacrilege to him. Alex had no way of knowing or understanding that this was a whole different world, which had nothing to do with their own.

Joe drove Nick back to his trailer then, and they saw women in the now-familiar costumes on the way. Joe recognized several of them as trapeze artists, but to Nick they were just pretty young women in short skirts. He noticed them, but for now he didn't care. And none of them were the kind of woman he would ever have looked at. He had always been attracted to the women in his own world. These girls were young, all foreign, and giggling like school-girls. But Joe gaped at them, as he always did, and nearly hit a young boy practicing on tall stilts in the road. There was constant foot traffic on the fairgrounds, everything from midgets to giants. Nick couldn't help staring as an enormously fat woman, who Joe said was very well known, and a man covered with tattoos walked past them, deep in serious conversation. It was a totally exotic crazy world.

And when they got back to Nick's trailer, he saw Lucas laughing and talking to a dwarf, and a man in clown makeup, dressed as a mime and wearing a beret, short pants, ballet shoes, and white tights. Once out of the truck, Nick approached them with interest, as Lucas smiled up at him with wide eyes and introduced his new friends.

"Papa, this is Pierre. He's a clown. And this is Thomas. He's a clown, too, but he doesn't have rehearsal today." Lucas said it as though he'd been there forever and knew their routines perfectly and what they meant. Nick wasn't even sure Lucas knew what a rehearsal was.

Nick shook hands with the young Frenchman, who smiled broadly. He'd been having fun with Lucas, and the dwarf had been laughing when Nick arrived. The threesome were having a good time. It was odd to think that these people would be their friends now, and that Lucas and Toby would grow up among freaks, acrobats, and clowns. Lucas had been begging to see the tattooed lady since they arrived. Joe had made a point of saying there were no "freaks" in the circus, only "acts," "artists," and "performers."

"They said I could be a clown," Lucas said, "and ride in the little car with them during intermission, and Thomas is going to take me to see the elephants." They had seen several in the parking lot that morning, including two babies following their mothers with a handler running alongside.

"That sounds like fun," Nick said with a tired smile. He had a lot to adjust to since they'd arrived that morning, and he didn't have a signed contract yet. It would all depend on his performance at rehearsal the next day, and if John Ringling North liked what he saw. "Toby and I have rehearsal tomorrow morning, for the president of the circus. He's coming to watch us. Where is Toby, by the way?" Nick asked, looking around. His older son was nowhere to be seen.

"He's inside," Lucas said, pointing to the trailer, just as a little girl walked up. She had golden curls that danced all over her head, and big blue eyes. She looked like a doll in a pink dress, and she was about the same age as Lucas. She had wandered over from her trailer nearby. She looked him over with interest, and smiled, as Nick watched.

"Do you speak English?" she asked Lucas boldly, and he nodded, although he wasn't fluent yet. But he had been managing well with the dwarf and the clown. The French clown spoke a few words of German, which helped. "Where are you from?" she asked him with a curious look, as the clown and the dwarf left, promising to visit Lucas the next day. He was already making friends.

"Germany," Lucas answered, and she

nodded. There were lots of Germans in the circus, and she knew many of them.

"I'm Czech, but I've been here since I was two. I speak Czech and German too," she said matter-of-factly, and began speaking to him in German. Lucas looked relieved, and thrilled to have found a friend he could speak to freely, without struggling for words. "I'm Rosie, and my mama dances on the high wire, without a net sometimes. She made my dress," she went on in German. He thought she had a funny accent, but she spoke it well. "My papa is Czech too. He's on the trapeze, and he can do a triple. Sometimes he does the high wire with my mama. He doesn't like it when she doesn't use a net, but everyone applauds more when she doesn't. What does your papa do?" She glanced shyly at Nick, and he smiled. She was an adorable child, from a typical circus family. And to her, it all seemed normal. It was the only life she knew. To Lucas, it was all new and exciting, far more so than his six quiet years growing up in Bavaria, in the country.

"My papa rides horses, and my brother will help him. We just got here today."

"I know. My mama said to leave you

alone until you settled in. My sister thinks your brother is handsome. She saw him when you arrived." Lucas thought it was interesting information, as Nick realized that his sons would be part of the large group of circus children now, and these would be their friends.

"My brother is fifteen, and I'm six," Lucas volunteered.

"Me too," Rosie said, and when she smiled, Lucas could see that she had recently lost her front teeth. He thought it made her look cute, and so did Nick. She was wearing pink ballet slippers with her dress. She usually did. She didn't need to wear other shoes here, only when she went to school.

As they chatted, Nick went inside to find Toby and remind him about rehearsal the next day, and tell him the president of the circus would be there to see their act. And when he found him, Toby was listening to the radio, and he looked up at his father with a glazed expression.

"Something wrong?" Nick asked, instantly worried. Toby looked like he'd seen a ghost.

"There were attacks all over Germany

two days ago. They burned synagogues
and businesses and people's homes. They
took people away. They said that they were
ridding Germany of the criminal element,
but it sounds like it was all Jews. They said
on the report that thirty thousand Jewish
men were put in prison, and several thousand women, in Germany and Austria. They
called it '**Kristallnacht**.' It happened the day
before we got off the ship. Would that have
been us, Papa, if we were still there?" Toby
looked terrified at the thought, and sad for
the people who had been hurt and put in
jail. They had been isolated from the news
while they traveled. Nick had heard something about it on the ship, but he thought it
was just another bout of violence after one
of Hitler's rallies. He had no idea that the
persecution of Jews had taken such massive proportions, and was so out of control.
He realized then that was probably why
General von Messing told them to leave immediately. He knew what was coming and
tried to warn. **Kristallnacht** was no random
roundup. It had been planned.

"I'm glad we didn't have to find out. Hopefully that wouldn't have been us if we were
there, but it could have been. The country

is in a sad state, and Hitler is a very dangerous man." Nick was relieved for the boys and his father that they had left. If he had stayed, they might have punished Paul for harboring them, and Nick could have been taken to jail, and even Toby. And now that they were gone, Paul was safe, and so were they. It seemed as though no one was secure in Germany now, not only the Jews, but anyone related to them, even by marriage, involved with them in any way, or doing business with them. Any Jew or person protecting a Jew was in danger. **Kristallnacht** had been a night of incredible violence that shocked the world.

Nick was suddenly even more grateful to be here, and knew he had done the right thing. His father was right. He was determined now to give the best possible performance he could, so they would offer him a contract and he could stay. Nothing was sure yet, until North approved their performance the next morning. He tried to get Toby to focus on that, in order to get his mind off what he'd heard on the radio. And he told him exactly which tricks he wanted to do. He was going to try and get Pluto to do all his most spectacular feats, and he wanted Toby riding around the ring on one of the Arabians both at the beginning and the end of the act. He didn't have to do anything more than that. For most of the act, Nick would be using liberty commands, and standing in the center of the ring in his top hat and tails. Toby would be wearing tails too.

After a sleepless night in the unfamiliar surroundings, the two men looked very elegant the next morning when they set out for the tent where they were keeping their horses. Lucas went with them, to help them lead the horses to the main tent. And Nick had found two handlers to assist him. The three men and Toby each took two horses. Nick led the two Lipizzaners, and Toby and the two handlers each led two Arabians, while Lucas walked along and told his brother that he had heard about a girl who liked him.

"Oh really?" Toby said skeptically. He hadn't met nearly as many people as Lucas in a single day. But his brother was irrepressibly gregarious, and he was far more reserved. The only girl he wasn't shy with was Marianne at home. He had written her a letter the night before, about the ship and their arrival at the circus, and he had posted it that morning. He told her how much he missed her and how strange everything was here, and how much he missed his grandfather and her father, and their home. "What's her name?" Toby asked about the girl Lucas had mentioned. He looked older than his years in the top hat and tailcoat, and very handsome. And Nick looked incredibly dashing as he led the two Lipizzaners toward the main tent. Several of the women's heads turned as he passed them, but he was oblivious as he worried about the act he was about to do for such an important man, with so much resting on his performance, their lives and his job.

"I don't know her name," Lucas said about his brother's admirer. "Her sister told me. Her name is Rosie and she's six. She's from Czechoslovakia, but she speaks German like us, pretty good too. I'll bet her sister does too." It was a definite plus in Lucas's mind, and he thought it might be to Toby too. He could see how quiet he was, and was trying to cheer up his older brother. But Toby was nervous about their performance too. He could see that his father was tense.

The handlers helped them tether their horses to a pole when they got into the huge tent. A trapeze act was just finishing its rehearsal, and Lucas wondered if it was Rosie's father, but he heard them speaking Spanish when they left, so he knew it couldn't be him. And he thought they were amazing as he watched them.

Another group came in after them, and Nick heard them speak Polish. A young woman emerged from the group and did a low-wire act, which she practiced quietly, doing a ballet on the wire, as a man in a wheelchair watched, and corrected her and told her what to do. As Nick glanced at her, he saw that she had the face of an angel, and the body of a fairy as she leaped into the air and then found her footing instantly on the wire. He was mesmerized by her, and she never raised her eyes. She just concentrated on what she was doing, and listened to the man in the wheelchair's commands. Nick thought he had never seen anything as graceful, and she looked like barely more than a child, she was so small, but she had a womanly grace about her. He thought she might be in her late teens. And then he turned his attention to the horses, and spoke to Pluto in a low voice.

"You know this is important, right? We won't get the contract if you miss the capriole or the croupade. I'm depending on you. This is just as important as the night you got back on your legs again on the ship." The big horse nodded his head as though he understood. And then Nick spoke to Nina, who was looking sleepy, and gave her a similar speech. The Lipizzaners were decked out in their finest bridles and saddles without stirrups and looked as elegant as their riders. The Arabians were already prancing, in need of exercise, and didn't seem skittish as Toby rode them one by one around the ring. And he looked comfortable riding them too. Like his father, he had been watching the girl on the low wire, being commanded by the man in the wheelchair, but once he started to warm up the horses, he forgot about her. Then Nick rode Pluto several times around the ring. The horse seemed ecstatic to be ridden again, and Nick felt as though he and Pluto had bonded on the ship when he was sick. Ever since, Pluto seemed to heed his every command and do whatever he could to please him.

Nick rode Nina after that, to warm her up, and then Toby got astride her when Nick dismounted. They had given themselves an hour to loosen them up. And by ten o'clock Nick knew they were ready. And just as he thought it, John Ringling North appeared, crossed the ring to where Nick was standing, and shook his hand. Nick didn't know it, but North had never done that before. It was a sign of respect, and then he discreetly took a seat in the stands, at a good vantage point to watch Nick and his horses perform.

Lucas put a recording of Mozart on a phonograph they had plugged into a light pole next to the ring. And their act began with Nick galloping elegantly around the ring on Pluto, going ever faster, and ending with the spectacular white Lipizzaner doing a levade, where he stood on his hind legs and held the stance for a seemingly endless time. The beautiful horse had never done it more smoothly or better, and then he hopped easily into the courbette, where he moved forward in little jumps. Then Nick galloped with him again, as Toby joined him on Nina. The two Lipizzaners looked like poetry in motion, as they moved with infinite precision through their ballet, mirroring each other's movements perfectly around the ring. Nick dismounted just as Toby did, and they left the ring, leaving both horses standing side by side, as Nick began the liberty commands. They executed each movement and exercise with flawless precision, doing exactly what Nick wanted. They didn't let him down. And after half an hour of impeccable exercises, Nick got onto Pluto's saddle again and led him into the challenging capriole, where the splendid horse kicked his hind legs out in midair, and then transitioned instantly into the croupade, where Pluto literally flew through the air, with all four legs tucked under his body, as though the powerful beast were weightless, and he landed as gracefully as he had left the ground.

The people who had watched him, handlers and a handful of acrobats, gasped when they saw it. Pluto had been exquisite, and Nick looked like the most elegant rider in the world astride him. The performance had been perfect, and Pluto took a bow, as

Nick sat erect and took off his top hat in the direction of John Ringling North, and then Nick and Pluto left the ring, and he dismounted. It had been a grueling performance for rider and mount, but Nick knew that neither of them could have done it any better. It had been the best that Pluto had ever given, and Nina had done extremely well too.

As Nick stood there, breathless with excitement after his performance, stroking Pluto, John Ringling North left the stands, and came to where Nick was standing. North was wearing jodhpurs and riding boots and carrying a crop with a silver handle, and he was beaming.

"They're the most beautiful sight I've ever seen. And perfectly trained. They're as good as the Lipizzaners I saw at the Spanish Riding School in Vienna. Welcome to Ringling Brothers, Mr. Bing." He smiled broadly at him and held out his hand, and shook Nick's. He turned to look at Pluto then, barely winded by what he'd done. He was powerful and young. "He really does fly, doesn't he?" And then he turned to Nick again. "That's it. That's his name. Pegasus, the flying horse of Greek legend. And

Athena," he said, glancing at Nina. "You have your act, Nick. They're perfect. Welcome to the Greatest Show on Earth. You're worthy of the name." And with that, he took an envelope out of his pocket and handed it to Nick. "I've already signed it. You do the same, and drop it off at my office. I want you in the center ring as our second act after the tigers, in the first performance after the winter break. You'll open in Madison Square Garden."

And then he turned to Toby with a warm smile. "Good work, son. You looked great," he said, and Toby beamed. There were tears in Nick's eyes when John North left. They were safe, they were home, he had a job. And Pegasus and Athena had been born. He smiled as he turned to Pluto and tried out the new name. The horse whinnied as though he were laughing, but didn't seem to mind.

"Thank you," Nick whispered, as he stroked his head. "Thank you, Pegasus, for taking care of us. I won't let you down. Sorry about the new name." But the newly renamed Pegasus just tossed his head and whinnied again, as though he approved. And as Nick turned to lead him from the ring, he saw the elfin girl from the low wire standing beside a post, half hidden, where she had been watching him perform. She had enormous vibrant blue eyes, like his own, and a halo of pale blond hair. Her eyes met his for a minute, but she didn't smile, she just stared at him, as she had at the astounding horse, and then she seemed to float off and disappear, and she was gone. She was like a vision, as though he had imagined her and not really seen her, a benevolent spirit that was observing him.

"Pretty girl," Nick said casually to one of the handlers who was helping them get the horses back to their tent, to cover the fact that he had been staring at her as intently as she had watched him.

"She's a Markovich," the handler said with a shrug, as though that would explain everything to Nick, but it didn't. He knew nothing of circus lore, or the names of the performers, except for the few Lucas had met. "They're Polish. They're all crazy. High wire. Without a net. Her father's in a wheelchair. He killed her mother that way—she was a beautiful girl. They'll kill her too. She was just practicing on the low wire today. She works up there," he said, pointing to the top of the tent. "The crowds love it. I think it's a terrible thing to do to a young girl. He doesn't care," he said about her father. "He does it to thrill the crowd. And if she winds up in a wheelchair like him, or dead like her mother, he thinks it's fine. She has four brothers who do the act with her. Her aunt's in a wheelchair too. I can't watch them. They make me sick," he said as they left the tent.

"What's her name?" Nick asked, intrigued by what the handler had said.

"Christianna. Christianna Markovich. She's the grand finale, the last act before the parade at the end. It keeps people in their seats till the end of the show, waiting to see if she'll fall and die." The way he described it sounded grim to Nick.

"She looks like a child." She appeared to be about fifteen when he saw her at close range.

"She's older than she looks. She's twenty-one. She's been in the circus since she was born. They're one of the oldest circus families here. There's another high-wire act that's been here for four years. Czechs. Big rivalry between them. The others work with a net most of the time, so the Markoviches treat them like dirt," he said with a grin.

Nick was beginning to learn about the circus and the people he now lived with, the intrigues between them, the jealousies and the dangers, but he had been struck by the ethereal-looking girl he had seen practicing, commanded by what must have been her father. Her eyes had electrified him, and then she had disappeared. He wondered when he'd see her again, and if he'd have the courage to see her act. It horrified him to think that she worked without a net and might fall. And even more so to think that her own father was willing to take that risk.

He and Toby fed and watered the horses, and Lucas helped them, after the handlers left. He had been excited to see his brother and father performing, and even more so when one of the handlers had taken him to see the elephants afterward, and he got to sit on one of them. His new life was full of thrills and wonders for him. And as they walked back to their trailer, still in top hat and tails, Nick felt suddenly more at ease, among the odd people walking past them. Several of them smiled at Nick and the boys, and Lucas waved at the dwarf he knew, who was standing with a group of his friends in the distance. It wasn't a bad place to have landed after all, just very different. Rosie was sitting on their front step, waiting for Lucas when they got home.

"Where've you been?" she asked him, in English this time.

"My father and brother had to work," he explained in German, and she nodded, and Nick noticed then that she had brought an older girl with her, who was obviously her sister. She gazed at Toby adoringly as he blushed beet red. He looked very handsome in his top hat and tails.

"This is my sister Katja," Rosie said, lapsing into German, as Toby tried to look nonchalant and couldn't pull it off. He looked mesmerized by the beautiful girl Rosie had brought with her. She was wearing a simple blue dress, she had dark hair, long graceful legs, and looked like a young ballerina. When Toby started talking to her in German, her face lit up. It was an international community of dozens of nationalities living together, a microcosm of the world.

Nick invited the sisters to join them at the mess tent for lunch a little while later, and the girls went to ask their parents and then returned and said they could. They were very well behaved and very polite to Nick as the five of them chatted in German on their way to eat. Katja was fifteen, like Toby, and they had only been with Ringling Brothers for four years, since she was eleven, she said, so her English wasn't as good as her little sister's, who had spoken it since she was two. They had been with a circus in Czechoslovakia and one in Germany before that, until scouts found them and brought them over to the States. Katja said she liked it very much, better here than at their old circus in Europe, and Rosie didn't know any life other than this.

"They're very nice to us here," Katja said to Toby, and he was fascinated by her. She was a very pretty girl. She told them her father was training her on the trapeze. Their family were the Markoviches' archrivals, Nick realized as he listened, and the girls' mother was the other high-wire act, but she usually used a net in her act, unlike the Markoviches, who never did. Nick realized he had a lot to learn about the intricacies of the circus, what these people did, the risks they took, and how they lived.

He slipped away from lunch for a few minutes to drop off the contract he had signed. He left it at John Ringling North's office, with one of his secretaries. He was one of them now. He had been reborn. He even had a new name. Nick Bing. And so did Pluto. He was Pegasus, the flying horse, and he was worthy of the name. Their new life had begun that day.

Chapter 9

"I had a letter from Toby today," Marianne said to her father mournfully, three weeks after they had seen them off at the ship, and her father looked at her in surprise. Germany and all of Europe were still reverberating with the stories of the destruction on **Kristallnacht,** and the people who had disappeared, all of them Jewish. It had proven to Alex and Paul how wise they had been to urge Nick to leave quickly. They were both relieved to know that he and the boys were safely in Florida now. They had nothing to fear there.

"Already?" Alex answered her. "He must

have written to you the moment he arrived. I had a telegram from his father when they landed in New York, to tell me the horses were all right, but I haven't heard from him since. How are they?"

"Toby sounds sad. It was the day they got to Florida, and he said everything there is very strange."

"Well, life in the circus certainly isn't familiar to any of them, but at least they're safe. Being in a circus in Germany would seem strange to him too."

"I suppose so. He said they're living in a trailer smaller than our boxcar for the horses. It must be very hard." Marianne sounded sorry for him, and Alex nodded. He was sure it was difficult, but less so than a labor camp, and he was grateful they were safe, particularly after **Kristallnacht** had stunned the entire world.

Alex went to see Nick's father the next day. Paul had been sick for the past two weeks, and looked as though he had aged twenty years since Nick and the boys left. His solitude now was hard on him, with no hope of seeing his son and grandsons anytime in the near future, if ever again. The turmoil in Germany appeared to be increasing, and certainly not diminishing. Paul had a bad cough, and Alex thought he looked feverish and said he should call the doctor. But Paul insisted he was fine. He didn't look it, but Alex didn't want to make a fuss, or send the doctor to him against his will.

"Marianne had a letter from Toby," he said before he left, hoping to cheer him up with news of the boys, but Paul just looked sadder, and hearing about them made him miss them more.

"Are they all right?" he asked, and Alex nodded, and didn't want to tell him they were sad, or at least Toby had been when he wrote.

"They're fine. He wrote it the day they got to Florida, so they hadn't settled in yet. It's all very new to them. They'll adjust." Paul nodded, and thanked Alex for the visit when he left. The house felt so empty to him now, whenever he went to the main schloss. It echoed and seemed ghostly without his son and the boys. It was a lonely life for him now.

Alex was equally sad without his friend. Marianne wrote to Toby now every day, with news from home, however little there was. She didn't tell him that **Kristallnacht** had frightened everyone. It had been so violent, and so many people had gotten hurt, been put in jail, or simply disappeared. She was happy to be in the countryside, where none of the chaos and turmoil in the cities affected them. She did mention that her father had decided not to give their Christmas ball that year. It was only a month away, but with so much disruption in Germany, and people being taken away and losing their homes in the cities, he had decided that it seemed wrong to give a ball. And without his friend Nick to share the festivities with him, he said it wouldn't have been fun anyway, and Marianne agreed. She wasn't in the mood either. Nick and the boys moving away, and so suddenly, felt like a huge loss to all of them. And the winter seemed cold and dark. It felt like a time for mourning, not joy.

She told Toby that she had gone hunting with her father, but even that hadn't been enjoyable, and like a bad omen, the fox had gotten away. She told him, too, that the little Lipizzaner foal was growing, and loved to run now, and he was still coal black as he would be for several years. And they were expecting another one soon.

She said that she hoped that Pluto and Nina and the other horses were doing well. She told him whatever she could of her daily doings, which seemed very dull to her now. She didn't tell him that her father seemed sad, and so was she, that life without her friend Toby and his little brother seemed empty to her. They had seen each other almost every day since they were born. And the days were so lonely now without him.

When Marianne got Toby's letter, it was the day before Thanksgiving in America, and by then Nick and the boys had been in Florida for almost two weeks. Nick had been assigned a rehearsal schedule, to develop his act, in one of the rings in the huge tent, and he was practicing there every day, with Toby most of the time. Sometimes he just went there with Pluto and Nina—Pegasus and Athena now, he was getting used to their new names. He was practicing their liberty commands and the precision training, and he was learning a great deal every day. And Toby's skills were improving too. The Arabians were easier to work with, although less interesting to watch.

Nick hadn't run into Christianna Markovich again. She was obviously practicing at a different time, and he hadn't thought of her since his performance for Mr. North. Thanks to Lucas, he was meeting many new people, Eastern Europeans, and Germans, and some French. Through Pierre, Lucas had met many of the clowns, and brought some of them back to the trailer to meet his father and brother, and he always had fun with them. He had finally met the tattooed lady and was thrilled. And he and his little friend Rosie had become inseparable, and whenever possible, got up to mischief together. They played marbles and hopscotch, hide-and-seek among the trailers, and all the games other children did around the world, and they visited the elephants and got a ride on them whenever possible. They went to watch a new contortionist, and Lucas wanted to learn to walk on stilts, and Pierre the clown showed him how. He brought him a small pair, and Lucas practiced with them every night. All he wanted to do was use them to perform during intermission with the clowns. Nick tried not to comment on it, because this was the world they lived in now, but the prospect of

his son becoming a clown one day didn't
sound like a worthy goal to him. But like it
or not, they were circus performers, just
like everyone else there. Nick tried to accept it as their destiny for the time being,
although it was hard to imagine being there
forever.

Nick finally met Rosie and Katja's mother
one afternoon when she came to pick up
the girls at Nick's trailer. She was wearing
a leotard and a tutu, and had just come from
rehearsal herself.

"Thank you for being so kind to my girls,"
she said with a warm smile. Her name was
Gallina. She was a strikingly pretty woman,
as lovely as her daughters, and she moved
with agile grace and had a lithe athletic
body.

"They're beautifully behaved and lovely
girls," he said kindly, and meant it. He liked
them both, as did his boys.

She and Nick chatted for a few minutes,
and he noticed that despite her Czech accent, she was well spoken when she spoke
German, as though she had been properly
educated when she was young. He was curious about them. She explained that she
was from Prague, and her father had sent

her to boarding school in Germany as a child, while her parents traveled with the circus. She had only come back to them at fourteen, and she had insisted on training for the high wire, despite their protests. Her parents had been gymnasts and trapeze artists, not a high-wire act like the Markoviches, and she had eventually married the girls' father, Sergei, whose family was famous for their work on the trapeze. Nick was beginning to understand that there was a real hierarchy in the circus, a kind of nobility, depending on which acts they performed, where they came from, and how long they'd done it. Her husband's family was Czech too. He had five brothers who had come to Ringling Brothers with him, and his parents had since retired. They stayed in Czechoslovakia, as had her own, and her brother and sister were still working with her parents, as gymnasts in a German circus.

She smiled as she looked at Nick. She had spent enough time in Germany that she was entirely aware of how aristocratic he was, and how little he belonged here. And she was touched by how courteous he was to her. She had seen him work with his horses and knew just how good he was. Several of the performers had been talking about him and his exquisite Lipizzaners since he arrived.

"I don't need to ask you what circus you came from," she said, smiling shyly at him. She had heard through the grapevine that he was a count, and it didn't surprise her. "Why did you come to the circus?"

"Political problems at home," he said simply, and she didn't ask him for further information. She already knew from Lucas that Nick's wife had died, and Toby's younger sister, who would have been nine by then. Gallina felt sorry for them. This was a strange place for them to land, and she wondered how long they'd stay. She wondered if he'd lost his money, and all he knew how to do was train horses and ride, which was painfully close to the truth. But she knew for a certainty that he was many, many social strata above them, but he never let her feel it, he was courteous and gentlemanly, and always kind to her girls.

"I came over to ask you if you'd like to join us for Thanksgiving," she said warmly. "It's an important family holiday here. We make turkey, and dumplings of course, and traditional Czech dishes. It's our version of Thanksgiving." She laughed. "We're hoping that you and the boys will come."

"I'd like that very much," he said graciously. "May I bring something? I'm not much of a cook, but I could bring dessert." He knew he could go to a bakery in town and buy some pies. He had been told that pumpkin and apple pies were traditional for Thanksgiving.

"No, my sisters-in-law do most of the cooking. I'm not much of a cook either. But it's your first Thanksgiving here, and we didn't want you to be alone. Besides, my Katja is crazy about your Toby." He had noticed it—it would have been impossible not to. And Toby was rapidly becoming equally crazy about her. They were smitten. "He's a good boy," she added, and Nick was touched. "And Lucas is a little monster, and we love him." They both laughed at that. Lucas had friends now all over the fairgrounds, and Nick wouldn't have been surprised if he had met each of the thirteen hundred performers at least once. He seemed to have friends everywhere they went, and he knew everything about them, what they did, and where they came from. And his English was improving by leaps and bounds. "He wants my brothers-in-law to teach him how to juggle."

"That should be interesting." Nick laughed at the idea. "Preferably on stilts, I imagine. He's been working on that diligently since we got here." As he said it, Lucas came down the road on his short stilts with Pierre, who was showing him how to keep his balance. Rosie was walking along beside him, looking as adorable as always and holding one of his hands while Pierre held the other. And Toby and Katja were following behind on a tandem bicycle they had borrowed from someone. "Speak of the devils," Nick said, as the ragtag group approached the trailer, and saw their parents talking.

"Are we in trouble?" Lucas inquired with an unconcerned glance at his father. If so, it wouldn't have been unfamiliar to him. Nick had scolded him several times for disappearing. Nick wanted to know where he was at all times, just as Gallina did with her girls. They both had fairly stern European values and rules for their children. Others were more haphazard and less vigilant with their kids.

"No, you're not in trouble for a change," Nick reassured Lucas. "Rosie and Katja's mother was kind enough to invite us for Thanksgiving." As he said it, all four children gave a cheer. "I think that's a vote of approval," he said, smiling at Gallina.

"Well, see you tomorrow then," she said, rounding up her girls to take them home for dinner. "Come at four o'clock. We'll have dinner at six." Nick thanked her again, and after she left, he went to a nearby liquor store and bought two bottles of decent wine. He didn't want to show up the next day empty-handed. He was grateful for the invitation, and talked to the boys about their new friends that night, as they ate dinner at the trailer's tiny dining table that was barely big enough for two men and a boy. Most of the time they were bumping into each other in the narrow, confined space.

"Gallina and her husband fight a lot," Toby filled him in, over the chicken Nick had cooked in the tiny oven. Nick was learning to cook as well as everything else. For the first time in his life, he was doing their laundry and making his own bed, and he had borrowed a vacuum cleaner from one of their neighbors to clean the trailer. "Sergei doesn't like her doing the high wire. He wants her to do the trapeze with him and Rosie's uncles, and she doesn't want to. She thinks it's too tame, even when they do a triple, which is really hard. But they use a net. I watched them do it," Toby said, as though it were commonplace to know people who could do that. A month before, he wouldn't even have known what a "triple" was. Now he was explaining it to his father. "It's a triple somersault in the air on a trapeze. He told her to go live with the Markoviches, if she wants to be crazy. They don't use a net."

"So I've been told," Nick said quietly. Some of the gossip was familiar to him now, and he knew the names of the star performers of the big acts. He had recently talked to the trainer of the big cats, who was an interesting person, had lived in Africa for many years, and was also German. It was an extraordinarily varied group of people, from all social classes and educational backgrounds. Some had had considerable schooling. He had talked to a man from another horse act and was intrigued to discover that he'd gone to law school but preferred the circus. Others looked as though they had come from some very dark places to join the circus. There was a huge sampling of humanity, with all kinds of people, even though they seemed strange to him at first. But the newness of it was starting to wear off. And the invitation to Thanksgiving dinner with Gallina and her family had touched him. He was intrigued to meet her husband and his brothers. He missed male companionship without Alex and his father.

Gallina and Sergei and his brothers and their wives turned out to be very friendly, kind people, when Nick and the boys went there for dinner. They had seven or eight children between them, mostly boys, all of whom were expected to eventually join the trapeze troupe, and some of whom already had, in their teens. And Nick liked Sergei a great deal. He had a good sense of humor, and immediately stashed one of the bottles of wine Nick brought, and said it would be wasted on his brothers. They drank the other one, along with several other bottles, at dinner. But they were a wholesome crowd, who loved their families and had fun with their wives, and Nick and his children had a terrific time at their first Thanksgiving dinner.

Toby and Katja went outside immediately afterward, and sat in the warm night air, talking about the things that mattered to them. Katja confessed to Toby that she wanted to leave the circus one day and have a normal life and a home and not live in a trailer, which seemed reasonable to him. She said her parents would be very upset if she said it to them. They thought this was the best life in the world, and Katja didn't. She wanted more.

"What about you?" she asked Toby with her big blue eyes, and he thought about it for a minute before he answered.

"I don't know. I don't know what I want to do, except go back to Germany one day." Just saying it made him miss his grandfather again, and Marianne and all his friends.

"I want to stay here," Katja added, "in America, not Florida. I liked New York when we went there. It's always great at Madison Square Garden when we start the season." Her eyes lit up as she said it. "I don't want to go back to Prague, it was boring. I think my mother misses it, but I don't. It's better here." Toby didn't know if that was true yet. He hadn't been there long enough to decide. All he did know was that he liked her a lot, and after they talked for a while, he kissed her. He didn't tell her, but she was the first girl he had ever kissed, and his head was swimming when they stopped. And so was hers. He kissed her again then, and they were better at it. It seemed to be something one had to learn. And they were both more than willing to apply themselves to it. They were still working on it when Lucas came around the trailer, saw them kissing, and stopped dead in his tracks, and then giggled and disappeared. He went to tell Rosie what he'd seen.

"How stupid," Rosie said with a disgusted look. "My father will be mad if he finds out. Katja's not allowed to kiss boys. He doesn't want her acting like 'some little tart in the circus,' whatever that means. He tells her that all the time."

"I think they like each other a lot," Lucas confided, and Rosie agreed. "I don't think we should tell." She made him pinkie-swear not to then, which she said was something she had learned at school. They went to school in Florida in the winter, but the rest of the time, on tour, they were tutored, which she liked better. The teachers at the circus didn't give as much homework, but sometimes her mother did instead. She wanted her to get a good education, which Rosie thought was boring.

When Nick and the boys went home that night, everyone looked sated and happy. Nick had had several glasses of wine, and had relaxed for the first time in a long time. He had played chess with Sergei and won, and enjoyed talking to his brothers. They had all spoken German to him and his boys, and Czech among themselves, and the children had spoken English to each other. It had been a wonderful family evening, and Nick had been touched to be included. He felt as though he had friends there now, and Sergei wanted to come and watch Nick work with his horses. He wanted to see Pegasus do his croupade, which several people had told him was amazing and hard to believe, and made Pegasus look like he was flying. People were beginning to know him by name now, by his new name, not the old one.

"They're good people," Nick said to Toby and Lucas as they walked into the trailer, which didn't look quite as bleak now, knowing they had friends nearby. Toby had stars in his eyes and only nodded, and Lucas giggled as they went to get ready for bed. He didn't tell Toby he'd seen him kissing Katja. Toby was totally besotted as he brushed his teeth, put on his pajamas, and went to bed. He was in love. And Lucas wandered into his father's room to kiss him goodnight. Nick was on his bed writing a letter to his father to tell him about his first Thanksgiving. It was so different from anything Paul knew. An evening with six men who performed a trapeze act, and their wives who were gymnasts, and Gallina on the high wire. It was hard to find the words to describe everything, but it had been a perfect evening in his brand-new life.

"Goodnight, Papa," Lucas said, brushing his cheek with a kiss. "Maybe I'll be a trapeze artist one day, instead of a clown," he mumbled with a yawn and shuffled off to bed, as though those were his only two options, as his father mused about how strange life was, how rapidly things changed, and wondered what would happen to them all. If only he knew. But for now, this was enough. It was a safe refuge from the storm brewing in Europe.

Chapter 10

The circus did a Christmas show every year in Sarasota, for the locals, and to try out some of their new acts. They wanted Nick in the show, and advertised it heavily: the Count, with the flying horses Pegasus and Athena. They had a photographer take some impressive photographs of Pegasus in midair during a croupade, and Nick cut a dashing figure in top hat and tails astride him. And when he did his act in the show, the audience went wild and loved him. He was in the parade at the end, riding Pegasus, and Toby on Athena, waving their top hats at the crowd. He was a new face, and both women and men seemed to be excited by him. The women liked his striking good looks, he was a very handsome man, and the men admired what he did with his horses. The introduction of his act was a resounding success, much to the delight of John Ringling North, who had come to watch him from a seat in the front row, and even he thought Nick's act was perfection. And several of the other performers had come, too, and all congratulated Nick when he went backstage after his performance.

Nick was hanging around afterward, waiting for the parade, when he heard the ringmaster announce the Markovich family in the main ring as the last act after the intermission, and Nick wandered out, to stand at the edge of the ring to watch Christianna. He had seen her practice on the low wire a few times, with her father coaching her, but he had never seen her perform on the high wire. He was curious, and stood silently as she shimmied gracefully up the rope to the tiny platform near the top of the tent, as the crowd watched without uttering a sound. The band was playing the music from **Swan Lake,** which Nick recognized instantly, but he paid no attention to it, as he watched her move with infinite grace from the platform onto the wire.

And instinctively he lowered his eyes to see what was below her. There were handlers, and her father in his wheelchair, and her brothers watching her closely, standing below the high wire, in case they had to catch her. But there was no net, and as he saw it, Nick held his breath and kept his eyes glued to her. He was mesmerized by the tiny waiflike figure who seemed to glide through the air, standing on nothing. She was up so high that it was hard to see the wire beneath her feet. She looked as though she were suspended in midair, dancing, and she smiled as she did it, as though she loved what she was doing.

The wire bounced once, and the entire crowd gasped, but she maintained her footing effortlessly. She turned backward then, and forward again, and as he looked, Nick started to feel sick. He couldn't bear the suspense and the tension as he stared at her while she took such terrifying risks. It was easy to see why she was the star of the show. She deserved every bit of it for what she was doing. Her performance seemed interminable as the tension mounted, and Nick felt chilled as he continued to watch her.

And then finally, with a last graceful leap, she landed on the platform on the other side, barely bigger than her tiny feet, and the audience burst into thunderous applause. She grasped a loop in the rope and slid effortlessly down until she landed on the circus floor and took an elegant bow. The crowd got to their feet immediately and cheered her. She had risked her life for them, and they considered it entertainment, and as he stood there afterward, Nick realized he was shaking. He had never seen anything so terrifying in his life.

She whisked past him as she left the ring, but didn't see him, and her brothers followed like a palace guard, with her father wheeling his chair behind them. He had once been as good as his daughter and notoriously more daring, and her mother had been as graceful, everyone agreed, until she fell to her death. Nick couldn't imagine anything being worth taking that kind of risk. He had watched Gallina perform earlier, and she had been far more cautious. Her act was exciting, but nothing like this. Christianna's performance was a combination of

exquisite grace and agility, remarkable balance, and sheer terror. And she was much
too young and beautiful to die. Her mother
had been scarcely older when she lost her
life, when Christianna was very young. She
had been brought up by her father and aunt,
Nick had been told.

He was still shaken when he mounted
Pegasus a few minutes later for the parade.
Christianna had been the grand finale, and
deservedly so. And then the parade light-
ened the mood again, with every performer
in it, all the animals, the stars of the show
riding elephants, and Christianna among
them, while the clowns cavorted around
them, and the music celebrated the close
of the show. There had been no mishaps,
but Nick had felt as though his heart would
stop as he watched Christianna. Pegasus
pranced past her at one point in the parade,
as she rode the largest elephant, standing
on his back, and she looked at Nick. Their
eyes met, and he saluted her with his top
hat, and then she smiled. She looked as
light as air as she danced along beside him
for a moment, and then he led Pegasus into
a slow canter and moved ahead. Nick realized there was something riveting about

her every time he saw her. He didn't know if it was the shocking risks she took with her own life, or her sheer beauty. But either way, he felt haunted for hours afterward whenever they met. And he couldn't imagine why her father let her do it, particularly given what had happened to him, and her mother. Clearly, as Gallina said, they were mad.

At the end of the show, he and Toby took the horses back to their tent, and brushed and fed them, and then he walked slowly back to the trailer with his son. He felt dizzy and almost drunk from the sounds and smells of the circus that day. He could still hear the music in his head.

"I watched Christianna Markovich tonight," Nick said casually to Toby as they wandered home. Their own performance had been exhilarating that night. Pegasus had been the hit of the show, and Nick along with him. "That's an insane thing to do," Nick said, still feeling queasy when he thought of what he'd seen Christianna doing. At any moment, she could have plummeted to her death, with the smallest slip. Gallina's high-wire act was entertaining. Christianna's was death-defying magic. There was a huge difference, and Nick had been aware of it instantly.

"Everyone says they're crazy," Toby said nonchalantly.

"Her father certainly is, to let her do it. I would kill you if you ever wanted to do something that dangerous." Nick still couldn't understand it. Nothing justified the risk.

"It's what they do," Toby said with a grin. In six weeks, the circus and everything that went with it had begun to seem normal to him. And now that he was infatuated with Katja, he was having fun there. Their romance was blazing. Both families were aware of it, and thought it was sweet, as long as it didn't get out of hand. And Gallina watched Katja carefully and had strict rules. Nick had warned his son not to go too far—she was a nice girl. Toby had promised to be reasonable. It was innocent and sweet, and their parents wanted it to stay that way.

That night as he lay in bed in his trailer, Nick thought about Christianna again, and her extraordinary high-wire act. He couldn't get her out of his mind. He could still see her dancing on the wire, turning backward and then forward again, high above the crowd. He had nightmares about it that night, as though he could see her falling, and in his dream he reached out to catch her, but couldn't get to her in time, and she fell into a deep hole in silence, her eyes watching him until she disappeared. Nick woke up in a cold sweat, and was still thinking about her when he went back to sleep. He felt better in the morning, but he hated what he had seen the night before. That much danger seemed like too much to him. He said something about it to Gallina that afternoon, and she rolled her eyes.

"That whole family has a death wish," she said with disapproval. "I think her father pushes her to do it. He's a crazy old man who thinks that the only thing that matters is the high wire. She should at least use a net, but then I suppose the audience wouldn't love it the way they do. I'm not willing to take those chances. I have children," she said simply. Nick knew that she occasionally worked without a net, too, but less and less now. And when she didn't, Sergei stayed angry at her for weeks. The circus didn't expect her to take that kind of risk—they had Christianna to do that. And Christianna had a younger sister their father was grooming too. She was only thirteen and too young for the high wire. But soon she'd be up there.

Two days after the Christmas show, Nick and the boys celebrated a quiet Christmas Eve together. They had bought a small tree and decorated it in the trailer. Nick bought lights, and Toby helped him string them up outside. The trailer looked festive, but still pretty bleak. It was the thing Nick disliked most about circus life. He hated the trailer, and living less well than his horses. But it was their life now. And they all lived the same way in the circus.

Nick lit candles on the Christmas tree on Christmas Eve, and it reminded them of Germany. He felt a lump in his throat as he sat with his children, trying not to think of the people they'd left behind and a lifetime of Christmases at the schloss. They'd been in Florida for almost two months, but in some ways it felt like an eternity to him. His sons were adjusting well, but there were times when he wondered if he would ever have a normal life again, among the people he'd grown up with, in the home his family had lived in for centuries. Everything here was new and totally foreign to him, except his children, and their horses. Everything else still felt strange. He questioned if he'd ever fully adjust to this life, or be allowed to go home again, or if he'd be an outcast forever.

All three of them were quiet as they watched the candles on the tree, thinking about what they missed most. And when the boys went to bed, he blew the candles out. He didn't want the trailer to go up in a blaze, but it had been nice to light them for a while. He thought about Alex and his father as he lay in bed that night, how they were faring, what kind of Christmas it was for them. He was worried about his father being alone, and he wrote to him often, but there was nothing he could do to help him now, and he knew that Alex was dropping by to see him as often as he could. And he assured Nick in his letters that his father was doing well. Nick hoped that was true.

There was a festive feeling on the fairgrounds for the week between Christmas and New Year's. People invited each other into their trailers for meals and a drink. Others went out and had dinner in town. The circus gave a big party in the main tent right before New Year's, which almost everyone attended, and Nick and his boys went too. It gave them a chance to meet new people and see the few they already knew. Nick heard every imaginable language around him, and was surprised by how many Germans there were, as well as numerous Italians and French.

With the emotions of Christmas behind them, there was New Year's to get through, and then the boys would go back to school after their vacation. They liked the school that other children from the circus went to. And their English was getting better. And they were to leave on tour in April. Nick was looking forward to it as a welcome change that would keep them busy. And it would be interesting to see new places, and discover America town by town, from one coast to the other. The boys were excited about it too.

They spent New Year's Eve with Gallina and Sergei and their family, and Nick and the boys went home shortly after midnight. He had let both boys have a taste of champagne, Toby more than Lucas, who only got a drop. He and Rosie played checkers and fell asleep long before midnight, and Nick carried him home when they left. It had been a nice way to end the year, with their new friends, and comforting to speak German with them and share similar traditions.

The next day, Nick was grooming the horses when he saw Lucas walk down the road with Rosie, heading toward the big top. He told him to be back in time for lunch, and Lucas promised that he would. And he had just finished brushing Pegasus, and started on Athena, when Rosie came running into the tent, in tears.

"Lucas got hurt!" she shouted at him in German. Nick stopped what he was doing and stared at her, terrified at what might have happened. He could have been trampled by an elephant, stuck his hand in a tiger cage, or been run over by a truck. In the world they lived in, anything could happen, and might have. There were plenty of dangers at the circus for a child, particularly one as adventuresome as Lucas.

"What happened? Where is he?" Nick asked her with a frantic look, dropping the brush.

"The big top . . . he wanted to try the low wire, and he fell. I think he hit his head. His eyes were closed after and he didn't get up." Nick didn't stop to question her further—he ran as fast as he could toward the big tent, which was the center of activity of the fairground. He couldn't imagine what would have gotten into Lucas to play on one of the low wires, set up for practice for the highwire acts. He ran into the tent, looking for him, and saw a small knot of people near one of the low-wire setups, and pushed his way through, fearing the worst. He had already lost his wife and one child, he couldn't bear the thought of losing another, adrift in this unfamiliar land, which made everything seem even worse. And he saw Lucas immediately, lying on the ground in his short pants and plaid shirt, but his eyes were open and he was talking when his father got to him, and then Nick saw who he was talking to. It was Christianna, in a white leotard and ballet shoes, kneeling on the ground, stroking Lucas's head. Lucas was smiling at her, and she had put a damp cloth on his head and told him not to get up.

Nick turned to her immediately, wondering how she came to be there, and if she had seen Lucas play on the wire. Maybe it had seemed normal to her.

"What happened?" he asked her in a sharp tone.

"I don't know," she said softly in English, in her strong Polish accent. He had never spoken to her before. "I came in right after he fell. He's all right, his eyes are fine. He got a bump on the head, but he can see clearly. We can call the doctor, but I think he will be better in a little while. And his neck is fine too." She knew what to look for and had checked. Her voice was very soft as she spoke to Nick, but she seemed sure of herself and unafraid, and she had been very gentle with the child.

Nick nodded and turned to Lucas then. "What made you do that? That was a very stupid, dangerous thing to do. You could have broken your neck." His own terror made him sound harsh, but he was scared more than angry. The low wire was only five feet off the ground, and was nothing compared to the high wire, but it was high enough for him to have done himself some serious damage. Nick was relieved he hadn't. He looked gratefully at Christianna, as he lifted the boy into his arms. And when he did, Lucas closed his eyes and said he felt sick to his stomach.

"I think he has a concussion," she said quietly. "But if you keep him in bed, he'll be better tomorrow." And then she smiled. "It used to happen to me all the time, in the beginning."

"Is that why you're brave and foolish enough to work without a net?" Nick said, only half-joking. Every time he'd seen her do it, it upset him. And as he gazed at her, he knew he had never seen such brilliantly blue eyes in his life, and they bored into him like a bright light she was shining on him. It took his breath away when he saw them and made him want to close his eyes. But he couldn't stop staring at her now. She was mesmerizing.

"It's what my family does," she answered simply, undisturbed by what he'd said. But it was also how her mother had died, and her father had gotten hurt. It sounded like a bad family tradition to him. "Would you like me to come and watch him with you for a while?" she offered, and Nick didn't know why, but he nodded, and the girl in the leotard followed him out of the tent, and walked quickly to their trailer with him. "I'll get the doctor if you like," she offered, but Lucas was talking animatedly on the way back, and seemed to be recovering rapidly, despite the nasty bump on his head.

"I think he's all right," she said again, and walked cautiously into their trailer behind Nick with his son in his arms.

"You scared me to death," he scolded Lucas, who looked sheepish as his father laid him down on his bed, and went to get another damp cloth. Christianna already had it ready for him, and handed it to him when he turned around. He put it on Lucas's forehead and told him to stay there for a while, and then he came back into the living room to thank Christianna for her help. "He shouldn't have done that," Nick said, upset.

"They shouldn't leave the wire up. I always take it down after I work. People don't realize that it's still high enough to get hurt." He nodded and couldn't resist asking her a question, as her eyes burned into his. Her gaze was intense. And standing next to her, he realized what a tiny person she was. She was barely bigger than a child herself, but she was a woman, with infinite gentleness in her gaze as she looked up at him. There was something totally fearless about her that intrigued him, and the wisdom of the ages in her expression.

"Why do you do that? It's so dangerous.

I watched you at the Christmas show, and it made me feel sick. I was frightened for you," he said gently. She fascinated him. "I'm sorry if I sounded harsh before, but I hate to see you do it."

"It used to make me feel sick too," she admitted, "but it doesn't anymore. I'm not afraid. That's why I can do it. It's the fear that makes you fall. If you're not afraid, you don't fall."

It sounded overly simplistic to him, and too confident and optimistic. "And if you slip?"

"I never do," she said quietly. He could see, talking to her, that she had no fear at all, at least not of the high wire. But something had happened to bring her parents down, other than fear. And they had been experienced too.

"You might one day. Isn't there some other way you can thrill the crowd?" he asked her bluntly.

"Not like that. That's what they want. It's why they come." And he knew that in part what she said was true. They loved the danger and the risk, he could sense that when he saw the crowd's reaction to her act. "Your horses are very beautiful," she said, changing the subject away from herself. "I like the white ones. They look like dancers, and what you do with them looks like ballet."

"It almost is, and when I work with them as a pair, it's called that." Nick smiled as he said it. "Do you ride?"

"I have. Horses frighten me," she said, with a small smile.

"I find that hard to believe. A woman who dances on the high wire without a net can hardly be afraid on a horse a few feet off the ground."

"They're unpredictable. You never know what they'll do. On the wire, I only have to depend on me." What she said was true.

"With a good horse, you can depend on them too. I'll show you sometime." She nodded and seemed to like the idea, and then they went to check on Lucas again. He was lying on his bed, playing with a toy, and he seemed fine. Lucas looked up and smiled at her.

"Thank you for helping me," he said with a shy smile.

"Don't play on my wire again," she said with a look that told him she meant it. She had a will of iron, and it showed in her eyes. She was a tiny person, with an enormous spirit. She had to be in order to do what she did. And then Rosie walked into the trailer looking for Lucas and Nick. Nick called out to tell her they were in Lucas's room. She appeared in the doorway looking panicked, and then burst into a broad smile when she saw he was all right.

"I thought you were dead," she said to her friend.

"I wasn't," he said proudly. "Just resting for a minute."

"You rested for a long time," Rosie said matter-of-factly. "I called your name and you didn't wake up."

"I hit my head, but it's better now. She helped me," he said, glancing at Christianna again, and she smiled.

"You were already awake when I got there, just a little dazed." She had gone to practice and found Lucas on the ground, coming to. Rosie had already run off to find Nick.

"I don't want you two out of my sight from now on," Nick scolded them both. "It's my fault for letting you go off on your own. I didn't know you'd be foolish enough to play on a wire."

"My mama won't let me play on it either,"

Rosie confessed to Nick, as Christianna walked slowly out of the room. There was nothing more for her to do, and she didn't want to intrude. Nick followed her to the front door.

"Would you like to come and see my horses sometime? You can ride Pegasus. I'll hold the reins."

"Not if he stands on his back legs," she said shyly.

"He knows not to do that if I'm not riding him or telling him to," Nick said with a warm look. "I won't let him frighten you. He's very tame. And Athena is even more so, if you'd rather try her."

"Maybe sometime," she said cautiously.

"You're welcome anytime," he said as she stepped out of the trailer into the winter sunshine. It was a warm day. "And thank you again for helping Lucas. He's lucky you were there and knew what to do." She had kept him from getting up too quickly, which would have been dangerous. He might have fainted and hit his head again.

"I'm glad he's all right." He could have broken his neck, too, which was what she had feared at first. It was how her mother had died. She smiled at Nick again then, and left, with her perfect tiny body molded by the leotard as she headed back toward the big tent. Nick stood and watched for a minute and then went back inside.

"She's pretty," Lucas volunteered as soon as his father came back into his room. "I like her."

"I do too," Nick said, smiling at him.

"Why does everyone say she's crazy? She's nice."

"Because she works without a net," Rosie explained. "That's a stupid thing to do. My mama says she does it because her father makes her do it, and he's crazy too. He must be really mean to make her do a thing like that." And as he left the two children to their conversation, Nick wondered if her father really did force her or if Christianna actually liked what she did. She seemed to, and had no qualms about it. To her, it was just work, like any other job. Most of the people in the circus seemed to feel that way, with no sense of how unusual it was. And many of them had done it for generations, unlike Nick.

He went out into the winter sun again, and sat on a chair someone had left out-

side the trailer next to them. There were
four acrobats living in the other trailer, and
they were often noisy at night. They were
Chinese, from Hong Kong. And as he sat
there, and lit a cigarette, Nick thought of
Christianna again, how beautiful and delicate she was and how brave. He hoped
she'd come to visit his horses sometime,
and then he scolded himself. She was
twenty-one years old, and he was about
to turn forty-four. He couldn't even think
about pursuing her as a woman, and yet
she appealed to him immensely. He was
riveted by her eyes. He went back inside
then and pushed her from his mind. The
last thing he needed was to get involved
with a young girl at the circus, and he told
himself that she probably thought he was
too old anyway.

But in spite of his good intentions, she
haunted him all day. He kept thinking of her
expression when she talked about not being afraid of the high wire, or when he found
her in the big top leaning over Lucas. There
was something so gentle about her and at
the same time so strong. He tried to forget
about her and found he couldn't, and by the

end of the day, he felt bewitched. All he could think of were those bottomless blue eyes.

He was still thinking about her when he went to feed the horses that night, and after he did, he turned and saw her standing there. She was silently watching him with the gaze that had him in her thrall.

"I thought about you all day," he said, not knowing what else to say. "I think you cast a spell on me." He smiled. He felt like a boy as he looked at her, and not a man of his age. The age difference between them seemed to melt as their eyes met and held.

"I thought about you too," she said slowly. "I came to see the horses." He nodded and beckoned her to him, and when she stood next to him, he lifted her up gently onto Athena's back. She was as light as a feather as he held her, and he led the mare out of her stall, holding her bridle.

"She probably can't even feel you, you're so light." He smiled at Christianna, who looked at him solemnly.

"But I'm very strong," she said proudly, pointing a graceful dancer's leg, and he laughed.

"I'm sure you are, Christianna. Strong

enough to distract me all day." She didn't look afraid, despite what she had said earlier about being frightened of horses. And then he turned to look at her seriously. She looked like a fairy sitting astride the horse as she gazed down at him fearlessly. Neither of them said a word. They didn't need to. She had come to see him, not the horses, and he knew it. "What are we going to do now?" he asked her, as though they both knew what was going on. He wasn't sure of anything except that he had never known anyone like her. And whatever happened now was entirely up to her.

She leaned toward him then and put her arms around him as he held her on the horse, and he kissed her gently, knowing it was what he had wanted to do all day and what he felt compelled to do now. She kissed him back, and when they stopped, she smiled at him, as though it was what she had come here to do. He kissed her again, and as he did, he lifted her gently to the ground, and she stood in front of him, looking up at him. And all he knew was that wherever he was, no matter how far he had come, he had come home. He had come from another lifetime, another world, across an ocean to find her, and there was no doubt in his mind about what he was doing with her, and she appeared to feel the same way.

"I've been waiting for you. You took a long time to come," she said quietly.

"I had some things to do," he said, with his arms still around her. "We're going to have a problem about the high wire, Christianna," he warned her, which only seemed fair.

"We'll see," she said, not promising him anything either way.

"I didn't come here to watch you kill yourself." He had been widowed once, and he didn't want to fall in love with a woman who risked her life every night. He couldn't go through that again. "I need you here with me."

"I need you too . . . maybe in time I won't need the high wire anymore."

"Is that why you do it? For the thrill?" He looked surprised. She didn't seem like that kind of person. She was serious and strong and wise beyond her years.

"No. I do it because it's expected of me. It's what my family does, and needs me to do. I'm the only one who can right now. My sister is too young, and she's afraid. My brothers are too big." Nick had noticed that her father was a far slighter man than his sons.

"Some of your family have been gravely injured or died. I don't want you to be next," Nick said as he nuzzled her neck and kissed her again. It suddenly felt as though this had always been meant to be, as though their paths had been destined to cross, and it was written years before, in another life. He couldn't get enough of her, just kissing her was dizzying, as was feeling her skin when he touched her face, or she touched his with gentle hands. She felt like velvet to him. "We'll talk about it later," he said, about the high wire. He couldn't think anymore. He just wanted to be with her, and feel her in his arms. She felt so small and frail, he was afraid to crush her.

"I can never be yours," she said in a sad, gentle tone, but her words surprised him.

"Why do you say that?" He looked hurt and worried as she lowered her eyes, but she didn't pull away. She was happy in his arms and didn't want to leave them.

"Because of who you are. I'm just a girl from the circus, and you were someone important in your other life. I can tell. And one day you'll go back. I don't know why you came, but I know you'll leave. You don't belong here. I do."

"I don't know if I ever will leave, or be able to go back," he said honestly, in a whisper. "And if I do, I'll take you with me. You're not just a girl in the circus, Christianna. You're a very special person." He already knew that. She had a quiet dignity about her, a nobility and grace that made where they had met and where she came from irrelevant to him. He would have been proud to be with her anywhere, and he said it to her without hesitation.

"I will always be less than you because I come from this place," she said sadly. She understood it perfectly, but it wasn't how he felt about her. She was the most exciting woman he'd ever met. And he didn't care about his lost world now or the people in it. In an instant, she had catapulted into his life and made him feel part of hers. "One day you'll be ashamed," she said as though she knew that about him, but it was no longer true for him, and he knew it.

"Never," he promised her as they stood there. "You have nothing to be ashamed of.

Nor do I. I will be the luckiest man alive if you're with me."

"You're a nobleman, Nick. I'm just a girl in a high-wire act."

"Be quiet," he said firmly, "shhh . . ." He silenced her then with a kiss, and Pegasus turned to look at them, and nodded. And Nick knew that all he could do now was prove to her that he meant what he said. Whoever she was, and wherever they had met, he was sure. The bond between them had formed, irreversibly, from the instant they first saw each other. And as they left the horse tent together that night, it was sealed.

Chapter 11

Everything was different and infinitely better in Nick's life once Christianna entered it. They kept their romance quiet at first, which seemed wise. They went for long walks at night, away from the fairground, where people wouldn't recognize either of them. He just wanted to be with her, and talk to her, and learn more about her. They shared many of the same views of life, and about people, and even the circus, despite the difference in their histories and age. She was wise for a girl of twenty-one, and she made him feel younger than he was. On their next birthdays, he would be exactly twice her age, but neither of them cared.

"What would your father think about us?" Nick asked her one night, as they sat down on a bench to talk. They had been walking for an hour, and it felt good to get away. They had agreed not to tell her family yet, or his sons. They wanted to give themselves time first to get to know each other better, and protect what they shared.

"He'd be worried that you'll take me away. There's no one else to do the high wire, except me. My sister Mina is too young, she's only thirteen. And there has never not been a Markovich on the high wire for forty years. Until Mina is old enough, it's up to me. And she's afraid." Christianna never was, which added magic to her act.

"And if you fall, there won't be anyone either. Your father got hurt, and it killed your mother. How can he want you to do that?"

"It's our heritage. It's a tradition. My grandfather owned the best circus in Warsaw, and then he lost his money gambling and sold it. My parents came here when I was a baby, twenty years ago. The circus has always been our life. But it's not yours, Nick. One day you'll leave. My father will be afraid of that when he knows about us."

"Will he care about our age?" Nick was more worried about that and what people might say, that he was a cradle robber, or had seduced her, which he hadn't. Thus far, their relationship had been chaste, although they were falling in love with each other. But he didn't want to take advantage of her in any way, he loved her too much to do that. It was the first time he had ever felt like that, even with his late wife. Everything about Christianna was different. He felt as though he had come back to life again.

"He won't care about that," she reassured him. "He was twenty-eight years older than my mother. She was his second wife." Her father was seventy years old, and her oldest brother, by her father's first marriage, was almost forty, three years younger than Nick. "All he'll care about is that I don't leave the circus."

"What if you want to one day?"

"I've never known any other life," she said simply. But Nick wished he could share a better life with her, but he had no other life to offer her now, and even if he did, she was happy there. She had never wanted to leave. This was as much her heritage as his life in Germany had been his. And it was the only life she knew. It was enough for her.

They walked back to the fairground, taking their time, enjoying being together and getting away from the chaos they lived with, the jugglers and clowns and elephants, and people constantly swirling around them. And everyone was busy now, working on new acts and costumes, and getting ready to leave on tour in the spring. In spite of everything that had happened, Nick had never felt as peaceful before. Christianna had a calm about her that brought balance and strength to his existence. He saw everything differently now, and instead of contemplating his losses, he saw his new life now as a tremendous blessing, with her in it. He looked happy and relaxed, and so did she.

They did several shows before they left Sarasota, and warm-ups for the season. And when he watched her on the high wire now, he felt physically ill, even more than before he knew her. He was breathless with terror until she came down. He knew he couldn't stand it indefinitely—he was too frightened for her, and twice she nearly lost her footing. He was angry at her about it later, at night when they were alone.

"Do you realize what you're doing, Christianna? You're risking your life **every** time. You can't be that lucky forever." He looked miserable as he said it. He had been near tears while he watched her. It was the only thing they disagreed on.

"Yes, I can. My grandmother never fell. She died of old age."

"She's probably the only one. I know I have no right to change what you do, but I want you to keep your life, and stay alive for me."

"I will," she said solemnly, but it didn't calm him. He was frantic with worry for her now every time she went up the rope to her platform.

At the end of January, Nick saw in the newspapers that Hitler had openly threatened the Jews in his Reichstag speech. It didn't surprise Nick, but the rest of the world was shocked. Hitler saying that Europe would not have peace "until the Jewish question had been disposed of" made everything clear. It made him even more grateful that he had left after the general's warning to his father. He had obviously known what was coming.

A few weeks later, John Ringling North asked Nick and Christianna to come to his office, together. They were sure that he had found out about their budding romance and was going to scold them and voice his disapproval. There was nothing in their contracts that prevented them from being together—people in the circus had affairs with each other all the time, as they both knew, and some got married. But Nick was afraid he'd reprimand them anyway, and he looked tense when they walked into North's office. They both felt as though they were being called into the principal's office at school. But instead, he smiled broadly when he saw them. They had no idea what was on his mind, and tried not to look at each other for reassurance.

"I wanted to bring you both in to discuss a thought I had. Christianna has been our biggest star since she turned eighteen," he said as he smiled at her. "And Nick, I think you're going to be. You're already heading there, and you haven't been on tour yet."

But his Lipizzaners had been the hit of every show since he'd joined them, and Nick was a dashing figure. The women in the audience were crazy about him. He was a handsome aristocrat from Europe, riding a white horse. He was the essence of every woman's fantasies. And even the other performers talked about what a good-looking man he was.

"I'd like you both to think about doing part of an act together. I don't think we're going to get you up on the wire, Nick," he said, smiling at him, "but I love the idea of Christianna on one of your Lipizzaners. If you could work up part of an act together, during yours," he looked at Nick, "I think it would bring down the house. The handsome prince and the fairy princess. Can you ride?" he asked Christianna.

"A little," she responded, shocked at his suggestion, and relieved that they weren't in trouble.

"I can teach her," Nick volunteered quickly. He loved the idea. "We could do a waltz together on horseback. I'll need to work with my horses for a while. We can do something simple in the meantime. I think it's a wonderful suggestion." Nick was ecstatic, they talked about it with him for a while, then left North's office in a daze. It seemed providential. It was the perfect opportunity to be together for shows and rehearsals. They had six weeks to learn the act North wanted, before they left on tour.

"Wow, I thought we were in trouble," Christianna said with a giggle that made her seem even younger than she was.

"We will be if we don't come up with a good act for him. Leave that to me. I'll start thinking about it today." It took Nick six days to choreograph a routine that his horses were able to execute, and that was simple enough for Christianna to follow. Nick rehearsed it with her a week after they'd seen North. And they had time to work on it before they opened at Madison Square Garden. It was still rough, but it worked, and with practice, once set to music, it would be elegant and romantic. Nick could hardly wait to perfect their new act and perform it in New York. He knew the audience would love it.

They rehearsed diligently every day, and by the time they left for New York at the beginning of April, Christianna looked like an angel on Athena's back. She was nervous at first, but she had exceptionally good balance, for obvious reasons, and she managed to stand on the Lipizzaner's back for part of the routine that Nick had designed, and was comfortable in the saddle the rest of the time, riding beside Nick on Pegasus, the two horses moving in split-second precision around the ring. Nick was thrilled with how far they'd gotten with the new routine, and Christianna learned quickly. And she had gotten better every day. They still made mistakes, but very, very few, and none the crowd would see. And he loved doing it with her. John North had been right—it added a measure of elegance and excitement to Nick's act. He could hardly wait to try it out in front of an audience. They were both excited about it when he walked her back to her trailer, the night before they left Sarasota. And they ran into her father and brothers and younger sister when they finished their rehearsal. Nick greeted them politely, chatted with her brothers for a few minutes, and then left to get back to his boys. Like everyone else, he still had a lot to do before they left the next morning.

The day they left Sarasota to begin touring, later than usual this year, everyone was excited to leave, and Lucas thought it was the most exciting day of his life. The big cats were loaded onto the train, along with the elephants and other animals. Nick loaded all his horses in a trailer early that morning after feeding and watering them. There were roustabouts and handlers on the train to feed the animals and tend to their needs. Many of the performers were taking the train, but some were driving their trailers, as Christianna's family was planning to do, and Nick with his boys, following the train. The big equipment was being transported by rail and a fleet of trucks. It looked like the whole town was leaving, which was nearly true, and it would be eight or nine months before they returned, after touring the country, stopping in small towns along the way, and occasional big ones, usually for only one night, and rarely for more than two days, except when they opened in New York, where they always spent four weeks at the beginning of their tour. And everyone loved performing at "the Garden" because the conditions there were so good.

Nick had been told the tour would be grueling, but his boys didn't care. And they were looking forward to being in New York for almost a month. Toby had asked to ride with Katja's family, and Rosie was going to travel the first day with Lucas and Nick. It seemed a fair trade.

Nick stopped briefly to see Christianna before they left. It would be many hours, or even the next day, before he could see her again. She was wearing a white cotton sundress and dance shoes that were too worn for the high wire. He gave her a quick kiss before they took off. Her brothers and sister were already waiting for her in their trailer, and her father and aunt were taking the train.

"My brothers are getting suspicious," she whispered as he kissed her again. They had been talking lately about saying something to them, but they were both sure there would be a reaction. His presence in her life, and his concern for her well-being was a huge threat to them. And they weren't pleased that John Ringling North wanted her to perform with him. They thought it diluted the impact of her own act later in the show. According to them, high-wire artists didn't perform on horses like acrobats. But

North was the president of the circus, and as Christianna pointed out to her brothers, his word was law, and they had to agree. And Nick and Christianna were delighted at the legitimate excuse to work together and no one could object. And the act that Nick had designed for them was beautiful and artistic.

"See you later," he whispered after a last kiss and hurried off, and she was smiling as she got into the trailer and they started on the long journey to New York.

They had been driving for several hours when her oldest brother, Peter, asked her about Nick.

"What's going on with you two?" he inquired as he took a bite of an apple. Their little sister, Mina, was asleep next to him on the couch. And their three other brothers were taking turns driving. Their wives had gone on the train to take care of their aunt and father-in-law.

"Nothing. Why?" She had never lied to him before, but she didn't want to share what was happening with Nick. She wasn't ready to yet. What they had belonged to them, and she felt loyal to Nick, and wanted to protect him, and herself. "We've been working on the act Mr. North wants us to do."

"And what else?" Her brother was smiling at her. "You can tell me," he pried with a knowing look. He always treated her like a child, no different than her thirteen-year-old sister.

"There's nothing to tell. He's a nice man. We're friends. I like his boys."

"They're more your age than he is. He's old enough to be your father, Christianna. I hope you realize that."

"There's nothing going on," she repeated with a cold look. She didn't like being pushed, and she got on less well with her older brother than the others. He was too much like their father and had old-fashioned ideas about their act. And he was jealous, and always had been, that she was the star of the high wire. He had always wanted to take their father's place, but he was heavy-set, and the audience liked watching Christianna better. She was a lot prettier to look at, and steadier on the wire. Peter had fallen off the low wire many times. And none of her sisters-in-law had ever performed with them. They were just part of the entourage, and several of them were jealous of her, too, especially Peter's wife. Christianna was wary of them both.

"Well, don't get any ideas about him, just because he looks good on a horse. He'll throw you away in five minutes, and he won't be here long. I know his type. Some fancy aristocrat with a title, down on his luck, so he joins the circus with his horses to bail himself out. As soon as he does, he'll be gone. And don't let him make you believe anything else." Christianna didn't think he'd be there long either, but for different reasons. He deserved a better life than this, and wasn't suited to it, even if he was a good sport about it. He had long since told her why he had left Germany and what he was doing there, but she couldn't imagine him staying either, once Germany returned to normal, which they all felt sure it would one day. The current insanity, under Hitler, couldn't last forever.

And if he didn't go back to Germany, Nick talked about breeding horses one day, Lipizzaners, maybe on a ranch. He didn't have the money for it now, but maybe he would in time, while Pegasus was still young enough to breed. There was plenty of time for that, the stallion would live for another twenty-five years. But it was his dream. And in twenty-five years, Nick would be the right age to retire. She would have to leave the high wire long before that, no matter how good she was now. She could do it for another ten or twelve years, if she was lucky. And then Mina would have to take over, or someone else. But at least she and Nick could dream. For now, it was all she had.

"Has he said anything to you?" Peter asked persistently, as he finished the apple and tossed the core out the window of the trailer, while looking intently at her.

"Why should he? All we do is work together, and I have a lot to learn." Peter nodded, satisfied for the moment. He wasn't sure if he believed her. He had seen how Nick looked at her, especially when she was on the wire. Everything he felt for her was in his eyes. Peter was glad Christianna hadn't noticed. It would only be trouble if she did, but he knew she was an innocent girl and never looked at men. Her brothers and father wouldn't have been happy if she did. There were plenty of loose women in the circus, and he wouldn't tolerate his sister being one of them, although he had been known to be enticed by them himself, unbeknownst to his wife. Christianna knew that her brothers all misbehaved with the circus women, but she was a girl, and they had different rules for her. She never let on to her brothers about what she saw or knew, or that she'd heard talk about them with other women. It was one of the reasons she was never interested in circus men. A lot of them played around and cheated on their wives.

"I'd say he has a lot more to learn than you do," Peter said disparagingly about Nick. "He has no idea what the circus is all about."

"He's a decent man," she said coldly to her brother. "And a good father. And I'm sure he was kind to his wife." All of which was more than she could say for her brother, who slapped his wife around whenever he drank too much. It was common in the circus, both drink and bad treatment of their women, who got even with them by sleeping with other men. Christianna didn't like their morality or values, or some of the games people played. She just did her work on the high wire, and took care of her father, aunt, and little sister. It was enough for her, or it had been until Nick arrived. Now she wanted more, with him. And he was so infinitely better than her brothers, such a gentleman, and so good to her. She couldn't imagine ever being lucky enough to have a life with a man like him. In that, she knew her brother was right, and believed it herself. Despite his promises, she was sure that when Nick got back on his feet and had enough money saved, or when Germany got sane, he would leave the circus, and he wouldn't be taking her. She could never fit into his real life. She was just a girl in the circus, but she was grateful to be in his life now. She was living their love from day to day.

"Just see that you don't get any fancy ideas," her brother warned her, and then went up front to ride with the others, while Christianna lay on the couch with her sister and thought about Nick. And after a while, she fell asleep, dreaming of him.

Nick was having fun with Rosie and Lucas, playing guessing games with them along the way. The convoy of trailers and circus trucks seemed endless, as they wended their way north. Most of them drove late into the night, the riders taking turns driving. But Toby was too young to drive, so Nick usually did it all himself. He went to check on the horses when they made a stop, and they were doing fine. He made sure that they had enough water and feed, cleaned their trailer, and got back in the truck. Nick was thinking of Christianna and wished they could have traveled together. And he wanted to go and visit her when they stopped for the night. She had asked him not to before they left Sarasota, and he agreed. He was thinking about her when she suddenly appeared next to his trailer late that night.

"What are you doing here?" He looked happy to see her, and surprised. The boys were already asleep, and he'd been out-side, smoking a last cigarette before he went to bed. The air was cool, and he was relaxing, thinking of her. "Did you escape?" he asked, and she nodded with a mischie-vous smile, and looked like a naughty child. He laughed with pleasure and pulled her into his arms to kiss her and hold her for a few minutes.

"Everyone's asleep," she giggled, "my

brothers drank too much when we stopped."
It was a bad habit they had. And it had been
a long boring day for them all.

"I wish we could just run away somewhere," he said longingly, as they sat next
to each other on the trailer's front step.
There were a million stars in the sky, and
they could hear murmurs and soft laughter
in the distance, but for the most part, the
trailers were quiet, and most of them were
dark. It was late.

"Where would you run away to?" she
asked with tender eyes. There was a sliver
of moon overhead. "Back to Germany?"

He hesitated for a long moment. "I don't
know. It's not a good place to be anymore.
Back to the way it used to be, yes. Now, I
don't know where I'd go." He no longer had
a country or a home. All he had now was a
woman he loved, which suddenly seemed
like a lot, and much more than he'd had before. He pulled her closer to him, and then
smiled into her eyes that turned a deep
ocean blue in the night. She was the most
beautiful woman he'd ever known.

"Where would you go if you ran away?"
he asked her, and she looked up at him so
innocently that it tore at his heart.

"To you," she said simply. The answer seemed easy for her. He held her tight and closed his eyes, wishing that the world were different and he could give her what he'd once had. He had nothing to give her now, except his love.

They sat for a long time in silence and then she stirred. "I'd better go back, in case one of them wakes up." He wished for an instant that she could stay there with him, but there was no way that was possible, and his boys were with him.

He kissed her again, and she scampered off as silently as she had come. She was like a vision that he conjured up whenever he thought of her or needed her, and suddenly there she was, and then gone again, like a dream in the night.

And when she got back to her trailer, she could hear her brothers snoring, sprawled out in the living room and on the floor. She quietly slipped into her bedroom, put on her nightgown, and went to bed next to her sister, thinking of Nick.

The next morning they set off again at dawn, to travel the rest of the way to New York. They made it at nearly midnight, and from then on, the roustabouts worked hard, unloading equipment and setting things up. It was an enormous undertaking, which required nearly all the heavy manpower they had. The performers had nothing to do with it, but the roustabouts and handlers had a big job.

The cages had to be rolled into place for the first acts and the tunnel cages that led to them. The high wire, the trapezes, the poles, and the ropes all had to be put in place. They worked all night and into the next day, and some of the clowns helped. And they had to rehearse after traveling for two days. The acrobats and gymnasts always complained of being stiff. The wardrobe mistresses had to organize costumes. There were a thousand things to do. And Nick and Toby had to exercise the horses before they rehearsed. Pegasus was prancing the moment Nick got on his back, the young stallion was tired of being confined and excited to see Nick.

Once he had exercised Pegasus, Nick went to look for Christianna, and found her balancing on a low wire that had already been rigged. He had ridden one of his Arabian horses over to find her, and she looked happy to see him. She smiled the moment she did. She was alone.

"Do you have time to rehearse with me?" he asked her, as she dropped off the wire easily and hopped to the ground.

"Sure. I just finished." They had put together a practice ring for the horses, and Nick had already arranged for rehearsal time between two other acts.

"Come on," he said with a warm look, and held out a hand to her. She took it, and he lifted her easily onto the horse, sat her up in front of him, and cantered off with his arms around her as he loosely held the reins. She was becoming more comfortable with his horses, and they went back and got Pegasus and Athena and walked them to the rehearsal ring. And once there, he led them through their liberty commands for a few minutes to warm up as Christianna watched him. He had gotten even better with them in the past five months, although he knew he still wasn't as good as Alex. And a few minutes later, he helped her into Athena's saddle, and they rode side by side on the Lipizzaners, taking them through their paces. And as Christianna had commented earlier, it looked like a ballet. She appeared more confident than she felt in the saddle, and Nick corrected her gently and gave her pointers. And in the end, she stood on Athena's steady back and rode around the ring, as he pulled Pegasus aside and then joined her for their finale. It was perfect, and her blue eyes were blazing when they stopped.

"How was it?" she asked him with a smile of pure pleasure. For a moment, it almost reminded her of being on the wire. She had felt like she was flying. "It felt great!"

"You are fabulous!" he complimented her, and knowing that no one was watching, he leaned over and kissed her, and they exchanged a warm smile. They looked like royalty on his spectacular horses, and after rehearsal, he walked her to where her trailer was parked. "See you later," he said, and then went back to the boys, who were thrilled to be in New York and wanted to go sightseeing the next day. Lucas insisted he wanted to go to the Empire State Building, since he hadn't gotten there after the boat. It was going to be an exciting month, being in the city and performing at Madison Square Garden. Christianna was as happy to be there as his children, although the

Garden wasn't new to her. But this time she would be performing there with Nick, who was her proverbial Prince Charming, and she felt like a fairy princess, riding the beautiful Lipizzaners with him. And they both hoped that the audience in New York would be dazzled by their new act.

Chapter 12

Their opening-night performance in New York was almost flawless, and Nick was thrilled with Christianna. She had added a new dimension to his act, and the audience responded with thunderous applause. It just got better and better for the month they were there. And they loved being in New York. Christianna went sightseeing several times with Nick and his boys, whenever they had a day off. Lucas got them to go to the top of the Empire State Building three times. And Nick invited her to go everywhere with them. They even managed to go out to dinner alone a few times.

There was tension among many of the Eastern European performers when they first arrived in New York, as Hitler had occupied Czechoslovakia in March, and many of them still had relatives there. Gallina and her family were particularly worried and upset. There was much talk about it and deep concern, which was still ongoing when the circus left New York in early May, and headed to Boston.

Lucas and even Toby were sad to leave New York. After Boston, they went south to Connecticut, then to Baltimore, Washington, and Philadelphia for two or three days in each city. It was a grueling schedule after weeks in one place in New York, which they all loved. After New York, the roustabouts had to set up the circus and tear it down every few days. They were used to it, but it was an incredible amount of work.

After Philadelphia, they went to rural Pennsylvania, and then New Jersey, Ohio, Kentucky, Michigan, Wisconsin. They were literally all over the map. They made their way west in August, north into Canada for a week, and then dropped down to Washington and Oregon at the end of the month.

They were in Eugene, Oregon, on September 1 when Germany invaded Poland, which panicked everyone in the circus. They had just gotten to Redding, California, when England, France, Australia, and New Zealand declared war on Germany on September 3, and the entire world was stunned. Europe was at war.

Despite the terrible news and his concern for his father, Nick was excited to be in California, and had looked forward to it for the entire trip. Nick had felt a pull toward California ever since he had come to the States. They went to San Francisco for two days, which Nick and his boys found thrilling as they walked along the Embarcadero and looked at the big ships, and admired the Golden Gate Bridge, which had recently been finished, and another bridge that spanned the east side of the bay. The views of the city were beautiful from all sides. And then they went to Los Angeles and San Diego, and back up to Santa Barbara, where they were given two days off. It was the opportunity for Christianna and Nick to spend time together. Nick and Christianna had been hoping for it for months.

Nick had no idea how she pulled it off,

but Christianna told her father, brothers, and aunt that she was going back to Los Angeles for the night with three of the Ukrainian female gymnasts. They had friends in the San Fernando Valley, and they had actually invited her to come along. And she asked them to cover for her instead. They were happy to help, and two of them suspected the reason, but didn't know with whom.

Nick asked Gallina to keep an eye on Toby and Lucas, and he borrowed a car. Pierre the French clown had said he could get him one, and Nick burst out laughing when he saw what it was. It was the yellow "taxi" that the clowns used during the intermission as part of their act, with the familiar logo on it that said "The Greatest Show on Earth." Nick was waiting in it for Christianna when she came running in a white dress and proper shoes, carrying a small bag, and she laughed, too, when she saw the car Nick had gotten for their two days away. They had been planning this for ages. And she was laughing and smiling as she got in beside him. The car had no backseat so it could accommodate more bodies when the clowns piled in on top of each other, so they could spill out in the center ring and make the audience laugh. It was a far cry from Nick's blue Bugatti or his father's Duesenberg, and all he could do was laugh as he kissed Christianna and drove away. They had actually managed to escape. He took her to the Santa Ynez Valley, which he had been told was beautiful horse country, and he wanted to see it with her. It was a two-hour drive from Santa Barbara, and the countryside was beautiful as they drove along in the ridiculous car.

"Well, no one will have any doubts about where we come from," he said as they parked outside a restaurant for lunch, and he followed her inside. They had hamburgers, and afterward drove the rest of the way. Once they were in the valley, they saw a small hotel that looked like a Swiss chalet. Nick went inside and rented a room, and then they went upstairs. It was a beautiful day, the sun was shining, the weather was warm, and the room was cozy with a big four-poster bed, and the moment he closed the door behind them, Nick took her into his arms and felt the sheer joy of just holding her and being alone. He had been desperate to share this moment with her for so long, and so had she with him.

"I can't believe we did it and we're finally together," he said as he breathed in the clean smell of her hair, and then kissed her neck. They hadn't had a day and night off in months, and she was constantly surrounded by her family and could hardly ever get away. The time they shared was always too brief and infinitely precious, and now finally they had two whole nights away to do whatever they wanted. It was a luxury and a gift beyond belief, and they intended to spend it well, discovering each other and the ecstasy of being together alone at last.

Christianna was so overwhelmed for a moment when they got to their room, that she didn't know what to say, as he slowly undressed her, and gently put her in the big comfortable bed. He slipped in beside her an instant later, turning his back to her at first as he slipped off the rest of his clothes. He didn't want to frighten her, he knew she was a virgin, but she held her arms out to him as though it were their wedding night, and for them it was. They had waited six months for this, and he wanted it to be perfect. He took her as gently as he could and made love to her with all the passion he had felt for her since the day they met. He had never loved anyone as he did her.

She lay in his arms afterward, with a peaceful look, and she smiled at him with her enormous blue eyes.

"I belong to you now, Nick," she whispered.

"And I to you . . . I love you so much." He wanted her to promise that she would never do the high-wire act again. He didn't want to lose her or have anything bad happen to her. But he knew he had no right to ask her to give it up, at least not yet, but he hoped that one day he would. He wanted her far away from all the dangers in her life, and wanted to keep her safe.

He looked at her then with everything he felt for her and kissed her, and then made love to her again, and this time it was even better for her. He taught her all the wonders of their bodies, and reveled in the beauty and joys of hers.

They stayed in bed until the sun was almost setting, and then they showered together and dressed. She was totally at ease standing naked before him, and he couldn't believe how perfect she was. Every inch of her was in proportion and delicately carved.

She was like a statue of a beautiful young woman, and all he wanted to do was gaze at her in awe. It was hard to force himself to get dressed, but he wanted to go out walking with her and look around the town. And after they did, they drove out into the countryside, wending their way around the Santa Ynez mountains, and he stopped when he got to a bluff. They got out of the car, and stood looking at the sun, which was setting over the mountains by then, and he knew he wanted to come back here with her one day.

She slipped her hand quietly into his, and leaned her head against his shoulder as they stood looking down at the valley, and he spoke as though in a dream.

"I want a horse ranch here one day, where I can breed Lipizzaners." He turned to her then with a serious expression. "I don't know how we'll do it yet, but I want to do that with you." It was as close as he had come to a proposal so far, and she gazed at him wistfully.

"I can't leave the circus, Nick. You know that." She was always honest with him.

"We will one day. I want a better life for my boys, and you and our children, than I can give you there. I don't want you on the high wire for the rest of your life," or at all, he almost said. "We'll know when it's the right time, Christianna. I can't afford it yet anyway. But I hope that one day I will, and I want you to come with me. I know this is the place. I knew it the minute I heard about it." It was the first thing he'd seen that made up for the country he had lost. He could easily imagine a life here one day, with her. And he wouldn't leave the circus until she was ready to go with him. He felt like he'd come home as he looked out over the valley from their vantage point, and he put an arm around her just as the sun disappeared behind the hills, and then he kissed her, and they got in the car and went back toward their hotel.

He took her out to dinner that night at an Italian restaurant. They laughed and talked, and she told him about growing up in the circus and wanting to be a clown, which made him laugh.

"You would have made a beautiful clown." He chuckled. "I'm afraid that's what Lucas wants to be now too. Toby says he wants to be a vet, for horses, which isn't a bad idea. We could use a vet if we're going to have a ranch one day." He spoke of it as though it were a reality, and she looked at him with worried eyes.

"You're serious about that, aren't you?"

"Yes, I am." She could see that he was.

"What if I can't go with you?" she asked in a sad whisper that touched his heart.

"Then I'll have to kidnap you. I know it will be the right thing for us," he said quietly, but she couldn't imagine leaving everything she knew.

"I've never been anywhere but the circus. I don't know any other life." Her eyes were huge as she said it to him, and he could see that she was scared. He reached across the table and took her delicate hand in his own.

"I want to share my life with you, Christianna. I can't give you the life I left behind in Germany, but I think I can give you a good one here one day, when we're both ready. A happy life for us and our children." It was the second time he had referred to their children that day, and she smiled as he said it.

"It's what I want too," she said softly. "I just don't know how to get there." Her family would be a major obstacle to overcome.

They would fight her every inch of the way if she tried to leave with him, and he knew that too.

"We'll find a way. Together. I'm here with you." She nodded, and he lifted her fingers to his lips and kissed them. "Don't worry. It will be fine."

"I hope that's true." She wanted a life together as much as he did, but she couldn't imagine it away from the circus, and he could.

"It is true," he said quietly. And then he paid for their dinner, and they left the restaurant and went back to their hotel and made love again. It was the most perfect night of her life, and when she woke next to him in the morning, he was smiling at her. He had been watching her for hours as she slept peacefully.

They spent the day exploring the area, and talking about his imaginary ranch and where it would be. They went wading in a stream, and lay under a tree together until they fell asleep. They bought sandwiches and had a picnic, and they went back to the bluff and watched the sunset again, and they brought dinner back to their room that night. He wanted to savor every minute they had together, and then they talked about what they would do when they went back. She said her brothers would kill her if they knew she had spent these two nights with him. And Nick had been as careful as he could be not to get her pregnant. He didn't want anything to go wrong for them.

"I want you to get to know my family," she said softly. "Maybe you could come to dinner with them, with the boys."

"I'll do anything you want, Christianna." He kissed her and looked at her seriously. "I'm here to stay, if you want me."

"I do," she whispered, and she believed him. And in all her beauty, with her lovely body lying naked across their bed, she looked like a fairy who had floated into his life like a dream.

"I want to go away with you again whenever we can," he said quietly. It had been perfection for both of them. And they knew that when they went back to the circus, they'd have to be discreet. There was always so much gossip about who was sleeping with whom, Nick didn't want them to be part of it, and he wanted to protect Christianna in every way.

He made love to her again that night

before they went to sleep, and in the morning when they got up, and then slowly they
got ready to leave the room that had been
their honeymoon suite, without benefit of
papers or a ring, but the feelings they
shared were the same. And when they left
the little inn, they both knew that they had
formed a bond that would carry them
through everything, whatever they needed
it to. No one and nothing could come between them now. She felt entirely his.

On the way back to Santa Barbara, they
talked again about his getting to know her
family. She wanted her brothers to like him,
and her father and aunt. It would make
things easier for her.

"How do they feel about your performing
with me now?" He knew they had been unhappy about it in the beginning, but she was
so good at it that he hoped they had calmed
down.

"They still think I should only do the high
wire. They think horses are dangerous, and
they're afraid I might get hurt." She smiled
as she said it, aware of the irony, and Nick
laughed.

"But the high wire without a net is fine.

Oh God," he said ruefully, as she smiled and leaned over to kiss him.

"I'm going to miss you tonight," she said sadly. It had been so wonderful to wake up next to him for two days.

"Maybe we can work things out," he said hopefully, "not every night, but whenever we can. I'll figure out something with the boys. And we can go away again. If we get a night off, we can disappear somewhere." It wasn't going to be easy, but they were both determined to try.

They were sad when they saw the Santa Barbara fairground come into view. It had been such a wonderful two days. She smiled as she looked at him. She felt like a woman now, not just a girl, and he was her man.

She told him to drop her off as far from her trailer as possible, and she would make her way back on her own. She didn't want to run into her brothers on the way back, or worse, see them while she was with Nick. And he had to return the car to the clown.

"I think our chariot is about to turn into a pumpkin," Nick said, laughing, as he stopped some distance from a group of trailers that neither of them recognized. She wanted to stop in and see the Ukrainian girls to match up their stories.

"I think our chariot turned into a pumpkin before we left," Christianna said, and laughed too. It had been a ridiculous car for their romantic vacation, but it had gotten them where they were going.

"I used to have a very fancy car," he told her, somewhat nostalgically. "I never thought I'd go on the most romantic holiday of my life, with the most beautiful woman in the world, in a clown car." They both chuckled at that, and she kissed him and then reluctantly got out of the car with her bag.

"I'll see you in a little while," she said softly. They had a performance together that night. "Thank you for everything. I had a wonderful time."

"So did I." He smiled at her from across the car. "The first of many," he promised. "See you tonight." And then he added for good measure, "Say hi to the Ukrainians, and thank them from me."

"I'll be sure **not** to do that," she said, grinning. She didn't want anyone to know who she'd been with, and had no intention of telling them, although they had been curious when she asked for their help. The age difference between her and Nick would throw everyone off the scent, for now at least. And they'd been extremely discreet, so her family wouldn't know. She set off on foot toward the Ukrainian girls' trailer, across the fairground, to see if they were back.

When she got there, they had just returned from L.A. themselves, and were getting ready for rehearsal.

"Did you have a good time?" one of them asked her with a sly wink, which Christianna ignored.

"Yes, thanks," Christianna said blithely, and thanked them again, and left. And it worked out perfectly, she was just leaving their trailer with her suitcase when she ran into her oldest brother. He didn't even look suspicious when he asked how her trip was. It had never occurred to him that she'd go on a romantic weekend.

"We had fun," she said as she smiled innocently.

"I don't know how you stand those girls," Peter said, lowering his voice so they didn't hear him through their open windows. "They're so loud. Did you all get drunk?" He teased her. He knew they drank a lot, too, when they weren't working. Most of the Russians did, cheap vodka, but her brothers often did, too, so he was in no position to talk.

"Of course not," she answered demurely. And he obviously didn't see anything different about her, since he didn't accuse her of being with a man. But she felt as though she had come back a changed woman, and as though everyone could see how happy and in love she was. But Peter said nothing. "Did you and the boys go to Las Vegas?" she asked. They'd been talking about it before she left.

"No, I wasn't in the mood, so we stayed here."

"That's too bad."

"We'll be there anyway in a few days. We can gamble anytime." The casinos in Vegas stayed open twenty-four hours a day. They went on tour every year, and most of the cast loved it. This would be the first time she was old enough to go to the casino, but she didn't really care except to see it. Drinking and gambling were her brothers' favorite pastimes, not hers. And chasing women.

She made her way to her own trailer then,

and her aunt and sister were in the living room when she got there. Her aunt was talking about the news she'd heard that day of how badly things were going in Europe, but her sister Mina made no comment. She was used to their aunt rattling on endlessly, always with bad news. None of them paid any attention to her. She always had some catastrophe to announce. Christianna said hello to them both and then went to shower. They didn't have rehearsal that day, and she didn't have to be ready until her performance with Nick and his Lipizzaners. She could hardly wait to see him again.

"I don't know why you bother with those horses!" her aunt shouted after her. "No one cares about horses!" It was the opinion of her entire family, but John North had asked her to do it, and they couldn't argue with it.

"Some people do," Christianna called back, as she undressed in the tiny room she shared with her sister. She was acutely aware, as she stood in her underwear, that only hours before she'd been making love with Nick, and wished she still were. She just hoped that she hadn't gotten pregnant. He had assured her he was careful. She wasn't entirely sure how he'd done that.

She knew several girls who'd had to have abortions, and she knew that they were dangerous and painful. Two years before, one girl went to a bad abortionist in New Jersey, while they were on tour, and died three days later of an infection. Her aunt had told her that would happen if you had sex with a man before you were married. It had terrified Christianna. But everything was different with Nick. Her two days with him had been perfect.

They had a light dinner that night in the trailer, before she had to be at the big top to meet Nick. She took particular care that night to wear a new white leotard and tutu, with silver sparkles on it, and she dusted a few into her hair from the box where she kept her makeup, so they would shimmer in the spotlight. She had her hair wrapped in a tight bun, and was wearing white satin ballet shoes. She wanted to look perfect for him tonight. It was their first performance together since their honeymoon in Santa Ynez.

And in his trailer, Nick put on his best tail-coat, and a white piqué shirt that had been made for him in Paris, and his favorite top hat. And he wore diamond studs in his white vest that he had brought from Germany and never wore while he performed. He hadn't worn them since the ship coming over. He shaved extra carefully before he dressed, put on cologne, and shined his boots, as he always did. He looked impeccable when he left to saddle Pegasus and Athena. Toby was already there, and had exercised all the horses that afternoon. And Katja was with him in the horse tent. Whenever possible, she went everywhere with him, and he seemed to like it. He was as crazy about her as he had been when they first met. And Lucas made fun of him often. He was with Rosie just as much, but they were just friends, at their age. By now, Toby and Katja were boyfriend and girlfriend, and both had just turned sixteen. She was dressed for work that night too. She was going to be in the trapeze act with her father and his brothers, while her mother performed on the high wire. Nick chatted amiably with the two young people, as he checked the horses and found everything in good order, and Pegasus in high spirits. He looked as though he couldn't wait to start.

"Where did you go?" Toby asked him with interest. His father had never left them

before, since they'd come to the circus.
Toby didn't mind, since he got to spend
even more time with Katja and her parents,
which suited him just fine.

"Santa Ynez," Nick responded, sounding
relaxed. "It's beautiful country, great for
horses. I'd love to have a ranch there one
day." Toby nodded. "Maybe one day," Nick
said as he got into the saddle on Pegasus,
trying to settle him down. He was high-
spirited tonight, as though he knew something was different. Like Christianna, Nick
felt like a new man. He had come alive in
Christianna's arms.

A little while later, Toby and Nick left for
the tent. And as they walked the two Lipizzaners, and led the Arabians, Katja followed at a safe distance, so none of the
horses could kick her if they reared. She
had learned that the Arabians did it often.
The Lipizzaners were better behaved. And
once they got to the tent, Nick and Toby
were busy, getting their horses ready for
the show. Christianna met them there, she
was already waiting, and right before they
went on, Nick lifted her into the saddle.
She flew into it easily, and put her feet into
the stirrups he kept short for her, and a

few minutes later, the spotlight was on
them. She and Nick looked magnificent,
and everyone agreed, it was the best show
they'd done so far. And the audience
cheered them loudly when they were finished. They had moved with total precision
that night, without a flaw. It was as though
they moved as one body now, and Pegasus and Athena seemed to be part of their
new bond as well. Christianna and Nick
had galloped through the finale holding
hands. They really did look like royalty that
night, and the costume mistress had given
her a little rhinestone tiara that glittered like
Nick's diamond studs. They were by far
the most elegant couple in the show.

Nick went to tie up the horses outside the
tent, and Toby helped him. And Nick had
plenty of time for a cigarette and to relax
for a while after their show, before he heard
Christianna's music start, and he walked
back into the tent just as she scampered
up the rope to the high wire. She got onto
her platform with her usual grace, and her
act began as Nick stared upward, as always
now, with his heart in his mouth. He was
careful to stay out of the spotlight and out
of her brothers' way. He could see her

father in the distance, watching her, as she glided through her routine with more than her usual grace. And she was beaming as she took the first turn, changing directions on the wire, and when she switched back, he saw her nearly stumble, and the crowd gasped and so did he. His eyes never left her for an instant, and he wanted to reach out and catch her if she fell, but she regained her poise and her balance instantly, and a moment later she was at the other side, and made the small leap to her platform. Nick felt almost faint with relief when she did. He couldn't imagine a lifetime of watching her like this, fearing for her life every night. It would have to change one day, but not yet. He knew it was too soon, but he could hardly wait to get her off the high wire for good, whatever it took.

She was down the rope a moment later, to thunderous applause, and smiled as she flew past him, with her brothers following her closely. Nick went backstage after that, but didn't see her. And he hated the fact that the crowd loved knowing that she could fall at any instant, but didn't. The extreme risk she took was what thrilled them,

and nearly drove him insane. It rattled him
to his core every time.

And the next time he saw her, she was
astride the elephant she always rode in the
finale. She looked like a perfect white elf
covered in silvery fairy dust, as she stood
on the elephant and held the handle on its
saddle, as Nick rode by on his stallion. He
stopped for a moment, held a hand out to
her, and she leaned toward him and touched
it, and then blew the crowd a kiss. They
loved it and ate it up as Nick rode alongside for longer than usual and then cantered
away, as Toby followed on Athena. The two
Lipizzaners were a spectacular sight. The
show was over minutes later, and he caught
a moment alone with her before she left.
Her brothers were waiting outside.

"You almost fell tonight," he said severely,
with a look of agony in his eyes. "I saw
it, you stumbled."

"I was distracted," she said apologetically. "I caught it very quickly."

"And if you hadn't?" He questioned her,
his eyes never leaving hers for a second.

"I would die," she admitted, aware of the
pain in his eyes.

"No, I would," he said softly. "Don't forget that."

She nodded, and quickly so no one could see it, he touched her hand, and then kissed it. "I love you," he whispered to her.

"I love you too," she whispered back, and was gone.

Chapter 13

After Santa Barbara, they went to Solvang, a funny little town modeled on a Dutch village, with windmills, and from there they went east to Las Vegas, which the crew always enjoyed. They only had one night there, so they had very little time to gamble, but they managed, and went to the casinos before and after the shows. They had a matinee to do as well.

And then they headed for the last leg of the tour. They had been on the road for seven months, a little less than in previous years, as they headed south and east on their way home. They only spent one night in each town, which was grueling for the roustabouts to set up and tear down, all in one day. More often than not, they worked straight through the night to tear it down, so they could leave again in the morning and move on.

They went all through the South, stopping in nearly every state, which would finally lead them to Tampa, Florida, for their last night.

All through September, the entire circus and the world had followed the war news from Europe, when finally Great Britain, France, New Zealand, and Australia declared war on Germany. And everyone in the circus was terrified for their relatives in Europe, and so was Nick. It particularly affected the people in the circus since so many of them were from Europe, especially Germany, and various Eastern European countries.

Despite the shocking news, they continued the tour and finished in Tampa on October 30, although their mood was subdued. Nick had had no news from Alex or his father for several weeks, and the letters he'd gotten after war started had been heavily censored, with official stamps and seals on them, but they'd gotten through, since the United States was not at war with Germany.

Nick had been worried about his father since he left, and he never said it in his letters, but Nick was concerned for his health. When Paul wrote to him now, he sounded old, and discouraged about the state of the world. And it could only get worse now, with Germany at war with much of Europe. He hoped that Alex would write to him again soon—he usually gave him more news than Paul. All Nick's father ever did was reassure him that as soon as things calmed down, he and the boys could come home. But it was clear now to Nick, even more so than it had been, that that wasn't going to happen anytime soon. Maybe never, if Hitler remained in power. And Nick couldn't help wondering how his mother had fared in the random removal of Jews to concentration camps in the past year. He wondered if she had fled, too, and could only hope that she had, even though he didn't know her.

Nick and Christianna had managed another romantic night together in a charming bed and breakfast in Savannah, Georgia. The Ukrainian girls covered for her again, and Nick confided to her how worried he was about his father, and she was deeply sympathetic and always gentle with him. Her family was anxious about their relatives in Poland, too, although most of them were in the States, with the circus, but they still had relatives in Warsaw, who were at great risk now with the war on.

Christianna was still under the spell of Nick's lovemaking after the stolen moments they shared, and she stumbled on the high wire again on the last night in Tampa. And when she slipped, it nearly stopped his heart. It had been a close one, and the crowd had gasped as they watched, and Nick nearly cried. They argued about it afterward, as they had several times now, and he always made the same plea for her to stop working on the high wire without a net.

"Don't ask me that, Nick," she said finally in frustration. "I can't stop doing it. I have no choice. If I stop, we have no act, and we'd have to leave. My father isn't going to let that happen, nor will my brothers. They depend on me. This is what I do. Just like you do with your horses." Her eyes were two deep pools of sorrow gazing into his. She didn't like causing him pain, but had no choice. No one in their family had ever worked with a net. The Markoviches were known for it, and their daring feats.

"And your father and brothers are entirely willing for you to risk your life, all of them." He got angry every time they discussed it, and she always vowed to herself that she wouldn't talk to him about it again. He didn't understand, he was not a circus person, and he'd only been there with them for less than a year.

"So you're not going to give it up?" he asked bluntly.

"No, I'm not. So maybe we shouldn't talk about it all the time."

"Probably not, if you're not going to be reasonable about it. And I know your family certainly won't be." He was seriously upset, because her working without a net filled him with terror, for her and himself. Nothing was resolved, and they were cool with each other the next day when they got back to Sarasota. Neither of them would concede, let alone take action about it. But the tension between them relaxed again as they settled into Sarasota for the winter break and no longer had to perform every night and travel every day. The issue was shelved for now, during their break, and they were all focused on the war news, none of which was good. Nick listened to the radio constantly to get all the news he could of what was happening in Europe. It appeared to Nick that Hitler wanted to rule the world, which had occurred to everyone by then.

Nick was often quiet now when he was with Christianna, thinking of his father and Alex, wondering how they were holding up in the face of the war. He felt guiltier than ever now not to be there to help.

"I'm sure they understand," Christianna said soothingly, as they talked about it late one night. "You couldn't stay."

"I don't know why they would understand," he said honestly. "I can't comprehend it myself. It makes no sense to me at all. It never did. I should be there with them." But he was here now and the others were in Europe, living it, and no longer safe. And there was nothing he could do, for them, or anyone else. He was too far away. And as she looked at him, Christianna could see the loneliness and helplessness in his eyes, and her heart ached for him. It made her want to console him for all he had lost, if she ever could. Their relationship had grown stronger, and the bond between them was continuing to bring them ever closer to each other.

Toby and Lucas were happy to be back in Sarasota, too, and had had a seven-month geography lesson traveling across the States. Lucas played with the clowns every day after school, just as he had before they went on tour. In the year they had been there, Lucas had become a circus child—he hardly seemed to remember their previous life. He was seven now, and he had friends all over the circus, among the children and adults. Lucas never met anyone he didn't love, or who didn't love him. Toby was far more reserved, and he and Katja were still in love, in a gentle and respectful way. They spent long hours talking, doing homework together, and kissing whenever they could. They were sixteen, after all. And they attended the same school.

It was pouring rain in Sarasota one November afternoon, when Christianna appeared at their trailer, soaking wet, and asked if he and the boys would come to dinner with her family. With nothing else to do, her brothers had been grousing about Nick all week, making comments about how fancy and what a snob he was, and she wanted them to see for themselves that he was a decent person, surprisingly modest, and always kind to her. She was tired of their snide remarks. She said her sisters-in-law were cooking dinner that night, and it would be a simple meal of Polish sausages, dumplings, steamed vegetables, and the things they liked to eat and knew how to cook. She hoped Nick wouldn't mind.

"I was going to take the boys to the cook tent." He smiled at her. He tried to take them out for hearty meals whenever he could, they were growing boys, but sometimes they ate whatever was on hand. Nick got tired of the mess tent and readily admitted that he still wasn't much of a cook. Fortunately Gallina and Sergei were generous about inviting them to join them, often for deliciously prepared Czech meals, which he and the boys thoroughly enjoyed. "We'd love it." He thanked Christianna for the invitation, and she told him to come around seven.

The camp had been bustling recently with talk of Warsaw surrendering to the Nazis a month before, which had many of them panicked. And Nick was sure Christianna's family was upset about it, too, and there would probably be talk of it that night. There had been fights recently around the circus on that subject. Sentiments were running high, and fears for loved ones at home in their countries of origin affected them all. Some of the Polish gymnasts had attacked a group of Germans at the commissary, and John Ringling North had sent out a general memo warning everyone to behave, whatever their national allegiance, or sympathies with the war. There was a British troupe with another horse act that had come to blows with the Germans too.

Word had gotten out that Nick and his sons had been forced to leave Germany, due to a Jewish connection of some kind, so the anti-German contingent left him alone. Without that gossip about him circulating, he would have been at risk for attacks, too, but thus far there had been none. And he was careful never to talk about politics except with Christianna, Gallina, or Sergei, who were his closest friends. It was no secret that he hated Hitler, and he had good reason to, but most of the time, he kept it to himself. It seemed smarter that way. One of the tiger acts was run by two Germans who were sympathetic to Hitler, and Nick stayed away and made no comment to them. He wanted no trouble here. There was enough at home. He was worried sick about his father, and Alex and Marianne. Their letters took much longer to arrive now, and he was without news for longer periods of time, except what he saw in newsreels in local movie theaters, which he went to whenever possible, so he could stay informed of the latest news from Germany, or what he read in newspapers, but most of the smaller towns they'd been in barely mentioned the war in the press. America wasn't involved, and in the rural areas, no one cared.

The Markovich family occupied four trailers, and Nick and the boys arrived promptly at Christianna's father's trailer, as Christianna had told him to do. Nick had managed to go into town and buy flowers for her aunt and her four sisters-in-law, and a small bunch for Christianna, and a bottle of vodka for the men. He hadn't wanted to show up empty-handed, and her aunt in the wheelchair was wreathed in smiles when he handed the first bouquet to her.

"Thank you for having us to dinner, Miss

Markovich." He knew the aunt had never been married. She had been injured when she was still young, barely eighteen, although she was in her fifties now. She was Sandor Markovich's sister, and he had always taken care of her, long before he was in a wheelchair himself. She sewed costumes for them, kept track of their money, and babysat their children for them, and she had been like a mother to Christianna after her mother fell. She was a cantankerous old woman, and Christianna said she was not a happy person, but she was very attached to her, more so than to her brothers or their wives, who weren't always kind to her, and Nick suspected they were jealous of her since she was the star now. Her brothers' wives weren't part of their act, but they resented her anyway, for her looks and grace, her youth, and her skill on the high wire. And they would have resented her even more if they'd known about her relationship with Nick. They thought he was too good for her. And the fact that they were the stars of the show together now made them both the target for other people's envy. And the adoration of the crowds for Christianna didn't sit well with them either. It just fed the

flames of the jealousy they already har-
bored against her.

The smell of sausages and European
cooking was strong, and it reminded Nick
instantly of the smells in their tenant farmers' homes. He had always liked it, and
longed to be invited to dinner at their homes
when he was a boy, instead of the more elegant fare they served him at his house, like
goose and venison and duck and pheas-
ant. His father loved to hunt, and they often ate game. He had preferred sausages
as a child, and Lucas's face lit up immediately when he saw what they were serving
for dinner. It was very much like German
country food, and familiar to them. And Nick
was perfectly content to eat a simple meal,
and get to know her family better. He
scarcely knew them at all, but her family
was definitely considered the royalty of the
circus world. And Christianna had the dignity of a princess when Nick and his sons
walked in and handed all of the women their
bouquets. It was royalty meeting royalty.

Her brothers were pleased with the vodka
when he handed it to them—he had bought
as decent a brand as he could find at the
small market near the fairground.

The men talked about the war for a while, and one of her brothers asked him why he had left Germany. He hadn't heard the rumors about Nick, and Christianna hadn't explained. She stayed among the women as they prepared dinner and left the men to themselves. Her aunt was having a lively conversation with Lucas about wanting to be a clown when he grew up, and she told him he should be a trapeze artist instead, which didn't appeal as much to him. And Toby was sitting politely listening to them, answering questions when he was asked. He had told her that he wanted to be a veterinarian for horses, which sounded dull to her.

"Why did you leave Germany last year, and come over here?" her youngest brother asked Nick.

"I discovered that my mother was half Jewish. I never knew her," he answered simply, looking him directly in the eye. He knew that the Markoviches weren't, and he had no idea what their feelings were about it, but there was no point hiding it, it was a fact. "They were persecuting Jews and trying to chase them away. It was right before **Kristallnacht**. We had to leave to be safe, or we could have been sent to a labor camp or put in prison," which was the truth.

"You don't look like a Jew," one of her older brothers commented, passing each of them a shot of vodka from the bottle Nick had brought. They all tossed it off in one gulp, and Nick tried not to make a face as he did. He didn't want to be rude, but he rarely drank and it burned his throat.

"I'm only a quarter. My father is Catholic and my mother was half," Nick explained.

"And a count, from what I hear," he said with an edge to his voice, as he took another shot. Their father rolled in and helped himself to a shot as well and seemed pleased, as he glanced at Nick. "This must be quite a change for you." There was still a sarcastic tone as he spoke to Nick.

"Coming to the circus saved my life, and my boys. I'm grateful for that. A friend gave me the horses I brought with me. This is the only thing I know how to do, ride horses and train them. I've learned a lot in the last year." The simplicity and honesty with which he said it silenced all of them for a moment. Nick didn't put on airs, he was modest and told the truth.

"Don't worry," one brother said with a

sudden laugh, warmed by the second vodka, as he glanced at Nick with a kinder look in his eyes. "We don't know how to do anything else either, except our trapeze act, and watch our sister on the high wire. It's enough. So is what you do." Then generously, he added, "You're good. I like what you do with the white ones. How do you teach them to stand up like that?"

"It's in their blood." Nick smiled. "They're born and built to do that. There's a school in Vienna where they teach them all the exercises they do. My friend was training them before he gave them to me. I want to breed Lipizzaners one day."

"They must be worth a lot," he commented, and Nick nodded. And then one of them asked him the question they'd all been wondering, and predicting darkly to Christianna: "Do you think you'll stay?"

"I hope so. I need the job. I have my boys to take care of. And by the time Hitler is finished, Germany will be in ruins. This is all we have now." What he said discounted the schloss and the land he had left in Germany, all of which he would inherit one day, if he was allowed to, and Hitler was no longer in power, or lost the war. But for now, Nick had no access to any of it, and lived on his salary, just as they did, and knew he might have to for a long, long time. He saved his money, knowing it was all he had for now. "What about you? Do you still have relatives in Poland?"

"Only some cousins. Most of us are here. And we're not Jews," Peter said matter-of-factly. "Some of the juggling acts are Jewish and still have relatives there. They're trying to bring them here, but they haven't been able to. You're lucky you got out when you did."

"Yes, I am," Nick agreed. There had been pogroms in Poland, Russia, and Czechoslovakia, and Jews were being taken to labor camps and severely persecuted, or killed. Nick had heard about it on the news. "Things are bad over there. We're all lucky to be here."

"We're Americans now," Peter, the oldest brother, said proudly, "and so are our wives. My father is now too. We've been here for twenty years. Christianna is a citizen now too. My aunt was the last to give up her Polish citizenship. It's better for us here, for all of us. America has been good to us," he said gratefully. Thus far it had been to Nick, too, but he still felt German, not American, and thought about going back one day, when things changed again, although he was no longer sure after everything that had happened. And he felt attached to neither country, the old, nor the new. He hadn't adopted his new country sufficiently to want to give up his heritage and his homeland yet, no matter how cruel they had been to him. He had been betrayed, but by Hitler, not by Germany. And he didn't feel American, and didn't think he ever would. But he admired Christianna's family for embracing the country that had been good to them, and where they'd lived for so long.

"Why do you let her work without a net?" Nick asked quietly, during a lull in their war talk. It was the burning question he had wanted to ask them since he had first seen her on the high wire, and there was a sudden silence. None of them answered him for a moment, and then her father spoke from his chair. He had been watching Nick closely since he first walked into the trailer with his boys. He liked him, better than he expected to. He seemed like a good man, and he had well-brought-up boys, which her father respected too.

"It's what the crowd wants, and what we do. They don't want to see a little girl tripping across a wire five feet off the ground with a balancing bar and a canary on her head. People respect courage. She's a brave girl. So was my wife. You don't win anything in life if you don't take risk. They don't understand it, but they respect the skill. It's not easy to be up there, and Christianna is very good at it. She has a gift, more than I did, or her aunt, or her mother, and we don't know about her sister, if she ever tries it, which she may not. Christianna has it in her blood. Not everyone does. It's a talent to be up there, not just something you learn or decide to do. Like your horses. You said that they are born to do the tricks they perform. So was Christianna. She must use the gift."

"And if she falls?" Nick asked, trying to understand the deeper meaning of what he said and what motivated them. They were gladiators in a way, prepared to ride into battle and face their death every day. But they weren't staring death in the face, Christianna was. And he didn't want her to do it anymore. He loved her too much to lose her to the high wire.

"She won't," her father said with confidence. "She's too good at it. Much better than her mother was. She won't fall. And every day she learns that she can do something difficult, something that may frighten her, and she conquers it again and again. It will make her strong." It could also make her dead, Nick knew, but he couldn't convince them of that. They were warriors who were letting a tiny, graceful girl fight their battles for them, at her expense. He hated it, but he didn't want to say too much the first time they met. It was obvious how he felt about it. "You could break your neck falling from a horse. It doesn't stop you. You know what you're doing. So does she." He had a point, and Nick could see he wouldn't win the argument, at least not tonight. "It's hard for other people to understand."

"Maybe we're all very brave and foolish," Nick said philosophically, but he and Christianna were taking all the risks, they weren't. Her father had, and her aunt and mother, but her brothers were nothing more than observers on the ground who ran along next to the princess when she came back down to earth. It was the princess who fought the dragons every day,

fearlessly. And she did it because they expected her to, and so as not to let them
down. As far as Christianna and her family were concerned, it was her heritage
and her duty.

Her youngest brother poured a third
round of shots, which this time Nick refused,
and their wives put dinner on the table, and
a moment later they all sat down, crowded
into the trailer, holding plates heaped with
food, and Christianna sat down next to Nick,
in the only empty seat, which she didn't realize her brothers had left free for her. It was
their way of saying they approved of him.
He wasn't one of them, but they respected
his honesty and clear, simple way of expressing what he thought and who he was.
Her father talked to him at length over dinner, and afterward they cleared the dishes
and invited Nick to play poker with them. He
was happy to oblige, as it was a game he
loved, too, and played well. They beat him,
but not without a fight, and all the men
pounded each other's backs and embraced
when he left. Her brothers were fairly drunk,
but Nick and her father weren't, and their
eyes met as Nick was leaving. The women
had gone to bed long before, and Christi-

anna had played a quieter card game with the boys. Lucas was winning, and squealing with delight.

"Thank you for having dinner with us," Sandor said diplomatically. It was his way of saying he approved, without uttering the words.

"Thank you for having us. It was delicious." Nick smiled at the man in the chair, who was looking at him with curiosity and new respect.

"You're an honest man. I like that. And don't worry about Christianna. She won't fall," he said again. He could see now that Nick cared about her, although he didn't know to what extent or for how long. And he didn't want his daughter getting hurt or having her heart broken, going after a man who was from another world, which her father understood too well Nick was. And if he went back to Germany, he would never take her with him, back to his old life. She would never be accepted there, nor fit in.

"I hope not," Nick said quietly, referring to his assurance that Christianna wouldn't fall. It would be an unthinkable loss to him if she did, but he didn't say that to her

father. He didn't have to. It was in his eyes.
"I hope you're right."

"Just don't let her fall off one of your
horses," her father warned him, and was
only half-joking.

"I would shoot the horse myself if she
did," he said with feeling. He was deeply in
love with her, and he wanted to protect her
from all harm.

"Come to visit us again." Sandor Markovich meant it, and smiled as he and Nick
shook hands, and Christianna watched
from where she sat.

"Thank you. We will. I would invite you
to our trailer, but I'd have to buy hot dogs
from the mess tent. I'm a miserable cook,"
Nick said humbly, and the man in the wheelchair laughed.

"We'll take you to a Polish restaurant," he
promised. "They have very good food, better than what my daughters-in-law cooked
tonight. We go there a lot during the break."
It sounded like fun to Nick. He rounded up
his sons then and told them it was time to
leave. They picked up their jackets, and
Christianna walked them out into the cool
air of the Sarasota night. It had been rain-

ing, and finally stopped, and the air was fresh. They could see stars in the sky.

"They liked you," she said softly, so no one else could hear, and the boys were a few steps away, talking to each other and not paying attention to them.

"They just liked beating me at poker." He had lost ten dollars, which was a lot to him, but he was willing to sacrifice it in the interest of better family relations between their two camps. He thought the evening had gone well too. And he liked them, although he hated their attitude about her, and how cavalier they were about the dangers to her, as though they were satisfied to leave her well-being in the hands of fate, and not protect her.

"No, they really liked you, and so did my father. You were very nice to them." She thanked him with her eyes.

"They were nice to me too." They were rough around the edges, but he could see their merits, and they came from a different culture than he did, and lived by the mores and traditions of the circus, but he respected it. He just didn't want it hurting her. "See you tomorrow," he said, wishing he could kiss her, but he didn't dare, in plain sight of her family and his boys. He still wanted to protect what they shared, although they had been together now for many months. They had taken an important step that night, with her father and brothers, and he didn't want to do anything to jeopardize it now. He had proven to them, or tried to, that he was an honorable man worthy of their daughter and sister, and hopefully in time, they would respect what he and Christianna felt for each other. And in the meantime, he had held his own among the men. That was important in their culture, and he knew it was to Christianna as well. He wasn't the elitist that they had believed he was. He kept no secrets from them, about why he'd come there, or how long he planned to stay. In truth, he didn't know his plans. They all lived in an uncertain world. But he had shown them that he was an honest man, and could be one of them, and fought his battles bravely too. It was enough for now.

"I love you," she whispered to Nick before he left, out of earshot of the boys.

"I love you too," he mouthed back, and then he walked to his trailer with his boys.

"They were nice," Toby commented, surprised that the evening had been as pleasant as it was, and the food had been good.

".I beat Christianna at cards," Lucas chortled, and his father laughed.

"Well, that's a good thing. I hope you made some money at it, because her brothers beat me at poker. They're a tough bunch."

"I like her, Papa," Lucas said quietly with a yawn as they got home.

"So do I," Nick confessed just as quietly, and Toby smiled at him. He had already figured that out for himself, months before. "Now go to bed," Nick said, not ready to admit more than that to his sons. And five minutes later, their teeth were brushed, they had on their pajamas, and they were in bed. He went in to kiss them in bed and could hardly get around it, their bedroom was so small. And then he went and sat in the trailer's living room, thinking about the evening, and the family Christianna had grown up in.

He had said the truth, they were a tough bunch, but a lot of people in the circus were. They played by their own rules, and they respected the hierarchy established by what

they did. And in circus life, they were nobility, just as he was in his own world. The
Princess and the Count, he thought to
himself, as he leaned his head back and
closed his eyes, thinking about her. In his
mind's eye, he always saw her now standing on Athena's back, as they performed
their act together, with him on Pegasus.
He never thought of her on the high wire
anymore, only as the magical elf who rode
the Lipizzaners with him. And in his mind,
they always rode around the ring together
on the two spectacular white horses,
holding hands. It was the only image he
wanted of her. She was the woman of his
dreams.

Chapter 14

At the end of November, while Americans celebrated Thanks-giving, things continued to get worse in Europe. Polish Jews were forced to wear a yellow star of David on their chests, or an armband, to identify them to others. Five days later, the first Polish ghetto was established.

In Germany, rationing had been introduced when war was declared, but only to a mild degree. Hitler didn't want Germans severely deprived, and to affect morale negatively, so despite ration cards, the changes were not too extreme. There was enough food and clothing, although shortages of fuel. And Jews were allotted lower food rations, in keeping with Hitler's views about them.

Young men were drafted when war was declared, and men in uniform were everywhere, even in the sleepy Bavarian countryside where Alex and his daughter lived. And although they had enough food, it was almost impossible to heat the schloss now with the fuel available to them. They constantly built wood fires in the fireplaces, but the schloss was large and drafty and Marianne was cold all the time. She had stopped attending classes, and spent her time at home, running the household for her father, and rolling bandages for hospitals to be used for the injured men.

All Alex's grooms and stable boys were gone, drafted into the army, and he and Marianne were caring for the horses themselves, with the help of young boys from their farms, who were still underage to be drafted. It was a full-time job tending to the horses now, and Alex had been warned that the Wehrmacht might commandeer them, since they were so fine. Civilians no longer needed horses of that caliber, he'd been told, when two officers of the cavalry came to visit him, and examined his stables. They were a country at war.

The meals Marta served them were still healthy. She used their rationing cards with "marken" on them to obtain the food they needed, even if in slightly lesser quantity. But she managed to prepare the same excellent meals. The only things noticeably missing were coffee, oranges, bananas, and chocolate. But they had enough meat, eggs, and produce. The rationing cards were used in restaurants too.

Alex was just grateful that he had no sons to send to war and could keep Marianne with him. He was relieved for Nick now that he had escaped with his boys before war broke out in Europe. Alex hated Hitler and everything he stood for with a passion, and he knew that Nick's father felt no differently, after what had happened to them. The revelation about Nick's mother had left Paul alone and lonely in the manor house on his estate, hungry for every letter Nick sent them.

Alex went to see Paul almost every day, and he had watched him age radically in the year since Nick had left. He was a different person, angry, bitter, disgusted by everything he saw happening around him. He went for days without speaking to any-one, unless Alex came to visit. He had no desire to go anywhere, and was losing in-terest in running his own estate. There were no young men to help him, and if Nick and his sons could not inherit the property, it be-gan to lose all meaning to Paul.

Alex didn't like what was happening any better than he did, but he was younger and could still envision a world and a life after the war, where Hitler would hopefully no longer exist. Paul could only imagine the to-tal destruction of his homeland, and had lost hope of ever seeing his son or grand-sons again. The days were long and the nights longer, as Hitler continued to devour the smaller countries of Europe, which were defenseless against him. And Alex noticed just before Christmas that Nick's father had developed a nasty cough. He had been sick several times in the last year, which weak-ened him, although he wasn't very old, but he didn't look well. Alex had invited Paul to spend Christmas Eve with them, but by then Paul had a fever and couldn't come. Alex rode over to see him instead before having dinner with Marianne. And when he got to

the von Bingen schloss, he found Paul de-
lirious from the fever and asked his
housekeeper to send for the doctor, and
she promised she would.

"Is he very sick, Papa?" Marianne asked
him with worried eyes, and her father nodded, as they dined on chicken that night,
with an excellent sauce Marta had made,
and potatoes. It was a very good meal that
showed no evidence of rationing, although
Marta had used their cards with marken to
buy the food.

To some extent, Alex was considered untouchable in the area because of who he
was, but he was also expected to do everything possible to support the efforts of the
Third Reich, materially and in attitude, to set
an example in the community. And Marianne looked tired and pale. She was working hard in the stables, to take care of the
horses with him. She was doing men's work
and freezing in their house at night. The
hardships of war had come quickly, and
Alex was worried about her, and keeping
her in a country at war. He almost wished
that she was in America with Nick and the
boys. At least they were safe there, and
America had no intention of entering the

war. Franklin D. Roosevelt had assured everyone of that, so the Allies had to defend
themselves in Europe, with no hope of help
or rescue from abroad. It was a frightening
situation, the importance of which was not
lost on Alex, although he didn't discuss it
with Marianne.

Toby's tales of life in the circus seemed
even more surreal to her now, compared to
what they were living in Germany. What he
was doing sounded so interesting, riding
the Lipizzaners with his father, and traveling all around the country, while Lucas
played with the clowns, and rode an elephant in the finale. Nothing in her experience now or ever bore any resemblance to
her friend's life, particularly while Germany
was at war and they were living with the
stress and worry of that at home. In addition, it was a freezing cold winter, by contrast. Toby said it was warm in Florida. They
were back in the winter quarters at Sarasota, where he was going to school and enjoying his friends. She felt a hundred years
old whenever she read his letters, and she
couldn't tell him just how depressing it was
in Germany, or censors would black out her
letters or destroy them, so she had to say

that all was well and they were fine, which wasn't true at all.

"Yes, I think he's very sick," Alex told her honestly, about Nick's father. Worse, he had the strong feeling that Paul had lost his will to live. He hated what had happened in his homeland, he had been deprived of his family, and the war was liable to last for a long time, too long for Paul. He had lost a considerable amount of weight in the past few months, and was malnourished, never wanting to eat alone. Alex feared he was too old and frail now, and mostly disheartened, to survive long years of war.

"I hope he'll be better soon," Marianne said quietly as they finished dinner, and when she saw her father leaving to visit him again later, she asked if she could come. He hesitated, not wanting to take her out in the cold so she didn't get sick herself, but when she begged him, he finally relented. They rode over together on horseback, so as not to waste gas for their car, which was harder to come by now.

They tied up their horses outside the manor house, after riding past the darkened schloss. There were never any lights on there at night, since no one lived there.

Paul's housekeeper Ursula came from one of the farms where she had spent her entire life, and the rest of the time, Paul was alone. Ursula was still there that night, looking concerned. The doctor had just been there, and had said he would come back in the morning. He had few medicines to give him, as medical supplies went to the army to be used for soldiers, and were in shorter supply. But Paul said he didn't want medicine anyway, and insisted he was fine.

Alex went into Paul's bedroom alone, and left Marianne with Ursula in the kitchen, where they drank hot water to stay warm. The manor house was almost as cold as the Hemmerle schloss.

When Paul opened his eyes, when he heard him, Alex didn't like what he saw. Paul's eyes looked glazed, and his cheeks were flushed and blazing. He looked tired and wanted to go back to sleep.

"How do you feel?" Alex asked him as he pulled up a chair next to the bed and sat down, and gently stroked the old man's hand. It was thin and veined and covered with spots Alex had never seen there before. Until Nick left, Alex had never thought of him as old. He had never seemed it, but he did now.

"Tired," Paul said in a whisper, and then was seized by a racking cough. Alex waited until it subsided, and gave him a sip of water, before speaking to him again.

"You have to get better. Nick won't like this. He's counting on you to keep running everything here until he gets back."

"I'll be dead by then," Paul said simply, as though he had made peace with it himself.

"No, you won't. Nick will blame me if that happens." Alex smiled at the man who had been like a father to him since he had lost his own at an early age. Paul had frequently advised him on how to run his estate, and taught him everything he knew, although he had been unable to teach his own son. But Alex had inherited all his lands when he was young. Nick had been able to rely on his father.

"It will be a long war," Paul said quietly after he caught his breath again. "The British will fight hard, and hopefully so will the French. And others. They won't let that little monster take over Europe. Who knows?

The Americans might come into it one day.
But it won't be over soon. He won't give up
until they destroy him, and by God, I hope
they do, before he destroys all of us and everything this country stands for. I'm too old
to watch them wage this battle. I'm tired."
He turned to Alex with eyes so sad it nearly
tore Alex's heart out. He could sense the
man dying right before his eyes, and had
no idea how to stop it. Nick's father had lost
his will to live. "I miss my son. When I die,
tell him how much I love him. This will all
be waiting for him when it's over. I want him
and the boys to come back then. Everything
is his. They can't prevent him from claiming his inheritance forever, especially once
that monster is gone."

"Then stay and take care of it for him until he returns," Alex said in a stronger voice,
trying to urge him to hang on, but Paul only
shook his head and turned away, and a little while later, Alex saw he was asleep and
left the room.

"How is he?" Ursula asked when Alex
came back to the kitchen. He was certain
that if Nick and the boys were still there, his
father would be fighting to live, but without

them, and no hope of seeing them again anytime soon, he no longer cared.

"Not well," Alex told her honestly as tears sprang to Marianne's eyes while she listened. Paul von Bingen had been like a grandfather to her, the only one she had ever known. "What time is the doctor coming in the morning?"

"He said he'd try to come at eight."

"I'll come back then," Alex told her, and she assured him that she'd spend the night at the manor house even though it was Christmas Eve. And a few minutes later, he and Marianne rode back to their schloss, and made a detour to the village, to attend midnight mass in the village church. They were singing "Silent Night" when they got there, and the crowd was thin. It was all women and children and old men. For any young man, it was considered a disgrace to still be at home, and Marianne had asked her father many times if he would be called up too. But at forty-eight, he assured her that he was too old.

After mass in the little church, they both went home to the schloss, and sat huddled in her father's library, building up a fire and trying to stay warm. It felt like the saddest Christmas they'd ever shared. All they had left was each other.

And in the morning after a short night, when he tossed and turned, Alex went back to check on Paul again, and was alarmed to find him worse. The doctor was still there and after listening to Paul's chest, he said he had pneumonia and told Alex honestly that he had little hope that Paul would re-cover. It would depend on how hard he fought, and from everything Alex could see, Paul had no desire to survive. He dozed for the rest of the day, and by the next day he had slipped into a groggy, nearly comatose state. Alex stayed at the manor house with him, and every day, Marianne rode over to keep her father company, but she had to go home to take care of their horses. She came back before dinner, and they sat together in the living room, and ate in the kitchen.

For a few brief moments on New Year's Eve, Paul finally opened his eyes and looked at Alex, and seemed as though he was go-ing to make it after all.

"You're still here?" He seemed surprised, as Alex leaned toward him in the darkened room and smiled at him. "Don't you have better things to do?"

"No, I don't," Alex said firmly, "I just want you to get better. Marianne is here too. She's downstairs. How do you feel?" Alex asked, looking hopeful, but he could see Paul was still blazing with fever, although he was more lucid than he had been in days.

"I feel fine," Paul said in a strong, clear voice, and he sat up in bed for a few minutes, and took a sip of the broth Ursula had left beside his bed. "I feel much better. Have you heard from Nick?" It was the only thing that interested him, and the same question he had asked Alex for the past year whenever they met, although Nick wrote to his father regularly too.

"They're still in Florida, at their winter headquarters. He and the boys are fine." Nick had never told Alex that he had fallen in love with Christianna. He knew that what he was experiencing now would be so foreign to his friend that there was no way he could explain it to him, so he never tried. He was sure that Alex would disapprove and say that he had gone mad, but Alex had no way of understanding the life they now led, or the people in it. And his father even less. "They were going to put candles on their Christmas tree, just as we do here." Nick hadn't told him that the tree was two feet tall and sat on a table in their trailer and they'd have to put the candles out quickly, so it didn't set fire to anything.

"It's good that the boys don't forget our traditions," Paul said with a satisfied look, and then lay down again and closed his eyes. He seemed tired, and Alex decided to spend the night, sitting beside him, although Paul seemed better and stronger when he went back to sleep. Paul opened his eyes once just after midnight, in the first moments of the New Year, and smiled at Alex, who realized instantly that Paul thought he was Nick.

"Come home soon. They need you here," he said in a whisper.

"I will," Alex promised, speaking for his friend. "I need you, too, Papa," he said then on behalf of both of them. He couldn't bear the thought of losing the old man he loved, and he knew that the loss would devastate Nick.

Paul just smiled as he looked at him again, nodded, and drifted off to sleep. He slept for several hours as Alex dozed beside him, and when the sun came up, Alex looked at him and knew instantly what had happened. Paul von Bingen had died peacefully in his sleep. He was gone. Alex sat looking at him for a long time, and gently stroked his hand, which was already cool, and his heart plummeted as tears rolled down his cheeks and he realized that the worst lay before him. Now he would have to tell Nick.

Chapter 15

Nick spent Christmas Eve in his trailer with Toby and Lucas, and he gave them each a game and a sweater he bought for them in Sarasota, and he gave Christianna a tiny heart-shaped gold locket, which she put on immediately. She cut out a small photograph of him from one of the pages in the circus program and put it in the locket, and she was thrilled. She had knitted him a scarf herself from soft black wool to wear on cold nights when they were on tour. They spent as much of the holiday together as they could, without arousing suspicion, and she joined them when they spent Christmas

Day with Gallina and Sergei and their children. And despite the alleged rivalry between them, the two women laughed with the others and had a good time. Nick and his children had spent Thanksgiving with them too, they were his closest friends.

"She's a sweet girl," Gallina said to Nick afterward, and looked at him with the same motherly look she gave Toby. "So when are you two going to admit that you're in love? How long has it been now? Don't you think you have the right to be happy? You can't keep it a secret forever, and anyone who sees you knows."

"How long have you known?" he asked her sheepishly, wondering if they had been less discreet than they thought. But Gallina was a smart woman, and by now she knew him well. And his deep feelings for Christianna were hard to hide. Even his sons had figured it out and were pleased. They loved her, and Lucas said he hoped his father would marry her one day so they could keep her, and Toby agreed.

"I've known for several months," Gallina answered, and he laughed.

"Well, so much for keeping secrets around here. I just wasn't sure how her family would

feel about it, and I don't want to compli-
cate things for her. They're very protective
of her."

"Except when they put her on the high
wire," Gallina said with a strong look of disapproval. She had completely given up
working without a net herself the month
before, at the insistence of Sergei. But
Christianna was still in the main ring every
night, risking her life, to the thrill of the
crowds. Nick hated every minute of it, but
he was always there, watching her. He
couldn't stand being anywhere else. And
whenever possible, they managed to spend
a night together, but they had been very
careful not to be discovered. He didn't want
to hurt her reputation in any way, and
treated her with profound respect. And
fortunately, there had been no slips in their
sex life either, and she hadn't gotten pregnant. He was always careful to protect her.

Gallina's words were not lost on Nick. He
and Christianna spent New Year's Eve with
them. And the next day, Nick talked to Christianna before they went to dinner with her
family at her father's favorite Polish restaurant in Sarasota. He had invited Nick and
his boys, to celebrate the New Year.

"What do you think about saying something to your family one of these days?" Nick asked her cautiously when he fed and watered the horses, and she came to keep him company. She liked feeding Athena, and had gotten used to her from their act.

"I've been wondering the same thing," she admitted.

"Will they be upset?" Nick asked her, looking worried. He could handle it for himself, but he didn't want them taking it out on her. It was a problem she didn't need, with four brothers and a father who watched her every move.

"They like you," Christianna said with a shy smile, as she stroked the Lipizzaner mare who nuzzled her. "And they suspect anyway."

"They might not like my age."

"They're afraid you'll leave," she said simply. They had questioned him about it too. "Or interfere," she added. His comments about the wire hadn't been lost on them, and they had mentioned it to her, that he was worried about her on the high wire.

"I'm not planning to leave anytime soon," Nick said quietly. "There's a war on in Europe. I had to flee Germany, and I have nowhere to go. And I don't know if I'll ever go back there, even after the war. I can't, unless things change. So leaving isn't an issue. And yes, I might interfere if they don't take you off the high wire one of these days. I'm not going to stop objecting to that. You know how I feel. All I want is for them to let you work with a net. I don't think that's too much to ask. If they give you a net, you can stay up there till you're ninety years old for all I care. Without a net, I'm going to interfere every chance I get." He was always honest with her. And he had been with her family too. But he was polite enough not to make a constant issue of it. He had let them know how he felt, and then let it go. He was respectful and polite, if nothing else, and Christianna loved him for that too. "What do you want to tell them, if we say something?" Nick asked curiously.

"That we love each other. I think that's enough."

"What if they want to know more?" Nick asked her.

"What more is there?"

"They might want to know if I intend to marry you," he said gently. It was the kind of thing fathers wanted to know.

"You don't have to tell them that," she said, blushing, as she turned away and busied herself with Athena. He smiled as he watched her then, and walked over to where she was hiding behind the white horse.

"Don't run away from me," he said with a smile, gently pulling her away from the horse and turning her face up to his. "You don't have to hide from me. I love you. I want to marry you one day, but not until I can give you a good life." He had never said that to her before, and she buried her face in his chest. She had wondered, but would never have dared to ask.

"This is a good life," she said, as she looked up at him again.

"Not good enough. I want to give you more than this, a trailer, and a net for your act, if I can talk your father into it. You deserve a lot more, Christianna. And one day, I want to give it to you. I'd love to buy a ranch in the Santa Ynez Valley." It had stayed in his mind from when they had seen it together. "Or somewhere else. Somewhere where we can breed horses and have a peaceful life."

"And what would I do?" she asked him, smiling at him mischievously. It was a big conversation they'd never had before, about their future and his dreams, although she knew some of them but not all.

"Take care of me," he said with a broad smile, "and have babies, if you want to. That's up to you. I'd like that, but I have the boys. I'd love to have a baby with you when we're married. But as long as I have you, I'll be happy. The rest is your decision."

"And not Germany?" she asked him, curious about his answer. Like her brothers, she had the feeling that one day he would want to go back to his own world, even if he was bitter about being forced to leave.

"I don't know. It depends what happens there after the war. I'm not sure what I would have left, or how I would feel after they made us leave." It was a cruel blow. "I have my father in Germany, which is important to me. If he's old and he needs me, I'd go back. If not, I honestly don't know. Maybe we'd be happier here. We'll have to see what it's like after the war. I don't know if I'll be able to reclaim our property. And who knows how badly they'll destroy the country? I don't trust Hitler, and Germany is at his mercy now. It might never be the same again when it's all over." That was honest, too, and he was trying to be fair with her. "I can't ask you to marry me now, Christianna. I have nothing to offer you. But when I do, I will, and I hope you'll say yes." He took her face in his hands as he said it and kissed her. He had told her all she needed to know, and all that her father would want to hear. "I love you," he added for good measure.

"I love you too. And when you ask me, I will say yes, whatever you have. I don't care." He knew that about her, too, and loved her for it.

"I think we got that all worked out," he said, smiling broadly as they left the horse tent, and they both looked exceptionally happy when they picked up Lucas and Toby and joined her family at the restaurant for a New Year's celebration. Her father noticed how jubilant they looked too. And after dinner he turned to Nick with a question in his eyes.

"Do you two have something to tell us?" Sandor prodded them. He and Nick were on a first-name basis now, which was a sign of his approval.

Nick looked at him innocently, teasing him a little. "Like what?" Nick smiled as he said it, and Christianna giggled.

"We're in love, Papa," she said softly.

"I knew that much months ago. I'm not blind, for God's sake. Anything else? Any plans?" He suddenly looked concerned, as his eyes went back to Nick's.

"As soon as I know that I can offer your daughter a good life, I will come and speak to you, I promise. I give you my word."

"And you will stay in the circus?" Sandor pressed him. He drove a hard bargain.

"For as long as Christianna wants to, if that's reasonable," Nick said diplomatically. "I'll do whatever makes her happy." But he had already told her what he wanted and hoped for them. And he hoped he could convince her to try it, a life in the real world with him. "And I want a wedding present from you, on the day we get married," Nick said smoothly.

"Of course," Sandor said, waving his arms magnanimously. "What is it?"

"A net for my wife," Nick said, looking him straight in the eye, and for a long moment the senior Markovich didn't answer, and then slowly he nodded and shook Nick's hand.

"You will have it. You have my word as well." The two men looked satisfied, and as

Nick thought about it, it was enough incentive to make him marry her sooner, just to preserve her life. But both men looked happy with the bargain they had struck and the assurances that had been given. Now that their love for each other was no longer a secret, Nick and Christianna could court openly, with her father's approval. He ordered vodka for the entire table, and everyone but Toby and Lucas drank it. There was a mood of celebration that night, and it was nearly midnight when they went back to the fairground. Nick wanted to get the boys home and Christianna joined him. Her brothers stayed to continue drinking with her father, while their wives and her aunt went back to the fairground as well. It had been a joyful evening, and they no longer had to deal with the pressure of hiding what they felt for each other. Nick was glad that Gallina had prodded him to broach the subject. So far, she was always right. And Sandor seemed satisfied with his promise to ask for her hand at a later date, and Nick's answer about staying with the circus seemed to satisfy him as well. Sandor couldn't imagine Christianna ever wanting to leave them, so obviously Nick wouldn't either. And Nick would make a very distinguished son-in-law one day. And at the restaurant, after several more vodkas, Sandor was bragging that his daughter was going to be a countess. As he said it, she was sitting outside his trailer, talking to Nick, and the boys had just gone to bed. The New Year was definitely off to a great start.

As they talked softly, Nick noticed a boy wearing a Western Union uniform ride up to the trailer on a bicycle. He squinted in the darkness as the boy in the uniform approached after he set down his bicycle. He took an envelope out of a bag slung across his chest.

"I have a telegram for Nicolas von Bingen. Is that you?" he said in an official voice, which startled Nick. He wasn't used to hearing his own name anymore. Everyone at the circus called him Nick Bing now. And he only saw his name on letters from Alex and his father.

"Yes, it is." Nick looked surprised as he took it from him, signed a log sheet the boy kept with him, and then opened the envelope as Christianna watched and the boy left. Nick had no idea what it was. He could just barely read it in the moonlight, and his eyes went immediately to the sender's name at the bottom of the telegram. It was from Alex.

"Deeply regret to inform you your father died in the early hours of New Year's morning. Peacefully from pneumonia. Nothing we could do. I am so sorry. Fondest sympathy and all our love. Alex." Nick read it and said not a word, unable to absorb what was written, and then read it again as it sank in. He felt as though he had been struck by lightning. He looked at Christianna and his eyes filled with tears as he handed it to her. He hadn't expected this final blow. He couldn't imagine a world without his father in it. Other than the boys, all he had had all his life was his father, and a mother he'd never known and probably never would now, thanks to Hitler.

Christianna took the telegram from him, read it and gave a gasp, and flew instantly from where she sat to put her arms around him and console him. He was crying silently as they held each other, and they sat that way for a long time as the full meaning of the words hit him. He had lost his father. Christianna stayed with him that night until early sunrise. The sun was just streaking into the sky when she left him dozing on the couch and went back to her own trailer. No one heard her tiptoe in. The others had all had too much to drink the night before, and would be hung over when they woke up.

And when the boys got up and found Nick, he stirred, and they saw the look in his eyes. He hadn't looked that way since he told them they had to leave Germany, and they knew something terrible had happened.

"What's wrong?" Toby said immediately. Maybe they were going to have to leave the circus and they were losing their home again. Lucas was scared too. The telegram was folded and put away in Nick's pocket so the boys wouldn't see it. He wanted to tell them himself.

"It's Opa," Nick said sadly. "He got very sick, with pneumonia." He took a breath before he dropped the bomb. They were waiting. "He died yesterday. I got a telegram from Alex last night when we got home." Both boys burst into tears, and Nick pulled them into his arms. The three of them cried all morning, and then they went for a long walk together, and after that they went back to the trailer. When they got there, Joe

Herlihy was waiting for them, to express his sympathy, with a personal letter of condolence from John Ringling North, and Nick was very touched. He stayed for a few minutes and then left, not wanting to intrude on them in their grief.

Nick and the boys were heartbroken as they talked about his father all day. Christianna didn't want to disturb them, and she left them alone and told her family what had happened. News had already traveled around several families in the circus, and Gallina and Sergei paid them a condolence visit that afternoon too.

Christianna's sisters-in-law prepared them a big casserole, and Christianna dropped it off that evening, and was going to leave quickly. But Nick asked her to stay and have dinner with them. She could see how sad they all were. It upset Nick even more knowing that he couldn't go to his father's funeral, but he was sure that Alex would have him buried properly in the cemetery on the estate, with a mass said in the chapel. It was agony not being there for something as important as this. And he knew exactly why this had happened. He and the boys had been banished from

Germany, and it had killed his father. And at that exact moment, Nick knew that he would never go back. He didn't say it to anyone, but now he was certain that he had come to America to stay. The door to his past had just closed behind him forever.

Chapter 16

As Nick had hoped he would, Alex arranged for Paul's burial in the family cemetery, attended the mass for him in the chapel on the estate, and ordered the headstone to mark his grave. He and Marianne were bereft at the loss.

And two weeks later, there was a flurry of activity in the village. Alex was working in the stables, cleaning stalls, when one of the young boys who helped him came running in, red-faced and excited. Alex turned to see what had happened. He had been solemn and depressed since Paul died, and he could only imagine how Nick must feel, after receiving the telegram. Alex had written him a letter immediately after, expressing all he felt, and his deep sympathy for his friend. He assured him that Paul's absence would be sorely felt by them all, and that he and Marianne were heartbroken as well.

"They're taking the von Bingen schloss!" the boy shouted across the stable, as Alex looked at him in confusion.

"Who is? Taking it where?" What he had said made no sense.

"The soldiers. A colonel, I think, or a general. They came in a big car and they're moving in." What he said chilled Alex to the bone, and he felt a rage rise up in him, like a tidal wave of bile.

"What do you mean?" Alex's eyes were blazing.

"There are a lot of soldiers there with boxes, and big cars, and officers. The schloss is open, and someone told me that they are taking it over. It will be headquarters for the area now, and the officers will live there." Alex wanted to kill someone as he strode out of the stables without comment and marched across the courtyard to his own home. Marianne was out visiting a woman who had just given birth on one of the farms, to bring her some food for her other children, and see how she was. The thought of them taking over Nick's home, two weeks after Paul died, was more than Alex could bear. He put on his most dignified suit, combed his hair, got in his Mercedes, and drove over to Nick's schloss. And just as the boy had said, there were cars outside, trucks in the courtyard, boxes everywhere, two dozen soldiers, and a colonel in charge, shouting directions. Alex took a breath and looked calmer than he was, as he walked over to where the colonel was standing. Alex looked at him with a pleasant smile.

"Welcome to the neighborhood," Alex said as he extended a hand to the colonel, and noticed with a pain in his stomach that there were two flags with swastikas flying from the colonel's car, and two lieutenants were standing at his side.

"And you are?" The colonel eyed him coldly, seemingly unimpressed.

"Alex von Hemmerle. Schloss Altenberg. Five kilometers from here." He pointed vaguely in the right direction. "I see that you're visiting Count von Bingen," Alex said, trying to keep as much sarcasm as possible out of his tone, and barely succeeding.

"Count von Bingen is dead," the colonel said bluntly. "Two weeks ago. We are taking over the schloss for the army."

"I was referring to his son, Count Nicolas von Bingen," Alex said innocently. "I assume he'll be inheriting the title and the estate from his father."

"I regret to inform you," the colonel said with an icy stare, "the late count was married to a Jewish woman, and 'Count Nicolas,' his son, fled a year ago as a Jew, as I'm sure you know. Jews can no longer inherit or own land in Germany. This schloss now belongs to the Third Reich. I have claimed it in the name of our Fuehrer, Adolf Hitler." His salute could have sliced an iceberg, and stopped just shy of his hat, and then his right arm shot out in the familiar salute that turned Alex's stomach. Alex did not return the salute, and as a civilian, he wasn't obliged to, although some zealots did.

"I see," Alex said with surprise. "I didn't know. They kept it very quiet." He feigned ignorance, and the colonel nodded.

"Understandably. I'm told you have very handsome stables," he said with a pointed

look at Alex, "and some very fine horses."
So he knew exactly who Alex was, and it
was only a matter of time before he paid
them a visit, and possibly took whatever he
wanted. Including the schloss, if he chose
to. The army had license to do whatever
they wished.

"Thank you for the compliment. I hope
you will pay me a visit now that you're so
close by." Alex executed a formal bow, and
clicked his heels in the style of German aristocrats, not soldiers. It was as respectful as
the colonel's salute, and far more elegant,
and reminded the colonel of just how noble Alex was, which was his intention.

"Thank you, Count. I will visit you soon,"
the colonel assured him, and then he disappeared through the front door of Nick's
home, followed by a trail of officers and soldiers. Alex looked after him and wanted to
burst into tears or scream. It was the most
horrifying sight he had ever seen. And it
would be the next piece of bad news he
would have to share with Nick, to tell him
that his elegant home, inhabited by six centuries of his ancestors, had been comman-
deered by the Third Reich, and was now
being lived in by officers and soldiers. With

any luck, when the Reich fell one day, if it did, it would be returned to Nick. But God only knew when that might be or what they would do to it in the meantime. Alex was shaking like a leaf as he drove home, parked his car, strode into his own schloss, and slammed the door. Marianne could hear him from the library, where she had returned to warm her hands by the fire, and she knew from the sound of the front door that something bad had happened. She hurried out of the library to see her father cross the landing. He had murder in his eyes.

"What's wrong, Papa?" she asked, frightened. He lowered his voice to answer her. He trusted no one now. There were people everywhere, longing to become puppets of the Reich, and spy on people they had known or worked for all their life.

"The army just took over Nick's house. They're moving in. I want you to go nowhere now. You do not leave this house without me. Do you understand?" he said to her harshly. "There are soldiers everywhere, and it will get worse. They could come here, and even move in with us. I don't want them anywhere near you. You do **not** leave this house!" he said again, and she could see that he was shaking with fear and rage. The fear was for her, and the rage against a government that had violated everything he held dear, including his best friend and his home.

"How can they just move in?" she said with a look of amazement, as they walked back into the library and her father closed the door behind them.

"I do not want you speaking to anyone. Make no comment. Say nothing. We can no longer know who to trust or who will betray us even in our own home." It was a reign of fear and larceny. The country had been taken over by boors, who were prepared to take anything they wanted. "I think the colonel is after our horses." And worse than that, Alex was terrified that one of them, or several of them, would be after her. She was eighteen years old and a beauty, soon to be nineteen, and he was afraid for her. He had a strong sense that these men would stop at nothing.

He realized now that there were several things he had to do. One of them was write to Nick, to tell him what had happened. And the other was to write to his old friend Lord Beaulieu in England. They had gone to school together thirty years before, and had remained close friends for many years. Nick knew him well too. Like the English, he pronounced his name "Byew-lee," not as the French did. But Alex realized now that he needed his help. He could not keep Marianne in Germany for long.

The letter he wrote to Nick that afternoon was one of the hardest he'd ever had to write, other than the telegram about his father. And Alex also knew that he had to word it carefully, lest he arouse the suspicions of the censors. But a letter to America might not be of great interest, and rather than using Nick's full name as he normally did, he addressed it to Nick Bing, in the hope that an uneducated censor reading it wouldn't make the connection. And he would try to make it sound like a fortuitous event, rather than the disaster both he and Nick would consider it to be.

Because of the delicacy of it, it took him a long time to write the letter. He explained that he was sure that Nick would be pleased to know that the old schloss near his own had been put to good use. Due to the departure of its once-rightful owner, and a recent death, it had now been taken over by the Third Reich and the army, and officers and soldiers would be living in the house, and had already moved in. Alex said that it would finally add life to the area and the right spirit, and he was sure that Nick would be pleased to hear such good news. He could only imagine the horror on Nick's face when he read it, but there was nothing he could do. He thought he should know. He added only one cryptic line to cheer him. "All of that could change one day, and surely will, if the family returns, but for now it is very happy news." There was nothing happy about it.

And after Alex had shared other minor news with him, he began his letter to Charles Beaulieu, which was equally hard to write, and the routing of it was complicated too. He wrote it enclosed in another letter, to a mutual school friend of theirs in New York, and asked him to send the letter on to Charles. Alex was almost certain that he couldn't get a letter from Germany to England now that they were at war. It would be a great deal easier from the States, and Alex could only pray that the letter would arrive. He apologized to his old friend Beaulieu for asking such a large favor, but he had no one else he could ask. He took both letters to the post office that afternoon, and hoped that they would reach their destinations, particularly the one to Charles. And then he went home and sat by the fire with Marianne, and tried to reassure her. It had been a distressing day for them both, and one thing Alex was certain of now, it was only going to get worse. And he didn't tell her so, but he wanted his daughter out of Germany before it did. It was in Charles Beaulieu's hands.

Chapter 17

Alex's letter to Nick arrived and he understood it perfectly although Alex had billed it as "good news," which they both knew it was not. Nick fully comprehended that the Third Reich had taken over his estate, and his father was dead, which he already knew from the telegram. And since Nick no longer existed civilly, only as a Jew with no right to own property in Germany, according to the Reich, the estate and the schloss were up for grabs, and now theirs. He no longer owned his own land or anything in Germany. He was not only displaced, but penniless as well, with no inheritance. All

he had was his title and his name. He was
less upset than he had been when his father died, but he was shocked nonetheless.
And he also understood Alex's cryptic ref-
erence that if the Reich fell, if they lost the
war, his land would revert to him again. But
who knew if that would happen, or when?
He could no longer count on anything, except himself. And like Christianna and her
family, the circus was Alex's life. He had
been disinherited by Adolf Hitler. After six
centuries of his family in the same place,
he was now without a country or a home.
In barely more than a year, he had lost everything, including his father. It was hard to
imagine. All he had left of the past were his
boys.

He told Christianna about it later that day,
and she was shocked.

"Can they just do that? Take your house
that way and move in?"

"Apparently they can," Nick said with a
bitter, angry look. "I have virtually nothing,
even in Germany now. I have nothing to
go back to, and I never will. I never want
to go back to Germany again." He looked
as though he meant it, and she felt sorry
for him.

"Maybe they'll lose the war." But it didn't look like it. Hitler was being aggressive with all the neighboring countries on his borders and across Europe, and gave the impression of wanting to swallow them whole.

The next day Christianna told her father and brothers about Nick's family home being seized by the Nazis, and they felt sorry for him. And others in the circus grew increasingly worried about their relatives, especially those that were Jewish and were now in countries under Hitler's control. None of them could go home again either, and they were afraid for their loved ones.

At the beginning of February, Hitler ordered unrestricted submarine warfare against his enemies, while England blockaded Germany. And German U-boats were sinking ships. He hadn't heard from Alex again.

Alex's letter to the friend in New York had found its way to Charles Beaulieu in Hertfordshire within three weeks, in early February, and Charles's response via the same route took another month to get back to Alex, but his response was immediate and sincere. First, he said he was sorry to hear

about Nick's father. He also shared Alex's
concern with what was happening in Germany, and he suggested that Alex get Marianne to England as quickly as possible, if
he could get her there, which they both
knew would not be easy to do. Many German children had been sent to England just
before the war, as well as Hungarians and
Poles, mostly Jewish children, who had
been gotten out by the British on the Kinder-
transport trains, but since war had been declared six months before, it was not easy
to seek asylum in England, nor find a way
to get her there. And Marianne was not a
child. She was considered a woman at
nineteen. So she would have to leave Germany as an adult, with all the ramifications
and risks of any woman.

And both the British blockade and Germans sinking ships made sailing across the
channel extremely risky. But Alex thought
keeping her in Germany with soldiers all
around them was worse, and he wanted to
take the chance, although his heart ached
at the thought. He had to get Marianne into
France, to cross the channel from there, or
by a safer route if he could find one.

Charles and his wife Isabel were more

than willing to have her—in fact, they said they'd be delighted—for the duration of the war if necessary. They had two sons, both in the RAF, and no daughters, and Charles said in his extremely kind letter to Alex that Isabel would be delighted with the company, since life in Hertfordshire was very dull these days, and they rarely saw their boys. And he assured Alex that she would be safe with them, as safe as anyone was in England these days, but surely more than Germany. He said that many people were sending their children and families to the country, whenever possible, even to strangers who had signed up to take them in. And he and Isabel had been thinking of having children stay with them, on their very large estate. Charles was the seventh marquess of Haversham, and a member of the House of Lords, and he and Alex had been in the same class at school.

Alex was greatly relieved to get his letter, and all he wanted now was to find a way to get Marianne safely to England, without alerting anyone in the Third Reich while he did. And since Germany and England were at war, he couldn't just book a ticket and send her. He had to find a discreet way to

get her out. And after careful examination
of the problem, he thought the best way to
do so would be through Belgium, which was
neutral. But he had no idea who to contact
to set the wheels in motion. Alex had no
connections in government or the army, and
although there were some aristocrats in the
Wehrmacht and the SS, he thought most
of them a bunch of badly behaved riff-raff.
And he wasn't willing to take a chance on
any of them, and surely not with his daughter. He had no underground connections either, nor wanted to use them for Marianne.
He wanted to get her out of Germany le-
gally, with proper papers. He was still thinking about it when the colonel came to pay
him a visit to see his horses.

He went through the stables and stopped
in amazement when he saw the four Lipizzaners that Alex still had, two mares and
two stallions, whom he needed for his
bloodlines. They were as fine as Pluto and
Nina had been, though slightly older.

"Are they trained?" the colonel asked with
a look of awe.

"Fully, to liberty commands," Alex said,
hating to even show them to him, but he

couldn't deny him. The colonel could do anything he wanted.

"May I see?" he asked, skeptical, and one of the young boys helped Alex bring the four horses into the main ring he used to train them. And wanting to impress him and show him how insignificant he was, Alex let all four horses loose in the ring and commanded them in the precise exercises of the Spanish Riding School that he had trained them for. The horses were exquisite, ending in a levade, followed by a croupade one by one in perfect symmetry. The colonel nearly had his mouth open when they finished. "You trained them yourself?" he asked in disbelief, and Alex nodded with amusement. He was tempted to tell him that aristocrats were far better at training horses than soldiers, but he said nothing.

"I usually send them to the Spanish Riding School in Vienna, but I kept these four for breeding." He didn't mention the two that had left the year before, with Nick.

"Do you ever sell them?" the colonel asked, with stars in his eyes. He could just imagine himself on one of the two stallions. But Alex had no intention of giving him any.

He would have to take them, and Alex realized he might.

"No, I don't. I place them with the school in Vienna, I keep them for breeding. And I've given two away. They're not for sale."

The colonel turned to him with an angry look then, and he had mean little eyes. "You realize I could take them all if I wanted to, don't you? In the name of the Reich." Alex didn't answer for a long moment as he stared him down. The colonel didn't frighten him. Alex loathed him.

"You could," Alex responded slowly, "but I don't believe that an officer of the German army would want to demonstrate such execrable manners, particularly among gentlemen, unless I'm mistaken, of course, about the Fuehrer's officers being gentlemen." His eyes never left the colonel's as he said it, and the little officer backed down immediately. It was clear he desperately wanted one of the Lipizzaners, but he couldn't find a reasonable excuse to just confiscate them. He had no reason to, the army didn't need them, and he wasn't an officer of the cavalry, which was an honor guard he didn't belong to, and Alex knew it. He was a colonel in the regular army, the Wehrmacht, not even SS, the elite corps. But one of the Lipizzaners would have lent him status and dignity. Alex could see how badly he wanted them, and it gave him an idea. It was bold, and dangerous, but worth it if it worked.

"I only give them to people who are extremely important to me, as a tribute of respect and my admiration for them. Like the Fuehrer, for instance," Alex said with a serious expression as the colonel nodded. "By the way, would you like to ride one of the stallions? They're quite easy, particularly the big one." The smaller one was in fact better bred and had trained better, but the bigger one was showier, and he could see that the colonel liked him, and thought him a good match for his sense of self-importance. The colonel nodded immediately at the suggestion, and Alex helped him into the saddle he put on the big horse. The colonel looked like he was going to explode in ecstasy as he rode around the ring on the beautifully trained horse. Alex commanded the others to stand still. "He's a nice ride, isn't he?" Alex said casually as the colonel rode several times around the ring, and then came to stand next to Alex and looked down at him.

"You would give such a horse to the Fuehrer?" The colonel looked impressed, but it still wouldn't get one in his possession, and he could hardly steal it from the Fuehrer if Alex were to offer such an extraordinary gift. He would have to commandeer it or confiscate it, but he realized it would make him look like a horse thief to Alex, which he didn't like either. Aristocrats like Alex had made him uncomfortable all his life, and Alex could sense that too.

"I would," Alex confirmed, "or to someone I respected equally." He looked at the colonel sitting on the stallion. Their eyes met and held, and the colonel understood instantly that there was something Alex wanted from him. All he had to do was find out what it was, and if he could deliver it easily. He had a feeling Alex was about to tell him, and perhaps they could strike a deal. The colonel was uneducated but he wasn't stupid, and the two men understood each other without words. "Travel papers and safe passage to Ostend in Belgium" was all Alex said, and the colonel looked at him intently. It was a port town, and the colonel could guess that it would only be a midpoint in a journey to somewhere else.

"For a Jew?" That he couldn't do, even for a Lipizzaner. He was no traitor, and he had strict orders about that, from the high command.

"Not at all. For a lady of high rank. Her papers are in order."

The colonel understood immediately. "Your daughter?" he asked in a low voice, and Alex was terrified to admit it and put her at greater risk, but he had no choice. He had to say it, if he was to get her out of Germany, and this might be the only way he could. Alex nodded, and the colonel took a long time to answer, sitting on the stallion he wanted so badly and could have confiscated, at the risk of looking like a boor to this nobleman who seemed fearless and at ease. But he could well imagine how much his daughter meant to him. Enough to give away a priceless stallion in exchange for travel papers to Belgium, to get her out of Germany, and probably to England from there. If he wanted her in Belgium, it was likely he was sending her to England across the channel.

"It could be arranged," he said quietly. "When?"

"Whenever you like, as soon as possible." Alex had exposed his whole hand, and prayed he didn't lose, or her life and his own would be at stake. He had played a high-stakes game of poker with the colonel and hoped he hadn't been wrong to do it.

"I'll give it some thought," the colonel said, and dismounted smoothly. "I'll get back to you in a day or two." He strode out of the ring then, and the stables, without ever looking back, while Alex's heart pounded in his chest. He knew he had been crazy to say what he had to him, with Marianne as the pawn he was risking. It had been a very dangerous game, and it wasn't over yet. The colonel drove off with his driver minutes later. And Alex stood in the stables wondering what to do. There was only one choice. He had to play the hand to the end now, whatever happened. The die was cast, win or lose.

He put one of his hunters on a lead rein, and tightened the saddle on the big Lipiz-zaner. He told the boy helping him to put the other three in their stalls. And he mounted the big stallion and walked it out of the ring, leading the hunter, as the boy looked at him in surprise.

"Where are you going?"

"To deliver a gift," he said, and then trotted off on the familiar road to Nick's schloss. The hunter followed the stallion easily, and when Alex got to the schloss, he tied the hunter to a post that he and Nick had used since they were children, and dismounted. There were soldiers in the courtyard, and he saw the colonel's car with the flags, and walked up to a young sergeant. He executed a curt bow and handed the reins of the stallion to him.

"With my compliments to the colonel," Alex said formally. "Please remind the colonel that he forgot his horse Favory in my stables. I wanted to return him." The sergeant smiled at what he said. He knew the colonel had no horse such as this. He had never seen another one like it. He was a spectacular beast, and he seemed perfectly calm and at ease standing in the courtyard. "His name is Favory, of the original bloodline of Lipizzaners. Good evening, Sergeant." Alex bowed again, and walked back out of the courtyard, untied his hunter, and rode away. He had no idea if it would work, but it was worth a shot. He had gambled everything on the last play.

There was no word from the colonel that night or the next morning, and he said nothing to Marianne. He had risked his own child's life and possibly his own, in order to save her and get her to safety. And as he sat down to lunch with her, a corporal arrived in a Jeep. He said he had a letter for Count von Hemmerle, and one of the maids brought him to Alex. Alex took the envelope and opened it with shaking hands after he left. There was no note. There were only travel papers, to Ostend, Belgium, signed by the colonel, in Marianne's name. They were for the next day. The poker hand had worked. Favory had bought Marianne's freedom. Alex's eyes filled with tears as he read them.

"What is it, Papa? Is something wrong?" Marianne looked worried.

"No," he said quietly. He put the papers back in the envelope, slipped it into his jacket pocket, and had a civilized lunch with her. After they finished, he took her to the library with him and closed the door, and explained it to her.

"You may not like this, my darling, but you

must do as I say. It is dangerous for you here, too dangerous. These people will do anything, and I don't want anyone to hurt you. You must leave Germany now. There are soldiers here, too close to us. They play by their own rules, and you're a beautiful young girl. I am sending you to my old friends the Beaulieus in England. They have agreed to take you, and the colonel has given you travel papers. I have them in my pocket. You must leave tomorrow." He told her all of it at once, and she burst into tears immediately and tried to argue with him, but he wouldn't let her. He wanted her out of Germany as soon as possible.

"Oh my God," she said, staring at him suddenly. "You gave him Favory, didn't you? They told me this morning that he was missing. But now you only have one stallion left to breed."

"I'd much rather have you safe in England. I will put you on a train to Belgium in the morning. The papers he gave you will get you to Ostend, and you can take a ferry to Ramsgate, and from there you can get a train to Hertfordshire. You'll be safe once you get to Ramsgate. And in Belgium before that, thanks to the colonel. I'll give you

as much money as I have here. Charles will
take care of the rest, and I'll settle it with
him later. You must go, my darling. We have
no choice. Think of Nick and Toby and Lucas, and how brave they were. And they
went much farther, to be with people they
didn't know. You'll be safe and happy with
the Beaulieus."

"But I can't leave you here." She was
aghast at the idea.

"You have to. I'll be fine. They're not
after me. We're not Jewish. We've done
nothing wrong. We will coexist peacefully
until this dreadful war is over, and then you
can come home and we'll go on as before.
But I want you out of Germany before it
gets any worse. There's no telling what Hitler will do."

"What if it takes years?" she asked, wip-
ing away tears, trying to be brave.

"Hopefully, it won't take long. But this is
what we have to do."

"Who will take care of you?" she asked,
starting to cry again, and he smiled at
her.

"I will. I'll be fine. Don't worry about me.
I'm not an old man like Paul. I'm not sick.
I'll just be here, waiting for you." She had

just turned nineteen, and he had no idea when he'd see her again, but he was more than willing to deprive himself of the pleasure of her company, for her own good. "You must pack tonight. Don't take too much, as you'll have to carry it yourself. Take what you need. And if anyone asks you tonight, say that you are going to visit friends in Berlin, for a party or two." Berlin was very lively these days, with officers and pretty women going to celebrations and glamorous parties. They talked for a few more minutes, and then he sent her to her room to start packing. Alex sat in a chair and stared into the fire for a long time. It had been a terrifying gamble, but it had turned out well. And even though he would miss her terribly, he knew he had done the right thing for Marianne.

Chapter 18

When Alex took Marianne to the station at seven the next morning, there were mostly soldiers getting on the train, and a few old farmers. She was the only woman, and she looked panicked for a minute, as she held a suitcase in each hand and set them down in her compartment. Alex had bought her a first-class ticket, and she looked very grown up in a dark blue coat and a black hat with a small face veil, and ladylike high-heeled black shoes. She looked seriously dressed, well born, and demure. He had instructed her to hide most of the money he gave her under her clothing, and keep only a small amount in her purse.

"You'll be fine," her father reassured her. He had already given her her travel papers and her passport and as much money as seemed sensible, and she was clutching her purse as she looked at her father with tears bulging in her eyes. She could barely speak. She had no idea when she would see him again, and she was trying to engrave this image of him in her memory in every detail.

"I'll miss you so much, Papa," she said, as she hugged him and clung to him.

"I'll miss you too," he said, trying to keep his voice strong for her, and his face calmer than he felt. "Charles will write to me through friends in New York to tell me you've arrived. Be careful, Marianne. Don't talk to anyone." After changing trains at the border, she would get to Ostend in nine or ten hours, and she would cross the channel that night to Ramsgate, catch another train, and be in Hertfordshire by morning. She would have to take a taxi from the station to the Beaulieus', since they didn't know when she was arriving, and he had no way to tell them.

But Alex knew that she was responsible and enterprising enough to get there on her own. He just hoped that none of the soldiers bothered her on the way. And her papers were in order. He checked them himself. And with a colonel of the high command having signed them, no one would dare give her trouble. "Be a good girl, Marianne," he said in a hoarse voice as the train whistle blew. He hugged her fiercely one last time and then left her compartment and hopped off the train. She opened the window and leaned out to him, with her hat slightly askew. She looked beautiful, and he knew he would see her forever this way in his mind. It would have to last him until Germany was a safe place for her to be again.

"I love you, Papa!" she shouted, as the train started to move, and he stepped back, waving at her with a broad smile, hoping she couldn't see his tears.

"I love you too!" he shouted back, as he began to disappear with the station. Tears were pouring down her cheeks, and she was alone in the compartment. He was only a speck by then, and the train rounded a bend, and he was gone. She closed the window, and sat on the banquette crying softly. She still couldn't believe that he had made her leave and go to people she barely knew. She couldn't even remember the Beaulieus or what they were like, and now she was going to have to live with them, maybe for years. All she wanted to do was go back home and hide under the covers, or look for her father in the stables. She was leaving everything she held dear and that was familiar to her, going to strange people in a strange land. And she thought of Nick then, and Toby, and remembered what her father said about how brave they had been when they left sixteen months before. It seemed as though they'd been gone so much longer. And once she got to England, she was going to write to Toby and tell him what had happened to her.

Alex left the station with his head down, and tears rolling down his face. He got into his car and felt like a thousand-year-old man as he drove slowly home. There was nothing to look forward to now, nothing to wait for, no one to come home to at night, until after the war. He drove past Nick's schloss and saw all the soldiers standing outside, talking and walking in and out. And as he drove by, he saw the colonel leave the courtyard on Favory, and Alex slowed to watch him. The colonel turned and caught his eye, and Alex saluted him smartly in a gesture of thanks. The colonel returned the salute, and Alex drove home, thinking of his daughter on the way to Belgium. It had been a good trade. The best one of his life.

When Marianne reached the Belgian border, she changed trains carrying both her suitcases. They were heavy, but she could manage them. She was confused for a minute about which track her train would be on. She asked for directions and found it after that, and settled into the compartment. She had passed through customs with no problem, and the train went straight to Ostend. She dozed on the way, and didn't eat all day. She felt sick every time she thought of leaving her father. She could still remember his face in the station. She woke up crying a few times, and when they got to Ostend, she was exhausted. She had to take a taxi to the ferry, and several other passengers were going there too. It was raining, but the sea looked smooth when she got there. She had heard horror stories about crossing the English Channel, but it was a peaceful moonlit night, as she stood on deck and watched Belgium fade away behind her. Germany already seemed light-years away. The passengers had been warned that they could be torpedoed al-though it was unlikely on a Belgian ferry, but she wore a life jacket anyway.

It took an hour for the little ferry to reach Ramsgate, and it was nearly midnight when they arrived. A single customs officer stamped her passport, and although she was German, he let her through. She was pretty and young, and he decided to be le-nient about it. He could have stopped her pending further inquiry, but he didn't. There were two taxis parked at the dock, and she took one of them to the train station, and had to wait an hour for her train to arrive, and then for the first time all day, she finally ate. She was ravenous. She hadn't eaten since six o'clock that morning. She ate a sandwich of sausages, and ordered a cup of tea, and by the time she walked back to the platform with her bags, the train was pulling into the station. She got on it and settled into the darkened compartment with a little blue light on. There was already a woman on the opposite banquette sound

asleep, as she set her bags down and a
porter helped her put them in an upper rack.
And then she sat down, and watched the
darkness as they slid past the British countryside. She had been in three countries
that day, and she finally fell asleep.

The conductor woke her when they were
pulling into Hertfordshire, and she put her
hat back on without combing her hair. She
was too tired and sad to care how she
looked. She already missed her father terribly. She had brought a whole box of photographs of him in her suitcase, and a few
of her mother. She found a cab easily at the
station. It was eight o'clock in the morning,
twenty-five hours after her journey had begun. She had traveled easily out of Germany with the papers the colonel had given
her father in exchange for the Lipizzaner
stallion. Her life in trade for a horse.

She told the driver at the station that
she was going to Haversham Castle, and
he glanced at her in the rearview mirror.
He was an old man, and had been driving
a taxi for years. He didn't ask her where she
was coming from—she looked as though
she didn't want to talk, as she watched the
countryside around them. There were cows

in pastures, and sheep, and fields, and a few houses scattered here and there, and finally the castle came into view. It was ten times the size of their schloss, and terrifying-looking, as though it would be full of ghosts and scary old people, and she wanted to burst into tears as they arrived at the front gate, which was open, and the battered old car drove into the courtyard and she got out. She paid the driver, and he drove away as she banged the enormous brass knocker on the front door. She had no idea what to expect as she stood between her two suit-cases, and a butler in a morning coat came to find her, rumpled and exhausted, with her hat half falling off her blond hair.

She looked up at him with enormous frightened eyes and nearly choked, while she said her name in a whisper. "Marianne von Hemmerle. I believe the marchioness of Haversham is expecting me." Her English and her manners were excellent, but she looked like an orphan, and he felt sorry for her. He took her bags and led her into the main hall, which was a long, dark corridor filled with portraits of their ancestors. It was a gloomy place and freezing cold, as he led her into a small parlor near the front door.

And the moment he left her, he went out to the garden to find the marchioness, who was already gardening, which she did most of the time. She was a youthful woman, with a girlish face and prematurely white hair the color of snow, which she was wearing in a long braid down her back. She was wearing an old plaid jacket, yellow gardening boots, and a heavy sweater. The butler bowed politely as soon as he approached her. He seemed much more respectable than she did.

"Ma'am, there's a young lady to see you. Miss von Hemmerle. She looks as though she's had a long journey," he said sympathetically. "She arrived by taxi from the train station, I believe, with two bags. Should I take her upstairs to a room?" He was used to people coming and going at Haversham. The Beaulieus were hospitable, and frequently entertained their friends, their children's friends, and people they barely knew.

"Oh my Lord!" the marchioness said, as she dropped her gardening tools, and ran toward the morning room door. "Marianne . . . the poor child . . . where is she,

William?" She turned to him with worried eyes.

"In the front parlor, ma'am, with her bags," he answered as she rushed past him, and burst into the room where Marianne was sitting with a terrified expression. And as the woman with the long white braid exploded into the room, Marianne stood up, and vaguely remembered meeting her as a child. She was very thin then, very athletic, very British, and very pretty, in a disheveled aristocratic way. And before Marianne could say a word, the woman threw her arms around her and hugged her, and then backed up to observe her and gently stroked the tangled blond hair.

"My poor darling. Did you have a terrible trip?" She was all sympathy and kindness as two big hunting dogs came into the room and wagged their tails, and a Jack Russell followed a minute later, barking at his mistress and their guest.

"Oh, Rupert! Will you stop!" she shouted at the small dog, and went back to fussing over Marianne and insisted that she come to the breakfast room for something to eat and a cup of tea.

"William, please ask Cook for a decent breakfast and a pot of tea," she said. "I'm sorry, darling, we've been on rationing for two months, but she'll come up with something." The butler disappeared immediately, as Isabel led Marianne to the morning room, and she sank down next to Isabel on an overstuffed blue velvet couch, and looked around the room. There were bright chintzes and soft colors everywhere, an enormous fireplace, and a wall full of books, and through the windows and open door, Marianne could see gardens and trees and a lake, and the beautiful grounds of the castle. She felt as though she had landed in a dream, someone else's surely but not her own, as her hostess sat next to her holding her hand and trying to make her feel at home. She had never met anyone with such kind eyes. Everything about her was welcoming and warm, and she punctuated everything she said with giggles and little bursts of laughter and silly jokes, and then scolded the dogs. And as the delicious breakfast came in on an enormous silver tray, Marianne looked at her with wide eyes. The cook had come up with oatmeal, scones, and some jam she'd been saving.

"Thank you for having me. I'm so sorry to come as such a surprise."

"We were expecting you," Isabel Beaulieu said with a warm smile. "Now eat, and then I'll take you up to your bedroom so you can settle in." As she said it, one of the hunting dogs stole a piece of scone, and Isabel scolded him, and they both laughed. Despite the enormous, daunting castle they lived in, Marianne had never met a kinder, friendlier woman in her life. She was like the mother Marianne had never had and always wished she did. And it wasn't scary being here at all. "And how is your father? Charles was quite worried about the two of you."

"He's fine," Marianne said between bites, while the dogs stared at her mournfully, hoping for another bit of scone, but Marianne ate it all. She was starving. "He traded a horse to get me out of Germany, a Lipizzaner," she said, as Isabel looked at her in surprise.

"Well, apparently it worked, and here you are. Charles will be so pleased. We were quite concerned about when you'd arrive. This was a very good time to leave Germany, with that dreadful little man attacking everyone. We'll put him in his place very quickly. My boys are in the RAF, you know," she said proudly, as Marianne finished the breakfast and the dogs walked away in disgust. She was embarrassed by how hungry she'd been. She had eaten everything. "Now let's take you to your room, and you can have a little rest," Isabel said, as though Marianne had come from London for the weekend. And knowing that she might be there for a long time, and probably would be, she had given her their best guest room.

Marianne followed her up a wide marble staircase, to a room on the floor above, and when Isabel opened the door, Marianne could see an enormous canopied bed with a flowered pink bedspread and beautiful pink satin chairs. It was a room fit for a princess or a queen, and without thinking, Marianne put her arms around Isabel and kissed her cheek and thanked her.

"I've always wanted a daughter," Isabel confessed, and then showed Marianne a handsome white marble bathroom with a huge tub. And a few minutes later, a young Irish maid in a black uniform with a lace apron and cap came to draw a bath for her, and then with a flurry of hugs and promises to see her later and telling her to rest as long as she wanted, she left Marianne alone, as she walked around the beautiful room, and stood staring out the window at the grounds. It was the most impressive place she had ever seen, but as she stood there, and saw swans on the lake, Marianne missed her father and their drafty old schloss. This was magnificent, but it wasn't home. Isabel was so nice, and everything was perfect, in spite of the war. But as she gazed at the gardens that Isabel was so proud of and worked so hard on, the tears rolled down Marianne's cheeks, and all she wanted was to go home.

Chapter 19

After lunch with Isabel, on silver trays in the morning room again, and meeting Charles that afternoon, whom she vaguely remembered now, too, Marianne had dinner with them in the enormous dining room, where they sat at one end of a vast table, which Isabel said could seat forty-two. When Marianne went to her room that night, she wrote to her father via his friend in New York, telling him that everything was fine, how beautiful the house was and how nice they were to her, and thanking him for getting her there. She said it cryptically, so the censors wouldn't get suspicious, and it wouldn't cause trouble for her father. She then wrote to Toby and told him the truth, that her father had wanted to get her out of Germany, to come to friends of his in England, so she was in exile now too. She said she was in a beautiful place, and the people were really nice to her, but she missed her father and home terribly, even if it was dangerous there. She didn't mention that soldiers were living in his house, so as not to upset him. But she said she understood now how lonely he must have felt at first, and how hard it must have been to join the circus. She said living with the Beaulieus was nothing like a circus, but she felt like Alice in Wonderland down the rabbit hole. Nothing seemed real to her now, except the war. She told him about traveling through Belgium for a few hours the day before, and how nerve-racking it had been. She asked him to write to her, and told him how homesick she was, which she hadn't said to her father so as not to worry him or seem ungrateful. But she said she had never felt so out of place in her life. And she mentioned that her hosts, the Beaulieus, had two sons in the RAF, whom they were very proud of, but she hadn't met them yet. She even told him about the dogs and how her father had traded Favory the stallion for her travel papers. And she asked William the butler to mail both letters for her the next day, and he assured her he would.

It took her letter a month to reach Toby in New York, at their first stop on tour. Their mail was sent from Sarasota to various stops. And Toby was shocked when he got her letter, to hear that she had left Germany too. He told his father about it, when they were brushing the horses that afternoon, before their evening performance at Madison Square Garden.

"He sent her to England?" Nick was surprised by what Toby told him. Clearly, things were even worse than he thought if Alex had sent Marianne away. He knew Alex wouldn't have done it otherwise. "Did she say who she's staying with? People her father knows, or strangers somewhere in the English countryside?" Nick was curious, and he could only imagine how lonely Alex must be without her. He felt sorry for him now too.

"She's staying in some kind of castle," Toby said vaguely, "with people called the Beaulieus. They have two sons and a lot of dogs." He had picked up all the information that seemed pertinent to him, and Nick laughed.

"Oh my God, Charles," Nick said, recognizing the name immediately. "I went to school with him, although he's a few years older than I am. They're lovely people, and Marianne is right. They have an enormous castle. Well, she'll certainly be comfortable there while she waits out the war. Alex couldn't have picked better people to send her to. Isabel will love her to death. She's a sweet woman," Nick said with a nostalgic smile, thinking of what odd lives they all led now. He and the boys were in the circus, Marianne was in England with their old school friends, and Alex was all alone. Nick was even more worried about him now, knowing how terribly he would miss her. At least he was with his boys, no matter how odd their life was, performing in a circus. And he was happy with Christianna. He had never been as happy in his life. And now that her family knew about him, they had accepted him, and they were very nice to him and the boys. They had dinner with her family often.

Nick got his own letter from Alex a week

later, which was cryptic but essentially told the same story. He didn't mention trading Favory for Marianne's safe passage out, but Nick guessed accurately that there had been some fancy footwork involved. At least she'd gotten out. Alex said he was still waiting for confirmation from Charles, via New York, but he was hoping she was all right. Nick actually knew of her safe arrival before Alex did, which he knew must be hard on Alex.

And just after he got the letter in April, they heard that Hitler had invaded Norway and Denmark. And the RAF was bombing German ships off the coast of Norway, and German airfields. All-out war was on. And a month later, when the circus was in Pennsylvania, the news was far worse. Hitler had invaded France, Belgium, the Netherlands, and Luxembourg. And five days later, Holland surrendered to the Nazis. Hitler was devouring Europe. And in England, Winston Churchill had become prime minister.

Nick talked about the news sometimes with Christianna. It seemed as though nothing could stop the Nazis, or hadn't yet, and it was becoming impossible to believe that Europe would recover. And he worried about Alex more than ever, especially now that he was alone. He wondered what he did now, other than care for his horses. Nick's own life at the circus was full, with his boys, and Christianna, and their rehearsals and performances and traveling on tour. He still hadn't told Alex about her, and felt guilty about it. And now that Marianne was in England, she and Toby were corresponding more often. It was easier getting letters between the States and England. Alex's letters to them, and to his daughter, had to go by a far more circuitous route, still via New York, since the United States hadn't entered the war.

Marianne met Charles and Isabel's younger son, Simon, in May, two months after she got there. He was twenty-two, flying fighter planes in the RAF, and he had fallen in love with a Canadian army nurse in London, whom he'd met at a party hosted by his squadron, and Isabel said he was crazy about. He was very nice to Marianne when he met her, although he only stayed with his parents for one night, and was anxious to get back to London. He was stationed at Biggin Hill Airfield outside London.

And she met their older son, although
only by a year, Edmund, in June when he
came to spend a long weekend with them
on leave. He was an RAF pilot, too, and flew
Wellingtons, on special missions. He had
already run reconnaissance missions over
top secret targets in Germany seven times.
Isabel worried constantly about his missions. She treated them all like children, and
Edmund and Marianne laughed about it
one afternoon when he invited her to take
a walk on the grounds. He looked like his
father, but he had the kindness and easy
laughter of his mother, and he asked Marianne if she was very lonely there. She never
said it to his mother, but she still was. And
homesick for her father.

"It's not home for you, after all. And we
must all seem very strange. This isn't your
house, or your language, or your country.
It's quite normal to be homesick," he said
sympathetically. "And this is such a big,
drafty old place," he said, referring to the
remarkable castle he'd grown up in.

"I feel so guilty when I get sad," she admitted. He was easy to talk to, and strikingly
handsome. He had dark hair and green
eyes, and he looked very dashing in his uni-

form. He treated her like a friend, and she had fun doing things with him when he was home for the weekend. He took her fishing at a nearby lake, and walking on the moors, and he taught her to milk a cow on one of their farms, which she had never done on their own. Their lives had been similar growing up, except that his home was far grander than hers. But he was simple and unpretentious and down to earth, and she liked that about him. He reminded her a little of Toby, except that he was four years older than she was, instead of two years younger, and he treated her like a little kid most of the time.

"I'm nineteen!" she complained to him. "Not twelve!" He even raced her down the main alley in their garden after they made a bet as to who could run faster. "You cheated!" she accused him, laughing and out of breath.

"I did not!" And then he got her lost in their maze, and she threatened his life if he didn't get her out of it after an hour in the sun, and he finally took mercy on her and showed her the way out. They enjoyed each other like two children while he was there, and Isabel commented to Charles again what a good girl she was, and how much Edmund was enjoying her. She thought that Marianne was a good stress reliever for him after the tension of his missions. And Isabel was happy to see him so relaxed, and Marianne looking happier at last. She'd been sad ever since she'd arrived.

"She's not a girl, Izzie," her husband corrected her. "She's a woman, and a very pretty one at that. Our son's not blind, you know. I'm sure he's noticed it too."

"I don't think so," she said innocently. "They've been playing like children for two days." It had done them both good. By the end of the weekend, Marianne wasn't as homesick and Edmund had gotten a breather from his flying missions over Germany. Marianne was sad to see him leave on Sunday afternoon.

"Who am I going to play with when you leave?" she said mournfully when he came to say goodbye. He was wearing his uniform again, and looked much more grown up than he had while playing on the grounds with her. She liked him better as a playmate than all dressed up.

"You'll have to entertain yourself, I'm afraid," he said with a boyish smile. "Or chase the dogs around the lake. You can milk the cows again, if you like." But none of it would be as much fun without him. They had an easy time being together, and had had a few serious conversations about the war. He was touched that she had grown up without a mother, and seemed very normal in spite of it. And they had gone riding one morning, and he was impressed by what a skilled horsewoman she was. He didn't admit it to her, but she rode better than he did.

He promised to come back the next time he was on leave, and the house seemed too quiet without him after he left. Marianne said as much to Isabel, who regaled her with stories of all the mischief her boys had gotten into when they were young. She agreed that the house was awfully serious and sedate without their antics.

In the days after Edmund's visit, Italy entered the war against Britain and France. And France fell to the Germans. Marianne was grateful that she had left Germany when she did. She couldn't have gotten out now through Belgium, since it was occupied. And she doubted that the colonel would have given her safe passage, even in exchange for a Lipizzaner stallion. Her father had written to her that the colonel now rode all over the county on Favory, which always made him smile, and made him think of her.

And Isabel said frequently that she hated to think of Paris in the hands of the Germans, it was such a beautiful city. And by the end of June, there were photographs in the press of Hitler touring Paris, which enraged her even further. And General de Gaulle was recognized as the leader of the Free French Forces, as opposed to Marshal Pétain, who led the Vichy government, whom Isabel considered traitors for handing over France so easily to the Germans. At least de Gaulle was willing to put up a fight and was organizing the Free French from London.

Isabel, Charles, and Marianne were hoping that the boys would come home again in July, but the Battle of Britain began, and they were too busy flying retaliatory missions and never got leave. And a month later in August, the Germans started bombing airfields, and there were daytime raids and bombing missions over England, and toward the end of August, for the first time, the Luftwaffe bombed central London. Simon called home afterward, and with strong emotion in his voice, he told his mother that the young nurse he'd been seeing had been killed. He sounded devastated, and Isabel was very sorry for him.

And two days after the bombing in London, the RAF bombed Berlin, and they'd had no confirmation of it, but Isabel had a feeling that Edmund was part of that mission. And he finally came home for two days after that. He hadn't been home in more than two months by then, and they were all happy to see him. Simon hadn't been back since his girlfriend was killed, but he hadn't had any time off. And they were grateful to see Edmund alive and in one piece. He looked tired and admitted that he hadn't slept much recently, but he was in good spirits.

He and Marianne went swimming in the lake, but this time they had more serious conversations than before, about the war, and about dying, and living with constant uncertainty. He said he was glad she wasn't in London, that the devastation had been awful. He said that seeing that and all the people who had been injured made it easier for him to fly bombing missions over Germany, although he hated the idea that he would hurt women and children and civilians and not just army bases and military targets. He seemed more serious to Marianne than he had in June. It was a hard way to grow up.

"And you?" he asked her gently. "Are you still as homesick?" She had been there for six months by then, and she had gotten more used to it, and loved his mother.

"She's such a good person," Marianne said with open admiration of Isabel. "I feel badly sometimes that they're stuck with me. It could be years before I go home." Sometimes it embarrassed her to be such a burden for them. And Charles had to give her spending money, which her father planned to repay later, but she felt awkward to be staying for so long. "You really need to win this war, so I can go home," she teased Edmund, and he smiled as they strolled through the gardens.

"I rather like the idea of your being here," he said, as he looked at her. "I like it very much in fact, so maybe I won't win the war quite yet." He took her hand and held it as they walked along. She looked surprised, but he hadn't been as playful this time. The war was fraying everyone's nerves, even Izzie's, who was constantly worried now about her sons. They all wanted the war to be over, especially Marianne, who was anxious about her father.

Before he left, Edmund took Marianne out for a walk again, and looked at her seriously. "If something happens to me, take care of my mum, will you, Marianne? She loves you, and it would be very hard on her if something happens to one of us, me or Simon." It was an awesome responsibility he was giving her, and then he startled her even more. "Actually, I thought I should let you know, before I leave, that my mum isn't the only one who's fallen in love with you. I think I have too. I haven't stopped thinking about you since June." For a moment, Marianne didn't know what to say. Until then, she had thought of him as a friend, like Toby. She wondered if facing death every day made him more intense about everything, but as he gazed at her, she felt a stirring, too, and the next thing she knew, she was in his arms and they were kissing. She was breathless when they came up for air, and she looked at him seriously too.

"Please stay alive, Edmund. . . . I think I love you too." It had all happened so quickly, and he was certainly handsome, but she loved his boyishness and his love of fun, his great sense of humor, and his kindness. He was a lot like his mother.

"I'll do my best, and now that we've got that worked out, I really ought to tell you that I don't 'think' I love you, I know I do. I just didn't want to frighten you when I said it."

"Thank you," she said with a shy smile, her blond hair tousled and framing her face like an angel. "I love you too. And I meant what I said. Please stay alive, I need you." She had lost too many people she cared about now, and she had just found him— she didn't want to lose him.

"I'm not going to die," he said quietly. "I wouldn't do that to you."

"Is that a promise?" she asked, facing him, as they approached the house again.

"A solemn promise," he said, staring her in the eyes.

"I'm going to hold you to it."

"You do that." He kissed her then and held her in his arms for a moment, wanting to feel her next to him. "I'll come back as soon as I can. They're not giving me much time off right now, but I'll come back as soon as they'll let me." She nodded, and they kissed for a last time and then walked back into the house with a look of innocence that didn't fool his father for a minute, but disappointed his mother.

"She's such a pretty girl, and so sweet," she complained to her husband, after Edmund left. "I don't know why he's not interested in her. He treats her like a little sister."

Her husband burst out laughing at her comment. "My darling, I love you, but you are quite blind. I think he's head over heels in love with her, he just doesn't want us to know it." He knew his son better than she did.

"Do you think so?" Isabel was shocked. "Does she know it?" She was amazed.

"I'm sure she does. I've never known Edmund to be interested in your gardens. And he keeps taking Marianne out to look at them. I daresay they're doing something else out there than admiring your roses."

"Really?" She stared at him in astonishment. "Well, I certainly hope you're right. I'll be so disappointed if you aren't. They'd make a very handsome couple, don't you think? Very pretty offspring."

"I think you're getting a bit ahead of yourself," he reminded her. "I said I thought he's in love with her, not that they're getting married next week."

"Well, as long as you think he's in love with her, that will do for now. It would suit me very well, though. She wouldn't have to go back to Germany, and she could stay and keep me company here. And after the war, they could live here."

"You have it all worked out, don't you?" he teased her. "Maybe you should let them organize it for a bit, just in the beginning."

"Well, I might," she said pensively. "I just don't want him to miss an opportunity. She's a wonderful girl."

"I daresay he thinks so too. He's not a fool, you know. He sees her and talks to her, too, not just you. And I do agree with you on that—she's a lovely girl. I feel so sorry for Alex, it must be miserable in Germany now."

"At least he's out in the country the way we are. I wouldn't want to live in a city right now, with all these bombings, in any country."

Two weeks later, the Germans bombed London, Southampton, Bristol, Cardiff, Liverpool, and Manchester, and Britain had taken a heavy hit.

Three weeks after that, Germany invaded Romania, which upset a number of people at the circus. There were many Romanian gymnasts and jugglers in the show, and they were suddenly as worried as everyone else. Thanks to Hitler, the news was terrible from all over Europe. For Americans, it was still someone else's war, and they had no intention of getting involved, but most of the cast of the circus were from countries that were being severely affected. It put a damper on everyone's spirits, and as they wended their way through the last week of the tour, a pall fell on the mood of the entire crew.

And in November, when they got back to Sarasota, Nick and his two boys had been in America, and with the circus, for two years. It was hard to believe, and he had been in love with Christianna for almost as long. At seventeen, Toby seemed like an American boy by then, and his English was almost perfect, and Lucas, at eight, felt and acted as if he had been a circus child forever. He could barely remember any other life, and sometimes Nick felt that way too. And he had settled into comfortable routines in the circus. He and Christianna were still the stars of the show.

The tour had been successful, and they'd done well, but everyone was happy to be back in Florida for the winter. The boys were back in school and Nick could hardly wait for some time off to spend with Christianna. He had invited her to go to New York for a long weekend with him, and she loved the idea. And as they had before, they asked the Ukrainian girls to cover for them.

"Why don't you two just get married instead of sneaking around all the time?" one of the girls asked her, and Christianna shrugged.

"We're not ready," she said blithely, but it had crossed her mind too. But she suspected that Nick felt he didn't have enough to give her, or enough security saved up. He was much older than she was, and very responsible about things like that. He wanted to provide handsomely for a wife, or at least better than he could now. And he thought they had time, because she was only twenty-three years old. She seemed like a baby to him, and it always shocked him to realize that she was only six years older than Toby. And in Nick's mind, it gave him more time to save some money.

He and his children spent Christmas with the Markovich family that year. They had Christmas dinner together, and he brought two bottles of vodka since he knew now just how much Christianna's brothers could drink.

They were all in the Christmas show together, and her brothers teased him now whenever they walked past him, and they were no longer surprised when Nick stood by breathlessly whenever she was on the high wire. He knew he'd never get used to it, but at least now when he watched her, most of the time he didn't feel sick.

And as the year drew to a close, while they all enjoyed their winter break, Nick made good on his promise to take her to New York between Christmas and New Year's. They had no performances scheduled, so they could manage the time away.

They stayed at a little hotel near Madison Square Garden, and walked around Times Square. He took her to see the Rock-

ettes at Radio City Music Hall, and she
loved it. And it snowed while they were
there. It reminded Nick of Germany, and he
took her for a hansom cab ride in Central
Park. It looked like a Christmas card, and
when they finally went back to Florida, they
were sad to leave. It had been another perfect trip.

Edmund managed to get three days off over
Christmas, too, although Simon couldn't
and was still flying bombing missions over
Germany. At least Charles and Isabel had
one of their boys home, and they were
grateful for that. Edmund came straight to
Hertfordshire as soon as he got leave. And
Marianne was as happy to see him as his
parents were. The moment he saw her, he
picked her up and swept her off her feet and
spun her around.

"I have missed you so bloody much!" he
said, and she laughed. She hadn't seen him
in over a month, and his last visit had been
as romantic as the one before. They had
spent most of their time kissing and making plans. And this time, after lunch the day
he got back, Edmund spent some time
alone with his mother. And whatever they

talked about, Marianne noticed that he seemed very pleased. He and his parents got on extremely well, better than his younger brother, who was more independent and more standoffish and didn't come home as often. Edmund had his mother's warm, affectionate nature. Simon was just more reserved, and more like Charles.

It snowed the night Edmund got home, and he took Marianne out for a walk in their park. She made snowballs and threw them at him, and he retaliated in kind, and pelted her with them from behind a hedge.

"Stop that! That's not fair!" she shouted at him. "I'm a girl!" They were both red-faced and laughing with snow matted in their hair when he came out from behind the hedge, grabbed her, and kissed her.

"Thank you for reminding me," he said, as he kissed her again. "I almost forgot." And he kissed her so lovingly that everything else went out of her head, as they stood in the falling snow. She forgot how much she missed Germany, and her father, and Christmas at home. All she could think of, as he held her, was how much she loved him. And he had kept his promise, and was still alive. She worried about him every day, and prayed for his safe return from his missions. And so far, he was doing fine. "I love you, Marianne," he said softly, and then smiling at her, he dropped onto one knee and looked up at her with a gentle expression as he took her hand. "Marianne von Hemmerle," he said solemnly, "will you do me the honor of marrying me? I would be very, very happy if you will." She looked at him in amazement, and nodded silently as tears sprang to her eyes, and suddenly she felt an acute pang of missing her father again, wishing that she could share this with him, other than in a letter that would take forever to reach him, if it even did. But she knew he'd approve because of how much he liked the Beaulieus, and would be happy to know she was marrying their son. She felt sure of it, even though she was only nineteen. But they were all growing up quickly in the war.

"Yes," she whispered breathlessly, as the snow fell on her eyelashes and her hair. "Yes, I will." He got up then from his bended knee and kissed her, more passionately than he ever had before. "When?" she asked him as they walked back toward the house.

"Soon," he answered, and the moment they walked into the living room, he took a small black velvet box from his pocket. His mother had given it to him that afternoon when he told her what he intended to do. And he had told his father that afternoon, and Charles gave him his blessing. They were both happy with his choice of bride, and neither of them was bothered that she was so young. She was a very mature girl, and they thought she was perfect for him.

Marianne opened the box cautiously and gasped when she saw it. She had never seen anything as beautiful, and Isabel thought it would be lovely on her. It had belonged to Edmund's great-grandmother, and was a beautiful round diamond solitaire, far bigger than anything Marianne had ever expected to wear. Her own mother's engagement ring had been much smaller, and her father had always planned to give it to her when she turned twenty-one. Now she would have her own engagement ring before that. She kissed him, and he slipped it on her finger. It fit perfectly, and she stared at it in wonder on her hand. It was the most extraordinary thing that had ever happened

to her, and she looked sad for a moment.
It was bittersweet for her.

"Darling, what's wrong?" Edmund asked
with worried eyes, and there were tears in
hers when she looked at him.

"I wish I could tell my father, and that he
could be at our wedding." But neither of
them wanted to wait until the end of the war,
which could go on for years. Edmund took
her in his arms, and he held her, and then
he went to the pantry, and poured them
each a glass of champagne. She stood admiring her ring while he did, and then he
handed the glass to her.

"To my very, very beautiful bride. To us,"
he said, and they each took a sip. They sat
in the library after that, talking about their
wedding. Edmund wanted it to be very
small, with just the immediate family, in the
chapel on the estate. It was not very different from the wedding she would have
planned at home in Germany, in the chapel
at Schloss Altenberg.

"When do you want to do it?" she
asked him.

He looked cautious for a moment, not
wanting to rush her if she didn't feel ready.
It had all happened very quickly. They

had only been in love for six months, but everything seemed to move faster in wartime.

"I have to leave again at the beginning of February. Would that be too soon?" he asked hesitantly, and she shook her head, smiling at him. It was perfect. She didn't want to wait either.

"It sounds wonderful. All I need is a dress anyway." And then she looked solemn again. "Would your father give me away?" Edmund was sure he would be honored to stand in for his old friend.

"Of course. And I'd like Simon to be my best man, if he can get leave then too. Maybe Mr. Hitler will give us a break for a few days."

They sat and talked until the fire went out, and then he walked her up to her room. He stepped inside for a minute, but he didn't stay long. He didn't want to get carried away before the wedding. They were getting married in six weeks. He could hardly wait, and she was as excited as he was. And she shed more than a few tears when she wrote to her father about it that night, wishing he could share the moment with her. And she was even sadder, knowing it would be many weeks before he even got her letter, via New York.

She thanked her future mother-in-law profusely for the ring the next morning at breakfast, and showed it off to her. Isabel felt like her own family now.

"It looks very pretty on your hand." Isabel smiled at her with pleasure. "Best wishes, my darling girl." And then she clapped her hands with delight. "I'm finally going to have a daughter!" And with that, Marianne threw her arms around her and hugged her. And when Edmund came down to breakfast that morning, he looked even happier than his bride. It was a perfect Christmas for all of them at Haversham Castle. Edmund and Marianne were engaged. They had a wonderful Christmas dinner in the dining hall, talking animatedly about the wedding. And Isabel was going to help her get a dress made, by her own dressmaker in a nearby village, whom she said did very clever work. And Simon called them just as they were finishing dinner, congratulated his brother, and promised to do his best to come to the wedding. And Isabel had never been happier. Both her sons were alive and well, and Marianne was going to be a perfect addition to their family. And they all agreed, despite the war and their anxiety about it, that it was the best Christmas of their lives. But in her quiet private moments, Marianne thought of her father and the Christmases they'd shared. For her, more than anyone, it was a bitter-sweet night, of great joy for the present, and all she was gaining, and sadness over the past and everything she'd lost.

In Germany, with Marianne gone, Alex didn't bother to put up a tree that year. He knew it would only depress him. It had been a hard nine months for him. One of his horses had died, a big hunter he was extremely fond of. The weather had been terrible, and his house was freezing all the time, and without Marianne to brighten his days, his life had never been as bleak. With no von Bingens, and no Marianne, it was the darkest Christmas of his life, except when he lost her mother. And in some ways, this was worse. He had no one. When he lost his wife, he still had Marianne to light up his days.

He didn't have much in the house to eat for dinner. He hated to eat alone. And he was boiling some carrots and potatoes from their garden when he heard a knock on the back door. He wasn't expecting anyone, and when he opened the door, he saw one of his tenant farmers, supporting a man with an injured leg. For a long moment, neither man said a word.

"I'm sorry to disturb you, sir," his tenant said in a low voice, and Alex could see that they were both shaking from the cold.

"Come in," Alex said, and stood aside, still not sure what they wanted, and he noticed that the man he didn't know looked afraid, and kept glancing over his shoulder. "What can I do for you?" he asked his tenant.

"I need to borrow a horse," he said simply. "I didn't want to just take one."

"Well, that's a good thing," Alex said, turning off the stove, where he'd been cooking his simple dinner. "Besides, you can't take a horse anywhere tonight. There's ice on the ground. You'll lame him, and he'll break a leg in five minutes. Why do you need a horse?" The tenant farmer glanced at his friend and then back at the landlord he trusted and had known all his life.

"My friend needs to get to the Swiss border."

"That's a long way from here. Should I ask why?" The tenant farmer shook his head, and the injured man lowered himself into a chair with a groan. The leg looked painful. "I don't think your friend's in any condition to travel." Alex sized up the situation, and then noticed that there was blood dripping on the floor, and he realized that more than likely the second man had been shot. "Is anyone going to come looking for you?" he asked him directly.

"Not now. Maybe tomorrow. I think they may think I'm dead. They won't check until morning," the injured man said honestly.

"That's reassuring," Alex said, with a wry look at them both, wondering what he was getting himself into. And then Alex thought of something. "Are you Jewish?" The man hesitated, and then nodded. His friend had convinced him that his landlord was a man you could trust.

"They took my family away two months ago. I was at an auction, in another county, selling a horse so I could feed them. And when I came back, they were gone. All of them, my wife, my two children, my mother, and my aunt. All women and children."

"Do you know where they are?"

"They were sent to a camp. I don't know where. I've been hiding ever since. One of the patrols saw me two days ago. They don't know who I am. I was hiding in the woods. And then they saw me again tonight. I've tried to stay away from everyone I know," he said, looking at them both. "One of them shot me. I don't know if they even care enough to come back. I was going to try and leave tonight, if you gave me a horse." He sounded desperate and was obviously in pain.

"Is there a bullet in that wound?" Alex asked cautiously. If so, they would have to get it out. He'd never done that before.

"He just grazed me," he said, and Alex nodded, trying to think of what to do with him. His home had never been searched, but they might change their mind, if there was a man on the loose nearby, even if they didn't suspect him, and they had no reason to. Yet.

"We ought to get some disinfectant on it. Some whiskey will do," he said, looking for a bottle in a cupboard, and he took it out when he found it. "You're better off hiding somewhere for a few days, and taking off again when you can walk. I have a wine cellar downstairs. And then we can figure out how to get you to the border, but not on horseback. I'm not going to kill my horses for you," he said sternly. He wasn't thrilled to be pulled into this project. But now they were here, and it was Christmas. He had nothing else to do. He had the man lower his trousers and poured the whiskey on the wound. It looked clean. And then he led the way downstairs. The wine cellar was dry but it was cold. He went upstairs and got him a blanket, and then he went back to the kitchen and put a potato and some carrots on a plate, and brought it down to the cellar, and handed the bottle of whiskey to him along with it. "This might help." And then he and his tenant went back upstairs. There was no light in the cellar, but the man needed to sleep anyway.

"Look for blood in the snow when you leave," he told his tenant, "and come back in two days. He should be better by then."

"I didn't think you would take him in," his tenant said apologetically. "I'm sorry, sir. We just wanted a horse."

"It's all right," Alex said, looking tired. "I'd rather get shot for a man than for a horse. We'll figure out what to do. Merry Christmas, by the way."

"Merry Christmas, sir," his tenant said, and left an instant later, with a look of disbelief.

Alex checked on his unexpected guest then. He had eaten the food, he smelled of the whiskey, and he was already asleep. Alex didn't even know if he was telling the truth, but he trusted his tenant, and they had come to him. So he had decided to help. The story he had told was heart-wrenching. He had lost his entire family in one blow. And he wasn't unique. There were too many others like him all over Germany now. People who weren't lucky enough to join a circus with eight horses and a box-car before the war, and had no way out now. Everything about it seemed wrong to Alex, as he turned off the lights and went upstairs to bed. He tried not to think about Marianne's empty room, which he did every night as he walked by. He lay awake for hours, trying to figure out what to do for the man in his cellar.

He checked on him again in the morning. The wound was still clean and he felt better, and no one came to search the house. There were no soldiers anywhere, and his housekeeper was off for two days. He brought the man food again, and let him come upstairs to use the bathroom, and then took him back down to the wine cellar. They didn't speak to each other except for the man saying thank you in an emotional voice, as Alex locked the wine cellar again. The house was entirely quiet, and the next afternoon, his tenant returned.

"How is he?" he asked as Alex let him into the house.

"He seems all right." And by then, Alex knew what to do. He had filled his tank with all the gas they had, and calculated how far he could go. Almost to the Swiss border, but not quite. Close enough—if the man was clever, careful, and could move fast enough.

"I have a friend who can help him," his tenant said cautiously. "If you get him as far as the St. Lorenz Basilica in Kempten. He has a house nearby, and he'll take him the rest of the way." And then Alex understood. This was no accident that had just happened. His tenant was obviously helping Jews escape. He had heard about a few brave people doing what they could and his tenant was one of them.

"My car is in the garage. He can get from the wine cellar to the garage without anyone seeing him. I want him in the trunk—in daylight, at least when we start out. It looks less suspicious than traveling by night. I'll take him to your friend. And then we will forget this ever happened." His tenant looked at him gratefully and nodded. "Get him in the car now. I'll be in the garage in ten minutes." Alex went upstairs to dress then, in a suit and a hat. He wore a heavy topcoat, and he looked properly dressed when he left the house, as though he might be visiting friends. His tenant was waiting for him in the garage. "Is he in?" The tenant nodded, and then without a word, he handed Alex a pistol.

"You might need it." Alex hesitated, and then took it and slipped it in his pocket.

"Thank you." And with that he got in the Hispano-Suiza and turned on the ignition as his tenant opened the garage door for him, and he drove out, as the man lumbered off, looking like a farmer on his way home.

Alex took the main road instead of a back one, and drove past the von Bingens' es-

tate at a normal speed. A soldier stopped
him and recognized him immediately.

"Good afternoon, Count," he said re-
spectfully. "Everything in order?"

"Fine, thank you. I'm going to visit friends."
The soldier waved him on. He didn't check
his papers or look in the car. He knew he
didn't need to, and Alex drove on, until it
was dark, and continued on after that. He
passed one checkpoint and stopped, and
one soldier asked another if he should
check the trunk and was told no. And Alex
drove on with no problem. He remembered
the location where his tenant had told him
to go to meet his friend. It wasn't as close
to the Swiss border as his passenger in the
trunk might have hoped, but they would take
care of getting him over the border, and they
were undoubtedly better equipped than
Alex to do so, in his coat and hat and city
shoes. He didn't even want to think about
what might have happened if the soldier
at the second checkpoint had opened the
trunk and found him. Alex could still feel
the weight of the pistol in his pocket, but
he didn't want to use it.

He went to the address he'd been given,
got out of his car, and knocked. The man

who answered the door looked startled to see a Hispano-Suiza outside his door, and someone who looked like Alex. He nodded, and they exchanged a password his tenant had given him. They were on a backcountry road with no one around. The man who had answered the door opened the trunk and helped the injured man, who said a hoarse goodbye and thank you to Alex. He could hardly walk after the cramped ride, but he disappeared into the house. The door closed and Alex drove off without further comment or conversation, making his way back the way he had come. It had been shockingly easy, and he thought about it as he drove toward home.

He passed the von Bingens' schloss early that morning, and the colonel was out for a ride. Favory was prancing, and there was vapor coming from his nostrils as the colonel saluted the count, and Alex slowed down with a smile.

"Enjoying your Lipizzaner, Colonel?" he said politely.

"Very much so, Count."

"He looks well." The colonel smiled and patted his neck, and Alex drove on, and a few minutes later he was home, as though nothing had happened. His housekeeper came in a few minutes later and made him a cup of tea, as Alex went to put away his hat and topcoat, picked up the cup of tea in the kitchen, and went to his study. He could still feel the pistol in his pocket, and he took it out and locked it in a drawer. It had been a good night's work, the first of its kind for him, and as he took a sip of the steaming tea, he suspected it wouldn't be the last. A door had opened for him that night, and he had chosen to step through it. There was no turning back.

Chapter 20

Edmund and Marianne's wedding at Haversham was just as they had planned it. Simon got a day off to be the best man, and Charles gave her away. She wore a dress by Isabel's dressmaker that molded her figure and made her look like a young goddess in white satin, and she wore the veil that Isabel herself had worn twenty-five years before. And there were twenty of the Beaulieus' friends from the area in attendance, along with a handful of Edmund's closest pals from the RAF. All of the young men were in uniform, and Isabel urged everyone not to talk about the war for the rest

of the day. They were married in the chapel on the estate, which Isabel filled with
flowers from her hothouse, and she made
the bride's bouquet herself of white orchids
from the greenhouse. And the weather
was fair.

The bride looked exquisite and was
beaming, and the groom ecstatic. They had
lunch at the endless table in the dining
room, and nearly filled it. It was covered with
silver birds and fresh flowers, and at the end
of the day the bridal couple drove away to
Brighton for a three-day honeymoon at the
Grand Hotel, which was funny and old-
fashioned, and they both loved it, although
it had changed a great deal. Edmund had
childhood memories there, which he wanted
to share with her, despite the sandbags and
provisions for war. All they could see was
each other, and the life ahead of them. They
would have been happy in a tent under the
stars just so they were together, which was
all they cared about. They were madly in
love with each other. The boardwalk was
closed but they chased each other down
the beach like children, and retired to their
room at regular intervals to make love. And
when Edmund brought his bride back to

Haversham, she looked peaceful and happy, and he spent one last night with her in the big pink guest room, and she cried the next morning when he left and made him promise again that he would come back.

"You know I will, Marianne. Always," he said, as he kissed her for the tenth time in as many minutes, and finally he left. It had all been absolutely perfect, and she was in a daze for days. She wrote to her father to tell him about the wedding, and then to Toby. He couldn't believe she'd gotten married when he read it. They were only two years apart, and he was still infatuated with Katja, but he couldn't imagine marrying her for another ten years, if that. Marianne had become a grown-up, and he still felt like a child at seventeen. He told his father about the wedding when he got the letter, and Nick smiled and shook his head.

"That really makes me feel old. I remember when she was born, not that long ago. Don't you go getting any ideas," he said to Toby, who made a face and shook his head.

"No way. I'm too young. So is she." He wasn't sure he approved of her getting married so young, but it was different with girls.

It was hard to believe he hadn't seen her in two and a half years. The time had flown. And their life had changed so much. And now she'd always live in England, and she was a viscountess, in a castle bigger than theirs. And he and his father and brother were living in a trailer with the circus, and they were on tour again. This was their life now, and Toby had grown accustomed to it. They all had. It was comfortable for them, and they liked the familiar routines, although changing towns every night was hard sometimes. But they'd gotten used to that too.

When they got to California in July, Nick drove Christianna to Santa Ynez again. They had a decent car this time, and they stayed at the same hotel. And some Romanian girls covered for Christianna, but Nick had the feeling that her father knew the truth and chose to turn a blind eye to it. He had grown very fond of Nick and the boys, and he knew how serious Nick was about his daughter. Nick wasn't playing with her. He loved her, profoundly. And she loved him.

They drove to the same bluff as they had before, and he looked out over the land he hoped to buy one day. He called it "his ranch," and Christianna laughed at him. He was still talking about it when he turned to look at her with a gentle expression.

"I've been thinking," he said cautiously. He wanted to be sure this was right for her too. "What do you think about our getting married when we get back to Florida at the end of the tour?"

"Are you asking me?" she teased him. She thought he was joking or just thinking out loud. They talked about it sometimes, but he always said that he wouldn't marry her until he felt he had enough put away. And none of them were able to save a lot of money working for the circus, although Nick was always careful and had been saving for three years. He didn't have enough put aside for a ranch yet, and maybe he never would, but he had what he needed to marry her and feel right about it.

"Not yet," he said in answer to her question, and then he got down on one knee where they'd been standing at the top of the bluff. "Now I am," he said, smiling up at her. "Will you marry me, Christianna?" Her eyes opened wide.

"Are you serious? Now?"

"At the end of the tour." He wanted to take

her on a real honeymoon, and he couldn't do that until they got back.

"I mean, you're asking me now?"

"Yes, I am. I love you, and I want to wake up with you every morning for the rest of my life." They'd been sneaking around for two years. It was long enough. Too long.

"Yes," she said breathlessly. "Yes . . . yes!" She wanted to shout it off the bluff. He stood up and kissed her then, and he stunned her by taking a tiny engagement ring out of a box in his pocket. It had a small diamond in it, but it was a proper ring. He had been planning this for a long time, and had wanted to do it here, at their future "ranch." She didn't believe he'd ever really have it, but it was as good a place as any and a very romantic spot. He put the ring on her finger and kissed her again, and then he swept her up in his arms, put her in the car, and took her back to the hotel, where they made love to celebrate the moment, two years after they had made love there for the first time.

"It's going to be a big wedding if we do it at the circus," she said after they made love.

"I don't think we can do it any other way,"

Nick said practically. "The circus is going to make a big fuss about it." It was all part of the hype of being circus stars, but he was prepared for that.

They told her family when they went back to the fairground in Santa Barbara the next day. And word spread like wildfire that they were engaged. They even got a telegram congratulating them from John Ringling North, and suggesting that they hold the wedding at Ca' d'Zan, the original home of John and Mabel Ringling, which was their palatial estate in Sarasota. It was going to be an even bigger deal than Nick had thought, and the Ringlings wanted all the publicity they could get.

By the time they got back to Sarasota in early November, the date was set, Christianna had the dress, and John Ringling North was going to have commemorative posters made of the couple to sell at the big top for the next year. Nick and Christianna were the stars of the circus, and were treated like royalty. And this was going to be a royal wedding. They would be married, as he had offered, at Ca' d'Zan on the Saturday after Thanksgiving, and all the performers were invited. They were expecting eight hundred people at the wedding, with a special tent set up for dining and dancing.

Nick had asked Toby to be the best man, and Lucas was the ring bearer, although he was a little old for it at nine, but he took the job seriously, and stood clutching the rings at the wedding. And Joe Herlihy made a special toast. The bride was radiant and Nick was as handsome as ever in white tie and tails. It was a fabulous event, a true circus extravaganza, and the posters of them sold out the first night and they had to make more. They agreed to do a special show the day after the wedding, and she wore her bridal veil with her white leotard and tutu. And the day after that, Nick took her to the Breakers in Palm Beach for their honeymoon. It was an elegant hotel and they were treated like movie stars while they were there.

"Well, Mrs. von Bingen"—he smiled at her one night after they made love—"are you tired of me yet?"

"I'll never be tired of you, Nick, until I die," she said solemnly.

"That's liable to be long after I do." She was twenty-two years younger than he was, but it didn't bother either of them. Everything about their union felt right.

And when they got back to Sarasota, everyone congratulated them again, and they were the heroes of the hour. They got standing ovations at every show. No one was tired of their fairy-tale marriage yet, and when they appeared on the Lipizzaners together, the crowd cheered. And Nick went to talk to Sandor the day after they got back from Palm Beach.

"I came to collect on my wedding present," he reminded his father-in-law.

"What present is that?" Sandor teased him. "You got my daughter. Isn't that enough?"

"No, I told you that the only wedding present I want from you is a net for her act. I said it two years ago, and you agreed. She performs with a net from now on," Nick said firmly, and Sandor could see that he meant it, and looked worried.

"The audience won't like it," he warned him.

"They'll get used to it. I told you I'd marry her. And I kept my word. You gave me yours, Sandor. We shook hands on it. The net, or she gives up the high wire, today." Sandor

looked at him long and hard and nodded.
Nick drove a hard bargain, but he was a
man of his word. "Tonight," he reminded
Sandor, who nearly groaned.

And that night, when she went on, Nick
followed her to the ropes. And he saw it.
There were eight handlers holding it for her.
And she saw it, too, and turned to him in
surprise.

"Does my father know?"

"It's his wedding present to us." Nick
smiled broadly and kissed her. "Now go do
your act." He was going to enjoy it for the
first time in three years. And when the crowd
spotted it, they cheered. They approved.
Nick gave Sandor a thumbs-up, and he
waved back. She was never going to wind
up in a wheelchair now, or fall to her death.
Christianna had a net at last, thanks to Nick.

Two weeks after their wedding, they were
still the talk of the circus, and Christianna
was quietly sewing some of her costumes
in their trailer, listening to the radio, when
Nick walked in from feeding the horses. He
leaned over to kiss her, happy to see her,
and enjoying their newly married life, when
the program she'd been listening to was

interrupted and the announcer said that the Japanese had bombed Pearl Harbor in Hawaii. They both stopped talking and were mesmerized by what he was saying.

"What does he mean?" Christianna looked at Nick, thinking she hadn't understood.

"You heard him. American naval ships were bombed and sunk by the Japanese in Pearl Harbor." It was something no one in America had ever thought could happen. They'd been attacked on their own territory. America had finally been forced into the war.

Within minutes, people had come out of their trailers and were telling others. There was a huge hubbub everywhere. Some people were panicking, afraid that they'd be bombed in Florida too. The whole circus was ablaze with the news within an hour. People were glued to their radios. And John Ringling North announced that one of their special Christmas performances was canceled for that night. Everyone stayed home to listen to the news, and Toby and Lucas were with them in the trailer, listening to the radio.

The next day, the United States and Britain declared war on Japan. And three days after that, Hitler declared war on the United States. America was at war. Two thousand four hundred and three men and women had died at Pearl Harbor, and 1,178 were injured. The big top was still dark, and Nick wondered if life would ever be normal again. He was talking to his brothers-in-law about it that afternoon, when Toby came home with a sheepish look. Nick wondered what he'd been up to. And Toby told him half an hour later when they were alone.

"I enlisted, Papa," he said, looking half proud and half scared of his father's reaction.

"You did what?" Nick looked at him, horrified. "You can't do that!"

"Yes, I can. I'm eighteen. And they'd draft me anyway."

"You're not even American," Nick reminded him. He didn't want his son going to war, for anyone.

"They took me," he said quietly with a determined look. "Germany took away our citizenship anyway. I leave for boot camp in two weeks."

"That's insane!" Nick said, and stormed out of the trailer, near tears. He didn't want his son risking his life for any country, neither his old one nor his new one. But Toby was right. He would have been drafted. When Nick told Christianna about it, she could see how upset Nick was.

"Maybe he's right, and they would have drafted him," she said quietly.

"He's German," Nick reminded her. But that rapidly became an issue too.

Two days later U.S. Immigration authorities came to the fairground to question all German nationals who were employed by the circus. Many were roustabouts, and several important acts were German performers. All of the horse acts, two of the big cat acts, Nick, many clowns, several gymnasts, and their star contortionist. And one by one they were questioned, as to their loyalty. Those who were Jewish were immediately exempt and allowed to ask for asylum. The others were given the opportunity to go home if they wanted to, and some had more complicated status, Nick among them. He had been deemed Jewish by the Germans, so he and his children qualified for asylum, but he was also married to an American now. Christianna was a citizen. So he had the choice of requesting asylum, or asking for citizenship through his wife.

"What's it going to be, Mr. Bing?" the immigration officer asked him, holding a clipboard. He had handed him back his passport and the boys'.

Nick hesitated for only a second. "I'd like to become an American," he said quietly. It was his final act of renouncing Germany forever. The officer made a note on his clipboard.

"We'll be in touch with you in the next few weeks," he reassured him. "What about the name? I see your passport is issued in a different name from the one you use in the circus. Which do you want it to be on your citizenship papers?"

"Nicolas Bing," he said clearly. He had lost the "von" and his title, but he had a name he could live with, one that would never link him to Germany again.

"Got it," the officer said, and moved on to the next one, as Nick looked at Christianna.

"Do you mind?" he asked Christianna, and she shook her head.

"You can be whatever you want to be,"

she answered, but she thought he had made the right decision.

In the next few days, they learned that several of the performers, mostly the non-Jewish Germans, were going back to Europe. They had decided not to stay. They didn't want to be under suspicion for being spies.

And all Nick could think about in the ensuing days was Toby leaving for the army and going to boot camp.

The best thing in his life had happened only days before, when he married Christianna. And now the worst was about to happen. His son was going to war.

Chapter 21

Toby left for boot camp at Fort Mason in San Francisco right before Christmas and there were tearful goodbyes with Katja, as well as his father, stepmother, and brother. Christianna was as upset as Nick and Lucas, and dozens of people came by for days before, to wish him well. And Toby and Katja were inseparable for the days before he left. They spent as much time as they could together, kissing and holding hands, but everyone else wanted time with him too. Many of the other young men were leaving, but Nick and his family were much loved, and Toby was a sweet boy. Pierre came to pantomime his goodbyes, and actually managed to make Nick laugh, which was rare now. He had been stone-faced and red-eyed since Toby enlisted after Pearl Harbor. He wasn't afraid to show how much he would miss his son. And he sobbed openly the morning Toby left. Katja was equally inconsolable, and Lucas and Christianna clung to each other and Nick after their goodbyes. And Gallina stood by in tears to comfort her daughter.

Toby would be home again for a visit in February, before they left on tour in late March or early April. And then the army would ship him somewhere, no one knew where just yet.

It made Christmas for Nick and his family a bleak affair. Nick didn't have the heart to buy or decorate a tree, so Christianna did it for him, and she and Lucas strung up lights outside the trailer, but Nick was serious all the time now, and terrified to lose his boy.

Those who had decided to leave the circus were already gone by then, or packing up. Their decisions had been quick, and made Nick's horse act even more important, since the others were departing. The only time Nick smiled now was when he performed, and nothing Christianna did could cheer him. She worried about him constantly, and talked to Gallina about it.

"He's had a lot of losses in his life," Gallina explained gently. "He's afraid. Be patient. He'll cheer up." Christianna did everything she could to lighten the mood, but Christmas was awful, and New Year's was no better. Nick stayed home when she went to have their traditional New Year's Day dinner at the Polish restaurant with her family, but her father and brothers said they understood. Christianna and Lucas went anyway and joined the others. Nick just wasn't in the mood, he was still too upset about Toby.

And in January, Nick had a letter from Alex, in a more complicated way this time, through a friend in Geneva, who forwarded the letter to Nick, since America had entered the war. Alex said nothing about conditions in Germany, or his life, due to the censors, but he told Nick that Marianne and her husband were expecting a baby in the late spring. It was Alex's first grandchild and he was excited about it. He said he missed her terribly and couldn't wait to see her and the new baby and meet her husband one day. And when Nick put down the letter, he looked at Christianna with a rueful smile and a groan.

"Now I feel ancient," he told her. "My friend Alex is having his first grandchild. He's four years older than I am, but I could have one too." Nick was forty-six now, and Alex had just turned fifty, which seemed astonishing too. It seemed only yesterday when they were boys, and had lives they thought that nothing could touch or would ever change. And now everything was gone. Nick worked in a circus, and Alex was alone and hadn't seen his daughter in more than a year, and Toby was going to war.

Nick and Christianna hadn't talked again about having a baby. With Pearl Harbor happening only days after their wedding, Toby enlisting was all he could think about—the babies he had, not the ones they didn't.

And when Toby came home after boot camp in San Francisco, it was agonizingly bittersweet. Each second was precious, and Nick never let him out of his sight for a minute. He wanted to be with him every moment he could. Toby did a final performance with his father, in his corporal's uniform, at the ringmaster's request. And when he and his father rode the Lipizzaners through their final steps, the crowd stood up and cheered them. They were cheering for Toby as tears rolled down Nick's cheeks. The ringmaster had explained over the microphone that Toby was shipping out.

And there were countless others like him, at the circus, and in all walks of life. Every young boy in America was wearing a uniform and looked like a man overnight. Even Lucas seemed suddenly older and more mature. And Toby had come back from boot camp looking solid and strong and healthy. He was home for five days, which went too quickly, and the night before he left, he announced that he and Katja had gotten engaged. And she and her family were as tearful as Nick about his leaving. And on the eve of Toby's departure, after walking Katja back to her trailer, the two brothers lay in bed in their familiar bedroom, and Lucas hugged him and told him how much he would miss him. Toby had tears in his eyes as he embraced his younger brother, and Lucas was crying.

All of Christianna's family came to see him off in the morning. Sandor referred to him as his grandson, and told him how proud of him he was, and what a great American he would be. And Katja and her family came to see him off at the train to California, and no one could stop crying.

In the days after Toby left for Fort Mason, Nick tried to keep busy with the horses, and practicing new routines for his new act without Toby. But Christianna and Nick were the main focus, even more so now. Nick had written to Alex to tell him that Toby had enlisted, but he knew it would be a long time before Alex got the letter, and longer still before Nick heard from him, from Switzerland. But it was shocking to realize now that Nick's little boy was in the army, and Alex's little girl was about to have a baby of her own. Time had flown.

And in April, Toby was able to get a message to Nick from Fort Mason that he was shipping out. He wasn't allowed to say where, but he said it was in the Pacific. He knew two other Germans in his company, and none were being sent to Europe. But at least he was being allowed to fight for his adopted country. Nick wished he weren't going. And at the same time Japanese Americans were being sent to internment camps in the West. The government wanted to be sure that there were no divided loyalties among any of them. But Nick knew nothing more about where Toby was being sent. Toby promised to write to them as often as he could. Nick slipped the letter into a little box, along with the others Toby had written from boot camp. He had saved them all.

They had another letter from him in May, from Hawaii, while they were on tour, and he sounded happy and excited, although he could say little about what he was doing or where he was going. Between the restrictions on him and the censors who read Alex's letters, Nick felt like he was in the dark about both of them, but at least he had letters from time to time. He wondered if Marianne had had her baby yet, but he didn't know that either. And he hadn't heard from her since Toby left for boot camp. She usually wrote to him and not his father, and Toby gave him her news.

Marianne's baby was due in the first days of June. She'd had an easy pregnancy, although the days seemed long to her without Edmund. Isabel had her help in the garden, to keep her busy and walking and moving, and she thoroughly enjoyed having her daughter-in-law with her, and watching Marianne blossom like a lovely flower. And Isabel was over the moon about the baby. As was Edmund. He came home as often as he could, which wasn't often. And each time, he rubbed his hands gently on his wife's belly, amazed and thrilled by how much it had grown. He loved feeling the baby kick, and looked excited each time, as though it were the first time he'd felt it. It wasn't likely he could, but he had said he would try to get leave around the time the baby was due, in the first week of June, and his mother warned him that first babies were almost always late. She told him that he had been three weeks late, and she'd almost changed her mind by then if he was going to be so rude and tardy. But she had forgiven him the moment she saw him.

Edmund had also said that if she went into labor when he was on the base, he would try to trade watch with someone, or even a scheduled mission if they'd let him, and drive home as fast as he could, although he was based in East Anglia, which was several hours away. But he said he would do his best, and she knew he would. She had decided to have the baby at home in Haversham, since hospitals were so busy with injured men now, and she felt guilty taking up bed space and the nurses' attention for something so normal. She was having the local doctor and her mother-in-law at the birth, and with any luck at all, Edmund would be on leave, or come soon after, to see their baby. She wanted a son for him, which was what was expected of them, but Edmund had secretly admitted to her, since the beginning, that he wanted a girl, one who looked just like her. They wanted many children, at least five or six, and they were both delighted with the seemingly easy arrival of their first.

By sheer miracle, Edmund managed to get five days' leave at the end of May, into the first days of June, which was precisely when she was expecting their baby, and she hoped it would arrive on time before he left. Isabel promised to run her around the garden, and they'd had a spell of hot weather, which Isabel felt sure would bring it on, if gardening and long walks didn't. But Marianne wanted to sit very still before he arrived, so she didn't have it early either.

She was enormous, and Isabel kept saying it must be twins, although the doctor hadn't heard a second heartbeat. But Isabel found it hard to believe that one baby could be that size. Marianne's face and limbs had stayed thin, but her belly was huge, and Edmund made fun of her now whenever he saw her. He said she looked like she'd stolen some poor child's beach ball and was hiding it under her dress. And she was uncomfortable in the heat and felt like she could barely move. She could hardly get her stockings on, and had given up wearing them in the heat. There was no one at Haversham to see her, and her mother-in-law told her not to bother. They didn't care. And lots of girls didn't wear them now, since they were so hard to get.

The night before Edmund was due home, he called Marianne from the base. He had just been assigned to an important mission, and they wouldn't allow him to trade it, or start his leave for two more days. He said it would be over quickly, and to keep her legs crossed until he got there. She promised to do so, and he had to get off the phone quickly, as dozens of other airmen, if not hundreds, had to call about canceled leaves. All she had time to do was tell him she loved him and come home soon, and he said he loved her, too, in haste, and hung up. And she went to tell Isabel the disappointing news that he'd been delayed for a mission, but Marianne was surprisingly calm about it, and said she was sure she wouldn't have the baby for a few more days.

And the following night they heard them. Hundreds of planes flying over Britain toward Germany. She, Isabel, and Charles saw them, and they didn't know how many there were, but the night sky was full of them, flying relentlessly toward their target, and she knew instantly that Edmund was with them. She stood smiling at the sky, and whispered that she loved him. They didn't know until later that there were a thousand bombers and they were heading for Cologne.

"No wonder he couldn't come home," Isabel said as they went back into the house. They had heard the massive formation coming, and had gone outside to look. "There must be hundreds of planes there, even a thousand." Charles thought that an exaggeration, but as it turned out, it wasn't. There were planes in the sky for as far as the eye could see, and you could still hear them after they had vanished from sight. It was the same droning sound that filled them with dread at night, when the Germans flew in to bomb their cities. It was familiar to all now. Marianne could only guess that the German civilian population were as distressed as they were. Their cities were in ruins, and England had taken heavy hits—there was rubble everywhere in the streets of London, although Marianne hadn't been there to see it, since she arrived. Isabel wouldn't let her, nor Edmund once they were married. Marianne was enjoying country life, where they were safer than in London.

They shared a peaceful dinner in the dining room that night, while Marianne reported on signs from the baby, and whether or not it might arrive. It distracted all of them from thinking too much about Edmund. Marianne told herself that this was just another mission, no different from the others, and he would be home soon. Either tomorrow or the next day, he hadn't been sure, and he promised to call as soon as he could. And late that night, they heard the planes come back. It was too many to be the Germans and sounded like the same battalion that had left. Marianne lay in bed with a sense of relief, feeling the usual contractions she had had for weeks. He was almost home. And she was beginning to think that their baby would be home soon too. The contractions were stronger than usual that night, but by morning, nothing major had happened, and she waddled down to breakfast, still pregnant and looking tired.

"Sleep well, darling?" her mother-in-law asked her, with a kiss, as she helped herself to a piece of toast, and an egg from one of their hens. They hadn't seen bacon in a year. Those days were over for the duration of the war. But eggs were plentiful in their henhouses, and chickens on their table. It was the only meat they got. Isabel noticed that Marianne looked tired, but she wasn't surprised. The baby wouldn't be long now, she could tell. "I heard the boys come home last night."

"So did I." Marianne had been greatly reassured to hear them return. She wanted Edmund to come soon. He hadn't called yet, but she assumed he was either sleeping after the mission, or trying to get permission for his leave before he called to tell her when he'd be home. And Isabel took her out to the garden with her again after breakfast, telling her they had work to do.

"My roses are a mess!" she complained, as Marianne went outside and put on her gardening boots with bare feet.

They were still busy and Charles was reading the newspaper in his study when William the butler came to tell him that there was a gentleman to see him. He was a general of the army who lived in the area, and he and Charles were old friends. Charles looked instantly pleased.

"Show him in." He was glad to have some male companionship. Isabel's constant clucking about the baby had begun to wear thin. It was all she could think of. And he stood up as his friend the general walked into the study, and held out a hand in greeting.

"Bernard, dear man. What a pleasure to see you! We're expecting a grandchild at any moment, and it's all the women can talk about. It's driving me mad. How good to see you!" His old friend smiled at what he said, but he looked serious as he took a seat across from Charles's desk. He got right to the point. He didn't want to mislead him, or waste time in idle conversation. His eyes locked into Charles's, who felt his heart skip a beat.

"I have bad news for you, Charles," he said simply. He had wanted to tell him first, and preferably alone, in deference to their long friendship.

"One of the boys?" Charles said it in barely more than a whisper. It was all he could get out. The general nodded.

"Edmund. Last night. He was shot down over Cologne. We sent more than eleven hundred planes over. All but forty-three came back. Edmund didn't make it. I'm so sorry." He was desperately sorry for his friend. Charles fought for his composure, stood up and walked around the room, distraught, as the general came to stand with him and patted his shoulder. He had lost two sons himself since the beginning of the war. It wasn't unfamiliar to him, which was why he had come. Edmund's squadron leader had called him, knowing he was in the area and a friend of the young pilot's father.

"Oh my God, what will I tell his mother?" Charles looked into his friend's eyes with panic and despair. This was what they had feared and hoped would never happen, like every parent in England, and everywhere else. "And it's his baby that's due at any moment, possibly even today." The general knew just how hard it was. It was a terrible, unthinkably agonizing moment in any parent's life, no matter how it happened. At least this was for a noble cause, they could tell themselves, and not some stupid accident caused by a drunk behind the wheel of a car. Edmund had been defending England against its enemies. But that was small consolation now.

"I wish there were something I could do," the general said kindly, but he knew there wasn't. All he could do was deliver the news as compassionately as possible. Others were notified by the War Office by a phone call, or by a bicycle messenger arriving at the front gate with a telegram. The general had spared them that. Charles was grateful for his kindness, and thought of poor Marianne. He felt so sorry for her now, as well as himself. He couldn't imagine how they would survive it, but he knew they would. They had to. They had no other choice.

The general quietly took his leave then.

William had an ugly premonition as he closed the door behind him. Feeling shell-shocked, Charles walked out into the garden to find the women. The sun was too bright and the birds were too loud, and his legs felt like rubber under his body. He felt as though the world had come to an end. But he couldn't allow it to show until he told them.

"Did you have a visitor?" Isabel asked him, looking cheerful. "Who was it?" She smiled up at him, but the moment she saw his eyes, she knew, and froze to the spot. Their eyes met, and he nodded, as she dropped her gardening tools and her hand went instinctively to her heart, as though she could stop it bleeding immediately, but she couldn't. She felt like she'd been shot. "Edmund?" she said instantly. Charles nodded again and then took two strides and took her in his arms to console her, gathering Marianne with one arm along the way. She didn't know yet, she didn't understand the shorthand between them that happens after twenty-five years of marriage. Charles and Isabel had needed few words. Marianne looked confused.

"What about Edmund?" Marianne looked

panicked, suddenly sandwiched between her parents-in-law, with her enormous belly. She felt as though she couldn't breathe. "Is he all right?" Her father-in-law looked at her as honestly as the general had at him.

"No, he isn't," he said simply. "His plane went down over Cologne last night, on the mission we saw leaving. A thousand bombers. He didn't come back."

"Was he injured? Did they take him prisoner?" she asked frantically, not wanting to accept what had happened.

"They shot him down. The plane crashed," he said as gently as possible, so she would accept it, but she couldn't.

"Sometimes people survive that. How do they know what happened?" He didn't want to tell her what the general had told him before he left, that the plane had exploded, and it had been quick. There were no survivors.

"They know," he said quietly with an arm around her shoulders, holding her close to give her what little comfort he could, as Isabel clung to him with a glazed look and said nothing. She was worried about Marianne too. It gave them someone to comfort, other than themselves. She had lost a husband and the father of her unborn child.

"He promised me he'd never die," Marianne said angrily, shouting at them. "He said he'd always come back!" She choked on a sob, and then collapsed into her parents-in-law's arms, crying hysterically, as Isabel gently led her into the house, to lie down. "He said . . . he promised . . . it's not true . . . they're lying . . . he's coming home today. . . ." She tried everything, but nothing would change what had happened. No amount of denying or begging, no fury and no pain. All she wanted now was him.

Isabel soothed her with cooing sounds as tears ran down her own cheeks. She made Marianne lie down, and gave her water to drink. Charles came in and out of the room like a ghost, not knowing what to do for her either, as the three of them cried. Simon called later that morning, and he was crying too. They had just told him. He'd had an ear infection and couldn't leave on the same mission, although he'd been scheduled to. And Isabel thanked God he hadn't gone. If she'd lost them both, it would have killed her, and Charles, who was as distraught as his wife, and had no words to express what he was feeling. They were all in agony and Marianne sobbed all day, unable to believe what had happened. She finally fell into a light sleep, and Isabel left the room to find her husband. He was sitting in his study looking ravaged, and he looked up when she came into the room.

"I'm so sorry," he said to the mother of his firstborn and burst into tears again. And she came to hold him in her arms as she cried too.

"He was such a good boy," she said miserably, and he nodded. "But so is Simon," she said loyally. "We're lucky to have him," she reminded Charles, although she'd been closer to Edmund in recent years. He was a more expressive person. "What are we going to do for that poor girl?" she said, as they sat together and she blew her nose on the handkerchief he handed her. He always had one in his pocket.

"There's nothing we can do," he said honestly. "Take care of her and the child. She'll stay here with us, of course," he said, echoing his wife's thoughts. "She can't go home to Germany now anyway. God, I hate those bastards," he said with feeling, forgetting that his daughter-in-law was German, as was her father, whom he loved dearly. But they were exceptions. He had raw hatred now for a country and all its people, and the man who had started a war on their behalf and killed so many others, and his own, in the process.

"I hope she doesn't go home after the war," Isabel said sadly. "At least we'll have his baby. Maybe it will be a little boy who looks just like him." She was clutching at straws for comfort.

They had to plan a memorial service, and Simon had said he would come home for it. But she couldn't think of that now with the baby about to arrive any minute. It seemed too cruel to schedule it now, with Marianne still expecting his child. It would be too much for her to endure. Isabel could hardly think straight, as she went back upstairs to Marianne's room, and saw that she was still sleeping. She went to her own room then, and lay down, and fell asleep. She hadn't eaten since breakfast, none of them had, and a little while later she heard Charles come upstairs and felt him lie down next to her. He took her hand in his own, and they

lay there, holding hands and saying nothing. There was nothing left to do or say, except be there together.

The next morning Marianne didn't come
down to breakfast. She was usually up
early, and at ten o'clock Isabel went upstairs
to check on her. She knocked on the door
and got no answer, and found her in her
bathroom, on her knees on the floor, retch-
ing into the toilet, and the eyes she raised
to her mother-in-law's looked dead. She felt
as though she had died herself the day before. And suddenly Isabel was grateful she
hadn't given birth the day she heard the
news. It would have been too cruel to have
the anniversary of his death every year on
the birthday of their child. But at least she
had his baby. Isabel was wearing somber
black, and had instructed William the butler to put a black wreath on the door, and
Charles told him to fly their flag at half-mast.
By nightfall all of their neighbors knew, and
handwritten sympathy notes had begun to
drift in. Everyone felt sorry for them, and
there were too many other families like them
now. At least her son had died a hero's
death. She tried to tell herself it mattered,
but it really didn't. Her baby was dead. But

Marianne's was still alive, and she forced herself to concentrate, and put a damp cool cloth on the girl's head as she vomited miserably. She was pale gray, verging on green. The day before had been too much.

"How's the baby?" Isabel asked her quietly. Marianne had never looked worse.

"Not moving," Marianne said, and looked as though she didn't care.

"Any contractions?" Marianne shrugged. "Not really. My back hurts and I feel sick." And as she said it, she threw up again. Isabel flushed the toilet, pulled her hair back, and washed her face with cool water, as Marianne lay down on the bathroom floor, too sick to move or go back to bed. All she wanted now was to die. He had lied to her, and didn't come back this time, after he'd promised. It was a promise he couldn't keep, and she hated him for it.

"Let's get you back into bed," Isabel said, and helped her get up off the floor, but as soon as she did, Marianne doubled over, and a flood of water came from nowhere and covered the bathroom floor. Isabel knew instantly what it was, and Marianne looked panicked.

"I can't have the baby now—I'm too sick."

Isabel helped her take her nightgown off, and reached into the cupboard for a fresh one, as Marianne doubled over again and clutched her between sobs. She was in terrible shape, and Isabel grabbed a stack of towels, spread them on the bed, and got Marianne to lie down.

"I'll be back in a minute," she promised her, and left the room quickly while trying to look calm and ran into Charles in the corridor on his way downstairs with a funereal look. "Get the doctor!" she told him quickly, and he looked instantly worried.

"Is she all right?"

"No. Yes. She's distraught, but she's having the baby. She just lost her water, and she's quite ill. Tell him to come now." She hurried back into the room, and Charles disappeared to do as he'd been told. And when Isabel got back, she could see that Marianne was having serious contractions. She looked up at her mother-in-law with sad eyes.

"I don't want the baby," she said miserably, as tears slid down her cheeks in rivers. "He's never coming home again."

"I know, dear, I know . . . " Isabel said, stroking her hand gently, and then Marianne reached out and clutched her. The pains had started to come hard the moment her water broke. The baby was ready, whether its mother was or not. It was time.

The pains got harder and longer for the next half hour, as Isabel got more towels, and wished the doctor would hurry. She didn't want to deliver this baby alone and had never done so. She was no midwife. Marianne let out a groan and a scream as the door opened and the doctor walked in, carrying his bag. He looked somber and sympathetic, having just heard the news after he saw the wreath on the door.

"I'm so sorry," he said to Isabel, and then rapidly turned his attention to Edmund's widow. It had occurred to Isabel the night before that her daughter-in-law was now a widow at twenty-one. It seemed a cruel beginning to life, and equally so to lose a child, as she had. And as he looked at Marianne, he could see from the signs that things were moving quickly. She looked desperate as she glanced at him and clutched Isabel's arm and then her shoulder.

"I can't have this baby," she gasped at him. "I'm not ready."

"Perhaps not." He smiled at her kindly.

"But I think the baby is." He didn't tell her that we get no choice in these matters, whether birth or death, but it was true. And her baby was going to be born that day, whether she was ready or not.

He examined her as gently as he could, and she screamed, which Charles heard from the hallway, and scurried downstairs, terrified by the sounds. Isabel went to get the old sheets that she'd put aside for the delivery, asked one of the maids to bring in more towels, and returned to Marianne, who was vomiting again, and in agony with each contraction. "This is horrible!" she screamed. "I can't do this without Edmund."

"He's right here with you, Marianne," Isabel said calmly. "He always will be. He won't leave you alone. Just hear him in your head. He won't let anything happen to you." Marianne looked at her as she said it, and suddenly got very calm and stopped screaming. It was exactly what she had needed to hear, and the doctor nodded his approval as he felt Marianne's belly. The baby was moving down nicely, and then Marianne looked at them both wild-eyed as a force greater than any she'd ever known pushed through her, and the doctor told her to bear down as she braced her legs. It was all happening very quickly, and Marianne was frightened as she screamed with each push, and fell back against the pillows and gave up.

"I can't, I can't," she said, crying and then the force seized her again, and she screamed one long, horrifying, never-ending scream that went on forever and ended in a small but mighty wail. Marianne looked at them both in amazement and then saw a small face between her legs.

"Oh my God," she said, crying, and looked at them with smiles mixed with her tears. The baby had dark hair like Edmund, and Isabel thought the baby looked just like him. The doctor told Marianne to keep pushing, and the baby slid out with another long wail and began crying fiercely. It was a girl, just as Edmund had hoped. Marianne lay back against the pillows with a victorious smile, and tears ran down her cheeks.

"She looks like Edmund," Isabel whispered to Marianne, crying, too, with all the joy and sorrow of birth, especially now. And Marianne had seen it too. The baby was the image of him. Marianne looked suddenly grown-up and mature as she lay there while the doctor cut the cord, wrapped the baby in a small blanket Isabel held out to him, and put the baby to her mother's breast. She had lavender-blue eyes like her mother's, but the rest was her father, without a doubt.

The three of them exclaimed over the beauty of the baby, and then they laid her in a bassinette, and Isabel helped clean the mother up, and then washed the baby, and swaddled her and gave her back to her mother. The doctor was satisfied that all had gone well—in fact, it had been an easy birth, and had only taken four hours from beginning to end. Isabel suspected she'd been in labor the night before and didn't know it. And she left Marianne alone with the doctor for a few minutes to find Charles and tell him the news. He was in his study and drinking straight scotch. She smiled when she saw it. He deserved it, so she didn't comment.

"You have a beautiful granddaughter, your lordship," she said as she came around the desk to kiss him, and took a sip of his scotch. He smiled. She was a good woman, and a game one. She had come through the past two days admirably—she always did. She had never let him down in more than twenty-five years, and he knew she never would.

"Are they both all right?" He looked worried. He didn't want another tragedy, for any of them.

"Very much so. The baby is huge, but Marianne did fine. And she looks just like Edmund." He seemed pleased, although slightly disappointed that it was a girl.

"It sounded awful for a while."

"It always does. You've just forgotten. I nearly brought down the house with ours. You were probably too drunk to notice."

"I think I went out hunting." He smiled at her for the first time in two days, but this was a happy event, no matter how great their loss. And it was a piece of Edmund to have with them forever.

"Would you like to see her?" Isabel offered, but he looked nervous at the suggestion. It was a little too soon for him.

"Let the poor girl recover for a few hours at least." Isabel nodded and went back to Marianne and the baby and the doctor left shortly afterward and promised to return the next day. He had had to do a little stitching up, which was to be expected with such a big baby, and he predicted that Marianne would be sore, which she already was. But she was looking at her baby with rapture and smiled at her mother-in-law when she walked in.

"She's so beautiful," Marianne said softly, touching the tiny fingers, and she had unwrapped her feet so she could see her toes. She had everything she was supposed to. Marianne had never seen anything as exquisite as her child.

"What are you going to call her?"

Marianne thought about it for a long moment. She had been looking at her violet eyes. "Violet," she answered, looking peaceful. What Isabel had said to her had calmed her down, and reminded her that in some way Edmund would always be part of her life, through this child. "Violet Edwina Alexandra Isabel Charlotte Beaulieu," she said, and Isabel laughed. She was honoring the baby's father and all her grandparents at one shot, since it would be Edmund's only child. Isabel was touched.

"Good lord," Isabel said laughing, "she'll have to marry at least a prince with all that, or a duke at the very least. And sit on a throne." But Isabel was well pleased by her choices, as Marianne lay with her daughter in her arms. She thought of Edmund and felt him close to her, and quietly closed her eyes as she and the baby drifted off to sleep. Isabel gently smoothed the covers, and silently left the room to go back to her own. She still had much to do, and none of it as joyful as welcoming a grandchild. She had her son's memorial service to plan, and her heart was heavy as she left. Marianne's journey with her baby had just begun. And hers with her son had just ended. The two ends of life had come together too quickly.

Chapter 22

It was July on tour in California when Nick heard from Alex that Marianne had had a baby girl and lost her husband, all within two days. Alex said nothing of his own doings, but Nick imagined that there was little going on in the county and his life was quiet, although there was much going on on the war front, both on the Russian front and in North Africa, but the tides hadn't turned yet for the Allies. And Nick stayed constantly abreast of what was happening in the Pacific. News was scarce from Toby, although he had written to Katja that he wanted to marry her if he came home for

Christmas, or on his next leave. And it was all she could talk about whenever Nick saw her. It gave both young people hope and some kind of affirmation of life to make plans.

Nick read avidly about the first American air attack in Europe on occupied France, in mid-August. The United States joined Britain in continuing bombing missions against Germany.

The circus got to San Francisco and was set up for two days in Oakland. Nick was shining his boots, as he always did before each night's performance. Christianna always offered to do it for him, but he smiled and said it was one of those things a man had to do himself. He always looked impeccable, whether in work clothes, or white tie and tails. He was listening to the news on the radio and didn't hear the bicycle messenger stop at his trailer. And when he looked up, a young boy in a Western Union uniform was holding out an envelope to him with a trembling hand. For a second, Nick didn't want to take it, and then he grabbed it. He hated telegrams now. The messenger ran off before Nick could open it. He stood there, reading it, with his shined boots at his feet in the dust, and the brush beside them, and he read it again and again and it didn't sink in. He wouldn't let it. . . . **The War Department regrets to inform you that Corporal Tobias Bing . . . killed in action . . . in the highest service to his country . . . regret to inform you . . . regret to inform you . . .** the words were swimming before his eyes as he let out a low animal howl. Christianna heard it as she came down the road, and came running, thinking that an animal was injured. She found Nick looking dazed, and the telegram clutched in his hand. She took it from him and read it, and he sobbed uncontrollably as she held him. Thank God Lucas was off with the clowns—he was taking juggling lessons. She led Nick into the trailer, and he just stood there still crying.

"He's dead . . . he's dead . . . oh my God, they killed him . . ." he kept saying over and over. Toby was a baby. He was almost nineteen and now his life was over. Nick was inconsolable, and Christianna held him for hours as he rocked back and forth, keening for his son.

News spread through the circus within hours. There had already been many losses of boys who had enlisted or been drafted, roustabouts, performers, sons, brothers— the list was long, and now Toby was on it. They had a page in the program now honoring those who had died in service to their country. Christianna's brothers and father came over that afternoon to talk to Nick, but he was almost incoherent and he cried in his father-in-law's arms like a child, and Sandor cried too.

"He was such a good boy," Nick said. "He never gave me any trouble." Sandor sat with him for a long time, and finally Christianna asked him if he wanted to cancel that night's performance. He was in no condition to go on, but he knew that he was expected to, and he felt he had to. He and Christianna were their star act, and the audience would be furious if they didn't go on, whatever the reason. His private tragedy was not their problem, and he shook his head in answer to her question.

"Are you sure?" She was worried about him, and John Ringling North, Joe Herlihy, and the ringmaster came to see him too. Mr. North had ordered their flag to be flown at half-mast. Everyone felt terrible about what had happened, and Christianna could hear Katja scream when Gallina told her. All those who had known and loved Toby were devastated. And the worst was telling Lucas. He lay on his bed and sobbed, mourning his brother, who had been his hero and best friend all his life, even more than their father.

Nick looked like he was going to a funeral when he left for the performance that night, and he'd been in no condition for rehearsal, although they didn't need one. They could do their act in their sleep. And even if the performance was lackluster that night, the crowd probably wouldn't know it. The horses were so spectacular and Christianna so beautiful that all Nick had to do was be there. It was all he was capable of now anyway.

Christianna helped him dress, and he followed her blindly to the horses' tent, where the handlers helped him get the horses to the main ring, and all of them expressed their sympathy about Toby. The ringmaster asked for a moment of silence for one of their brave boys fallen in battle, and mentioned him by name, at the beginning of the performance. Fortunately, Nick didn't hear it, or he would have come unglued. Nick was devastated. His boys meant everything to him, and it was the second child he'd lost, after his daughter nine years before. Out of three children, only Lucas survived.

Their familiar music played, which was their cue to go on, and Nick and Christianna rode into the spotlight on Pegasus and Athena. Nick was smiling, which looked like a grimace, and Christianna tried to put more into it than usual, to compensate for whatever Nick was lacking, but his performance was flawless. She knew him well enough to see that he was going through the motions blindly, without paying attention to anything, but no one else could see it, and she smiled at him to encourage him, but he was in a daze and looked like he was sleepwalking. Pegasus did the show himself with almost no guidance from Nick, and as they were leaving the ring, Nick was holding the reins slack, and didn't see a pole someone had left on their path, and neither did the stallion, and he stumbled badly and nearly fell. The shock of it woke Nick out of his stupor, but too late. The Lipizzaner stallion had pulled something in his leg, and was limping badly when they left the ring. Nick was off the horse's back instantly to check it, as was Christianna, standing near him.

"What happened?" she asked in a frightened voice. She knew how much Pegasus meant to him, and this was no day for anything bad to happen. But the shock of losing Toby and the state Nick was in was why it had. For the first time ever, he hadn't been paying attention.

"He pulled a ligament," Nick said tersely. "It's my fault. I wasn't watching. I didn't see what was on the ground." He always looked for things like that, but hadn't tonight. All he had been able to see was Toby, who would never come home. Pegasus's safety had been the farthest thing from his mind.

He asked for a trailer to get the stallion back to the tent. He didn't want to lame him more by walking. And he asked one of the animal handlers to send him a vet as soon as possible. He got Pegasus to the tent, rubbed him down with liniment, and wrapped the injured leg, but Pegasus could hardly walk when he came out of the trailer. For any horse, it was a disastrous situation, and Christianna prayed that Pegasus would be the exception. She knew that if they had to put him down, it would kill her husband, and he was half dead with grief already.

For the first time in four years, Nick didn't go to see her act, nor ride in the finale. He stayed in the tent, waiting for the vet, who came after midnight. He seemed to know what he was doing, and he didn't mince words with Nick. "It's bad. I can't tell you it isn't. It's not broken, but I think the ligament is torn, not just strained. You may have to put him down." He was a heavy animal with a powerful body, and thin graceful legs. It was a lethal combination when a horse was injured, and many a racehorse had been shot because they couldn't recover. Nick refused to hear the vet's dire prediction.

"I'm not putting him down," he said grimly.

"We can put him in a sling off the ground to keep his weight off his legs," the vet suggested, "but you can't keep him there forever. Sooner or later, the leg has to heal, or you'll have to face that it won't." The sling sounded like a good idea to Nick, and he asked the vet if he knew any competent horse ranches in the area. He mentioned one in Santa Rosa. Nick sat with Pegasus all night and called the ranch in Santa Rosa in the morning. The day before had been the worst day in his life. Peggy Taylor, the woman on the phone at the ranch, promised to come and see Pegasus that afternoon. She sounded smart, and Nick hoped she knew what she was doing. She said they had saved a horse the year before with the kind of sling the vet was talking about, and they still had it.

Fortunately, the circus was staying in San Francisco for five days, and Nick had time to make a decision before they moved on. He informed the ringmaster that Pegasus would not be performing that night. He could ride on one of the Arabians while Christi-anna rode Athena. He had a black Arabian that would be a good counterpart to her, and the ringmaster accepted. He couldn't expect him to ride a lame horse.

The woman from the ranch in Santa Rosa came at two o'clock, and after they talked for an hour, she examined Pegasus. Nick liked her. She said they had an excellent vet. Nick agreed to drive Pegasus there before that night's performance. They left at three o'clock, and by five the vet had seen the horse, and they had him in the sling to keep his weight off his legs. It was all they could do for now. And Christianna had come with him. She was worried sick over Nick, even more than the horse. He looked ravaged and exhausted, and she knew he hadn't slept.

At seven they headed back to San Francisco, and arrived at the fairground just in time for their show, with no rehearsal, but Nick was more alert than he'd been the night before, although she knew how tired he was. And this time, he watched the ground for obstructions and random objects. And the black Arabian he rode performed well. The audience scarcely knew the difference, and Athena shone when Nick put her through her paces, with Christianna on her, looking like a fairy princess. The crowd loved it.

For the next three days, he drove to Santa Rosa every day to see Pegasus, and Lucas and Christianna came with him. Nick looked grim and barely spoke to them, and Christianna knew he was thinking about Toby, not the horse, but he concentrated on Pegasus when he got to the ranch. And so far nothing had changed. The vet he met with again said it would take several weeks,

or even months if he healed, and in the end
they might still have to put him down. Nick's
mouth was set in a grim line. And he made
the decision to leave him there for now and
continue with the tour. Later, he would come
back to Santa Rosa on his own, after
Oregon and Seattle, and catch up with the
circus again after that.

Nick was up most of the night, and Lucas
crawled into bed with him that night, and
they clung to each other and sobbed.

And when they left San Francisco the
next day, Nick looked morbid. He barely
spoke to Lucas and Christianna on the drive
north. He called the ranch in Santa Rosa
twice a day for the next two weeks. Nothing had changed, and he decided to leave
Pegasus there for another month. They
would be back in the Midwest by then, and
he was still using the black Arabian for their
act, but he would drive back for Pegasus
whenever the vet and Peggy Taylor thought
he was ready.

"How is he?" Christianna asked, after the
last call.

"The same," he said, disheartened. It was
Labor Day weekend, and they were in Ne-
vada. They played Las Vegas the next day,

and Nick went out gambling all night and got drunk, which she had never seen him do before. He was miserable all the time now, and he snapped at Lucas, which was also unlike him. He barely spoke to Christianna, and they hadn't made love since Toby died. He was mourning his son, and Pegasus being lame was the final straw. Christianna wondered if he'd ever be the same again. He was a different person, and not one she liked or even knew. She said nothing to anyone about it, except finally Gallina. She sobbed to her that he was so miserable now and nothing she did helped him.

"Give him time. This is the second child he's lost, and a wife. It's a terrible blow. Just pray that Pegasus gets better. That's not helping." Christianna knew her friend was right, and a month later, on the first of October, in Illinois, Peggy called him.

"I think you'd better come out here," she said sadly. "He's not eating, Nick. I think he's just tired of hanging there. Maybe he's losing hope." So was Nick, but he didn't want Pegasus to die. He took two weeks off from the circus, which he had never done before, and his brothers-in-law agreed to drive his horse trailers and tend to his horses with Lucas, and he promised that if he could get back sooner, he would.

He borrowed a truck, and it took him and Christianna two days and nights to drive from Illinois to Santa Rosa, driving hard and sleeping in the truck by the side of the road when they were too tired to continue. And when they got to the ranch and saw Pegasus, Christianna knew it was all over, and so did Nick. He was hanging off his feet and already looked half dead. He had lost all his spirit and his life. The vet was lowering him every few days, and his leg was stronger, but he didn't seem to want to stand up. The vet said he couldn't tell if the leg was weak from lack of exercise and still painful, or if Pegasus just wanted to lie down and die. The vet didn't want to give him the chance to do so, so he'd kept him in the sling, although it was six weeks now since he'd been injured, and Toby had died. Long enough for the Lipizzaner to heal if he was going to, though not long enough for Nick to recover from losing Toby. He was still deeply depressed, and even more so when he saw the horse.

Nick stroked his head and spoke to him

softly, and Pegasus seemed to revive a little when he saw him. He tossed his head
and whinnied and seemed to recognize
Christianna as well. It broke her heart and
Nick's to see the condition he was in. He
looked like a very tired old horse, although
he was only eight years old, which was
young for a Lipizzaner, and he had a good
fifteen or sixteen years ahead of him, if
he chose to live. But he didn't seem to
want to.

Peggy offered to let them stay with her
for the night, and they thanked her for the
small guestroom. She didn't say it, but Nick
had to make a decision about Pegasus. He
was avoiding it, but it was cruel to let Pegasus languish if he wasn't going to recover.
And thinking about it, he went out to the
barn that night. He was there for a long time,
and Christianna followed him there two
hours later, worried about Nick. Losing Pegasus was not going to help him get over losing Toby, or even adjust. It would only make
it worse.

She found him slumped against the barn
wall, in Pegasus's stall, talking to the horse
in a low steady voice. He was reminding
him of the trip over on the ship four years

before, when he had lain down and nearly died.

"You've got to make the same decision now," he said, looking up at him, and Pegasus nodded, as though he understood, as Christianna stood in the distance and watched them. Nick had no idea she was there. "You decided to stand up when we were on the boat. I needed you then, and I need you now. You can't just give up, and neither can I. Toby wouldn't want that for either of us. He was a good boy, and he'd still be here if he could be. I think he'd be real disappointed in both of us if we give up." As he said it, tears came to Christianna's eyes. "I promise you, if you give it another shot, I will give you a good life. I will take care of you for the rest of your days. We're in this together." Pegasus nodded again, and Nick stood up and stroked him, and then he saw his wife, watching them both. "I didn't know you were here," he said quietly, embarrassed by what she might have heard. He hadn't wanted to admit to her the depths of his despair, but she loved him and knew it anyway, and he could see it in her eyes.

"What did you do the night he got up again on the boat?" she asked, with a curious look at man and horse. She'd been thinking about it for several days, and hadn't wanted to bother Nick by asking.

"I just sat with him all night and begged him to stand up." Nick smiled at her, touched that she had come out to the barn. He knew how much she cared about them both. And he had been able to give her nothing emotionally for the past six weeks. He just didn't have it to give, and she understood. "I told him that my life would be over if he didn't stand up, and our lives were in his hands." It wasn't as true now, but in some ways it was. Nick was in no shape to withstand another blow and suffer another loss.

"Why don't we spend the night with him tonight?" Christianna suggested as she walked into the stall. "Let's just be with him, and tell him how much we love him and need him," she said, with a look of innocence, and Nick took her in his arms.

"You're an amazing woman. And I love you more than I've told you for a long time."

"I love you, too, Nick," she said softly, "and I love you, too, Pegasus. So get better, this has gone on for long enough. Everyone in the circus misses you, and that little black Arabian looks stupid compared to you, so you need to come back." She talked as though speaking to a child. Pegasus threw his head and whinnied as though he were laughing, as Christianna and Nick sat down in his stall, and Nick put an arm around her. He felt like the luckiest man in the world. And he hadn't felt anything like that for the past six weeks. He suddenly looked better than he had since mid-August, more like the old Nick. They sat in the stall and talked for a while, and then she leaned her head against him and fell asleep. And they woke up in the morning, with the sunlight streaming into the stall. Pegasus was looking at them, as though wondering what they were doing there, and there was an old familiar light in his eyes. Nick thought he could see something that hadn't been there the night before. Christianna could see it too. He looked the way he did right before a performance, when he heard their music and knew his cue to go on.

"Let's have a look," the vet said when he came. They lowered the sling, and gingerly Pegasus stepped out of it and looked around, and then he turned back as though laughing at Nick and trotted out of his stall. He roamed free for a few minutes, and then

Nick gave him his familiar voice commands, and he came back immediately, looking steady and strong on his legs. The vet was beaming, and Nick had tears in his eyes. "Maybe he was just missing you these last few weeks," the vet said with a puzzled look. "There's no telling with horses, particularly as highly bred as these. They have their own mind." Nick glanced at Christianna, and she was smiling through tears.

"What do you think, doctor?" Nick asked the vet. He didn't want to put him at risk or lame him again. The vet checked his injured leg again before he spoke.

"His leg feels strong to me, and he's not having any problem walking on it. I think you take him home and go easy on him for a couple of weeks and see how he does. And since he injured a foreleg, I don't think you need to worry about it when he goes back to performing. All his weight is on his hind legs with the kind of work you do with him." He patted the big stallion's head and looked him in the eye. "You behave yourself, Pegasus. No more of this feeling sorry for yourself. You had us all worried sick. Go back to work!" Pegasus whinnied again, and Peggy gave them one of her horse trailers, and they were ready to leave that afternoon.

"I can't ever repay you for what you did," he said seriously. She had charged him minimal rates for boarding Pegasus, and had given her whole heart to help him. "You brought him back to life."

"No, I didn't," she said firmly, and she was sure of it. "You did, when you sat with him last night. I've never seen anything like it." And then she patted Pegasus before they put him in the trailer to go home. "You be a good boy, and don't give them any trouble. They're nice people, and they love you." She kissed him right between the eyes, and then Nick led him into the trailer. They were ready to go.

It took them four days to meet up with the circus again in Kentucky, and they'd been gone for exactly a week, not the two they'd planned. And everyone was excited to see Pegasus with them. They'd been afraid Nick would have to put him down, and so was he. But Pegasus looked as lively as ever when he saw Athena and the other horses. And when Nick took him out to exercise him, he was spirited as he ran around the ring. It took him a little while to get his strength back again, but Nick worked with him every day, and on the third week of October, in Raleigh, North Carolina, Pegasus made his triumphant return. He was back. It had been a long, arduous two months, and the hardest time of Nick's life, even harder than leaving Germany, or joining the circus. He had felt as though he were drowning ever since Toby's death. But he had surfaced again, and so had Pegasus. They had survived the worst, with Christianna's help. She had never looked more beautiful than the night they performed together again, in the center ring. She was glowing. Pegasus was flying. Lucas made a brief appearance on one of the Arabians. And even though he still missed Toby terribly, and knew he always would, Nick was a happy man. They had come through the storm, and survived.

Chapter 23

By the time they got back to Florida for their winter break, Pegasus had hit his stride again, and Nick was almost back to himself. He was more subdued, and there were times when missing Toby still overwhelmed him, but he had good moments now too. And he was enjoying Lucas again. They even spent an evening with Gallina and Sergei. But poor Katja was still devastated. Toby had been her first love, and she still couldn't believe he was never coming home again. Nor could Nick, but it was the truth. It made him think of Marianne sometimes, too, losing her husband so soon, and widowed at twenty-one, with a new baby her husband had never seen. He hoped she was doing all right. And he was worried that he had heard from Alex very seldom recently, and hoped he was holding up, too, with the Nazis right in his backyard. Nick was glad to be in Sarasota, and that he hadn't stayed in Europe. If he had, they might all be dead by now.

And as they settled back into their winter quarters, he noticed that Christianna was sleeping a lot, and tired all the time, although she didn't admit it. The three months since Toby's death had taken a toll on her too.

"Are you okay?" he asked her with a look of concern, on a day when she'd slept unusually late, again.

"I'm fine," she said, smiling at him. "Just tired."

"You're not old enough to be tired," he teased her. "That's for old men like me."

"You're not old." She smiled back at him. He was forty-seven years old. But he had been through a lot in the past four years. He was still as handsome as the first time she'd seen him, although since Toby's death, there was still something sad in his eyes, and maybe there always would be. Only time would tell. But she knew that in some ways losing a child was a deep scar that would never heal. And that night she was back in bed and sound asleep at an unusually early hour again. It was starting to worry him.

"Are you sure you're okay?" he asked her again the next morning. "It's not like you to sleep so much." She answered him vaguely, and assured him she was fine, but he had a strange feeling suddenly that she was hiding something from him. He'd been so involved with himself, his loss, and Pegasus's injury that for the past three months he had paid very little attention to her. He felt bad about it, but she was always patient and understanding, maybe more than he deserved. "What are you not telling me?" He was afraid suddenly that she was sick and didn't want to burden him with it. She hesitated for a long moment before she answered, which confirmed his worst fears, and he pulled her into his arms with a look of terror. **Please God,** he thought to himself, **please don't**

let me lose one more person I love.
"What's wrong?"

"Nothing." She smiled up at him as he held her. "I'm fine." And then she realized it wasn't fair to keep it from him any longer. And maybe he was ready to hear it now—he hadn't been for the past two months, and it might only have upset him more. "We're having a baby," she whispered into his chest, and then looked up at him with love in her eyes. He didn't answer for a minute, thinking of Toby and the daughter he'd lost, and wondered if he could do it again. He was obsessed now with anything happening to Lucas. He was the only child he had left. But he also knew that he didn't have the right to deprive Christianna of having her own child, and theirs. He closed his eyes as he held her, and then he looked down at her with greater tenderness than he'd ever felt for her before.

"Why didn't you tell me?" he asked, but he already knew the answer to the question.

"It wasn't the right time." They both realized that was true. He was ready to hear it now, but he hadn't been for the past two months.

"How long have you known?" He felt

guilty that she hadn't been able to share such important news with him.

"Awhile. About two months, soon after Toby died, and Pegasus got hurt. I couldn't tell you then. And you wouldn't have been happy. Are you happy now?" she asked cautiously, and he kissed her.

"Very, very happy. I want a little girl who looks just like you. When will it be?"

"In June. But I can still go on tour. Everyone does." He looked at her in amazement and started to laugh. He had grown up with women who languished for months, rested, took naps, pampered themselves, and complained, and she wanted to go on tour with the circus, and deliver somewhere on the road.

"You're crazy," he said, laughing at her, and then he realized what she'd been doing and got instantly upset. She'd been doing her high-wire act, even if with a net, doing his horse act with him, riding elephants, and touring the country for these two months. He wondered if that was why she hadn't told him, too—because she wanted to continue doing it all, and she knew he'd have a fit. "Wait a minute, you. I don't want you doing your high-wire act if you're pregnant, or riding with me. Christianna, be sensible. I don't want you to lose this baby," he said earnestly with a look of panic. He wasn't used to women like her, and she was stronger than she looked. She was accustomed to working hard and the things they did.

"I won't lose it," she said peacefully. "I want to do the high wire as long as I can. They have no one to replace me. And you need me too. I could do our act for longer than the high wire."

"What? And give birth in the center ring on tour? Christianna, I'm not going to let you do this!"

"Yes, you are," she said stubbornly. "You can't stop me!"

"Yes, I can! And I will. Does your father know?"

She shook her head. "I didn't want to tell him before I told you. That wouldn't be fair." Nick was touched by the respect. "But he won't mind. My mother did the wire before she had me, without a net," she said proudly.

"Wonderful! So she could have fallen even before she had you, and where would I be? Christianna, please . . . please . . .

don't risk our baby, or you. I love you too much to lose you too. What if we take a year off and don't go on tour?"

"You can't do that in the circus. You lose your place." She knew more about it than he did, but the idea of her riding horseback, standing precariously on Athena's back, and doing a high-wire act, while pregnant, drove him insane. But even Gallina offered him no support this time, when he complained to her about it. She knew the ways of the circus too. It was a tough, cutthroat world.

"She's right," she told him. "She should work as long as she can, without taking insane risks. And there's no reason she can't have the baby on tour. There are hospitals everywhere we go." It was not the life he wanted to provide for his wife, but Christianna didn't seem to mind, and the argument raged on. Nick couldn't win it, no matter how hard he tried. She was loving and loyal, but also stubborn, and her family agreed with her and not with him. They had too many examples to prove him wrong.

She finally agreed to give up the high wire in March, during rehearsals for their tour, when she started to lose her figure. And he got her to ride a saddle and not stand on Athena's back, in their own act, and she wore filmier costumes so her growing belly didn't show. She was young and her body strong, so she was able to conceal it for a long time. But by late April even Christianna couldn't hide it any longer, and she had to bow out, for the next two months at least. Audiences were touched when the ringmaster announced it and told them why, and she took a bow every night, at the beginning of Nick's show. She looked beautiful in a pale silver gown, and he tipped his top hat to her as the Lipizzaner act began, but it frustrated her not to work till the end.

"Then you should have been a clown or a juggler," he teased her, loving to watch her and hold her as her belly grew. Lucas was thrilled about the new baby and hoped it would be a boy. And Nick was excited about it now too. The birth of their baby gave him hope, and a sense of starting life over again. It was the dawning of another era. The only thing that troubled him was that he wanted to give Christianna and the new baby, and even Lucas, a better life than they had now.

He had been with the circus for almost five years now, and he was feeling old, and tired. At forty-eight, he wanted to give them more. And he still dreamed of having a ranch one day.

While he cherished his dreams for his family, and they waited for the new baby as they went from town to town, the war droned on. The Germans surrendered in North Africa in May, and the Allies were gaining strength. And in the last days of Christianna's pregnancy, the eyes of the world turned toward the Germans' brutal decimation of the Warsaw Ghetto, and their horrifying destruction of human life there. Because it was in Poland, Christianna was particularly upset. The Germans were monsters, and they had been systematically eliminating Jews from Europe. Nick realized every day that if he had stayed, he and his children would be long dead, and his mother probably was by now too.

When they got to Santa Barbara in June, Nick drove her to Santa Ynez as he always did, as a pilgrimage to his dreams. But they didn't stay at the hotel this time, she was too big and uncomfortable, and she was already two days overdue, which made him nervous. He was much more anxious than he had been when his other children were born. Maybe because he was older, or because Christianna seemed so delicate and so tiny to have this baby and he was afraid for her, and because the losses of recent years had hit him hard. He was desperately afraid that something would happen to her, but she seemed totally calm and at peace when she reassured him. And she always reminded him that Gallina and her own mother had given birth in their trailers. Nick did not find it reassuring, and begged her not to do that to him. He wanted her in a hospital, with all the help she could get.

"I'll be fine," she said confidently.

"Yes, you will, in a hospital, with a doctor and lots of nurses in attendance. Let's not do this circus style, please." His origins showed in how he viewed it. He wasn't casual about her giving birth, and he wanted the best possible medical care for her. And he was relieved that for the next three weeks, they were playing all decent-sized cities. Santa Barbara, San Francisco, Portland, Seattle, Spokane. He was perfectly satisfied to have her deliver in any of those towns, which was why he had agreed to let her come on tour. And she bounced along happily with a big belly, full of energy as she watched his act every night, waved at the crowd, and took care of Lucas. He wondered if it was her nature, or just youth. She was twenty-six years old, and she still looked fourteen.

On their way back from Santa Ynez, after visiting the bluff he liked to visit every year, they had dinner at the Italian restaurant and went home. Lucas was staying at Gallina's for the night and still loved spending time with Rosie, although at eleven, she was less of a tomboy now and acted more like a girl sometimes, which annoyed him. But he forgave her for it most of the time, and they were still friends.

Nick smiled at Christianna as they walked back to their trailer, after returning the car they had borrowed, and he chuckled at how huge she was. She looked like a circus ball with arms, legs, and a head. Her middle section was totally round. He loved holding her at night and feeling their baby kick.

He was doing just that a little while later

in bed, when he felt her whole belly turn rock hard and Christianna made a face.

"What was that?" He looked startled, and so did she.

"Probably something I ate for dinner. Maybe the baby didn't like it." She had eaten very little, because she had no room, she said.

He felt the baby kick a few more times, and could feel a foot or an arm poking him, which made him smile, and then her stomach hardened again, and it worried him this time.

"Are you sure that's all right? Should we go to the hospital?" She laughed at him and rubbed her belly and it softened again.

"Of course not. You don't go to the hospital for indigestion." She smiled at him, but he wasn't convinced.

"How do you know it's indigestion?" He looked suspicious, but Christianna was unconcerned. She rolled over on her side and kissed him.

"I just know," she said, and kissed him again.

"I just want you to know," he reminded her, "if you get fresh with me, I'm not going

to touch you. You're having a baby any minute. I'm not going to be responsible for doing something wrong or hurting it or you."
She laughed again at what he said.

"I know, I know," she said, and they cud-
dled up together, and safe in his arms, she
fell asleep. He loved curling around her and
sleeping with her. Her existence in his life
had brought him more comfort than he'd
ever known, and he settled next to her
and drifted off to sleep. He woke up when
he felt her stiffen, and she gave a soft
moan.

"Christianna? Are you okay?" He wasn't
sure if she was awake or had been dreaming, but she answered him in a sleepy voice.

"I'm fine. My back hurts." He rubbed it for
her, and she started to drift back to sleep
and then jolted awake with a sharp stab-
bing sensation. He looked at her then and
sat up in bed. And he could see that she
was in pain.

"I think you're having the baby," he said
in a strong, quiet voice. "I don't think this is
indigestion." He suddenly realized that she
was in denial, and she'd been having contractions earlier. "Come on, baby, let's go."

"I want to stay here," she said in a small voice.

"We can't," he said firmly. "I don't want you to have the baby here." He was definite about that.

"They won't let you be with me," she said plaintively, and then in a smaller voice, "I'm scared . . ." And as she said it, a viselike pain gripped her, and she clutched his shoulders with both hands, and he could see in her eyes how bad it was.

"I'll stay with you if they'll let me," he promised. He got up, put on his pants and a shirt, his socks and shoes, then rapidly brushed his hair. "Come on," he said as he scooped her up in his arms, and wrapped her in the blanket. He tried to stand her up, but she could no longer walk, and he was panicked they had waited too long. He set her down on the couch in the living room. "I'll get the car." They had already arranged to borrow one from a trapeze act down the road, who had agreed to leave the keys on the seat. And when he got there, he found the keys, quickly started the car, drove it back to their trailer, and went inside to get Christianna. She was in the throes of terrible contractions and could barely speak. She stopped him when he tried to pick her up.

"I can't . . . I can't . . ." she whispered. "It hurts too much . . . don't move me," she begged him, and then she screamed.

"Christianna, don't do this to me . . . baby, please—let's go." But she was in agony, and he didn't have the heart to just pick her up and move her, she was in too much pain, and she wouldn't let go of him. He helped her lie down on the couch, and he ran next door to wake Gallina. "Get a doctor—an ambulance—somebody—she's having the baby!"

"I thought you were going to the hospital." Gallina looked at him in surprise, still half asleep.

"I think it's too late—she won't let me move her." Gallina woke up fast then, and promised to get someone there, the fire department if she had to. Nick ran back to their trailer, praying that someone would come soon. And by the time he got back to her, Christianna had gone back to their bed, and was writhing in agony.

"I can't . . ." she kept saying to him, "I can't . . ." and then she was racked by another pain, and he didn't know what to do, and finally he held tightly to her hands and looked her in the eye, and knew what he had to do. It was no different than Pegasus when he wanted to give up.

"Yes, you can," he said to her firmly. "Yes, you can. You're doing it . . . it's going to be fine . . . I'm right here—"

"No!" she screamed at him, as a pain bored through her that was so powerful, she felt like she was drowning and could no longer see him. Everything was underwater, except the pain that followed her everywhere, and she could hear him but she couldn't see him. And as he watched her, there was terror on his face. He didn't want to lose her or the baby if something went wrong, and then he laid her down gently, and when he looked, he could see the baby's head coming through, moving toward him, as Christianna screamed, one long unending howl of agony, until the baby lay in his hands, and she stopped screaming, and there was silence in the room. It was a girl, with the cord wrapped around her. She wasn't making a sound, but she was looking at him with wide-open eyes, and he was crying as he held her and turned her gently and tapped her back, and she took a breath and started to cry, and Christianna cried too.

"She's so beautiful," she said in awe. "And I love you so much." She touched his face, as they looked at each other and laughed and cried.

"I love you too." What he had just experienced had made up for almost everything that had happened to him. It was the greatest gift of his life. And so was Christianna. And their child.

He had no idea how to cut the cord, but he didn't have to. The fire department arrived five minutes later, and the firemen took over and knew what to do. They offered to take Christianna to the hospital, but she didn't want to, and the baby was fine. She was already at her mother's breast, and looking around with interest. And Nick knew he would never forget the instant she'd been born and what they shared. And maybe Christianna had been right. She didn't want to leave him, and if she'd gone to the hospital, he would have missed all of it. It was the greatest miracle of all.

The firemen checked Christianna's vital signs and the baby's, and helped them clean things up, and Gallina came to help too. And an hour later the firemen left and wished them luck. Other performers had gathered in the road by then, and Gallina told them what had happened, and everyone was happy for them. Lucas came to see his baby sister for a few minutes, and then went back to play with Rosie in the other trailer.

In their tiny room, Christianna lay holding their baby, and Nick looked at them both with adoration.

"You were fantastic," he praised her, "and so brave."

"No, you were. I'm so glad we were together," she said softly, as Nick stroked the baby's cheek and she slept in her mother's arms.

"Me too. You were right." She was right with most things. Christianna always seemed to know what was best for them. They had already agreed to call her Chloe if she was a girl, and Nick whispered her name, and then kissed Christianna. And as he looked at them, he knew that one day he'd give them a better life than this, in this tiny room in a trailer, touring all over the country, with no place to call home. He knew he would do it—he didn't know how, but he would. Christianna deserved it, and so did their baby, and Lucas . . . but for now, what they had just shared was a miracle in itself, and enough for them both. He curled up in bed next to them, and all three of them went to sleep. It had been a very big day.

Chapter 24

A year later, in the spring of 1944, when Chloe was nearly a year old, the tides were turning. The Allies were bombing Germany relentlessly, and landing in Europe, the Russians were pushing the Germans back, and Adolf Hitler's forces were finally losing ground. It was a long time coming, and it wasn't over yet. But there was hope at last that Hitler might not conquer the world. Things were moving in the right direction.

Nick was worried about his old friend Alex—he hadn't heard from him in nearly a year. The letters just weren't getting through anymore. He had heard from Marianne, and she had had no word of her father either. Nick just prayed he was still alive. Marianne's baby was two years old by then, and she was living with her parents-in-law at Haversham, and she said it was a peaceful life, but there was an unmistakably sad tone in her letters. At twenty-three, she had lost a country, a home, a husband, and possibly a father. She said the great joy in her life was her little girl. She was a year older than Chloe, Nick and Christianna's baby, who was the light of his life too.

After Alex had helped get the tenant farmer's friend close to the Swiss border, and concealed him in his wine cellar before that, there had been others, Jews who had remained hidden or been overlooked, and were trying to escape before they were sent to camps. Most were men who had the strength to survive the hardships, and were wily enough to flee the Germans, and live in hiding or on the run. There had been women on a few occasions, and once two little girls whose entire family had been taken—they were trying to get to their aunt in France, who was willing to conceal them there.

Alex had never planned to help them, but each time the opportunity came, he rose to the occasion and did what he could. There was no formal underground, just a handful of people who were brave enough to help. It was the only thing that gave meaning to his life now. Marianne was safely in England with the Beaulieus and her baby, he hated his countrymen, and he was willing to do almost anything he could to undermine the Nazis, and he had a perfect front as a distinguished aristocrat whom no one suspected. And in time it took over his life. It had become his reason for living, and he continued to help and conceal people, assisting them to escape. He knew it was his mission. And he had gotten bolder as he gained more experience. Still the local high command treated him with respect. He was just a local nobleman alone with his horses, and they saw him out riding every day. He was on cordial terms with all the officers, and had invited them to dinner several times. They thought him a charming man.

In June 1944, the Allies began landing on the coast of northern France. Hoping they would come soon, and wanting to clear a path for them, Alex helped a group of men

blow up a train carrying rockets and munitions, to do all he could to wreak havoc for
the Nazis. It had gone well.

Alex worked as part of a six-man team
that night, with one woman among them.
It was the first time he'd done anything like
it, but he had agreed to join them, when
they said they needed his help.

They had a surprisingly easy time laying
the wire for the explosives, and they were
bringing in the dynamite later that night, by
wheelbarrow and by hand and by car. Alex
was planning to walk through the woods to
them. He was fearless, and if they killed
him, he didn't care. Marianne was safe with
the Beaulieus, and the world he knew and
loved had been blown to smithereens in
the past five years. Nothing he had ever
held dear still existed. And whatever he
could do to destroy the Nazis as revenge
seemed fair.

He carried feed bags full of explosives
that night, and handed them man to man
to set them. And then they all waited in the
woods for the train the next morning, and
when it appeared at dawn, they lit the fuses.
The reaction was immediate. The train was
blown to kingdom come and everything in

it. Their mission had been accomplished. They disappeared like mist into the woods, and Alex walked home through the forest. He had just reached the path to the schloss, when the colonel appeared out of nowhere on Favory. The horse still recognized the man who had trained him and pawed the ground when he saw Alex. Alex smiled at both rider and man, and looked like a gentleman out for a morning walk.

"Going somewhere, Count?" the colonel asked him with an evil glint in his eye.

"Just out for a morning walk, Colonel. How's our friend there? He looks lively. Is everything all right? It sounds like you had some trouble this morning." The entire neighborhood had heard the explosion. There was no way to ignore it. Alex couldn't pretend not to know.

"And where were you an hour ago, Count?"

"Getting some air," he said innocently, as the colonel watched him. Alex could see he was suspicious, but he was fearless.

"Along the train tracks? It stinks of dynamite there," the colonel said angrily. It would go badly for him that the explosion had happened in his district and on his watch. And the high command was sensitive these days to betrayals and failures. The colonel didn't want that on his record, and Alex knew it.

"Does it?" Alex said benignly. And as he did, the colonel pulled a gun on him and pointed it at his head from the distance.

"You think I don't know what you've been up to, hiding Jews and making trouble! Always the innocent aristocrat, looking down your nose at us. And now you think you can blow up a munitions train and get away with it! We've been watching you for months." He was shaking with anger. Alex only smiled.

"Have you? It must be disappointing for you. I lead a quiet life." If he was trying to scare him, he hadn't, but Alex had his hand on the pistol in his pocket, just in case. It was the gun he'd been given the first night his tenant came to see him with the man he had hidden in his wine cellar for two days.

"Not so quiet as you'd like us to think. And when the Allies come, you'll welcome them with open arms?"

"Are they coming?" Alex asked, feigning surprise. "What interesting news. I haven't heard that on the radio."

"What have you heard?" the colonel asked, as the horse danced and he approached.

"About our victories on the eastern front, and how the British are cowering beneath our bombs. Is that not true, Colonel? Propaganda or truth?"

"You traitor!" the colonel said as he drew closer. "I hate your kind! Always supercilious! You think you're better than everyone else, because you were born with a title and a schloss, and can do anything you want."

"And you think you can steal it from us, and be one of us. You're not, any more than the Fuehrer. You can't steal it, Colonel. You have to be born to it. That's how it works."

"You bastard!" the colonel shouted at him, and cocked the pistol he held at Alex's head.

"You can kill me, or drive us out of Germany." Alex was speaking for Nick then. "But there are thousands more like us, and we'll win in the end. Truth is mightier than the sword, and so is honor. You can't dishonor us. You can kill us, but there will always be more of us than of you." As he said it with eyes full of hate and rage, the colonel pulled the trigger. He wanted to silence him forever. But Alex had had his pistol pointed at him, ready and cocked. And as the colonel fired, so did Alex—not at the man but at the horse, which Alex knew would be the final blow to him, and far more subtle. As Alex fell dead to the ground, so did Favory beneath the colonel. Alex had had the last laugh, and he had chosen the most elegant exit, which was so like him. He was a nobleman to the end.

Chapter 25

The summer of 1944 was a strange season for the circus, too, a summer of disasters. They had decided to change their route that year, and went north in the early months of the tour, planning to head west later, so instead of California in July, they were in Hartford, Connecticut. And on July 6, with the big cats in the center ring for the first act, a fire broke out in the first twenty minutes of the show. It began as a small blaze but ran up the sidewall of the tent. The band broke into "Stars and Stripes Forever" immediately, which was the agreed-upon SOS signal to all circus personnel that something

was amiss, without alarming the crowd. And
the ringmaster attempted to warn the audience to leave the tent and not panic, but
a power failure caused his announcement
to go unheard when the microphone died,
just as people began noticing the flames.
They stampeded toward the exits, two of
which were blocked by the big cat cages
and tunnels that funneled them into the ring.
Pandemonium broke out, as people became separated from their children, and the
paraffin-coated tent, which had been treated
for waterproofing, erupted in a blaze and
collapsed within eight minutes, to the horror of the audience, the crew, and all who
saw it. From then on it became a battle to
save those inside, rescue children, find parents, get the animals as far away as possible, and put the fire out. A hundred and
sixty-eight people were killed, and more
than seven hundred were injured, and everyone associated with the circus was devastated and shocked at the loss of life and
the damage. Some of the victims had been
burned beyond recognition, but many were
killed by the crowd trampling them as they
tried to flee. It was a tragedy like none other
they had experienced.

Five officials of the circus were later charged with involuntary manslaughter, and the circus accepted full financial responsibility to pay whatever damages were requested. But the tragedy had left its mark on them all. John Ringling North was no longer running the circus then and had left it a year earlier, but everyone associated with the circus was in deep grief over what had happened. Nick and Christianna and everyone they knew were deeply shaken. And tragically for those who knew and loved him, Joe Herlihy had been killed in the fire. He had just come back from a scouting trip and wanted to see some new additions to the show. Nick and Christianna were heartbroken by the loss of a good friend.

The circus closed down during the investigation, and opened in Akron, Ohio, a month later. Disheartened by what had happened, and working without a tent in heat and bad weather, they made it as far as Texas, decided to end the season early, and went back to Sarasota. And once back in Florida, after the disaster, Nick knew it was time. He wanted to leave the circus. It was an insecure, nomadic existence, and he wanted a normal life for their children, and he said as much to Christianna.

"This **is** normal," she insisted. She had never known anything else, but he had, and even if he could no longer provide the way of life he had grown up in, he wanted stability for them. He wanted more than tattooed freaks and bearded ladies, high-wire acts and big cats, and jugglers and contortionists, for Chloe and Lucas. He knew that Lucas would miss the clowns and the friends he had made in the past six years, but he wanted Chloe to grow up in a healthy, sane atmosphere, like other children. But no matter what he said, he couldn't convince Christianna. She wanted to stay at all costs. And what her father had predicted was proving to be true. Nick knew he would leave someday.

In November, Nick got a letter from Marianne that nearly broke his heart. He had been afraid of hearing it for months. British Military Intelligence, at the request of Charles Beaulieu, had been able to discover that Alex had been engaged in subversive activities in his area, against the authorities on a small scale, and had saved many lives. He had done all he could to undermine the Nazis and help Jews, and had even helped to blow up a munitions train as a final mission. And the same morning, he had been shot and killed and his body dumped on his doorstep. He was buried in the family cemetery by one of his tenant farmers. But there was no question now as to what had happened to Nick's old friend. Alex was dead and had been for several months, and Marianne was devastated when she shared it with Nick.

He wrote her a long letter of sympathy in response, but once again Nick had suffered another painful loss, and Christianna was worried about him. He was restless and unhappy and sad, and even Chloe's antics didn't always cheer him. The war had gone on for too long for all of them, and taken too high a toll.

And in England, Isabel said the same to Charles. She was frantic about Marianne, who was a young girl leading an old woman's life, and was seriously melancholy after she learned in October of her father's death. After the shock of losing Edmund two years before, she was deeply depressed again. She had been widowed for two and a half years. And although Marianne adored Violet, her sadness over her father's death was greater than any pleasure she derived from her little girl.

"There's nothing we can do about it," Charles said, looking tired. Isabel was always trying to solve everyone's problems, but there was no lightening the burden of the war until it was over. Simon had been injured the year before and was back in action. That was stressful enough for them after losing Edmund. It was a terrible time for them all. Charles thought they just had to tough through it.

"I think we should send her to London," Isabel said with her latest brainstorm.

"What, and have her killed by a bomb or falling debris from a burnt-out building? Are you mad?"

"Not everyone gets killed in London. I'll admit I don't like the idea much myself, but she's twenty-three years old, and she has no friends here, nothing to look forward to or to do. They may be dropping bombs on London, but there are parties and people and young officers to flirt with."

"Oh, for heaven's sake. Wait till the war is over, Izzie." But she was worried about Marianne and how despondent she had been since her father's death. She didn't even seem to be enjoying Violet these days, who was an enchanting child.

"We can keep the little one here. At least send her up for a visit. She's too depressed over her father's death. She needs to get out of here."

She argued with him for a month, and finally after Christmas, she sent Marianne to London to stay with cousins of the Beaulieus who had a lovely house on Belgravia Square, near a bomb shelter. At first Marianne said she didn't want to go, but by the time she left, she looked brighter again, and she was excited about her London visit. Isabel had chosen their cousins for Marianne to stay with because they had a daughter the same age, and she could introduce Marianne to some young people for a change. She had seen no one but her parents-in-law for four years. And Marianne herself didn't realize how much she had missed being with people her own age since Edmund died, until she got to London and their cousin Julie took her to a score of parties, and introduced her to everyone she knew. She convinced Marianne to extend her stay and got her a volunteer job at a hospital two days a week, and the rest of the time they were out every night. She missed Violet, but her time in London was therapeutic and restoring her, so Isabel urged her to stay there. Her trip to London was doing for her what Isabel had hoped. She sounded young again, and happier than she'd been in years.

Marianne called the Beaulieus regularly, and she sounded like a different person. And she didn't tell her mother-in-law, but on New Year's Day she had met a young officer from Virginia, an American named Arthur Garrison, and she had seen him almost every day since. She had never had so much fun in her life. And when she came back to Haversham in February to see her daughter, she looked like a different person. Even Charles had to admit it, and that Isabel's mad idea had been the right thing, as always. Her "mad ideas" were usually her best.

Charles had a serious talk with Marianne when she got back. The war was by no means over, but when it would be, she would have to decide what to do about Schloss Altenberg, and whether she would want to keep it or sell it. She couldn't imagine living in Germany again. Her life was in England with them, and it would be too sad for her at Altenberg without her father. She thought she would probably sell it, although she knew it would be painful to do so. For all this time she had hoped to go back, but without her father, it had lost meaning for her.

"I thought you'd feel that way," Charles said sensibly. "But I wanted to ask you. I'll help you when the time comes. And of course, my dear, we want you to stay here with us. You will always have a home here." And Edmund had left her a substantial amount in his will, which she hadn't expected. Charles knew that her father had had a considerable fortune and extensive lands. Germany was liable to be in very bad shape after the war, but she was his sole heir. And between Edmund and her father, she'd been left a very substantial amount of money. She was set for life.

Marianne went back to London after a week and saw Arthur Garrison again. They shared a passion for horses. He had a horse farm in Virginia where his family raised them. He had inherited it right before the war when his parents died, and she told him about her father's Lipizzaners. He was fascinated by them, and by her, but he also noticed how reticent she was to let any romance develop between them. She had fun with him, and loved talking to him, but she treated him more like a friend, and he finally questioned her about it one night after dinner.

"I lost my husband two and a half years ago," she said quietly, "in a bombing raid over Germany. And my father this year. I hadn't seen him in four years since I came to England. And my mother died when I was born." She took a breath and tried to explain to him what she was feeling. "I just don't want to lose any more people in my life. All I have are my daughter and my parents-in-law. I'm afraid that if I get attached to anyone else, they'll die too." It was as honest and direct as she could be with him, and tears stood out in her eyes as she said it.

"You're twenty-three years old, Marianne. You can't be afraid to love anyone for the rest of your life, because they might die. That's not fair. When the war is over, we'll all go back to normal lives. No one will be flying bombing raids, or having bombs dropped on them. We'll live with the risks of ordinary life."

"The only family I ever had was my father," she said sadly. "Now he's gone. My best friends died or left Germany. And I'll never go back to live in Germany again. My parents-in-law want me to stay here. And the only man I ever loved was Edmund, and he died the day before my daughter was born. I don't know if I have the courage to try again." Arthur was five years older than she was, and mature for his age.

"You've paid a high price for this war. Now you're going to have to learn to live with peacetime."

"It's not over yet," she reminded him. He could still die, as any number of people could.

"It will be soon. You can't live hidden away in the country forever either. You're too young to do that."

"Maybe I'll move to London," she said vaguely. She really didn't know what she wanted to do yet. He was kind and attentive, and they had the same interests. He was very attractive, and protective of her. And she truly liked him.

"Will you give me a chance, Marianne?" he said softly. "Please?" He had never met anyone like her.

"I don't know if I can," she said fairly.

"Let's do it together," he said with a kind expression. It was one of the things she liked best about him, his gentleness, and how well he treated her. So had Edmund and her father. Arthur reminded her a lot of Edmund in that way, although he was very American and soft-spoken with a Southern accent, and not British. And he didn't look anything like Marianne's late husband. He was as fair as Edmund had been dark, which was a relief. It would have been too strange if he looked like Edmund. But they had the same loving spirit. "I won't push you," he promised. He was smart enough to know that that was a bad idea. She didn't answer, but she smiled at him, and she seemed calmer.

And for the next several weeks, they went to dinner and saw friends. He was an adjutant to a general, so he was not flying missions, and she didn't need to worry about his dying from being in danger. He came down to Haversham to visit her one weekend, and her parents-in-law liked him too.

He was well bred and polite and as aristocratic as they were, in an American way.
And he was wonderful with Violet, and she
responded to him. Most of all, he was terrific to Marianne. But his circumstances and
"real life" worried Isabel greatly about him,
and she expressed it to Charles after he
left.

"What if she marries him and goes to
America with him?" she said sadly.

"Then we'll visit her, and she'll visit us.
You said it yourself, we can't keep her locked
up here forever. She's a young woman."

"I was thinking London, not Virginia," she
said wistfully. And she would miss Violet so
much if they left, but she knew Charles was
right, and she wanted whatever was best
for Marianne. And Arthur Garrison looked
like he might be it. Only Marianne still wasn't
convinced. She was keeping him at arm's
length.

By early April, Arthur was discouraged.
He had the feeling that Marianne would
never let herself love again, or not for a long
time. And he had fallen in love with her. He
stopped calling her for a few days to give
himself some air, and Marianne was surprised. She had gotten used to spending

a lot of time with him for the past few months, and hearing from him constantly, whenever he wasn't working. She mentioned it to Julie, who suggested that she might have finally scared him off, and Marianne spent the next few days thinking about it, afraid she had. And she suddenly realized that she didn't want that to happen. She liked him more than she wanted to admit.

She sounded relieved when he finally called her again. "I missed you," she confessed, and he beamed when she said it.

"Well, that's good news. I figured that you'd be relieved not to hear from me." He had almost given up on her.

"I'm not relieved, Arthur," she said honestly. "I'm just scared."

"I know you are. Me too. But good things can be scary sometimes. You just have to be brave enough to grab them."

"I don't know if I'm that brave," or if she wanted to be, but she knew now that she didn't want to lose him either.

She was warmer when she saw him for dinner that night, and animated when they talked, and when he took her home this time, he kissed her. She hesitated at first, and then let herself go and kissed him with a passion she had forgotten. He didn't press her for anything then. He kissed her lightly again and told her he'd call her in the morning, and she looked dreamy eyed when she walked into the house and Julie saw her.

"What happened to you?" Julie asked her, and Marianne smiled mysteriously and didn't answer. "Don't tell me Sleeping Beauty is waking up again. Good lord! Hallelujah!" Julie had been worried about her too. She'd been so frozen when she first came to London, as though everything inside her was dead.

"Maybe" was all Marianne would say, and went upstairs to bed. But when she saw Arthur again the following night, things were progressing nicely.

Two weeks later, after they'd been dancing all evening at a private club, they talked about Berlin falling soon, and she suddenly realized that when the war ended, he would be going home to Virginia. And thinking about it, she suddenly felt panicked. She said something about it to him, and he was happy to hear it.

"May I consider that a hopeful sign?" he asked her, and she smiled, and he kissed her. They had been doing a lot of kissing in the past few weeks, and she wasn't as disconnected as she feared. He could sense that she was a passionate woman. She had just been badly wounded. But he was a patient man, and he was willing to spend a lifetime helping her recover. He was trying to let her know that, and he thought she was hearing him at last.

For the next few weeks, as the war ended in Germany, Arthur did everything he could to reassure her. They were together when the German surrender to the Allies was announced, and it was a day of jubilation in England and all over Europe. It was bittersweet for Marianne, without Edmund and her father. Arthur said he'd probably be going home in June, back to his horse farm in Virginia.

"I'll have to go to my home in Germany to decide what to do with it," she said with a look of profound sadness. "I'm pretty sure I'm going to sell it. I could never live there without my father, and now knowing he died there. I think he must have come to hate Germany in the end. I don't want to live there anymore. Charles Beaulieu said he'd help me put it on the market."

"And the horses?" he asked sympathetically.

"They're all gone. The Germans took them. The stables are empty. And the house. At least the German high command never took it." And then she smiled at him. "It was probably too drafty and too hard to heat." He laughed at that. Most European castles seemed to be, from what he'd seen. She wondered if Nick would sell their old schloss now, too, or if he'd come home. After seven years in America and a life there, she didn't think so. Germany was over for all of them.

They talked late into the night. And two weeks later, Arthur told her that he was going home at the end of June. She nodded sadly when he said it.

"I'd like to ask you something, Marianne," he said quietly. "I'll understand whatever you decide. But would you do me the honor of marrying me? I know this isn't easy for you, and it would be a whole new life in America. But I love you, and little Violet. I would love you to be my wife." She hesitated for an eternity as she looked at him, and he was sure she would say no. And

then she nodded. He nearly fell out of his
seat, and he wanted to whoop with glee.
But he didn't want to scare her. Instead he
kissed her and promised to take care of her
for the rest of her life, and she believed him.
And she didn't ask him never to die. She
knew better now. Sometimes people died,
even if they didn't mean to. They couldn't
help it. And it didn't mean they didn't love
you.

"I love you too," she said softly. "I'll try to
be a good wife."

"You don't have to try to be anything," he
said, kissing her again.

"I have to settle my father's estate in Germany, and put the house on the market.
Maybe I could come in September."

"Whenever you're ready," he said peacefully. "I'll be waiting for you." And she knew
he would be, for however long it took.

Chapter 26

Arthur left for America at the end of June to be released from the army, and return to Virginia. And in July, Marianne went to Germany. It was the first time she'd been back in five years, and the country was a shambles. It broke her heart to see it. And it nearly killed her to see their schloss again, empty and sad and deserted. She took her father's old lawyer with her, and asked two of the tenant farmers and their wives to help her. She spent a week packing up the house. She had to dispose of her father's possessions, and many of her own. She had a big job deciding what to give away, and what to keep, or sell. She wanted to send a few family heirlooms to America, like their silver and her grandmother's china, and some furniture she loved, and a portrait of her father. And she spent a whole afternoon going through the treasures of her childhood. There were so many memories, and all of it made her sad now. In the end, she kept very little, and decided to sell a lot of the furniture and even the ancestral portraits with the schloss. She had never really liked them and had no use for them now.

And there was nothing for her to keep from the stables. All the Lipizzaners and Arabians were gone. She and the lawyer decided what price she wanted for the estate. Her father's cars had disappeared from the garage, even the Hispano-Suiza he had loved, stolen by the Third Reich as well. The objects mattered nothing to her. She missed her father. She had come to say goodbye.

She stopped at her father's unmarked grave, near the chapel on her estate. No one had ordered a headstone for him, since he had been killed by the Third Reich, and she asked the lawyer to do it. She visited the tenant farmers before she left, and thanked them for their many years of service to her father. She was a lady to her core, with all the sense of honor and responsibility that her father had taught her by his example.

And then she and the lawyer drove past the von Bingen schloss. It looked empty and deserted too. And she shuddered when she thought of who had lived there and that no one of the family would return. It was overwhelmingly sad.

Marianne felt as though she had crawled through hundreds of years of history when she left Germany and went back to Haversham. She hoped to never return. Her life there was over. It was finished. And it was a relief to go back to the Beaulieus. They truly were her only family now, other than Violet. She was going to America in September to marry Arthur, and Isabel and Charles were happy for her. She had promised to spend the summer with them, and to return as often as she could. And they were going to visit her in Virginia too.

She and Isabel walked in the gardens the day she returned from Altenberg, the way she used to with Edmund. She had come so far in the last five years, and the Beaulieus had been so good to her. She had grown up. Violet had thrived, and they had lost a son. The world had changed. And now she was going to America for a new life. She looked at Isabel and smiled as they walked back into the house, remembering how terrified she had been the day she arrived, and now this was home to her in many ways, and they were like her parents, not just Edmund's. And she could almost feel him with her as she walked into the morning room. Violet was there, playing with her grandfather, and looking so like her father.

It would be a new chapter for Marianne now, a new country, a new life, and finally she was ready. And she knew Edmund would have approved.

Nick had the same difficult decision to make as Marianne, once the war in Germany ended. He had a schloss, extensive lands, and tenant farms. The house and lands still belonged to him, now that the Third Reich had fallen and he could own his estate again. But unlike Marianne, he had no desire to go back, even for a visit. He was sure. His homeland had betrayed him. And he knew it would break his heart to see it all again, and the manor house where his father died of grief, upholding his duty to God and country till the end. And seeing Alex's deserted schloss now that he was dead would be no better.

Nick decided to sell all of it, and make his life in the States for good, in the country that had welcomed him. He told Christianna about his decision, and she wasn't surprised. She had always believed that he wouldn't go back to Germany, just as he said. Too much had happened there to hurt him.

Nick had contacted a Red Cross group and a Jewish refugee organization, trying to trace his mother, when the war ended, and in September, they told him what he had suspected. She had died with her husband, four children, and several other relatives, including her parents. The whole family had been wiped out, like so many others. It didn't surprise him, but it made him sad. She had had other children, but had never known him. He felt as though he had lost her again when they told him.

He was startled when his father's old lawyer contacted him, after their exchange of letters in the summer, asking for Nick's permission to sell the estate. He had been offered a handsome price by an Austrian count, to buy everything, and after a night's reflection, Nick took it. It wasn't a fortune like the one they'd had before the war, but it was a great deal of money, enough to do whatever he wanted. And he knew what that was. He wanted to buy the ranch in Santa Ynez that he'd been dreaming of for years. Either an existing one, once he started looking, or he would build one. But it was time. He had been with the circus for seven years. He had just turned fifty, and he wanted a home for them and their children.

He told Christianna that when they got back to Florida, he wanted to leave the circus, and buy a ranch in California. She was horrified when he told her. She had always hoped this day would never come. But he had the money to do it now, and provide a wonderful life for all of them. The days of poverty and hardship were over—and for him, his years with the circus.

"I can't go," Christianna said in a choked voice.

"Are you serious?" He looked shocked. "We can do whatever we want now. We don't have to live like gypsies in a trailer anymore."

"But this is all I know, Nick," she said, sounding panicked. She was twenty-eight years old, and this was the only life she'd ever known. And Chloe was two, and he wanted her to have more than the circus, before it became her only life, too, which it already was. He knew that Sandor and her brothers wouldn't like it, but he thought this was an important move for them. And he owed it to Lucas too. He was thirteen, and needed good schools now, and a future, not just clowns as his best friends, and the bearded lady.

Christianna was so upset that she wouldn't even talk to him about it. And she hadn't told her father, but whenever Nick tried to bring up the subject, she said she wouldn't leave the circus. He wanted to give notice immediately, but he agreed to wait until January or February, or even March or April when they left on tour. But he assured her again that they were leaving. And she refused to discuss it with him again. But Nick was determined, he had made the decision, and he had the money to buy or build a beautiful horse ranch and stock it with fine horses for breeding, even Lipizzaners if he wanted. He had freedom again now, but had learned so much in the meantime.

Nick got a sweet letter from Marianne at Christmas, and was surprised to learn that she had moved to Virginia, gotten married to a man who bred horses, and was already expecting a baby with him. She said her schloss hadn't sold yet, but she was sure it would soon. And most important, she was happy and at peace. And she sounded very much in love with her husband. She wanted Nick and his family to come and visit. She was longing to see him, and suggested they come in January. Nick talked to Christianna and told her how important Marianne was to him, almost like a daughter, and she agreed to make the trip with him. She was only four years older than Marianne, and Violet was a year older than Chloe. And it would be the first time Nick had seen her in seven years. Lucas's memories of her were already hazy, but Nick's were crystal clear.

The weekend after New Year's, they went to Virginia, as planned. Nick and Christi-

anna both thought that Arthur was a wonderful person when they met him, and
perfect for Marianne. Violet was adorable,
and Arthur's horse farm was spectacular.
He came from an old Southern family and
knew a lot about horses. And although she
was shy at first, Marianne was so warm and
welcoming, as was Arthur, that Christianna
had a good time too. And Lucas remembered Marianne, once he saw her. She was
sad not to see Toby, and it made his absence and Alex's seem more acute to Nick.
But in spite of that, they had a wonderful
time with Marianne and her family. The visit
was a great success. He and Christianna
talked about it all the way back to Florida.
And when they got back, he reminded
Christianna again that he wanted to give
notice. He was not going on tour again. His
years in the circus were over. And he wanted
a horse farm like Arthur's.

Inevitably, it turned into an argument that
lasted for weeks, and he couldn't win. She
brought her father and brothers into it, and
they argued with him too. Nick simply said
that he was too old to go on with the circus. He wanted a horse ranch, and to breed

horses, and that was it. And for Christianna, the circus was it. She wanted no other life, and was refusing to leave with him.

In March, they came to the conclusion that he had hoped to avoid. They were separating. He was going to California with Lucas to set up a ranch. And she was staying with her family and the circus, and keeping Chloe with her. It made his heart ache to lose both of them, but he knew he had to do it. He would visit Chloe whenever he could, and when she was older, she could visit him on the ranch. Christianna was as heartbroken as he was, but she agreed. Their paths were going separate ways, and neither of them would be happy doing what the other wanted. They weren't divorcing, but they were separating. Gallina was devastated when she heard it. And Lucas was unhappy too. He was going to miss his friends in the circus, and he loved Christianna and his little sister. But Nick was sure it was right for them to leave, and he didn't waver.

He handed in his notice before they left on tour, and John Ringling North came to see him himself to try to dissuade him. But when they finished talking, he said he understood, and thanked Nick for staying as long as he had. He realized that it was time for him to move on.

"You saved my life," Nick said to him gratefully. But seven years later, he needed to leave. "I'll never forget it." The two men shook hands. Nick had decided to leave for California the same day the circus left Sarasota on tour. There was no animosity between him and Christianna, it was just a very sad decision, and a fork in the road for both of them. They each had to follow their own path, and they were no longer the same, or headed in the same direction.

Nick had said goodbye to all his old friends that week, and he packed the horse trailers with everything but the horses the night before he left, and he and Christianna spent their last night together in the trailer. He wanted to make love to her but he didn't. He watched her sleeping all night, but didn't touch her. He knew he would love her forever. And she said the same the next morning when they got up. And he knew he would miss her every day from now on, but he had to follow his dream.

They walked to the horse tent together, and Christianna cried when she patted

Pegasus for the last time. She was going to miss him and Athena too.

Nick and Lucas went to load up the horses then, and Christianna watched with tears rolling down her cheeks. She smiled sadly at Nick, and he brushed the top of her head with a kiss, and turned away so she wouldn't see the tears in his eyes. And then they were all loaded up. He went to kiss Chloe, and he looked long and hard at his wife.

"Take care of yourself. Don't give up that net again because I'm not watching." She shook her head and knew she never would. She was trying not to think of all the ways he had made her life better.

One of her brothers got into their trailer to drive it away, and he waved at Nick. They were sorry he was leaving. And then the convoy of circus trailers and vehicles headed out. Nick and Lucas got in line to leave the fairground in the new trailer Nick had bought. They had just gotten to the exit, when Nick stopped with a look of panic. He looked at Lucas and then turned around, and headed back into the fairground.

"What are you doing, Dad?" Lucas asked, looking confused.

"Never mind. Wait here," Nick said, pulling their trailer off the road and jumping out. He ran back to where the other trailers were in line. He ran until he saw her, by the side of the road, with her suitcases, holding Chloe, and Peter was carrying the rest of their bags. She looked like a refugee in a war zone, with big, terrified eyes. "Okay, I give up. We're staying. We'll stay in the circus forever. I love you," Nick said, feeling like jello inside. The dream was worth nothing to him without her. And he loved her more than any ranch.

"We're coming to California," she said in a trembling voice. "We're leaving."

They had each been willing to give up everything they wanted for the other. Her brother smiled at them and set down her bags.

"You're both crazy. You deserve each other." But he was happy for them. "So which way are we going?"

"California," she said clearly as she looked at her husband and smiled.

"Are you sure?" Nick asked her. "I'll stay if you want to. All I want is you. The rest isn't important."

"Yes, it is. To all of us. It will be good for

Lucas and Chloe. I don't want her growing up on the high wire, or terrified like my sister." She and Nick walked to his trailer then, and her brother followed with the rest of her bags. Peter kissed them both, and Nick opened the door to speak to Lucas.

"We forgot something," he said matter-of-factly.

"What?" Lucas asked him, confused by the delay.

"Christianna and your sister. They're coming." Lucas's face exploded in smiles. Christianna settled Chloe in the backseat with a bag of toys, and slid in next to Lucas.

They waved at her brother as they left the fairground, and headed for California. It was a long trip, and took them ten days, going slowly with the horses, but they never looked back.

Chapter 27

It was six months before Nick and Christianna found their ranch in the Santa Ynez
Valley. They looked every day, and the
right property finally fell into their hands,
on the bluff that Nick had always loved on
their annual pilgrimages to Santa Ynez.
Finding a ranch there was his dream come
true.

They rebuilt the ranch house while living
in a rented house, and by the end of the
year, Pegasus Ranch was off and running,
and Nick had bought six more Lipizzaners
and a few Arabians. He wanted to breed
the best Lipizzaners in the country, using

Pegasus as his champion stud, which had always been his plan.

Lucas missed the circus and the clowns, but he liked his new school and made lots of friends, and Chloe was thriving. And even Christianna agreed that a normal home life was better for them all.

Nick exchanged letters with Marianne at Christmas. Her baby, a boy, had been born in July, and she was already pregnant again. Having lost her father, she was grateful for the contact with Nick. He was the last vestige of her lost life in Germany before the war.

Christianna's entire family came to stay with them for several days during the holidays, and again when they were on tour in California the following summer, and they made it a tradition to come twice a year every year from then on. The house was bursting at the seams the moment they arrived, with lots of cooking, laughing, talking, and riding horses around the ranch. Although her father was still unhappy that Christianna had left the circus, he was pleased to see her with a good man and a solid life. And despite her earlier reluctance, Mina had stepped into Christianna's shoes on the high wire. She had no choice once Christianna left, and she had taken on the role without complaint, and seemed more confident about it now. She was dating a Romanian gymnast, and her brother thought they'd get married. They were happy he was in the circus. Only Nick had gotten away with absconding with his bride.

For Nick, and even Christianna, the circus began to feel like a dream that was fading behind them. They loved living on the ranch. The circus had been exciting, but they had a life now that she had never dreamed of before. They had a beautiful home, friends, and Lucas loved his school and friends too. Christianna also loved their horses, and in time Nick had the finest Lipizzaners in the state, and wanted to have the best ones in the country. Pegasus's foals had begun to be born, and were finer than Nick had ever hoped.

After they left the circus, Marianne sent them a Christmas card every year, announcing a new baby. She had four with Arthur now, three boys and a girl, and Violet of course. In her letters, she said that the Beaulieus came to visit them at Garrison

Farm once a year, and she and Arthur and the children stayed with them in England at Haversham every summer. Marianne said they were wonderful grandparents to her other children as well. And best of all, she was happy with Arthur. She said he was the kindest man alive, and they shared a terrific life together. Just as Nick and Christianna did on their ranch. They had each found the life of their dreams, after the turbulent years of the war.

For nineteen years after Nick and Christianna left the circus, Marianne was busy with her kids, her husband, and their farm. She and Arthur added on to it, and she was always taking her children to horse shows, as all of them were serious competitive riders. She never made it to California for a visit during those years as a result. Her life was too full where she was, with five busy children and a husband. And Nick was no better. He could never get away, nor wanted to. And Lucas and Chloe kept them busy too. And monitoring Pegasus's breeding and that of the other horses kept Nick present and intensely occupied on the ranch.

Nick was ashamed and often felt guilty

at how much time had gone by without getting together with Marianne, and she felt badly about it, too, but the years passed too quickly. It was 1965 before Marianne and Violet were in Santa Barbara for a horse show Violet was in. She was training for the Olympics, and Marianne wanted to drive to the Santa Ynez Valley with Violet, and visit Nick and Christianna at last, even if it was only for a day. She was planning to leave the other children at home with Arthur, and she had a free day with Violet after the show. Nick wrote back and invited them to stay for the weekend. He felt as though he had let his old friend down, that he hadn't seen Alex's daughter for so long. And she was a woman now, with five grown children of her own. Nick was seventy, Christianna was forty-eight. And Chloe had turned twenty-two that year, while finishing college at a Stanford program in Florence, and speaking Italian fluently, or so she claimed.

Lucas was thirty-three, married to a terrific girl from the Valley, and working on the ranch with his father. They had only been married for a year, and didn't have kids yet, but Nick figured they'd get around to it eventually. Lucas and Sally were in no hurry. And

Nick liked her a lot. She was from a family that owned a ranch nearby, and she was as horse crazy as the Bings, and was both knowledgeable and helpful on the ranch. Nick had invited Marianne and her family to Lucas's wedding, but she couldn't get away, and had missed it. She wanted to at least meet Sally now, and hadn't seen Lucas since he was fourteen, which she was sad about too. In her heart, they were part of her family, and always would be.

When Marianne got out of the car at the ranch, after the horse show in Santa Barbara, she looked no different to Nick at forty-four than she had at twenty-five, nineteen years earlier when he'd last seen her, or barely. She was the same beautiful, tall, aristocratic-looking, lanky blonde that she had been as a young girl in Germany, and when she'd married Arthur nineteen years before. And like Nick and Lucas, she'd been American now for years, ever since she married Arthur. And Violet was a beautiful young woman at twenty-three.

Marianne was bowled over when she saw Nick's Lipizzaners—they reminded her of her father's so long ago. And she was pleased to find Pegasus still alive at thirty-one. She considered him an old friend and went to the stables where they kept him, to say hello. He was quiet and old now, but still a spectacular-looking horse, just as he had been when she was in her teens and her father had given him to Nick. He had served Nick well to establish their bloodlines. The success of the ranch was thanks to him. And Violet was excited to see Pegasus and the other Lipizzaners too. She was a horsewoman to her core, like the grandfather she had never known. And she had the exuberance and slightly British eccentricity of her paternal grandmother, Isabel Beaulieu, with whom she spent her summers. Violet said the Beaulieus and her stepfather were close too. And although Arthur had never adopted Violet, out of deference to her father and the Beaulieus, Violet was extremely close to him and he had always been wonderful to her, and treated her no differently than his own children.

Marianne and the Bings had a wonderful visit, and spent a terrific weekend together, as Nick rode all over the ranch with Marianne, and they talked about her father, and some of the memories Nick hadn't allowed himself to think of in years. He still missed Alex, and Toby of course. But life in Germany had faded into the mists for him, except for Alex, Toby, and his own father, Paul. It was part of another lifetime, for both of them. It all seemed so long ago.

Although Violet was ten years younger than Lucas and Sally, they were all such passionate horse people that they talked about horses all weekend, and her training on the Olympic equestrian team. They saw her ride at the ranch, and it was no surprise three years later, when they saw on TV that she won the gold medal. She was beaming during the ceremony, and Nick was proud watching her, and knew Alex would have been too.

Lucas and his wife, Sally, were so busy on the ranch that they were married for six more years before they had their first baby, Nick's first grandchild, a little boy they named Alex, after Nick's old friend. Lucas wrote and told Marianne, and she was touched, and sent them a tiny pair of riding boots as a baby present, in memory of her father, and her beloved old friend Toby, Lucas's older brother. Their families were inextricably woven together, even all these years later.

Chloe was studying equine medicine at Davis by then, in order to become a vet for the horses on her father's ranch, and her parents were thrilled with what she was doing.

They had sad news four years later, when Violet wrote to tell them that Marianne had been killed in a car accident on the way to a horse show. She was only fifty-four. It was the end of an era for Nick, and saddened him deeply. Marianne had been the last survivor of a lost world, other than Lucas, who was too young then to remember anything except his life in the circus, once he came to the States. Marianne was part of Nick's extended family, through his bond to Alex, and a last link to him, and now she was gone too. Her early death hit Nick hard, and her daughter Violet maintained the friendship in the ensuing years. She was running her stepfather's horse farm since none of her siblings were interested, and Arthur had turned the farm over to her on her mother's death. He said he wanted to travel, and without his wife, no longer wanted the responsibility of the farm.

Violet married a year after her mother died, to another horse breeder on a neighboring farm, and she had a baby girl a year after that, whom she named Nicola, after Nick. He was eighty-two by then and very touched by her gesture. He was still in good health and very active, although Lucas took over running the ranch that year. But his father went to all the auctions with him when they bought new horses, and Nick still had an unfailing eye. The horses Nick purchased were superb, to maintain their bloodlines, and Lucas had learned his father's lessons well. Lessons Nick had learned from Alex forty years before.

Little Alex, Lucas's son, was six when Violet's daughter Nicola was born. And he was the apple of his grandfather's eye. Nick taught him all about the Lipizzaners, and told him stories about the circus, and the clowns who had been his father's friends when he had been the same age Alex was now. He loved listening to his grandfather's tales of Pegasus, the circus, and the clowns. He knew all about Pegasus, although the stallion had died before Alex was born, and was buried on the ranch.

Nick and his grandson rode together every afternoon, usually just before sunset, while Nick told him stories about the circus, his uncle Toby who died in the war, his father as a boy, and their friend Alex in Germany, whom Alex had been named after, and the beautiful horses he had, how well he trained them, and how brave he was in the war. Alex was fascinated by his grandfather's stories, and they were riding together one day when Nick stopped talking, and seemed to be resting in his saddle, and the beautiful Lipizzaner he was riding, one of the sons of the great Pegasus, just turned slowly home toward the barn, and Alex's horse followed.

"Grampa's sleeping," Alex told Lucas, his father, when they got back to the barn. The little boy didn't look worried, and Lucas glanced at his father and saw what had happened. Nick had been busy and alive until the end, in love with his life, happy on his ranch, and passionate about his horses. He had died just the way he would have wanted to, riding a Lipizzaner, cantering across the fields of his ranch with his grandson, and enjoying his life and his world as the sun set on the mountains he had loved.

Lucas sent his son in to see his mother,

and then he gently lifted his father down from the saddle for the last time.

They buried him on a peaceful corner of the ranch, near where Pegasus was buried, on the bluff he had visited for so many years with Christianna. They took him to the spot on a horse-drawn carriage, pulled by two Lipizzaners, with his favorite one, saddled and riderless behind it, as Christianna walked beside him.

She visited him every day, and talked to him. And sometimes she rode there on one of the Lipizzaners herself. He had given her a wonderful life, and she had never regretted coming to the ranch with him. He had been right for both of them, and even at sixty, she was a beautiful woman. And she had loved him to the end.

Chapter 28

The bidding took off at a rapid clip in the auction, near Haversham Castle in Hertfordshire in England. It was an auction that happened every year, and drew aficionados from all over the world. The most knowledgeable people about horses, and the most serious buyers, turned up to buy Arabians, fabulous show horses, hunters, jumpers, and whenever possible Lipizzaners. It was the second Lipizzaner on the list, a stallion, that drew the highest bids, and one of the locals, allegedly a family member, a Beaulieu staying at the castle, wasn't letting go. She moved her paddle almost imperceptibly, and kept her eyes locked on the auctioneer's. She had no intention of losing the fabulous stallion to someone else. And she had stiff competition from a tall man in a cowboy hat, standing languidly to the side. But his eyes were keen and sharp, and one of the spotters had him in his sights, as the bidding continued to go up at a rapid pace.

"The lady in the pink shirt," the auctioneer said again, as the spotter reported yet another bid from the side an instant later. Eventually everyone else dropped out, and finally with a nod and a smile, the man in the cowboy hat gave up. And the woman in the pink shirt gave a victorious grin, and was patted on the back by two attractive women on either side. The woman who bought the Lipizzaner was tall and blond and looked to be in her early thirties. She gave her information to one of the spotters, as the bidding went on for the next horse, and she left her seat a few minutes later and went to the cashier to pay for the horse. The man in the cowboy hat found her there and extended his hand. He was wearing well-worn cowboy boots to go with the hat.

"I just wanted to congratulate you. He's

a gorgeous horse," he said with a broad smile. He had been the underbidder, and hadn't wanted to lose. But he had sensed that the woman who had bought the Lipizzaner wasn't going to give up, at any price. And he had already gone well past his limit on the last bid. He had bought two other horses that day, fabulous Arabians that he was happy with, although the Lipizzaner was what he had come for. The Arabians were extras he just couldn't resist.

"Thank you," the blond woman said pleasantly, with a slightly embarrassed smile. "I'm sorry, I have a thing about Lipizzaners."

"So do I," he said easily. "Did you buy him to show?"

"No, to breed."

"So was I. Maybe we can talk about that sometime. I'm from Pegasus Ranch in California." He was sure that if she knew horses, she had heard of his ranch. And he could hear that she was American, although the women she was with were English.

"Garrison Farm, in Virginia," she said. He knew it. "I'm staying with my cousins nearby." She didn't want to say that she was staying at the castle, which belonged to her cousins. It made her sound like a snob. He was very understated and casual in his demeanor. And she had been very intense during the bidding. She was a pretty woman, and she was wearing riding boots and jodhpurs. She'd been riding that day right up till the auction. "To be honest, I bought him for sentimental reasons. Lipizzaners are part of my family's history." She felt as though she had to explain why she had been so fierce in the bidding, but he didn't seem to mind. He had lost to her with good grace, and looked intrigued by what she said.

"It's part of my family history too," he said vaguely. There was something in her eyes that looked familiar to him, but he didn't know what it was, as though they had met before.

"My great-grandfather gave his best friend two Lipizzaners in Germany before the war and saved his life. They've kind of been good luck charms for us ever since." She smiled, and he noticed how blue her eyes were, they were the same color as his, although he was as dark as she was fair, and he had a California tan, and lines around his eyes from squinting in the sun.

He was in his early forties and a handsome man.

"My grandfather was given two Lipizzaners by his best friend in Germany, and he joined the circus with them, which saved his life," the man in the cowboy hat said carefully, as they compared stories which, strangely, were matched, like two halves of a whole.

"Oh my God," she said, staring at him as though she'd seen a ghost. "I didn't say the part about the circus because that always sounds so crazy, and I've never been absolutely sure the circus part was true. My mother told me about it, but she was always a little vague about the circus, and my grandmother died before I was born, so I couldn't ask her."

"If we're talking about the same two men, the circus part was true. My grandfather left Germany with two Lipizzaners and six Arabians in a railroad car in 1938, and joined the circus. What's your name?" he asked her, looking mystified. How was it possible that two people who were related to that story had come to England to buy the same horse? It felt like destiny to him.

"Nicky Steele. My grandmother's maiden name was von Hemmerle. Marianne von Hemmerle. Her father's name was Alex. He sent her to England to stay with friends and get out of Germany in 1940. She married an RAF pilot—my grandfather—here during the war. He died, and then she went to America and married again. My mother, Violet Beaulieu Steele, is the daughter of the Englishman, so she's half English, and I have cousins here."

"I'm named after your great-grandfather. I'm Alex Bing. My grandfather's name was von Bingen. Nicolas von Bingen, he changed it to Nick Bing when he joined the circus, and it stuck. He never changed it back after he left the circus. I guess it was easier."

She looked equally stricken by what he said. "I think I'm named after your grandfather. Nicola, people call me Nicky. This is so weird." The hair was standing up on her arms. "I wish my grandmother were still alive so I could tell her. Wait till I tell my mom. I run their farm in Virginia."

"My dad is still alive, Lucas Bing. He was six when they came from Germany, and joined the circus with his brother and my grandfather. My father had an older brother,

Tobias, who died in the Pacific in '42. My dad is eighty-two and still going strong. My grandfather Nick passed on when I was six, thirty-seven years ago. I was riding with him when he died on our ranch. He just went to sleep while we were talking. All our bloodlines at the ranch came from the original Pegasus, the stallion they brought from Germany before the war."

"I've heard about your ranch. All the names sound familiar. The part about the circus always threw me. It sounded so weird to me, I was never sure it was true," she said, looking slightly embarrassed, and he laughed.

"It always sounded strange to me too. But kind of fun. My grandfather's stories were fantastic. He married a high-wire artist from the circus. She died last year at ninety-six. She was terrific, Polish, and a beautiful woman. Would you like to talk about this over a drink?" His eyes searched hers, looking for something more, as though she were a ghost from the past.

"I'd love it." She smiled at him. "Do you want to come to the house after the auction? Brace yourself, though, 'the house' is the size of Buckingham Palace, although it's falling apart. But it's an amazing place. It's where my grandmother lived during the war, and where my mother was born. My grandfather had just died flying a bombing mission the day before." Their crossed paths were rife with history and sounded like a movie.

They both felt as though they were in a time warp. Alex showed up at Haversham two hours later, and had tea and eventually a scotch with her cousins, who told Nicky later that they thought he was incredibly good looking, and she had noticed it too. It was hard not to. He was striking and at the same time very low key. She had mentioned to her cousins that they were linked by history and two Lipizzaners, and gave them a quick rundown on the story before he arrived. They thought it was fascinating, and that he was even more so. He looked like a genuine cowboy to them.

"Fate, my dear," her cousin Fernanda said. And her raised eyebrows nearly flew over her head, and she shot Nicky a meaningful look, when Alex said he was divorced, and had no kids. Nicky was thirty-seven and never married, she had been too busy raising horses. He was roughly six years older than she was, from what he said, although Nicky didn't really care. She loved their story.

The three women and Alex had a nice time together, and eventually Alex said he was meeting friends from the auction at his hotel and had to go.

"Enjoy your Lipizzaner," he said to Nicky with a warm smile as he left. "You won him fair and square. Stay in touch." He was anxious to tell his father about the meeting. He was going back to California in the morning with the two horses he'd bought. And Nicky was flying back to Virginia with the Lipizzaner two days later. Alex reminded her of the name of his ranch before he left. And she repeated the name of her horse farm in Virginia. Neither would be hard to find on the Internet.

"Let's Google him," her cousin said, giggling, after he left. They felt like schoolgirls, and were impressed by the size of the ranch, and there was a nice picture of him, and one of his father, an older but still very attractive man. They were a good-looking family. And there was one of Nick Bing, the late founder of the ranch. And of Pegasus, the stallion for whom the ranch had been named.

"I think you ought to call him sometime,

or drop in for a visit," her other cousin suggested after another scotch.

"And say what?" Nicky said with a sheepish look. She would have felt silly calling, despite their common history.

"Call him for advice about the horse you just bought. I think your meeting was fated. The hand of destiny. Think of it, his grandfather and your great-grandfather were best friends. Yours saved his grandfather's life, and now here you are seventy-six years later."

"It's just a coincidence," Nicky said, brushing it off. "Though weird, I'll admit." Nicky called her mother in Virginia that night and told her, and Violet was touched by the story and remembered meeting Alex's father and his grandfather when she visited the ranch with her mother Marianne, after a horse show in Santa Barbara in 1965, when she was training for the Olympics, three years before she won the gold.

"That was all before I was married, and before I had you, and before the man you met today was born. What's he like?" She was curious about him, the two families still exchanged Christmas cards every year, but she had lost track of the details. And the man her daughter had met at the auction was an echo of her own history, their two families somehow intertwined.

"He's nice. Kind of a handsome cowboy," Nicky said thoughtfully.

"Was he upset you got the horse?"

"No, he was very gentlemanly about it. I wasn't about to give up that horse," she said, and her mother laughed.

"I'm sure that's true." Nicky never gave an inch once she made up her mind. She was strong-willed and independent, which was why she wasn't married. She had never met her match, and wasn't sure she wanted to anymore. She liked her freedom too much. "Well, I can't wait to see the horse. He must be gorgeous," Violet said warmly. They were all horse mad. It was in their blood.

"He is gorgeous," Nicky said, referring to the Lipizzaner and sounding delighted, and she told her mother all about him. And two days later, Violet saw him for herself, when Nicky brought him home. He was even more beautiful than she'd expected, and a gorgeous specimen of the breed.

Nicky started working with him immediately, and trying to break him, but he was the fiercest, most stubborn horse she had ever seen. He was strong and independent. And for the next month, he resisted all her efforts to train him, although she had trained several Lipizzaners before him, and knew the breed well.

She called him Snow, and he tried to bite her whenever she said his name, as though he didn't like it. The rest of the time, he threw her every chance he got. She had never been thrown as often by any horse she tried to train, and she was black and blue from head to foot, but determined not to give up. She almost called Alex Bing once to ask him for advice, for real, not as a ploy, but she didn't want to admit she was having trouble with the horse. It was embarrassing. She had never had a horse she couldn't break, except this one. He was totally wild, and after two months, she was wondering if she should sell him. She thought again about calling Alex Bing, to offer the stallion to him for breeding, but she didn't want to sell him a bad horse. But she was beginning to think that Snow would be good for nothing except breeding. He had flawless bloodlines and a rotten disposition.

She decided to take him to a horse show with her, when she went to Santa Barbara for a jumping event. She was thinking of selling him to a breeder there.

After the show, she left her jumpers at the stable in Santa Barbara and, on the spur of the moment, decided to drive to Santa Ynez to check out Alex Bing's ranch. She took a single-horse trailer with her, with Snow in it, to ask Alex's advice. She didn't call before she got there. She wasn't planning to stay long, and if he was busy, she would just leave.

She was impressed as soon as she drove onto the property, and saw the beautifully maintained ranch, and the enormous barns. They obviously had a lot of horses. She saw him walk out of one of the barns as she drove up. She stopped her trailer, and he turned to look at her. He smiled as though he'd been expecting her to come, and she laughed as she got out of the front seat in jeans and a crisp white shirt. He was wearing the same cowboy hat he'd worn in England or one just like it.

"Well, what brings you here?" He looked pleased to see her, and recognized her immediately when he walked over to her.

"I brought a friend to visit," she said, pointing to the trailer.

"Anyone I know?"

"Could be," she said, as she opened the door of the trailer and led Snow out. He was a splendid horse, and they both stood admiring him for a minute. Alex was happy to see him again, and her.

"How's he doing?" Alex asked with interest, as a much older man stood in the doorway of one of the barns, and watched them with a smile. He had a feeling he knew who she was. Alex had told him the story when he got back from England, and Lucas had been impressed by the sheer coincidence of their meeting at the auction. He sensed that this was the same girl and the horse.

She laughed at the question and was honest with him. "He's a huge pain in the ass. He throws me every time I ride him. He bites me if I say his name. I don't think he'll ever be any good for anything but breeding. He can't be trained." She had trained a lot of horses, but not this one.

"Are you selling him to me?" Alex asked with a look of serious interest, feeling the horse's legs and flanks with expert hands, and Snow stood peacefully and let him do it, while Nicky waited for him to go wild. But he didn't. He looked at Alex like an old friend, and as she watched them, she knew why she had come. It was suddenly crystal clear in her mind.

"No," she said quietly, "I'm giving him to you. I have this crazy feeling that he wants to be here. Besides, it's a family tradition. My family gives yours horses, Lipizzaners, every seventy-six years." Alex laughed and shook his head. He knew what she had paid for him. A fortune.

"I can't accept a gift like that." He smiled as he said it.

"I'm sure your grandfather said something like that to my great-grandfather in 1938."

"Maybe so," Alex said, watching her quietly, and then he looked at the stallion again. "What did you call him?"

"Snow," she said, and the horse turned and gave her a filthy look, but he didn't try to bite her.

"What about Pegasus?" Alex said, and the horse turned again and looked like he was smiling.

"See what I mean? He doesn't even like

the name I gave him. I swear, he hates me. I think he wanted to go home with you all along." It felt that way now, watching him nuzzle Alex. He was wearing a bit and bridle, and Alex swung easily onto his bare back and led him around. The giant Lipizzaner was as meek as a lamb. And Alex looked at Nicky and smiled.

"Want to go for a ride? I can grab you a horse from the barn." She was wearing riding boots, and she nodded, still unable to believe that he was riding the huge stallion bareback with no problem. He had a magical way with horses, and the Lipizzaner looked like he knew he was home and had a friend. He had treated Nicky like the enemy since she bought him.

Lucas saw what they were doing, and brought her a horse a minute later. He introduced himself, and Nicky explained who she was. He had known it the minute he saw her.

"Beautiful stallion," he commented about the Lipizzaner she had brought with her.

"He belongs here," she said simply. And a moment later they cantered off, and Alex had no problem with him at all. They rode for a long time and were still on his enormous ranch.

"I don't know why, but I had a feeling you'd come here. And I felt like I was going to see him again," Alex said quietly, referring to the stallion.

"You must be psychic," she said, and he laughed.

"No, I just felt like our meeting was so strange, as though it were meant to be, or happened for some odd reason." And then he realized where he had taken her, without thinking. They were walking their horses past the peaceful place where his grandfather was buried, and Christianna beside him, looking out over a bluff, and Pegasus was buried nearby. He looked at Nicky then, and saw again that her eyes looked familiar, as though he had known her for a long time, or in another place. And she had the same feeling about him. It was as though they had been linked long ago, and their paths had been meant to cross that day at the auction. It felt as though forces more powerful than they were at work.

"I'm glad you came," Alex said quietly. "I thought about you a lot after we met. I almost called you a couple of times, but I didn't know what to say."

"Me too," she admitted. "I just rode in a show in Santa Barbara, and I knew I had to bring him here. He was meant for you. He doesn't belong to me. He never did."

"Pegasus," Alex said quietly, and the horse gently moved his handsome white head at the sound of his name. "Welcome home," he said, patting him, astride his powerful bare back, and as he said it, he looked at Nicky and she smiled.

He gave Pegasus his head then, and Nicky followed beside him, as they galloped through the fields. They had come through generations to find each other, and the white stallion that had bound their ancestors to each other and saved three lives had come with them.

Pegasus had come back to them. They slowed their horses to a walk as the barns came into sight, and Alex reached out and gently touched Nicky's cheek. She felt as docile as the stallion when he did it, which wasn't like her. He had a magical touch. "Welcome home," he said again. He was saying it to her this time, and as their eyes met, it was the most peaceful feeling in the world. And as Lucas watched them from the distance, he smiled, too, and walked into the barn, knowing that all was well in their world. Pegasus had come home.

About the Author

DANIELLE STEEL has been hailed as one of the world's most popular authors, with over 600 million copies of her novels sold. Her many international bestsellers include **A Perfect Life, Power Play, Winners, First Sight, Until the End of Time, The Sins of the Mother, Friends Forever,** and other highly acclaimed novels. She is also the author of **His Bright Light,** the story of her son Nick Traina's life and death; **A Gift of Hope,** a memoir of her work with the homeless; and **Pure Joy,** about the dogs she and her family have loved.

Visit the Danielle Steel website at daniellesteel.com.